The Gods
Lightning and Fire

Levi K. Castle

THREE SKILLET

THE GODS, LIGHTNING AND FIRE, Castle, Levi K.

1st ed.

 THREE SKILLET

www.ThreeSkilletPublishing.com

ISBN: 978-1-943189-44-1

"O you gods, think I, what need we have any friends, if we should ne'er have need of 'em?"

— Shakespeare, "Timon of Athens" —

The
Gods
Lightning
and Fire

— Part 1 —

Ship

— Part 2 —

Gods

— Part 3 —

Rebirth

Book of the Gods

Chazah 2:1-8

*A*ND BEHOLD, *a door was opened in the heavens, and a great Throne was set out for all to see. Ten gods sat upon the Throne, one to rule and nine to follow, and they were clothed in suits of iron and glass. They wielded power over all that was in heaven and on the ten precipices. In the right hand of She who sat upon the Throne, a Book was sealed with ten seals, one for each god upon the Throne. Inside the Book were the names of the Faithful Five Thousand who traveled to the Promised Land.*

*I*N THOSE DAYS, *the Five Thousand slept. They had confidence that one day they would arise once more at the Gate Beautiful.*

*F*OUR BEASTS *crawled out of the Throne, wielding great weapons of destruction in their hands. They wished to claim the Book as their own. In time, the door opened a second time, and a lesser throne appeared. The four beasts were banished to the lesser throne.*

*S*HE WHO SAT *upon the great Throne spoke, saying: Behold, the last of the ten seals will not be broken until* *the end of time has come.*

AS SHE WHO sat upon the Throne prepared to break the final seal and read the names of the Five Thousand, the four beasts shattered their bonds. They bound all of Creation, from the smallest grain of sand to the vast expanses of the cosmos, into one tightly-held fist, threatening to crush it all, leaving the Five Thousand without hope or reward.

SHE WHO SAT upon the Throne flashed anger from her eyes, and she caused Time to stand still. A great war erupted in the heavens. The four beasts wreaked havoc upon Creation, and for an eon and more, the skies were left bruised and streaked with blood. The ten gods and the four beasts tumbled from the sky in The Great Falling, and the Faithful Five Thousand fell with them.

SHE WHO SAT upon the Throne vowed that one day She would triumph over the beasts who stole Paradise from the Five Thousand. Time would be restored, and the fist binding all of Creation would be released. All of Creation would be restored to its rightful place in a great conflagration such as has never been seen before.

IN THE DOING, the world as we know it will be consumed by lightning and fire. Selah.

— Part 1 —

Ship

The Drive Glitches

One day.

It was one day since departure, and already trouble brewed.

"*Oy vey iz mir!*" Engineer Levitscn swore disgustedly, keying in a series of taps on his console. Engineering's massive overhead display twinkled, the image shifting and reformulating into a simulated image of the ship as it would look if seen from outside.

As if the ship could be seen from the outside. Not at the rate they were traveling, a hundred days to cross a hundred light years, with five thousand corpsicles safe in her hold until they could be delivered to their new home.

"*Pah!* We're flying a *tchotchke,*" Levitson muttered, tapping the board and watching the image expand to reveal the central space between the ship and the Cassel-Jackson Magnetic Resonance Drive.

"Who's flying a tchotchke?" First Mate Wendy Honda leaned in the door.

"I didn't know anyone was listening." Levitson didn't turn, keeping his eyes on the display. His hand moved, and the patterns overhead adjusted, the colors changing slightly.

"I'm always listening." As Honda spoke, her words repeated themselves faintly. She tapped her ear, and they ceased. "Are we up to speed?"

"And how. Too much up to speed." Levitson touched the board again, and a series of numbers scrolled along the bottom of the screen, the smaller place values flickering as fast as the eye could see, and the larger ones changing at a slower pace. The largest, a dozen decimal places over, remained stationary for a long time before clicking over once.

"That's good, isn't it?" Honda was bright and cheerful, almost chirrupy, like a kid at fourteen wanting the world to like her. With her short, black hair in a close-cropped pixie cut, her pert nose, black eyes, and tiny waist, she looked about fourteen. Her looks were one of the tools of her trade. No one who crossed her would ever be fooled a second time. "Like, we can get there early, right? I could use a little rest and relaxation."

She released the door, and it slipped shut with a soft sucking sound, the seal hermetically separating the corridor from the workspace. No sense in everyone dying if a micro collision caused decompression in another part of the ship. Live another day to die another time. Wasn't that how it went? There would be no dying on the *Higgs*, however. She had five thousand colonists to deliver, and then it was back home again with a shipload of *whatever* was produced on Deneb 4 Station.

"Look here." Levitson touched a roller, and a bubble appeared over the area just between the magnets separating the nose of the ship and the Drive, expanding it in a fisheye fashion. He enlarged the bubble until the center was clear and the fisheye effect was pushed to the edges. After Mission Control in Florida was breached by unknown hostiles just as their mission was getting underway, he'd been cautious about anything that seemed out of line. "What does that look like to you, Firstie?"

More numbers scrolled across the lower half of the bubble, pale blue and slightly translucent. One, many decimal places down, occasionally shimmered red, as if the computer couldn't quite tell if something was making it ill but didn't want to whine about it.

Honda put her elbows on the edge of the console and rested her chin in her cupped hands, peering at the image, her eyes narrowing in concentration. Her lips pursed in thought, making her appear about twelve. She began to smile and reached a finger towards the console, glancing Levitson's direction.

"May I?"

Levitson paused, taking a deep breath. His eyes relaxed, and he chuckled. "Sure. Why not? It's not like we're going to *die.*"

"Thank you." Honda tapped the console once, then rapidly several more times. The entire display rotated and magnified, sucking them in like a ship at light speed traversing a star field. Four meters tall, the display now centered on the magnets between the two sections of the ship. A grid erupted, as if netting the power emanating from the drive, and it shimmered with the magnetic field put out by the Casson Drive. Two bars had trouble aligning, the lines flickering repeatedly.

"There, that's your problem." Honda smiled pertly, as if the situation had required only her presence to resolve itself.

"Been working that spot for the last twenty minutes," Levitson growled, although he smiled to soften the comment. "That seems to be the reason for our phenomenal and unprecedented increase in speed. If only Deesy were here. He'd have this bagged and tagged. He was the best at tweaking the drives." He tapped an icon, shifting the image slightly, and shook his head.

"Until that decompression blowout at Earth Station. Never understood that. He wasn't assigned to Level C."

"A shame, but when it's your time. Still, he could work out anything just by feeling the control board. My question is, what if I can't decipher this before we need to reverse the drive to disembark our passengers?" The ship didn't *jump* through space, like in old movies. That far-fetched concept had been proven a fallacy long before. The *Higgs slipped through real space,* just very fast, in a warped quantum field—a warp bubble—powered by the ship's rapidly spinning drive kernel. When you went fast, you had a lot of slowing down before you could stop.

"I suspect no one on board's worried about that, me least of all. You, Asher, have our utmost confidence." Honda touched him gently on the nose and stepped to the door, hardly pausing as it released its hold on the wall and slipped aside to allow her egress. "I'll be at the Gym if anyone needs me." With a wave, she was gone, and the door closed with a whisper.

Levitson leaned over his console again, and he typed a long series of entries, once using his finger to swipe a display and erase a section, then reentering a slightly different configuration of numbers and symbols. As if hesitating, he held a finger over a red square, then with a grimace, dropped it and triggered the sequence. The numbers on the display blinked, and the two errant lines, fighting like disgruntled children earlier, seemed to shake hands and agree to get along for a time. Levitson smiled and leaned back in his chair, inordinately pleased with himself.

"I'm good," he whispered to the empty room. "Thanks, Wendy. You, girl, are an inspiration."

He stood, gathered his things, and reached his hand to blank the screen when he noticed a blinking information icon in the lower corner. Touching the roller, he enlarged it and tapped. A new series of numbers appeared, revealing the grid coordinates for another section of the drive configuration. He slid the display sideways to expose the new location, and he sat heavily in his chair. Two *different* children were now fighting. He tapped a bubble onto the display, and numbers pulled up. One far down the decimal register flickered red for a moment before turning translucent blue once more.

"You've got some *chutzpah,*" Levitson muttered, frowning, as he rapped his knuckles on the console.

18

Alarms Shatter the Silence

A massive floor-to-ceiling viewscreen surrounded the Bridge, offering the crew a 360-degree panorama of space and the stars around them. It was nearly blank. Then, the nature of space is to be empty. That's what space is, a vacuum. Nothingness. Planets suspended in a void near blazing balls of fire.

With nothing better to display, the five crew on duty had sections of the screen claimed for their own; small, vivid worlds of idiosyncratic beauty—or not—revealing their distinct and very different personalities.

Ranson Charles, Communications Chief (and sometimes esteemed and overworked technical advisor), bobbed his head as he worked. Barely nineteen, he was young to be aboard the ship, but his perfect ratings at the Academy—and at seventeen—had opened doors few other people ever stepped through. His red hair stuck straight up in a dozen directions, and the undershirt protruding from his uniform was even brighter than his hair.

Just above Charles' terminal, four sections of screen pulsed with blistering images, one of a Rez concert in full flower, with flashing strobes and flames; another showed two figures—not entirely human—involved in an intimate encounter; the bottom right was a live battle scene on a disturbingly alien world; and the last was the most bizarre: Jade lightning shattered a bruised sky, leaving ruby necklaces of blood running down the screen. Brightly colored ear buds told of music no one else could hear. He wasn't watching any of his personal Views, but he smiled when especially brutal scenes flashed overhead. His hands were busy inputting coded messages into a terminal that seemed more intelligent design than computer interface.

Weldon "Welly" Clarkson manned the Cybernetics Terminal. He was a big man in his forties, with graying, receding hair and perpetual rosacea across his cheeks and nose. Officially a Mission Specialist, Clarkson's primary job was anything to do with the colonists. His claimed area of the screen scrolled through all five thousand biometric readouts, one for each one, telling of ship's resources keeping them alive and how they were adapted to being a corpsicle. The passengers were grouped in fifties, so that a micro-collision or a failure in a supply line didn't doom the entire mission. It was better to lose fifty than an entire payload. Clarkson didn't intend for any to expire on his watch.

He paused the scroll with a laser pen, backed it up a few rows, and pointed to one. Clicking, it filled his section of the screen, showing a CorpseCase with a clear, frosted window and a boy about eight inside. He seemed at peace, as if sleeping, although he'd never wake if Mother's shunts, pumps, and resurrection fluids didn't cycle life through his veins at just the right moment as they neared Deneb. Day one on the trip. Ninety-five days until Wake-Up cycled on. It was nice to give the passengers a couple of days awake before arrival, although the ship would be crowded the final days before docking. Twenty-five kilos. Clarkson adjusted the nutrient feed. The boy was using too much. Didn't want him to be sick when he woke. It was better to lose a kilo or two than be a balloon upon arrival. He moved his pen, and the display began to scroll again.

Payload Specialist Imani Okotie-Eboh had a video game running. Her duties would commence when the return cargo was loaded in the hold. The trip out was a hundred days of playtime to her. In a skin-tight StretchSuit of shimmering purple Lycra, Okotie-Eboh thrust virtual weapons and dodged scorchingly fast images dancing above her. Bioelectric pickups studding the StretchSuit conveyed her every motion into the game and returned simulated—and very painful—feedback when she failed to defend her position.

At one point, she stumbled. On the overhead, a light flashed, red globules splattered the screen dead, and Okotie-Eboh grabbed her side, cursing loudly. Everyone except Charles looked her direction for a moment then casually tuned her out. Okotie-Eboh slammed her fist on the console, blanking the screen, and took the time to twist a length of cloth around her hair, leaving it a fountain of jet fireworks pirouetting ceilingward. Stepping into a circle on the floor, she worked her shoulders, put her hands on her knees, and thrust one leg forward. The display flashed into life with a blaze of color, and a hand dripping vitreous slime seemed to reach into the room for her. Okotie-Eboh ducked and slashed, and a gleaming sword appeared on the screen, severing the arm. The game was on.

Pilot Frederick Nielson was the old man of the group. Nearly fifty, he was a ramshackle scarecrow of an officer, with long limbs and wide features. His shoulders suggested contact sports in his past, although his hips were those of a runner. His face had gone craggy decades before, but his eyes were whip-sharp, and nothing got past him. He gazed at the same scene Engineer Levitson had pulled up earlier in Engineering. Nielson had access to anything aboard that impacted the operations of the ship, and he was certain no numbers should be red, not even for a moment. When the errant number resolved itself, he smiled. He figured First Mate Honda had joined Levitson on his shakedown. It felt like something she would do. As he moved to disengage the feed, he watched the

21

image shift to another section of the drive. A blue number blinked red for a moment, and Nielson withdrew his hand, watching with a new level of fascination.

The fifth crewmember on the Bridge was positioned strategically in the most prestigious location, the Commander's Chair. Jebena Pollock had captained two previous starships, and the *Higgs* was a step up for her. Literally. She intended to do this run twice—two years of her life—and then move into the more prestigious Centauri run. At less than five light years, the trip was only five days each way. Commander Pollock wanted to start a family, and that wasn't happening when one run ate two-thirds of a year. She'd just crossed thirty, and she was still attractive enough to snag a man once she got off these god-forsaken deep-space assignments. Her blonde hair and pert breasts didn't hurt, either, especially as she'd had both augmented just out of the Academy. Part of the job. It'd gotten her this one, anyway, one night with Admiral Lebo Eriksson, a small price to pay for being a stone's throw closer to the Centauri run.

Pollock watched a virtual screen just in front of her as she spoke rapidly into a VoiceCone. The Cone used active noise control engineering to absorb Pollock's voice, effectively giving her a very narrow cone of silence, if she didn't turn her head too far to the side. It was no help against lip readers, but her conversation wasn't private, just very animated. The virtual screen flickered on her face, at times rapidly, and often in response to something Pollock said. It looked like an argument, and it didn't seem to be working toward a quick resolution.

Four stations were empty, their portions of the 360-degree screen painted with jet, and only the occasional image of a distant quasar or supernova like a reverse inkblot on black to mar the night. Science Officer Jameson Kirkpatrick was in his science lab doing science-y things, and Interplanetary Education Liaison Liam Schlegel spent more time in the ship's Virtual Learning World than he did on the Bridge, but that was to be expected.

22

Their duties involved little that required Bridge time before nearing Deneb Station. Flight Doctor Elisabet Minkovski had no permanent station on the Bridge, and her hundred days were planned in precise detail as she studied the effects of Hyper-Flight on age-accelerated rodents, hoping to be the first to conclusively document the God-gene that offered hope for extended and perhaps eternal life. If it was discovered anywhere, she insisted to anyone who dared listen, it would be on board the *Higgs*. Men would one day live to see the end of the known Universe and perhaps view the ensuing Big Bang that would usher a whole new Universe into being.

Commander Pollock's armrest blinked red, and she frowned, pushing the Cone away. Her virtual screen became clear, and she thumbed the light to see Levitson appear before her. She smiled despite herself. He was cute, in a nerdy sort of way. Not advancement material, God, no, but still, a man was a man, and she did respond to them. Who could blame her?

"Yes, Engineer?" Keep it cool. She always did.

"Commander, Firstie was just here, and there's something we think you should be aware of." Levitson barely glanced at her before looking down. It appeared he was inputting something into his terminal, then his eyes jumped up, knocking about at something she couldn't see.

"I'm listening." She pressed her lips together for a moment before relaxing them. Levitson never looked at her, not really looked. Maybe it was part of what attracted her to him. The challenge of a disinterested man.

"I've made this trip half-a-dozen times—"

"No stories," she interrupted. "What should I be aware of?"

"There's a drive thing going on. It's getting ahold of it that's stumping me. Firstie'll be glad to tell you about it when she gets there. She stopped at the Gym on the way to the Bridge."

As Levitson talked, Pollock had her eyes on Nielson's personal display. It was an image of the ship's drive. She tapped a spot in the air, and a second virtual display appeared before her, mirroring Nielson's.

"I think Nielson's onto it. He might know—"

"Maybe, Commander. I don't think so, though. Ahh, not again," and he twisted away from her view, disappearing for a moment before dropping heavily back into his seat. "You're not going to believe this. Commander, how fast do you want to get to Deneb Station?" He looked at her directly through the display as he ran his hand across his hair, his fingers causing it to stick up in a comical fashion.

"Pretty fast," she said with an uplift at the end, like it was a question. "Just tell me, Levitson. I'm a big girl. Nothing much surprises me."

"This might," he said, his eyes still locked on hers.

"And?" She studied his, thinking, God, he really does look eighteen, sometimes. It's those eyes, black, with that nose. No one would mistake this man for a WASP. He was as kibbutz as they came. Her breath surged a little faster, whether because of the intensity of his upcoming revelation or that he was actually looking at her, who knew?

"We're one day out, Commander, and we're at 160 percent of speed." His eyes grew bigger, and he licked his lips.

"Hundred-sixty percent." She had to think. Top speed, one light year per day, making 100 light years in 100 days. Of course, that was the average. They traveled much slower at the beginning and end of the voyage, so along the middle they might easily be at two, three, or even four per day. She really had no idea. Still, it was fast, faster than any other ship out there.

"And increasing." Levitson's mouth was a hard line.

"And increasing," she repeated, trying to put his words into context. "You have it under control, of course."

"Commander, I'm just the engineer. I'm trying to decide *why* we're going so fast. Nielson, maybe. He might can answer that. I'm just passing on the word, so when we break the speed record,

24

you knew it was coming." He blew out his cheeks, and in the image, he reached to something off screen and tapped the console. He glanced back and whispered, "One sixty-five, Commander."

"Painted clear as day. Thanks, Levitson." She hit the light, now green, on the arm of her chair, leaving just Nielson's viewscreen mirrored before her. She noticed the red number. "My God," she murmured, reaching to the virtual image and enlarging one section. The numbers for their speed were increasing at a blurring rate, one she couldn't make out except as a bigger number replacing the one already there.

She touched another spot on her armrest, and across the room, the border of Nielson's display blinked once. He turned to her as if he'd been expecting her communication. He nodded, and as he began to speak, the entire 360-degree viewscreen began blinking red, and klaxons blared three times.

"Lockdown, lockdown. Security alert. All security doors are now sealed and operable only with Triad voice and retinal prints. Commander, if you are still alive, please reply." Ship's computer blared the instructions into the room.

"What the devil," Pollock let fly.

"Commander acknowledged. Thank you. First Mate, please reply." There was a short pause, and the computer said, "First Mate acknowledged. Science Officer, please reply." After a pause, the computer repeated, "Science Officer, please reply."

"Where is Kirkpatrick?" Pollock muttered the comment under her breath and was irritated to hear the computer reply, "Location unknown, Commander."

Then the computer rang out, "Science Officer acknowledged. Commander, your presence is required in Weapons. Please proceed to the retinal scanner for secondary confirmation."

Pollock stood. All eyes were on her. She took a deep breath, putting a confident expression on her face. She looked good, and that was important. She didn't know what was going on, but she was the one the crew looked to for answers, and she intended to get them. If they believed she had the balls to do so, whatever the cost, they'd support her to Deneb and back.

"Chief Charles, when I return, I want to know just what's going on. Got that?"

"Yes, Commander." His ear buds rested on his console, and as he spoke, he brushed them into his lap. Even subdued, his eyes carried an eagerness that said this was exciting, and he was ready for the ride.

"Good man." She strode to the door. It didn't open, and she peered into the retinal scanner on the wall. A light flashed, the door opened, and she disappeared through, the lift opening sealed once again before she could turn around.

The hush she left in the room was deafening.

Weapons Brings a Surprise

The interior of the lift flashed gently, washing Commander Pollock in a shadowless glow, each time in a different color indicating the levels of the ship: pink for Quarters; blue for Recreation; gold for Medical, yellow for Stores; silver for Cryo-Storage; and amber for Weapons. The lift dinged. The Commander paused before the retinal scanner, and the door slipped aside with no more than a pucker of released air. Even the elevators were under environmental lock, separated from the rest of the ship when in use. No one dies today. It was the ship's motto. Dying was for tomorrow, and not on anyone's watch. Pollock's eyes covered the corridor both ways. *Lockdown. What next, replicators chewing holes in the sides of the ship?* She shook it off, glancing at the video pickup in the ceiling, knowing everything she did was observable to anyone who cared to look. With determination, she pulled herself briskly towards the main Weapons bay.

"Commander." Science Officer Kirkpatrick appeared from an adjacent corridor. The lift that direction meant he'd been in the lab, just where Pollock would expect. He sidled in next to her, quizzing, "What's up—"

"Not now." She shook her head the barest amount, but her true feelings came out in her arm. It jerked into the air, cutting him off.

"Replicators, again?" Kirkpatrick had the nerve to grin. He referred to an old joke from the Academy.

"Stuff it, Kirkpatrick." She whipped around and stopped him in his tracks, hissing, "Not now means not now. Hear that?" A rising and falling crescendo filled the silence, and it didn't belong. "You think this is a drill? Spit it out if you do."

"No, sir." His mouth had gone straight, his neck newly pale.

"Good. Let's pick up Honda and find out what's going on." She smiled as she turned, remarking, "Sorry for the gruffness. This has me off kilter, the not knowing."

"Me, too, Commander." He didn't sound convivial.

"I said I'm sorry, James. I should have been less forceful." She glanced his way but didn't slow down.

"Thank you." He seemed to let something out and sounded less distant. He pointed, "There, sir. Honda!"

The petite First Mate dropped out of the ceiling as he spoke, settling gently to the floor in a crouch, her black hair catching up with her as she stood. She released two suspension bands, and they withdrew into the ceiling just before the drop chute overhead slipped closed. She was in all black, with workout trainers on her feet and a martial arts belt around her waist.

"Training, Commander. Sorry. I dropped in directly from the Gym. I was afraid I'd miss you, otherwise."

"I had no worries, Prime. You have a clue?" Pollock nodded at Honda's earpiece. The crescendo was about the same but more concentrated closer to Weapons, and it continued to grate on her.

"No, sir, but I'm ready to kick some butt." Her device whispered confirmation, the sound a soft echo in the quietness of the corridor. "Hold, sir."

The three paused as Honda tapped her earpiece in a broken pattern, a shortcut system that spoke of long usage with the small device and kept her input private from anyone who hadn't bothered to learn her special code. Her eyes went back and forth between Kirkpatrick's and Pollock's. "Stowaways, sir?" Honda looked incredulous.

"Where?" Pollock was furious. No, not on her ship. By the stars above, how could there be stowaways? "Maybe one of the colonists wasn't chilled properly. Kirkpatrick, is that possible?"

"Umm . . ." He looked perplexed. "Maybe, but I honestly don't think so. Levitson would be the one to ask. No, Clarkson. Yeah, Welly would know, if anyone would. You want me to . . ." He tapped his comm indicator on his uniform, with a question mark in his eyes.

The computer interrupted their tête-à-tête, stating, "Centrifugal Thruster Guns now coming online. Weapons hot in three minutes."

"Shut them down!" Pollock barked the command.

"Unable to comply. Override initiated. Will attempt to bypass Weapons egress for your convenience."

"You mean we're locked out?" They had Triad permissions. Weapons was just in front of them. The retinal scanners were green. They couldn't be locked out. Pollock was incredulous. No one had higher authority than the Triad, not even the computer.

"Yes, Commander. I am attempting backdoor access. Be prepared. You may access retinal scans as you wait. My access window may be brief, and you will need to be prepared."

"Me, first." Honda was already there, her face to the scanner. When finished, she pulled Kirkpatrick after her, slapping him playfully on the shoulder and remarking, "Don't be a pansy. Step up, Jameson."

He stuck his face to the scanner, then Pollock took his place, afterward indicating ready positions in front of the door. She pointed to Honda, indicating she would go right, then to Kirkpatrick to head left. A roll of her hand confirmed her direction was the bold one, straight into the fray.

29

"Computer," she whispered. "Anytime."

"Now, Commander."

The band around the door blinked amber one time, and the door whispered aside, revealing four figures cloaked in quantum camouflage. The light bending around them was barely noticeable, just a slight shimmer at the edges. The massive Thrusters were the giveaway. They weren't camouflaged, their matte casings stealing light from the suits, revealing the hands and the barest image of the interlopers directly next to the weapons. Each weapon showed five blinking lights out of ten. They would be fire-ready at six.

"Go," Pollock hissed, leaping and dropping into a roll. She had to do the unexpected, or she'd be dead as soon as those guns locked on her. She kicked as she reached the first intruder, taking out an ankle. A feminine oomph hit her ears just before the sound of the gun tumbling to the floor. A second gun rattled, telling her another minion was down. Pollock already had an arm around the neck of her prize, and she used the downed criminal as ballast to kick the feet out from under a camouflage suit turning a Thruster her direction. The weapon flew into the air, and Honda spun, kicking it to the far side of the room. Kirkpatrick had already disabled his culprit's suit. Pollock grabbed the neck of hers and pulled, ripping the contacts apart, and the suit flickered once before dying. She elbowed its occupant upside the head and was relieved when the woman went limp.

"Kirkpatrick, Honda, where's the fourth?" Pollock realized she was breathing hard. Honda seemed at ease, even relaxed as she held her charge's arms behind his back. Kirkpatrick? His face was red with exertion, but he was holding his own. He'd pulled the strap off the weapon and tied his gangbuster to a locker.

"In back," Kirkpatrick whispered. He'd swung a terminal input from the wall and was tapping furiously. "I've . . . about . . . disengaged the gun . . . now!" He pushed the terminal aside and stood, calling, "Your weapon's no good. It won't fire. You might

30

as well come out."

"Before we make you. You won't like it if we do." Honda kept her captive's arms locked as she barked her demand.

"Magill?" A pause. "Zealander? You there? Hollis?"

"Kaseem, take them out!" The man in Honda's arms got a hard elbow to the temple, and he fainted dead away, leaving Honda free to push him aside and begin moving down an aisle to intercept the final invader from the back.

"Star-sucking," they heard, as the weapon clicked uselessly. "Fire, frag you." Something banged several times, probably the weapon against a locker.

"Enough, Kaseem. We're through, here." Pollock stood with a smile, motioning Kirkpatrick to join her. "You've got no weapons and no rights. Make it easy on yourself."

A wet oomph told of Honda's success, as the fourth Thruster clattered to the floor. Honda appeared, dragging the limp intruder into the open. His face was cratered with long scars that seemed to run under his tunic. She dropped him roughly, his head banging to the floor and bouncing once before lying still.

"That's gonna hurt." Pollock turned to the one infiltrator still conscious, and she crossed her arms, tapping her index finger broadly and plainly against her skin. "Okay, interrogation time. Let's see what this one has to say."

He slid back against the locker as she walked his direction. Kirkpatrick grinned. Honda shook her head and laughed, looking away.

This was going to be fun.

Confusion Weds Dismay

"What *mishegas!* Are all of them nuts?"

It was Engineer Levitson, and he leaned forward, peering into a scene being broadcast to any crew who wanted to watch. It was inset into his larger screen, and an orange button glowed on his console, labeled Temporary Override. His search for the trouble in the drive system was on hold. The four insurrectionists were in the brig—more precisely an unused stateroom reserved for the colonists when they awoke in ninety-five days, but lockable, so doing double duty—with their hands tied behind their backs and bruises on their faces. Chief Charles, Specialist Okotie-Eboh, and Liaison Schlegel were with Levitson in Engineering observing the interrogation. Mission Specialist Clarkson had demurred at the impromptu meeting and was with the colonists on an inspection tour, making sure no surprises caught them off guard.

"I didn't know what to make of it." Okotie-Eboh still wore her StretchSuit, although she'd pulled the feedback sensors out, revealing a taut figure, toned and with little to no fat obscuring her muscular frame. Her hair still towered skyward. "The whole trip with nothing to do, and then this. I was shivering with fear." Her hair quivered as a shudder ran down her body.

"Nah, seen it a dozen times." Schlegel blew at the nails on one hand before taking his file and starting on the other. "The bad guys never win. Never. Trust me, I know." He blew again.

"Still," Levitson murmured, "what if they'd gotten the weapons charged? What would they have done, blown the ship up?" He was already on edge, first the drive configuration out of whack, and now this.

"Nah." Schlegel laughed. "Couldn't happen. I got me a direct line to a higher power. We're protected."

"You mean that boy you rescued back on the station and had the doc stitch up? Be serious." Levitson shook his head dismissively.

"Said he was a priest, the real deal. He was, if you ask me, on the station with no chip, then disappearing like he was never there."

"Crazy people do that, Liam. Doesn't mean anything."

"Means the bad guys never win." Schlegel grinned.

Charles sat at the back, out of the conversation. His feet were propped in a chair, and his earbuds were bright spots in his ears. A terminal filled his lap, with the ever-present virtual display hovering just above it. Pollock had demanded *answers,* and he was pulling them from the system, hidden or otherwise.

Only two of the condemned were alert. Kaseem Abdullah was still out, reflecting Honda's hand-to-hand expertise. His feet were splayed in front of him, and his head lolled at an angle across the back of his chair. His arms were hidden behind his waist, and a black strap across his chest kept him from rolling to the floor. Crystal Hollis swam in glazed soup, but her eyes were at least nominally open. She might have a concussion, if Dr. Minkovski pronounced it that way. The crew didn't much care at this point. Hollis had tried to kill the ship. Shank Magill had been Kirkpatrick's conquest, tied to a locker instead of being conked on the head, and he was alive and spitting fire. His arms were twisted behind his chair, and Kirkpatrick was behind him with a weapon at his temple, forcing him to play nice. Honda had ripped into Raytheon Zealander on the way to Abdullah, and the man had taken a hard hit. He wouldn't likely be alert for some time. One eye was already swollen, and with his crooked ankle, it was doubtful he'd walk anytime soon. Just as well; there was no place on the ship he'd be welcome, no matter his story when he woke to tell his lies. He was also strapped to his chair.

"Pollock'll fry 'em. Just watch." Schlegel was onto his third nail, and he pointed to the screen. He'd yet to look at it, as if the sound told him all he needed to know. "She's got the balls to do it, if anyone does. Seen it a million times."

"Christ, Liam. Virtuals don't count. This is the real thing." Okotie-Eboh shuddered again. "Why would they want the Thrusters? Everyone'd die. What's the point of that?"

"Not if they used a Daughter." Levitson tore his eyes from the screen, and he searched his companions' faces. "You don't think—" He slashed into his terminal, his breathing growing hard, his fingers dancing on the input sensors. His large screen blanked, becoming a neutral backdrop of undulating pixels. As he worked, various points of light brightened and faded in tandem with his jabbing fingers, a visual representation of his queries as he probed the ship's databanks.

"Think what, Ashe? Don't tease then leave us in the dark. What'r'u thinking, something bad?" Okotie-Eboh dropped into a chair, her voice climbing higher and higher in pitch.

"Found it," Levitson cried, his voice triumphant.

"Found it," Charles called at almost the same time, pulling his earbuds from his ears. Faint music thumped from the devices, a punctuated background to his announcement. His hair was a flame of excitement.

The two stood and faced each other. On the screen at Levitson's side, Hollis spat a wad of saliva at Pollock, and Kirkpatrick cuffed her upside the head as the commander wiped her face with her sleeve. "You bilge-head," Pollock muttered clearly over hidden speakers before motioning, and Kirkpatrick yanked up on the woman's arms, forcing her forward, causing Hollis to yelp in pain. The ship's medic was off to the side, but she made no move toward her. Her eyes were on Pollock, and there hadn't been a request for help.

"What'd you find?" Schlegel asked, finally looking up. He grinned, as if he thought all this amusing. "Ashe, Liam? Who's first?"

"You go," Levitson pointed, with a wave of his hand at the Communications Chief.

"You called it. Those jerks are in custody. Mine will wait. Go." Charles dropped into his chair, realized his keyboard was under him, and jerked up before removing it and seating himself more carefully.

"Yeah, okay. Well, see, a Daughter's already powered up. These guys knew everything. They weren't leaving anyone to rat on them." His face was pale, and it glistened with sweat. "What'd you get, Ranse?" Levitson dropped into his seat, blowing his cheeks out and running his hand across his face. He'd passed his conceptual threshold on the reality of imminent death about an hour before, and this wasn't helping.

"Anyone heard of the Society of Serpents?" Charles grinned. Of course, they had.

"They took out the London Eye back in '98, didn't they? They were ramping up for the 200th birthday celebration, then it was gone." Levitson seemed to sulk. Of course, Charles' discovery was better than his. Of course.

"And about 80,000 partiers. The reason why is what's important to us. It was payback for defunct British colonialism in Africa three centuries before. No matter that the people killed weren't alive then."

"So, what have *we* done?" Okotie-Eboh was interested. Her family lived in Africa, and life still wasn't good in many places.

She'd emigrated a lifetime before and had no hard feelings. The crew were her friends, or as close as she got, with her 100 days of play while they were working their butts off.

"I can't be certain, but I ran the corpsicle list, and we've got a possible target. American Klu Klux Klan. Extinct now, of course, but those old farts had children, and they liked to inter-marry. We've got a tribe of descendants in Section 8. I suspect all four of them," he indicated the interrogation on the far side of the screen, "have strong Serpent ties. No matter how you draw the lines, it looks pretty connected."

"We should let Welly know." Levitson reached for the comm switch. His hand hovered, and he waited for confirmation. His response was understood. There were a thousand freezer pops times five. Specialist Clarkson was there now, and that was a lot of popsicles to cover. However, any grease on his feet would be a bonus to everyone.

"My onus. I've got it covered." Charles stood, gathering his earbuds and slipping them into a pocket. He set his keyboard to the side, twirling once and pointing at the others, calling, "Later, dudes and dudette." Laughter followed him out the door.

"The London Eye?" Okotie-Eboh had her feet in her chair and her arms around her knees. She rocked. "I don't know what that is."

"Hey, Africa-born. Check this out." Schlegel had out his Kinnect, and he unrolled the screen and held it in front of him. "Pull up London Eye, year 2000."

It responded, "London Eye, Cantilevered Observation Wheel, Great Britain, CE 2000. Once located on the Thames River, it was destroyed in CE 2198. See attached image file."

Schlegel tossed the Kinnect her direction, and she caught it, shaking the screen flat. An image of a Ferris wheel-type device towered over a glittering night skyline, and it was lighted in bright pink. The colors shimmered in the Thames.

"That's beautiful," she cooed. "Pink. I love it."

The Kinnect responded, "The Eye attracted up to 5 million visitors each year before its demise. It was closed from 2113 until its grand reopening in 2117, after river water undermined a footing, and the structure developed an alarming tilt. A popular petition to stabilize the Eye at 3.5 degrees of tilt was rejected, and the tower was righted to 0 degrees. After its destruction, the five undamaged capsules were permanently installed at Hyde Park in London as a memorial to those killed in the blast."

"Oh, my God," she whispered, without looking up. "At least there was a memorial. We would have had nothing. Space junk. No one'd come to see that."

"It's a good thing they don't have to," Schlegel remarked, standing and retrieving his pocket computer. He slipped his file in his jacket and exited the door after Charles. He didn't bother to send his farewells.

"What're you going to do, Imani?" The scene with Pollock still played on the video. Minkovski was injecting Abdullah in the arm, and Zealander was rousing. He sported a spot in the crook of his elbow indicating the doc had already gotten to him. Levitson watched, interested and not. The grand adventure was winding down, and with the Commander fully in control. They had ninety-eight days of boring before unloading at Deneb. It was fun while it lasted, but it was over.

"Don't know." Okotie-Eboh still looked rattled.

Levitson turned to Okotie-Eboh and grinned. "I'd like to get my hands on one of those camo suits. Take it for a stroll when the popsicles wake up. A little quantum fun, find out what they really think of our delivery service."

She laughed, the ice water fright from the thwarted attack finally warmed. "Find out the truth. They know we're lazy pudzos, and they're too polite to say so."

"Some of us, anyway. The rest get no sleep." He winked, the expression barely there, given especially for the Payload Specialist. He might not notice Pollock's overtures, but Okotie-

Eboh was a gaming vixen, and she'd been on his radar since she boarded two trips past.

"I pay my dues." She stood and blew him a kiss, her payback for the wink. "Wait till we get there. I won't have time to wipe my own backside. Bye, Asher." She slipped out the door.

Levitson tried to place what he'd been on when the alarm had sounded. The tall screen overhead shimmered, the pixels telling of inactivity from his terminal. It had been a long day filled with entirely too much excitement. He shook his head and clicked off the scene in the brig. His stomach drew his attention, and he stood, adjusting his uniform to head to the Mess. He realized he'd missed lunch. Everyone had, except perhaps Pilot Nielson. God knew where he'd gotten to during the fray. Still piloting, Levitson presumed, even as the interlopers tried to do the dirty on board their ship.

As the door closed behind him, a section of the screen came to life, showing a red band reading, "Attention required. Acceleration now reaching 7,250 percent of normal speed. This is outside the safe operating parameters of the ship's design." Silently, it began to repeat, "Attention required . . ."

Impromptu Tribunal

"That machine's *gornisht helfn!*" Levitson tossed his supper tray onto a table, the forward motion carrying it just to an empty spot on the far side. Frost formed a winter scene on his cubed turkey, with a ski slope of gravy waiting to be thawed.

Three booths were in arched niches, giving a bit of separation to the all-white space. Overhead, the ceiling arched with lighted insets hidden in the folds. There were no windows, either walls, ceiling, or floor. Quarters were overhead, and below was Medical. Windows were reserved for the private spaces in Quarters and those in the Observation Bubble. Okotie-Eboh had Levitson blocked, and he put one hand on the back of the bench seat and leaped over, sliding deftly into place.

"I would have moved. Why's it beyond help?" Okotie-Eboh smiled at Levitson. The crew were familiar with his casual Yiddish and understood most of what he said, the intent, if not the actual words. She had changed from her StretchSuit into a diaphanous robe that revealed chocolate limbs and a neck that never seemed to end. Her hair was tucked in a knit bag at her neck, imprisoned by a jeweled tie with sparkling bangles. With no outstanding duties, she was the one crewmember who could get away with such flamboyant dress. She smiled at Levitson, and her face was that of an effervescent goddess.

"Nah, the food." He pulled a steam cover from above and slipped it over his tray. It hissed; released, it retracted, leaving his ski slope a steaming brown river. "I wanted a burger. Seems someone got the last one until Tuesday." He worked at a mound of gravy-covered flesh as he glared at Kirkpatrick across the table.

"Hoy! I got here first." He held up both hands, as if to say, keep your complaints on your side of the table, mate. His burger was half gone, anyway. "You can have my chips, if you want."

Levitson took one, scooping some catsup on the way. He turned when Honda, Nielson, Pollock, and Charles walked in together, bantering loudly. Pollock had on a fresh tunic. Honda was laughing.

"Magill's regretting coming aboard about now, and you, Commander, look fine, as always." Honda raised a hand to those already seated. "You got the last burger, Kirkpatrick, as usual? Two days out, and what's that, six, already?"

"Six!" Levitson glowered. "I haven't had one."

"Poor baby." Pollock put her hand on his shoulder, as if in commiseration, holding it there too long for something so simple. "The rest'll cycle up soon."

"Thanks, Commander." He tore into his food, keeping his eyes down until the hand was gone. He grinned at Okotie-Eboh. "Can't wait."

Charles was at the AutoVend searching the menu. His ear buds dangled from one pocket, and his hair was in greater disarray than normal. He tapped turkey and gravy, and added a double tap on the roll icon. When his tray slid out, he did it again, this time choosing chicken pasta with mixed vegetables. He placed the chicken across from Okotie-Eboh and nudged Honda, pointing, as he fell into the adjoining booth with his turkey. He pulled his table's steamer down, and it began to hiss. Pollock sat without anything in front of her. She looked at Levitson, and the lines around her mouth revealed her tension.

"Space the lot of them!"

The crowd turned to see Clarkson flood the doorway. His face was redder than usual, and he looked angry. He carried a canvas-covered pack with him, and he set it hard in front of Pollock. He blew his cheeks out and tightened his jaw, his eyes narrowing.

"And this is?" Pollock tore her eyes from Levitson and hit Clarkson with them.

"Open it," he said, his voice hard, and his words curt. "I can't even speak."

"Doing pretty well," Kirkpatrick said, with a smile, "if you ask me."

"Chief Charles, if you'll do the honor." Pollock nodded at him. The Mess was normally off limits for work, and her look said this had better be good.

"A Christmas present, for me?" He grinned and pushed his plate aside. He pulled it close, unzipped it from one side, across the top, and down the other. He separated the top before leaping from his seat, jarring the table, and bumping hard into Clarkson, only stopping once he was across the room.

"Thought you might like it." Clarkson snorted his satisfaction.

"It's a . . . it's a . . ."

"Don't worry. I disarmed it."

"I didn't expect you to actually . . . *find* one." Chief Charles tried to laugh it off. "You sure it's disarmed? I mean, it looks so *real.*"

"It *is* real." Clarkson pulled the bag away to reveal a block of explosives, together with an ignition device. "Right there in Section 8, exactly where you suggested."

"Feh!" Levitson started, but stopped when Okotie-Eboh placed her hand on his arm. His snow scene turned running river was mostly gone, and he pushed away the rest. "We would've been dead. What would have been the point, killing five thousand

41

people?"

It was more than that. For weeks before the corpsicles had been dropped into their cryo-cylinders, there had been opportunities for the prospective colonists to meet the crew. They'd still been on Earth, then. A few had shown up at every meet-and-greet. It was them Levitson was thinking of, and heads nodded, whispering names of several they remembered fondly.

"Five thousand and ten, but let's not quibble over the details. The next question is, what do we do with them? We can't let them loose, and we don't have enough drugs to sedate them the whole trip. Besides, it's not fair to Doc Minkovski to be forced to babysit. She's got an agenda planned. Ninety-eight days lost? She won't like that." Pollock still hadn't touched the canvas pack, and except for a brief glance, hadn't looked at it, either.

Nielson cleared his throat. He had coffee in front of him, and the steam swirled. It was one of the few items that came out of the AutoVend fully prepared and ready to consume. Nielson was nothing if not a man of economy, both in words as in action. The room quieted, waiting.

"Maybe Welly's right, but it wouldn't be proper, would it? Doing to them what they'd have done to us is just another way of showing who's in power."

"We could do that, space 'em?" Okotie-Eboh seemed surprised.

"You bet." Commander Pollock stood, using the table to push herself up, and she took a deep breath. "Out here, I'm king, and Prime's my queen. You're the court, and Doctor Minkovski and Liaison Schlegel, of course. You, Payload Specialist, you have full rights, also. We get to live with our decision, and that's the hard part. Any other options? I agree that using our store of drugs and committing Minkovski to jailer duty isn't my idea of okay."

"Drop 'em in CorpseCases for the rest of the trip?" Liaison Schlegel stepped through the door. "Didn't mean to eavesdrop. It was so interesting, I didn't have the heart to interrupt."

"No spares." Clarkson was seated, and he ran a hand through his receding hair.

"We always have spares." Honda was bright with enthusiasm. "Right, Imani?" Everyone looked the Payload Specialist's way.

"Usually." She smiled apologetically. "We've got some special cargo on board. The colonists paid extra to transport two simians and two canines."

Schlegel laughed. "I could manage a monkey for a pet for the next three months. Anyone want a dog? What would be so bad about that? Surely the corpsicles won't mind, so long as their pets arrive in good condition."

"They're pregnant," Okotie-Eboh explained.

"Yeah, that'd be great, Liaison Schlegel." Pollock finally laughed. "We'd have two dozen puppies under our feet, and anyone know how many young that monkeys have? Our food stores would run low by the time we reached Deneb."

"They may anyway, with four extra mouths to feed." Nielson took a final drain on his cup. "We need something better, hopefully without spacing our friends down on Medical or raising a couple litters of pups aboard the ship."

"Can we spare a Daughter?" Levitson didn't look up. It was a very bad option, but the Commander had asked.

"Hey, mate. Don't even suggest that." Kirkpatrick hissed the words. The Daughters were their shuttles for runs to and from a planet's surface. There were two. Similar in design to Mother, they were also their backup ships, and like Mother, could achieve relativistic speeds with independent Magnetic Resonance Drives. Launching while at speed, no telling how much acceleration a Daughter would be able to attain. They were their hope if something happened to the main drive, their *only* hope.

"Spacing our guests, not really an option." Pollock grimaced and looked to Nielson, as if she'd considered it before he'd laid out the moral boundaries for everyone to see. "Running out of food probably wouldn't happen, although we might need to consider short rations the second half of the trip. Can we manage with one Daughter? Levitson, what's your opinion?"

"I'm just Science Officer, Commander." He laughed deprecatingly. "Freddie or James," he motioned, "could say better."

"You're the one that brought it up. Why, if you can't commit?"

"Oh, that's easy." He brightened, now more confident. "One's powered up, already."

"By whose orders?" Pollock's ire bled through, and her eyes darted around the gathered crew.

"Sorry, Commander." Charles took charge of explaining. "Levitson found it while you were in interrogation. Our friends in camo were planning it as their escape route, we think. We hadn't had time to make a report. I think that's the only reason Asher mentioned it."

"Then, anyone. Can we manage with one Daughter?" It was Pollock's first trip as Commander, and her question was a good one. The crew who knew the ship understood what she needed and what she didn't.

"Never been tried. We might be able to use the rail launcher to avoid conflicts in the two Casson Fields. That'll be the real issue." Liaison Schlegel had his arms crossed. His tunic appeared freshly pressed, and he looked confident and in his element. "I could run a simulation, have the ship download current conditions, dovetail it into Virtual. You want?" He shrugged.

"Maybe, if we can't resolve this here. We'd still have one for backup. How would this work?" Pollock was considering it. "Levitson, you have an answer for that?"

"We could set the controls to anywhere we wanted, lock out the drive computer, and someone else could take custody."

"And turn them loose to try again." Honda brought attention to the elephant in the room.

"Okay, put them in a Daughter, but not to any particular location. How fast can we set the drive?" This was why Pollock

44

was Commander. She was good at nosing out the difficult options and making them palatable to people who were good and moral.

"Starting at current speed?" Levitson considered. "If we tweak the settings for the resonance field, unrestricted acceleration is possible. The problem isn't the speed but slowing back down."

"If we don't want them to slow down?" Pollock fought a smile.

"They'd have to slow down." Levitson looked to Okotie-Eboh and back to the Commander.

"Humor me. What if?"

"Let me." Nielson, as Pilot, saw what she meant. "If we push her out of flat space, time dilation will resolve our issue. Get fast enough, and inside the ship, time'll slow down, living out maybe, what, a week, two weeks of relative time, while a couple of centuries go by out here. They become a problem for the distant future, and all with plenty of air, water, food, and fuel. That what you're getting at, Commander? Moral issues resolved, with no deaths on our hands."

"If we consider this, we have to be unanimous. We do have other options, and I won't go forward without everyone committing." Pollock saw those considering it. Crew were catching each other's eyes, with nods of agreement. "The only one not here is Doctor Minkovski. If we're agreed on this, I'll speak to her, see if she's willing to trade nearly a hundred days of babysitting for one Daughter."

"She won't care." It was Clarkson. "She's already got mice to mind. I'll vouch for her."

"I'll ask, anyway. Thanks, Welly. You want to get this out of here? And no," she smiled, putting her hand on the bomb as if it were nothing, "you may not reset it and stow it on the Daughter if we decide to follow through on this. We're not taking any lives, not if there's any way to avoid it."

With the matter resolved as much as it could be for the time being, calm settled over the Mess. Clarkson set the bag in the corridor for later removal and chose a fine meal of beef stew, with hot peppers and garlic bread on the side. Pollock pulled a chef salad with chicken strips, flash frozen and best eaten cold. Kirkpatrick and Honda regaled those not present with the juiciest details of the interrogation and more, to everyone's delight, including moving the injured and uninjured detainees to the Medical level, where the Doctor had given them serious sedatives and was making necessary repairs to those injuries that needed them. It seemed that Magill had mysteriously managed to break a wrist in transit; Hollis hadn't known when to keep her mouth shut, resulting in a split lip; and Zealander might need a bone in his ankle pinned. Abdullah? That concussion of Hollis'? Attitude deemed Abdullah needed one, also.

The real conversation during dinner wasn't taking place in the Mess. It was one-sided and happening on Engineer Levitson's full-wall monitor. The ship, well-designed and fresh from a complete refit, worked seamlessly. There was no sense of acceleration or speed while traversing the emptiness of space. The micro-adjustment that Levitson had found earlier wasn't affecting the ship's stability. Rather, it was allowing the massively powerful magnets between the drive module—with its rapidly spinning drive kernel trapped in a warped quantum-containment field—and the nose of the ship to draw infinitely closer together (normal when under controlled acceleration), thereby bypassing the computer's fail-safe warning system. Silently, the red band, hoping for someone's notice, announced repeatedly, "Attention required. Acceleration now reaching 145,600 percent of normal speed. This is outside the safe operating parameters of the ship's design." The numbers changed, growing larger, as the words scrolled again, "Attention required . . ."

Taking the Path Less Traveled

"A piece of cake! Right!" Crystal Hollis' eyes were clear, too clear, and she vomited her fury over Shank Magill's relaxed form. She was a vixen with her thick, dark hair, darker eyes, and olive skin. Her naturally red lips and flashing anger did nothing to detract from her beauty. "We were set up to head back to Earth, and we wind up here. How the proton flush did that happen? I knew I should'a gutted that kid when I had the chance."

"Relax, Hollis. We're not done here, yet. The kid's gone, and you think they're gonna space us? This joint's got more weak links than a kid's swing set. You'll get home, yet." Magill was smug, and with his pale latte skin, he was hard to read. He claimed African ancestry, but she couldn't find it, and that infuriated Hollis more. He had no *right* to pass for white, when she'd been ridiculed for her skin all her life. What she *liked* about him was his life's mission: Eradicate the devils that had enslaved his forebears.

"Get up, Kaseem! Do something about that space turd." She glared at Magill as she hit Abdullah hard on the side of the leg. He was on a bed, his arms behind his head, watching the fireworks, and he claimed he still felt dizzy when he stood. "I thought you were *with* me. You becoming a wuss, too?"

He looked away and ignored her.

Raytheon Zealander—no one knew his real name—was to the side on his own, practicing martial arts moves. His ankle was taped, and he was being careful with it. He was probably doped up to be on it after the damage it had taken. It was rumored, quite believably, that he was on the lam after killing a woman on the mat, and that he had taken the names of his last four victims for his own. By the size of his arms, they knew better than to mess with him when he wanted left alone.

Magill stood, his ancestral heritage coming out in his long legs and smooth walk. "I got backup plans in here. That kid might have screwed with our plans, but there's always options." He tapped his forehead and moved to the door, placing his hand on the access panel. It blinked yellow, and he slapped his hand against it. He stood for a moment, breathing hard, before regaining control and turning with a smile. "Just gotta work it out, that's all. It'll come to me. We got 98 *days*. Ain't nobody stopping us."

"At's what you said when we donned those camo suits. In there, sweatin' like pigs, and you said they wouldn't know what was coming. Well, they did, space turd." Hollis had a hand on one hip, and the other dancing in front of his face.

"I said," Magill grabbed the wrist attached to the hand, "ain't nobody stopping us, and that's the way it'll be. Chick, you need to chill."

"Chill? I need to chill?" With her other hand, she swung and connected firmly with his cheek, throwing his head sideways with a loud crack. Before she could draw her hand away, he had her turned and wrapped in his arms, one around her waist, and the other on her forehead, pulling her head against him and exposing her neck. He laughed.

"Kaseem, what should I do with my prize?" Hollis squirmed, but she didn't cry out. Magill placed his face next to hers, and he licked her cheek. Her eyes narrowed, and she worked her lips, barely under control.

"You got what you want?" She spat the words.

"Nah, baby. I want some time with you." He whipped her around and kissed her hard on the mouth. She fought for a moment, then gave in to it. As soon as she did, he pushed her roughly away, laughing. "All women want it. You just ain't getting it."

"You . . . *turd,* you. You just wait!" In her fury, she leaped at him, her arms around his neck and her legs around his waist. They tumbled against Abdullah's bed, the tussle becoming more passionate than vicious.

"Idiots! You don't know how much I hurt. Get off!" Abdullah pushed them with his foot, and they crashed to the floor, finally separating. "That how you going to take down the man, with a little lovin' from a woman? Takes more than that to blow up a ship and not die in the process."

The door whispered aside, two bristling weapons clearing the opening. Even Zealander stopped what he was doing to pay attention.

"It's about time," Hollis shrieked. "We got rights, too. Who the jerks you think you are, keeping us in here without a trial. We ain't done nothing."

"Yeah, nothing." Honda was first in. Her weapon was almost bigger than she was, but she moved smoothly, and there was no doubt she ate with it, showered with it, and took it to bed with her at night. All sweetness was gone. She wore a riot helmet with a clear faceplate, giving her an insectoid appearance with the extra-large head on her tiny frame. "Specialist Okotie-Eboh, got the cuffs?"

She stepped in, closely followed by Kirkpatrick. Both wore matching riot helmets. Kirkpatrick's weapon matched Honda's, and they covered Okotie-Eboh as she stood between them.

"You first, Hollis. On the floor." Kirkpatrick pointed with his weapon. "You others, back. We do this one at a time."

"You gotta be friggin' out of your heads." Abdullah hadn't moved. "I've got a concussion; Zealander, or whatever his name is, is over there on drugs because you broke his foot. He can barely stand. How we supposed to come against you and break your faces?" There was a momentary lull, and in those few seconds, Abdullah leaped like an angry bull for Honda, so fast his body seemed to blur. She was quicker, the butt of her weapon coming around and connecting with his head. He crashed to the floor with a soft exhalation of air, pausing in a crouch for a short time before collapsing totally.

"Now we know where the scars came from, total stupidity. Anybody else?" Honda barked her question.

Zealander backed up a slow step, moving with a pronounced limp, giving in to his taped foot. He didn't speak, but his eyes calculated, taking in the open door, the distance between the three crew members, and Abdullah collapsed on the floor. Resting his eyes on the two guns and the riot helmets, he let out a tight breath, and his massive shoulders dropped several centimeters, as if giving in. It was unlike him to cede even the smallest amount. His apparent calm didn't inspire confidence in his caretakers.

Hollis was a caged tiger, her back riled, and she was next to Magill as her ally of the moment. She began to sidespeak in a pidgin code, her eyes narrowed at Honda before jumping to Okotie-Eboh. If they'd been lasers, she'd have fired already. Her arms quivered with fury.

Magill was a Cool Luke and held up both hands, one in a flexible splint-cast, and spoke in a reasonable and pleasant voice. "Hold on. That wasn't us." He pointed to Abdullah on the floor and chuckled. "Even I think Kaseem's a wild card. We had no idea that was coming. We're prepared to cooperate—"

"Cooperate?" Hollis whipped around, her hand flying towards Magill's face. He caught her wrist just in time. "Like hell, we will," she spat.

"Yes, my sweets. Co-op-er-ate." He said it like four separate words, slowly. Behind him, Zealander let out a short laugh, his first sound since they'd been locked up together. Magill ignored him, keeping his attention on Honda as the most dangerous of their jailers.

"Cooperate?" Kirkpatrick spat the word. "With camo suits and Thrusters? Hoy, I should just hit you now, save us the food and water you're likely to consume. Now, you ready to tell us how you got on board? Or you want to kiss your freckle good-bye as we stand here?" Sure enough, the light from a laser sight danced across Magill's chest.

"It's been a misunderstanding, that's all." Suave Magill, his hair thick and wavy, his dark eyes sincere, worked his devious magic. "We had no idea this was a personnel transport, have no idea how we got here. Colonists. Why would we have any interest in harming innocent families out to better their lot in life? We were told there were terrorists aboard, with ordnance and other such materiel destined for Deneb Station. Even we get incorrect information at times. Who can say? For your peace of mind, we'll be glad to remain in our quarters for the remainder of the trip."

Hollis still steamed, furious at his words of betrayal. Zealander's chuckle said he was following their leader's intent fine. Magill was giving them an opportunity for a second chance.

Kirkpatrick blew that wide open.

"You'll keep to your own quarters, all right, just not here. Imani, cuff the one on the floor. You, little woman. You're next. Hands behind your back; face the wall. I've got you covered, Imani. Cuff her next."

The cuffs were strips that interlocked, one end feeding into the other. It made a ratcheting sound as she pulled it tight around Abdullah's wrists. Standing and moving behind Hollis, she pulled a second band from her waist and interlocked it around the woman's wrists. She ratcheted it slowly.

"Tight, Imani," Kirkpatrick barked. "You saw what she did to the Commander."

51

"Sorry," Okotie-Eboh whispered, as she yanked the strap, causing it to click several more times.

Hollis hissed, "Sniveling boy toy. You gonna kiss his crotch when he says to?"

"Ignore her, Imani. She's trying to rile you." Honda kept her laser on Hollis' back the entire time. She knelt and with one hand snapped a cord onto Abdullah's cuffs, then walked to Hollis and did the same. Magill offered Okotie-Eboh his wrists in front of him, and Kirkpatrick called him on it.

"Behind you, Magill. These other three might be pawns, but you've got some brains. We're taking no chances. Imani, not too close until he complies." Kirkpatrick motioned with his weapon, his laser circling as he used it to punctuate his demand.

"So, what's the plan?" Magill kept his voice neutral, that of cooperation and reasonableness. "Are you putting us to sleep for the duration?" He chuckled as he said it, making it into a joke that was too extreme for belief.

"After a fashion," Kirkpatrick said. Magill was cuffed, and his laser centered on Zealander next. "You, mate. No fancy footwork. Just let us cuff you, and we'll be on our way."

When Honda got the cord latched to the last inductee—and giving them plenty of space—the team marched the four cuffed bandits down the corridor. Abdullah stumbled along with the help of Magill, who swore at his weight and awkward gait. Hollis kicked at Abdullah each time he went down. Zealander limped at the end of the line, his eyes in motion, looking as though he'd already be gone, even with the cuffs, if he didn't have three people, one of them a cripple, attached to his arms.

"Think they've got any idea?" Okotie-Eboh whispered the words to Honda. They tailed the group, Honda's weapon ready, while Kirkpatrick was ahead. When Zealander looked their direction, Honda shushed her, and they moved silently forward.

52

Terminal Abuse

Engineer Levitson was on the bridge of *Daughter Two*, and he was engrossed at his terminal. Chief Charles, Welly Clarkson, and Liaison Schlegel were with him, just not *with* him. Levitson was adjusting the ship's drive parameters, per the Commander's orders, for maximum acceleration. When finished, his next job was to disengage the braking sequence. Essentially, he would be setting the ship's downsized Cassel-Jackson Magnetic Resonance Drive on full thrust and leaving it on in full acceleration mode. God knew how they would be rescued. It was no more than theory how an out-of-control Casson Drive could be retrieved once it reached speed, not without the ability to internally slow itself down. That required full reverse thrust, the giant magnets pulling themselves apart rather than edging ever closer together. Levitson's guess was they'd go so fast, they'd still be traveling when the cosmos wound itself down to absolute zero and exploded into the next rendition of life, the next Big Bang, to quote 21st century scientific theory. He felt almost sorry for what they were doing to the poor suckers who'd be aboard. Having seen them on the video during interrogation mitigated his sympathy, however, and he continued entering instructions into the drive computer.

"Settings non-compliant with the drive's safe tolerance levels." The computer's cleanly enunciated words, spoken in a smooth and warm tone, were honey over the speakers. "The minimum allowable magnet clearance is—"

"Hush it." The computer fell silent, and Levitson continued to work. Drawing the magnets in beyond design parameters was how he could increase the acceleration to relativistic speeds, push the ship to the edge of flat space, and essentially trap the passengers inside, using time as the lock and speed as the key. Even if they did work out a way to unravel the drive system's computer lockout, it would take them days. By then, it would be decades or even centuries in the future on the outside. Problem solved for the *Higgs*.

"How's it coming, Levitson?" Chief Charles, his ever-present ear buds dangling from a pocket, leaned into the small bridge. "Need any help? This is my area of *ex-per-tise*." He grinned.

"Give me a bit of technical advice, Communications Chief. That's what you're paid for, right?" Levitson glanced at him and smiled.

"Among other things. What'cha need help with?" He seemed very pleased to be asked. On the screen, only a fraction of the size of Engineering's massive one, a diagram of *Daughter Two* lay with her intestinal workings out for them to see. The ship, only a fraction the size of the *Higgs*, was a bulbous rectangle, with a massive head at one end. That was the magnet. A short distance away was a second magnet attached to the Cassel-Jackson Magnetic Resonance Drive. The two looked completely separate, and they were. Just as with handheld magnets, they didn't have to touch to be stable. The attraction was there, seen or not. Just like electric magnets, turn on the switch, and the two couldn't be separated. Move one, and the other had to tag along the same direction. The Casson Drive provided the power, and the magnets dragged the ship after it. The magnets could never be allowed to touch. The Resonance Field must be continually balanced and dampened. The Drive absorbed energy as it accelerated, using that same energy to decelerate, rather like regenerative braking, except this was regenerative acceleration. Should the magnets touch while at speed, theoretically, the Field could release its total energy in a blast that would decimate an entire parsec of space. It was only theory, however, because it had never happened. The core of the Drive, enabling it to perform successfully, was the warped quantum field powered by the ship's rapidly spinning drive kernel. Kept offset, with one side flattened, the ship was constantly pulled toward an empty place in space, essentially a manufactured black hole, creating a massive wave in space-time. The closer one got, the bigger the wave, and the more acceleration was available. There was a down side. Just like playing on the rim of any black hole, too close, and you might fall in. The Casson Drive wanted to fall in the black hole. The ship kept it from doing so, and hence, travel through space at multiple light years per day was possible, riding a warp bubble of flat space across the cosmos.

Levitson had to get the *Daughter*'s magnets very close, because this ship would be accelerating more rapidly than any ship had ever done before. As the Drive tipped closer and closer to its manufactured black hole, the passengers on the ship would feel as though normal time was passing, but the rest of the Universe would see them hovering nearly motionless within their ship as the rapidly moving *Daughter Two* eventually achieved full acceleration.

"How foolproof is our lockout going to be?" Levitson continued to input adjustments, and the numbers on the screen scrolled, adjusting themselves as his fingers struck the input pads.

"Not very, I think."

"Oh?" Levitson sat back, surprised. "What makes you say that? We're stripping out everything technical. They'll have nothing to work with."

"You must not know about Shank Magill, certified genius IQ

and master programmer. I thought you might have recognized him. Remember the technician that replaced Deecy after that decompression accident on Earth Station LaGrange? I'm guessing he hacked in and built himself a backdoor, then accessed the *Higgs* when he got aboard. Nearly took us offline. Your job is to slow him down."

"Mac? I rather liked him. Who'd have thought?" Levitson rolled his eyes and gave a sour chuckle. "At this point, *our* job is to slow him down. I thought of doing this." He tapped in a series of instructions, and they bled across the display in an orange band, equations and instructions in computer code. "There. If I insert a white rabbit, then do this," tapping several more times on the terminal, "without knowing what's here," he tapped his forehead, "there's no way to override the computer."

"Unless they do this." Charles did a quick input, overriding the white rabbit, and the entire orange band disappeared. He sat back and grinned. "I got that from one of my simulations."

"Undo it," Levitson instructed. When Charles did, Levitson took the white rabbit and added a subsidiary code beneath it, then asked Charles to try again. After three attempts, the orange band remained intact.

"Good, my man. Now, help us get this stuff unloaded. Honda and all her friends are on the way. We're ready to send them packing ASAP. We've a load of colonists to deliver, and we plan to be on time."

"Early, maybe," Levitson chuckled.

"Early? How's that?" Charles was standing, and he looked at Levitson, puzzled. "What do I not know?"

"Ah, it's nothing, just an odd reading this morning. The Resonance Field was drawing energy at a faster rate than normal. I had Firstie look over it, and we made some tweaks. The good news is, we may be getting to Deneb a few days before our scheduled arrival window. How's that sound, a little vacation time on the company's tab?"

56

"I could do with that. Maybe spend a day in a Deneb Sauna Pool. Has the ship been feeling a bit chilly to you?" Charles rubbed his arms as if trying to warm them.

"Ha, ha. Funny, you. Let me wrap this, and I'll be right out."

Levitson turned to the ship's input terminal, but the Chief's words nagged him. He'd felt it, too, the coolness, and had dismissed it. Then he shrugged, adjusted his clothing, and leaned in to his input board once more.

Parting Shot

"Doctor, any last-minute suggestions for medical care? They were pretty roughed up. If we're taking the moral high ground, I don't want any doubts left in anyone's mind."

Commander Pollock watched three video feeds on the screen in her personal quarters. Doctor Elisabet Minkovski's surgery took up one, with the good doctor wiping down her surgery table. The video feed was high on the wall, and she looked up and held out a reddened sponge, then pulled down an overhead sprayer. The sound of water hitting the table was a hissing rebuke.

"I'll get back with you, Doctor." Pollock tapped the terminal, and the Medical feed shifted to show Pilot Nielson on the Bridge. He was hunched over, his lined face and wide shoulders giving him the look of impenetrable stone. He was, too, emotionally. Stable as a rock. Hard as one, too, something she had come to depend on. He could make a call in the heat of things, and it was the same call he'd make when the dust settled and minds were clear. He was someone she'd want at her helm during an emergency, which this had nearly been. She smiled when she drew in to the screen he watched. It was the Drive Field, a diagram showing an extrapolated image of the Magnetic Resonance Field binding the *Higgs* to her drive module. The larger and brighter it was, the faster they traveled. They'd use the accumulated energy, bleeding it off to slow the ship when they neared Deneb. It was fiery red close to the ship, fading to orange and yellow farther out. Numbers rolled across the bottom of the screen, but it wasn't Pollock's area of expertise. Nielson's either, although she was pretty sure he knew what he was looking at.

The rest of the Bridge was empty. Even with the upcoming maneuver, there was no need for her to be there. The computer had control, and anything she could do on the Bridge, she could handle just as well from here. The Bridge's purpose was face-to-face time with her crew. Currently, she had four crew preparing the smaller, secondary ship—Engineer Levitson, Chief Charles, Mr. Clarkson, and Liaison Schlegel—and another three transporting the prisoners—First Mate Honda, Science Officer Kirkpatrick, and Specialist Okotie-Eboh. Nielson was the one needed on the Bridge, doing piloting things. When they set the *Daughter Two* free, the *Higgs* would be a bucking bronc until the secondary craft cleared the *Higgs'* Magnetic Resonance Field. Break off at the wrong angle, and the daughter ship might easily be snared in the edge of the mother ship's warped quantum field. The small drive kernel in *Daughter Two* would be unable to compensate for the Event Horizon of the manufactured black hole driving the *Higgs* forward. She didn't care about that, but it would be problematic if their own course parameters were compromised, and that's what Pilot Nielson was ensuring *wouldn't* happen.

The other two feeds were of the *Daughter Two* and the corridor leading to her. The exterior of the smaller ship was fully visible in her bay, and small avatars in the lower part of the feed showed who was inside and if they were talking. Tap one, and the audio would come through, fed by their personal comms. The crew were all inside, and Pollock didn't bother switching to an interior view. In the third feed, she watched Science Officer

Kirkpatrick walking backward, his weapon in his hands, his riot helmet shield over his face. He seemed to know exactly where he was walking, even backwards. He made a hand motion with his arm held high, calling out something, though Pollock had the sound off, and she couldn't read his lips with the glare on his faceplate. He turned and strode forward assertively. She wondered that she'd ever found Levitson interesting. Kirkpatrick had a quite nice posterior, firm and expressive in his uniform. A nice back, too, a perfect complement to his thick, muscled arms. She tried to remember the color of his eyes. Green? Or blue? What color eyes did reddish-blond-haired Irish men have?

Pollock shook off her interest in the Science Officer. She had other things at hand to attend to. She keyed the Bridge feed over to Medical to find Minkovski out of the picture. She swiveled the camera and found her at an opened cabinet, facing away from the camera.

"I guess our guests are good to fly?" Pollock tried to make it sound light-hearted.

Minkovski partially turned. Her hands twisted lids onto small containers, setting each one into a foam gripper on its shelf. She glanced at the video before speaking. "If you call an oblique fracture of the fibula and two concussions good to fly, then I suppose I've done all I can to make them flight ready."

"Now, Elisabet, everyone had input on this. Is this a change of heart?" Pollock sincerely liked the good doctor, but the woman had a conscience of velvet. She supposed it was the woman's emotive side that brought out her best when dealing with her patients, but she'd been in interrogation. These were real criminals they were dealing with, and to keep them on board was disastrous on every level.

"No. I see the need for what we're doing. My empathy levels are high today." She closed the cabinet and crossed her arms, looking directly into the camera. "I'm cold, too. I've turned up the heat, but I can't get warm. I might be fighting off something. I'm sure that's what it is." She smiled, waving her hand at the camera to brush off any sympathy that might be funneled her way.

"So, good to fly?" Pollock needed verbal confirmation. It would be logged in the system, and that was important for possible litigation that might come later.

"Walking and talking when they left my surgery. I've given Mr. Zealander instructions to rest for a few days, and included some amitriptyline and gabapentin, standard Mayo treatment for concussion-induced headaches. If they follow my instructions, then, good to fly."

"Thank you, Elisabet. I know this is hard for you. Put on long sleeves and try to stay warm. You're the one person we don't need to be sick." Pollock laughed to show she didn't put anything into her comment. As Doctor Minkovski waved and stepped away, the video camera, now on, tracked her movements. Pollock keyed the sound off, pulling her uniform tighter at the neck. She had been chilled, too. Even her chair felt colder than the room's ambient temperature.

"Ship, have you changed my room temperature?"

"Your personal quarters are currently set to 72 degrees. Would you like me to make an adjustment?" The honey words melted through the room, coddling the Commander with concern.

"Up about two degrees. Raise the temps in Medical, too. Minkovski says she's cold, and we don't need her getting a chill."

"Thank you, Commander."

Pollock was already back to her video feeds, and the ship's words faded into the background. The corridor feed had reset several times, following the three prisoners and their ersatz guards, albeit ones behaving very professionally, towards the *Daughter Two*. When they entered the bay with the ship and were picked up on that feed, the corridor scene reverted to the Bridge. Nielson's eyes were on the camera, and Pollock noticed a blinking icon on her terminal. The man wanted to talk, and she tapped the icon.

"What can I do for you, Nielson?"

"You are aware of our drive peculiarities, I presume?" He said it as though she should be, and he pursed his mouth slightly.

"Enlighten me." Dear God, she thought. He's going to cut to the chase about something I don't want to know. At least she could trust him not to dramatize. Whatever he told her would be God's honest truth.

"This." He tapped his console, and his feed changed to the one she'd seen earlier, the ship's drive diagram. It pulsed a brilliant red close in, the looping whirls of the magnetism inextricably linking the two parts of the ship stretching far into space. They grew larger the faster the ship traveled, and in the diagram, they were enormous.

"Tell me what you see." She thought it was beautiful, the red deepening to near-violet in the narrow confines between the two magnets. A pointer icon was moving on the screen, controlled by Nielson, she supposed.

"The colors are off. Here." The icon circled the deepest red. "The size of the field, too. I'm having trouble getting a star-chart reading; I should be able to pinpoint our position to the parsec. I haven't mentioned our speed. I can't—"

"Levitson said he'd resolved this. It's his field." Let it go, Nielson, she silently pleaded. We have other fish to fry right now. Something in the adjacent video feed caught her eye, and she glanced over. "What next? Nielson, we've got a situation at *Daughter Two*—" The video image of the ship's drive diagram switched back to the bridge as she spoke. "—and we'll have to discuss this later."

"Should I join you?" He was already standing and gathering his things from the console.

"Can you bring a weapon, a big one?" She was belting hers on.

"Can a corpsicle take a hundred-light-year nap?"

Pollock smiled to see him already heading out the door. Her

smile fell away when she turned back to the adjacent video feed. Zealander had Okotie-Eboh in a chokehold—how he'd gotten loose was beyond her—and it seemed there might be a standoff in the hangar bay. He'd tossed her riot helmet to the side. At least he didn't have a weapon. Prime was on the gangway with her weapon aimed Zealander and Okotie-Eboh's direction. Hollis was gesticulating and yelling. She was still cuffed so had probably been flexible enough to step through them. Kirkpatrick's weapon was in one hand, and he was motioning to the three prisoners still attached to each other. A light blinked on Pollock's console, Nielson's icon flashing, and she tapped it.

"Sit tight, Commander. Ship's updated me, and I've got this."

"Acknowledged." She keyed the contact off. "Ship, give me sound on the situation." Pollock watched the feed for developments that might tell her if this was contained or would go sour.

"Who you freakin' space turds think you are, sending us out there?" Definitely Hollis' rant. "You booby-trapped this ship, huh? You gonna let us *die* out there? Look at prissy Honda, there, her cute little weapon covering her sweet little backside. Come fight, you vacated proton flush."

Proton flush? Pollock nearly laughed. That was pretty low.

"Calm down, Hollis." Kirkpatrick's voice. "You guys warmed up the motors. We're just letting you have your ride."

"Letting us walk? I don't think so." Abdullah looked blank behind the eyes, and his words sounded slurred. Pollock wondered what had happened there.

"At least we'll be in control. Back down, Kaseem." Magill was the only one with any presence. He seemed put together, dare she think suave, even with his hands secured behind him.

"Maybe not in *control*," Honda muttered. No one looked her direction, and Pollock knew she'd only caught it because of the comm Prime wore. A good First Mate, she kept it on, always listening, and always in contact.

Nielson stepped through the door and stood poised for action, facing the showdown. He held a Mag-stunner, an unwieldy weapon, but one that would get the job down without killing anyone, hopefully. Pollock relaxed. Good ole Nielson, always the master of every situation.

"Enough, Zealander. Or should I call you Cyril, Mr. Fassbinder?"

"How you—" Zealander choked. His tone toughened, and he called harshly, "I'll break her neck. I'll do it."

"How's that leg doing, Fassbinder? You able to walk on it?"

"I'll break her neck!" Zealander was breathing hard, and his words came out short and hard. He was perspiring heavily. "I'll do it!"

"The Doc fixed you up nice, didn't she? Did you say thanks to Doctor Minkovski? She even gave you medicine to dull the pain. It's about worn off, huh? You've been walking on that leg, and now it's about to explode in your brain. Want some more medication? It's on the ship, plenty to last you as long as you need. You've got to cooperate with me, though."

Pollock smiled at the scene coming over the video. Nielson had this sewed up, and Zealander—or Fassbinder, if Nielson was right—didn't even realize it. She wondered how he'd gotten that information. That man was a tricky devil, tricky good to have around.

She said to the computer, "Do you have anything on a Cyril Fassbinder?" Her eyes remained on the scene playing out in the *Daughter Two*'s bay. Zealander had relaxed his chokehold on Okotie-Eboh, although he still had his arm across her chest. Charles, Clarkson, Schlegel, and Levitson were just outside the Daughter's door. Weaponless, they were attempting to remain out of the way. Smart, Pollock thought. We don't need this to become a multiple hostage situation.

"Colonel Cyril Fassbinder," the ship purred, startling Pollock. "Special Ops, Delta Squadron, Earth Armed Forces. Court-martialed in absentia for desertion; implicated in death of an opponent during a military-sanctioned martial arts demonstration and suspected in deaths of multiple victims since. Whereabouts unknown. Considered dangerous and possibly armed at all times."

"Whereabouts not unknown. He's on board with us, I suspect. Is there an image available?"

A fourth display formed, showing a thick-necked but otherwise good-looking man in full uniform. His shoulders told of his dedication to weight training, and the intense look in his black eyes said he wasn't to be messed with. His bone structure suggested German, although his hair and eyes bemoaned polluted blood. Neo-Nazi leanings? Perhaps.

"Family?"

"Unknown. Records sealed. A general search found these pictures." The image shrunk, and three more filled the rectangle. One was of Fassbinder on a beach, shirtless, playing volleyball with a team of military types, all similar in build. He was at a picnic in another, his arm around a pretty, blonde-haired woman, with two children at their side. In the last, he stood on a podium, presenting information displayed on the wall behind him. Normal things, nothing to suggest a connection with what was happening in the bay. Still, he'd seemed to accept Nielson's accusation. That made him guilty, as far as Pollock was concerned. She was convinced they were one and the same.

"File for retrieval and remove from view."

Okotie-Eboh was released. She ran to Levitson, and he put his arm around her. Zealander was attempting to stand. He was soaked with sweat and quivering. Kirkpatrick had the first three sitting against the rail, his gun pointed at them, ready to enforce his request for cooperation. To the side, Doc Minkovski appeared, with her customary black case. She snapped it open, pulled out an air-powered injector, and she held it up to look at it closely. Nodding, she stepped toward Zealander.

"He's dangerous, Doc," Honda warned. Her laser sight painted a dot right in the middle of his chest.

"Without this," Minkovski held up her injector, "he's a basket case. You do your job, and I'll be safe doing mine." She knelt at Zealander's side, lifted a sleeve, wiped the sweat from his skin, and pressed the device to his arm. Almost immediately, the man's face relaxed, and the quivering in his muscles eased. Minkovski chided him, "I told you to take it easy with this foot. You staying off it is the best medicine for it there is." She stood, dropped the injector into her case, closed it, and disappeared out the door at a brisk and professional pace.

Pollock tapped an icon on her console. "Liaison Schlegel, is that everything we're removing from the ship?" In the image, he looked towards the video camera. He shot her a thumbs-up, tapping his comm device to engage it.

"Yes, Commander. Levitson has the drive configured and locked out. Chief Charles was with him to confirm the final details. Commander, it looks like the food stores are going with the ship, unless you want to wait another twelve hours. We can't risk the cold temperatures in the nitrogen stores without time for them to equalize."

"Noted." Ouch. She'd wanted those supplies. They were sending food for ten for 100 days, most of which would never be used under the circumstances. "Once you have this situation contained, get Nielson to the Bridge. I want things back to normal ASAP. We can't afford to risk our passengers any more than necessary."

"Aye, aye, Commander. We won't let you down."

She clicked off before whispering, "You'd better not." Her eyes were on Kirkpatrick, though, not even thinking of Levitson. The Science Officer knelt at Zealander's side, and his back flexed as he yanked the cuffs tight on the man's arms. Zealander grimaced but didn't complain. Minkovski's happy juice, probably. As Kirkpatrick stood, cradling his weapon, his legs pulled at the fabric of his uniform. Pollock's eyes jerked away when he yelled for the other three to stand.

"Oh, he's good," Pollock whispered. "He's very good."

The Berth of Your Dreams

Crystal Hollis was the first aboard the *Daughter Two*. She spat and cursed as First Mate Honda released her cuffs, spinning around to plant a wad of phlegm on Honda's riot shield.

"Thought you might like first choice of bunks, compliments of the prissy proton flush." Honda's weapon was between them, firmly grasped in one hand. They stood in a corridor lined with doors. She chuckled. "Choose wisely. It'll be yours for a very long time."

"I don't think so." Hollis swung her fist at Honda, attempting to connect with her face underneath the riot shield. Honda caught her wrist handily.

"Why do pissant miscreants think they're so tough?" Honda twisted until tears formed in Hollis' eyes. "You ready to give, or do I need to break it? I'm not calling in the doc for a feel-good prick like the Commander did. I'll let you deal with it on your own terms." She twisted harder, until the woman collapsed to the floor.

"Okay, I give. Let me breathe." Honda released, and Hollis held her wrist to her chest, sucking in gasps of air.

"You okay in there?" It was Kirkpatrick, still outside with the other three.

"Yeah, in a minute, okay?" Honda had no time for lady-like sweet talk. Hollis was standing, and Honda growled, "You ever really did someone, or you just like impressing the boys by barking really loud?"

"Grew up in the Venus mines." She still held her wrist, and her eyes were glowing coals. Her olive skin gleamed with her anger. "Alone."

"Alone?" That startled Honda. The stories about the mines on Venus were hardly believable, except news reports had proven them true. "And you survived?"

"A dozen of my fellow miners didn't. I made sure of that, and that was before I turned ten." Hollis was opening doors, checking out the spaces, finally stopping to look Honda point-blank in the face. "We don't get heat? What's this, powered down to save fuel? Space junket, it's cold in here."

Honda called out to the smaller ship's computer interface, "First Mate Wendy Honda, Starship *UEF Higgs. Daughter Two*, acknowledge."

"First Mate Honda recognized. How may I help you?" The voice was pleasant, if younger sounding than on Mother.

"Environment settings. What's the temperature?"

"Controls are currently set to 72 degrees. Optimal ambient temperature should be reached—"

"Enough, Ship. Thank you."

"You're welcome." The ship's computer went silent.

"See? All systems are at normal."

"So," Hollis stood at an open door and glared Honda's direction, "you have to pat the computer on the head to get it to jump up and lick your hand?" The words were sneered, peeling aside Hollis' good looks and revealing the black mire that roiled underneath. Without waiting for an answer, she nodded her head inside the cabin and barked, "This'll do for now."

"Step inside, please." Honda motioned with the business end

68

of her gun, not really pointing it at Hollis, but close enough to make her request unequivocal. Hollis had no choice. When the olive-skinned woman was clear of the door, Honda palmed the lock, sending it silently shut, sealed until the vessel was safely away from the *Higgs*. She smiled when the woman inside began beating against the door and yelling curses. "Sorry, sweetheart," she called through. "I'm a vacated proton flush, remember, and this is as nice as I get."

The string of resulting insults was as satisfying as locking the door and trapping Hollis inside. She made her way down the corridor, through the ship's small lounge, past the miniscule bridge, and onto the gangway. It was little more than a metal catwalk with rails on each side. Falling off wouldn't kill anyone—wouldn't *likely* kill anyone—but broken bones were another issue. On Earth, or even Deneb 4 Station, similar injuries could be healed in a matter of days, or hours if it wasn't a compound break. Here? Like Zealander, break something, and you had to live with the pain. It sucked, but that was space travel. Crews opted for videos and virtual sims, not massive medical facilities. Take care, and you didn't need to be taken care of. How hard was that to comprehend? She found Kirkpatrick facing his three captives, his weapon in his hand, although it pointed at the ceiling. His face was stone, his eyes narrowed to mere slits. Levitson and Schlegel were nowhere to be seen. Chief Charles and Mission Specialist Clarkson were conferring over a stack of supplies removed from *Daughter Two*. Charles pointed, and Clarkson moved one item, then carried another towards the door. Charles stooped to read the label on yet another and toted it after Clarkson.

"Next, James." Honda lifted her clear face shield. Hollis was why they'd worn them. "Send me the pretty one. He might like to spend some time with a real woman for a change."

"Magill, face away from me and kneel." Kirkpatrick answered Honda by his actions. "I'm untethering you but leaving the cuffs on. First Mate Honda will release your arms when you're

69

inside the ship."

"Thank you, Officer Kirkpatrick." Magill smiled and nodded. "I appreciate your thoughtfulness. Can I get you to loosen the cuffs? They're chafing my wrists. Watch the broken one, if you don't mind."

"Down." Kirkpatrick motioned with the live end of his weapon.

"Absolutely, Officer. The cuffs, please?"

"You are smooth." Kirkpatrick leaned in to his ear as he released the tether from the man's arms. "I'm ship's Science Officer to you. You tried to take out a group of our paying passengers, and for what? Because their parents once had power over your people? You're a misguided fool, Magill. A sorry scumbag, misguided fool. Now stand, and let's get you on your new ship, gratis the United Earth Federation. You don't even have to return it."

Kirkpatrick stepped back, keeping an eye on Abdullah and Zealander. Abdullah still looked glassy-eyed, and Zealander was smiling, tanked up on the Doc's happy juice. He motioned for Magill to move towards Honda, stepping back and following him with his weapon. The man walked smoothly past Honda, who had her shield back in place, and they disappeared into the ship.

"So, you're the brains of the bunch," Honda remarked brightly to Magill's back. "What happened? A flash of stupidity? The lights went out? Hormone override? I suppose you won't mind sharing Hollis' cabin for a bit of hormone suppression therapy." She snickered with satisfaction, enjoying her gibes.

"Can I?" He paused and turned his head. "Or is this supposed to be your version of macabre humor?"

"Okay, flash brain." Honda laughed. Magill could give as good as he got. She wouldn't be surprised if his reported genius IQ was actually real, and the master programmer could rewire the ship and gain control of navigation. As long as he did it about two hundred years in the future, it was no ablative off her suit. "Into a room. Your friend, Hollis, already asked if we were turning the temperature up. Ship confirms the heat is on and set to 72. How about this one?" She tapped a door with the muzzle of her gun.

"Any reason I should?" He palmed the door panel, and it slipped aside. Lights flickered on. "I suppose they're all the same."

"Close enough. This one do?"

"Where's Crystal?" He glanced up and down the corridor but didn't step into the room.

"Listen for the she-demon." She grinned. Sure enough, a door several down shook, and curses filtered through.

"We're locked in?" He backed away. "Who'll run the ship? And meals? We do have to eat."

"Only until you're under way. Inside, please."

He slipped through, running his hand along the doorframe as he stepped past. Honda stepped to the doorway, feeling where he'd placed his hand. She smiled and stripped a magnetic contact plate from the doorframe's sensor panel. It would have allowed the door to close, but Magill would have been able to manually force it open as soon as he was left unattended.

"Nice try, Magill." She held it up before slipping it into her pocket.

"You'd be disappointed if I did nothing." He shrugged with a smile. "I hope I've earned your respect."

"Nah, but nice try, anyway. Turn and face the wall if you want those cuffs off." The deed done, she lifted her visor and palmed the door, catching the faint whoosh of air on her face as it slipped shut. She attempted to slide it open manually, but it was firm, near as she could tell. She headed back towards the bay, yelling, "Next!"

Locked and Loaded

Kaseem Abdullah and Raytheon Zealander, if one wanted to accept the conjoined name, were simpler to install on the *Daughter Two*, and more difficult at the same time.

Crystal Hollis, spitfire, had been tricked into her bunk and installed on the *Daughter* with little unexpected fanfare, removing her from the equation, which was surprising, since by all accounts she had learned a few things in the Venus mines. A product of illicit Birthers, she had been hidden as a baby, kept from the eyes of the Overseers until she was four. It wasn't an easy childhood, but she'd known no other, so it was as any youthful existence, accepted for what it was, even if that included long hours alone, with crudely fashioned playthings of metal and stone, and hunger that would have defeated a lesser being. The Thracian-seam collapse had changed all that. Both her parents had been on assignment, and when the Maccabee-fission explosion fractured the substrate underneath the seam, 1,300 workers had given their daily breath to whisper their dedication unto the Thrax Collective coffers.

Hollis, independent and mature for four, although still a child, was left to survive on her own, becoming tougher than a vein of Thracian ore and deadlier than a Waldorf Fragmenting Laser. Her first kill was at six, a man who thought her daily rations were better housed in his stomach. A handheld boring screw to his neck, and his lifeblood darkened the Venusian soil, his flesh making its way to the recyclers. It was a good kill, because Crystal claimed his rations for six weeks before his body was found, and she grew fat on twice the calories.

Shank Magill had been the surprise of the four, for a moment letting his intelligence override his twisted nightmares. Once reasoned with, he'd walked right into his new and locked quarters. With his looks and his charm, he could have taken his life anywhere, achieved whatever he desired, possibly even a berth on the *Higgs*. It wasn't to be. He'd grown up on his grandparents' oft-regurgitated tales of cruelties foisted on his ancestors, their excuse for the family's misfortunes, until Magill internalized them as his own. To him, it felt as if he'd borne the manacles aboard the slave ships, stood naked to be auctioned to the highest bidder, and had crosses burned in his yard. It didn't matter that his hair was soft, his skin was light, and his speech was upper middle class. Black blood coursed through his veins, and he had long ago determined to take from the Man that which he'd taken from the Brothers: life; freedom; pride; self-worth; the chance to be secure; and the feeling of superiority in the face of conflicting views.

Shank wanted it all.

For a time, he'd pushed his demons away, integrating into the status quo, using his superior intellect to build one of the premier tech companies on Earth. Even in his success, he was defeated. In his head, he wore chains and sold himself for the right to live every day. His grandparents' stories were the iron keeping him locked within the churning morass of his blackened blood.

Not so with Kaseem Abdullah. He'd endured the torture of the South African Second Coming of Christ re-education camps. When the white minority rose up against the country's black

73

leadership, using the Church as their platform of superiority, whole subgroups of humanity had been swept aside, dumped into self-contained camps, with righteous overseers bursting with religious zeal no one thought to moderate. Kaseem and his husband had landed in the Sterkrivier Purity Camp. Black, coloured, Asian, it didn't matter. If you weren't white or were unable to prove moral purity, you were trash, cast aside and hidden away, and the world didn't care. Millions were re-educated through torture, disease, and death. Kaseem's husband and god-niece ascended into re-educated martyrdom, and the scars on Kaseem's back told of his fight to vindicate their deaths.

He barely survived, the torture teaching him one thing: The world is what you take. No one gives you a thing unless you crush them first to make them bleed. This was an unexpected opportunity not to be missed. He wanted the *Daughter Two*. He needed Pretoria to burn as he flung *Daughter Two*'s energy-swollen Casson Envelope through Earth's atmosphere. It was what he lived for, to have the deaths of the White Minority in payment for the family he'd had ripped from him.

It was also the reason Honda and Kirkpatrick dragged the man lifeless through the ship, installing him in a cabin of their choice. It would have been more considerate if he'd been willing to walk. He'd lunged for Honda's weapon, once again getting thumped upside his head, this time going down and staying there.

Raytheon Zealander—no one doubted any longer that he was Cyril Fassbinder of Special Ops fame—was doped to the gills. After Doctor Minkovski's generous contribution to his health and welfare, he'd been unaware of Abdullah's vendetta-fueled cry, his vicious subdual, or the curses from Honda and Kirkpatrick as they unhooked the man from the tether and struggled to drag the big man inside the ship. Zealander, with his massive shoulders and steely stare, became a man among friends, jolly, the youth on the beach, out with his chums, and he sang as he was walked, dragged, and supported onto the *Daughter*, down the narrow corridor, and

74

helped into a bunk in a cabin of his own.

"Don't think we need to lock this one in." Kirkpatrick was without his gun. It stood outside the cabin. Wrestling Zealander inside while wearing it had been near-impossible. Honda kept her weapon at the ready as he released the cuffs and slipped the plastic strap onto his belt. They exited the small room. Kirkpatrick shouldered his weapon as Honda keyed the door to close and locked it.

"Don't trust a one." Honda checked the door. She'd learned that after Magill's trick with the sensor. Down two doors, thumping noises told of Hollis' continued anger. "Hollis is still up and active," she remarked with a grin.

"I'd like to thump some ears." Kirkpatrick smirked as they exited the ship. The items removed from the *Daughter* were nowhere to be seen. Efficient work, Team, he thought, giving a mental nod to Levitson, Charles, Clarkson, and Schlegel. He looked back through the doorway, viewing the interior of the ship one last time, and he shook his head wistfully. "Waste of a good ship. I wonder if the Commander'd notice if we jettisoned the occupants and kept the *Daughter Two*. We wouldn't have to tell." He winked at his companion.

"Ah, you are such a tease. Our own private rendezvous. Just me and you." Honda had reverted to feminine vixen, and she batted her eyes. Tiptoeing, she rubbed her hand across his cheek, stroking his face sinuously. Then she tapped her earpiece and said, "Commander, you got that? We have an alternate plan for our inductees. Our Science Officer wants to send them sans ship, maybe a space experiment to see how long humanity can survive at hyper-parsec speeds."

Kirkpatrick laughed, clapping Honda on the shoulder, saying, "Dang, Prime. Ain't nothing private around you. You are wired and on all the time." He didn't sound irritated, and he adjusted his weapon as he turned away from the ship. "It is a waste, though, giving a ship to these losers. Too bad we can't ice 'em like our paying passengers. Yeah, I know—" a palm jumped up to stifle her rebuttal "—we already discussed this, but still, it's hard to see hardware tossed aside, knowing it'll be lost forever."

"It's insured." Their feet were clicking on the metal catwalk, and Honda held her gun in one hand, the high-tech weapon swinging slightly with each step. "It's company property, anyway. It's not like *you're* giving up anything."

"It's the dream thing, like wanting a little house with shutters and a picket fence. You know you'll never get it and would probably go stir-crazy if you did, but the idea is stuck in your head. A ship's like that for me. This takes the *Daughter Two* out of my dreams, like ripping a hole in my psyche." He didn't sound very ripped.

"You can take the *Daughter One* to bed with you and dream of her." Honda's tone was suggestive.

"Not the same." They were at Weapons, and Kirkpatrick unshouldered his gun, preparing to store it away in a locker. "I could take the *Daughter Two* and not leave you guys in a lurch. That's the difference. If I took the only ship left, you'd be stranded in an emergency. I couldn't live with that. See how considerate I am?"

"Considerate, my—"

"What a plunger!" Kirkpatrick yanked his hand from the locker door as it swung open.

"Did it bite?" Honda grinned, as she removed the live rounds from her gun and powered down the laser function.

"Nah, it's cold, like ice." Weapons nestled against the outside of the ship. A few meters down, the wall curved inward, accommodating the ship's hull design. Kirkpatrick moved closer and held his hand a few centimeters from the wall, frowning.

"And?"

"Check this out, Honda. I don't remember this." He pulled his hands back and rubbed them, as if chilled. "It's gotta be close to freezing."

"Food, Jameson. You need to up your metabolism. Maybe it's

time for a little competitive boxing in the Gym." She grinned, settling her gun into its individual foam bushing, the foam's built-in internal spring mechanism grabbing the weapon firmly and holding it in place. "Ship?" She tapped her ear. There was no audible response, but Honda spoke as if there were. "Check ambient temperature in Weapons. Our Science Officer is turning into a wuss, and I want him back in all his glory."

Kirkpatrick laughed, looking somewhat chagrined at her remarks, but he continued to rub his hands together. "What's she say?"

After a pause, Honda clicked her ear. "Set to ship standard, 72 degrees. I may need Levitson to reprogram the cleaning bots to check for obstructions in the ductwork. This place could be an icebox, and we'd never know."

"Until the next insurrectionist takeover attempt, anyway." Kirkpatrick hiked his weapon in one hand, clicking it into its foam receiver, and hit the locker door with his shoulder, slamming it shut.

"Afraid to touch it?" Honda's eyes twinkled with amusement.

"Once burned, twice shy."

"Freezer burned." Honda chuckled. "Our portion's done. Meet me in the Gym. I want to kick your butt." She was walking the opposite direction from Kirkpatrick, and she called back, "Half an hour. I'll be there."

Kirkpatrick palmed the door to Weapons, and the door slid silently closed. He looked at his hand with a frown, before rubbing it hard against his pants, and finally tucking it under his arm. He shivered as he walked away. He began to whistle, only stopping to whisper, "Kick *your* butt, Honda," before starting up again.

Anchors Away

Engineer Levitson hunkered at his station on the Bridge, oblivious to the others around him. Above him, stealing a section of the 360-degree display wrapping the space, a diagram of the *Daughter Two* hovered in a three-dimensional hologram. Numbers in crisp boxes shifted as he touched his console, the terminal sending his input into the main ship's computer, which interfaced with the secondary ship's drive computers. The area where the main drive unit was separated from the bow of the *Daughter Two* was encased in an orange flashing box, sending a warning to whomever happened to be watching.

Levitson ignored it, as it was no more than a confirmation that his settings were correct. Yes, the drive was overclocked. Yes, the magnets were adjusted too closely together. Yes, the smaller vessel would accelerate faster than its design parameters allowed for. No, there was no provision in Levitson's calculations for slowing the ship at any point in the near future.

Or in any future.

The *Daughter Two* would continue to accelerate, the magnets growing closer and closer until, just a fraction of a nanometer apart, the vast Magnetic Resonance Field would no longer be able to bleed off its accumulated energy, and the *Daughter Two* would become part of the future, lost to the present in the mists of relativity, no longer riding in flat space, but hovering at the edge of her Cassel-Jackson Drive's manufactured black hole and unable to pull away.

It was a sentence of death, although the occupants of the ship would still be living out their lives as if the end of time was no more than a few hours away. Days, if they were lucky. Months at the very most, still alive until they reached the end of the Universe, as far as the *Higgs* was concerned, unaware that everyone they knew or had known had lived out their lives eons before.

Levitson separated himself from the events on the terminal, letting the Bridge filter in to his awareness. The Commander was in a spirited discussion with Chief Charles as he corrected a minor detail in the plans to set the *Daughter* on her own course, even as the *Higgs* barreled along at hyper-parsec speeds, barely in touch with the Universe surrounding her. Yes, space was vast, and agreed, there was little likelihood another ship would intersect the *Daughter's* new course, but was it possible? Yes. The *Higgs* flew along a predetermined path, only slowing and adjusting direction to aim for Deneb 4 when they were at a precise and documented point in their journey. No one would know where the *Daughter Two* was if the *Higgs* failed to send that information. Pollock was satisfied with the signal from the smaller ship's transponder beacon. It wasn't failsafe, but they didn't need failsafe. Besides, the difficulty of broadcasting to anyone who might be able to receive the *Daughter's* new flightpath was very nearly an impossibility while at speed. The Magnetic Resonance Field that absorbed the energy the ship would repurpose to begin their slowdown at the midpoint of the trip was the same field that captured their communications signals, unless they narrowed the beam enough to punch through the noise.

Levitson spoke up, "The Commander's right, Ranse." His

eyes never left the display before him. Tapping his console, he brought up the feed from the Bay showing the real-time *Daughter Two*. Her access door was open and her umbilicals still attached. She was a ship ready to go, but she hadn't been released, yet. He would manually unlock the interior cabin doors after the exterior door was closed but before the umbilicals were disconnected. Once that happened, the blast tube doors would iris open, and the rail launcher would punch the *Daughter* through the Resonance Field, wreaking havoc on the *Higgs'* drive stability until she was outside the field and charting her own course through the cosmos. The *Daughter's* drive kernel was already spinning, her magnetics online, but her black hole was muted, wrapped in a proprietary Feynman-Hawking Containment Bubble, only to be released when free of the *Higgs'* Resonance Field.

"Nah, Asher." Charles bounced his way, his neon earbuds bobbing jauntily at his breast, and leaning one elbow on Levitson's console. "I've done it before. Load the coordinates, hit it with an extra kilojoule or two, and it cuts right through."

"Except," Levitson said, raising a hand and pushing Charles off his console with one finger, "you don't know all the facts." He leaned back, wrapping his hands behind his head. "Freddie over there knows, and I'm pretty sure the Commander does. If not, Firstie was there when I first found out. We're getting to Deneb a few days early."

"You were serious, earlier?" Charles' eyes found the back of Nielson's head, then jumped to Pollock's, to find her engrossed in two screens she'd pulled up before her. Her face was perfectly visible through the screens, with only the slightest hint what she was seeing. Charles knew she could see through the image also, but part of the skill in using the virtual screens was tuning out anything beyond what you were watching. Charles focused back on Levitson, his elbow once again finding the console, and at Levitson's frown and stern expression, he lifted it off. "How are we managing to arrive early? A hundred days, one light year per day. That's what we've always done. The magnets . . . I mean, what if they *touch*. Ka-blooie, right?" He puffed out his cheeks and blew the air out quickly, making a soft popping sound. His eyes found the orange box on the *Daughter's* drive diagram. "There, they touch, and they blow. Am I right?"

"You, asking me?" Levitson chuckled. "I'm only the Engineer, the man who flips the switches. You're the Technical Advisor with all the know-how."

"But they will, won't they?"

"How much energy would the drive have to pick up along the way to override the innate propensity of those two magnets to repel each other?" Levitson's eyes were on the orange box. He nodded its direction, waiting until Charles followed his eyes.

"Most of the positive energy in the Universe." Charles seemed to relax, and he laughed, grasping Levitson's shoulder for a moment. "I guess I'm jittery, what with those four we've got locked away. Even if we did absorb too much energy, we'd just bleed it into the Alcubierre Bubble caused by the black hole, and—"

"*Slowly* bleed it into the bubble caused by our black hole. Slow the drive module too fast, the ship would slam into it, and burnt toast is all that'd be left."

Nielson called, "If you two Schwinger-woods are through discussing non-essential Drive theory, I think we're about ready to initiate the departure sequence for our guests."

Pollock touched her two displays, moving them aside. The scenes were still running. One showed Clarkson on the lower level, and he was working with a bag of delicate tools, disassembling the bomb left in the freezer section. He wore a full energy-diffusion suit. It resembled the quantum camo suits, but rather than bend light, it would absorb energy from an inadvertent blast and channel it to a containment capacitor. A thick cable trailed from the waist of the suit, leading to a plug in the wall. Somewhere deep in the drive section was the capacitor that would absorb the energy and store it until it could be released in another form.

The second display revealed Minkovski. Pollock had requested she visit Okotie-Eboh in her quarters. She was still upset about her hostage ordeal, and Minkovski had agreed that a sedative was in order, if Okotie-Eboh would agree to it. Minkovski carried a small bag, and by the signage on the walls, was nearing the Payload Specialist's quarters.

"Nielson, you ready?" Pollock drummed her fingertips on the arm of her seat, the only sign of her concern. It was valid. Releasing the *Daughter Two* at speed wasn't exactly dangerous, but it was an infrequent maneuver, and it did involve a measure of risk. All starship pilots were trained in the procedure, but training and hands-on experience weren't the same. Sometimes you had to ride the bronc to learn to be a cowboy. They were about to open the gate and let the four-legged tornado shake them up a bit.

"As I'll ever be, Commander. Levitson, close up ship anytime you're ready." Nielson slipped on a pair of black gloves, with round, shiny tabs, one to each joint segment and on the palms. He pulled a black VR helmet from under his console and placed it over his head. The face was integrated, solid, allowing nothing from the outside to detract from the virtual experience inside. Small lights blinked on at various places on the helmet, indicating full linkage to the ship's computer, and the gloves came alive, a light on each tab. When Nielson next spoke, his words had an artificial, manufactured sound. "Launching the *Daughter Two* at your command." His hands moved in the air, touching controls no one else could see.

"Think Honda would like to see this?" Liaison Schlegel held a VR helmet in his hands, about to slip it over his head, and he dropped it to his lap.

"Asked already, Prime and Kirkpatrick both. They declined." Pollock had been focused on Nielson and his virtual connection, studying the blinking lights telling of connectedness with the ship's different systems. She pulled her attention away and looked at the arm of her chair, touched something, then looked up again. The view in one of her displays shifted to reveal Honda and Kirkpatrick in the Gym, both in StretchSuits, battling opponents in a virtual scenario only they were privy to. She touched her chair again without looking, her eyes on the display, and she spoke. "Prime, last chance. Want to observe the sendoff? Schlegel wants to know."

Kirkpatrick continued to battle, his arms rippling with muscle, and his posterior flexing his StretchSuit, leaving nothing hidden under the skintight fabric. Honda paused for a moment, glancing at the video feed, and calling out, "Thanks, Commander, but no thanks." Without waiting, she looked away and was back in the simulation. The display automatically reverted to Minkovski, who was now with Okotie-Eboh, sitting on the edge of her bunk and giving her an injection. They were speaking, but no sound came through.

"It's only polite to ask. Their loss. I want to see it all, in full, living color." Schlegel shrugged and smiled, showing white and well-maintained teeth. He disappeared underneath his VR helmet, smoothing his hair as he did so.

"Engineer, shut the hatch and prime the rails." Pollock nodded his direction.

"Aye, aye, Commander." Levitson tapped a pattern of moves on his console, and the exterior door on the *Daughter Two* flipped around and pulled into the hatch. "Unlocking the interior doors. Passengers are now unconfined." As he spoke, he tapped another icon. The screen was unchanged, but he began to move faster. "Umbilicals released." Tap. "Rail launcher charging." Three taps. Steam began to build, letting off pressure at several locations underneath the ship. Several massive clamps moved in toward the *Daughter Two*. When they were in place, each one a meter from the *Daughter's* hull, they powered up, and the ship flinched, now suspended, held in the massive magnets that would soon spew the hyper-parsec-capable ship out of the *Higgs* and into the black reaches of unknown space.

"*Higgs'* navigation under manual control," Nielson's mechanical voice intoned. "Ready for separation and Resonance bombardment."

"Rail door open." Levitson tapped yet again, this time four jerks of his finger, and in the video image, massively thick doors irised open, revealing the rail tube and the black night of space at the end.

"Fire in three." Nielson's fingers were twisted into an impossible configuration, waiting, prepared to intervene in his virtual environment as soon as the secondary ship punched through the *Higgs'* Magnetic Resonance Field. The *Daughter Two*'s warped quantum field, powered by her drive kernel, would skew the *Higgs'* orientation for a short time, and Nielson's job was to keep his vessel in line as the *Daughter's* spinning kernel brought her manufactured black hole online. Once there was enough distance between the two, he'd be able to relax and again let the ship do all the work.

"Two, one," and Levitson's finger jabbed. *Daughter Two* disappeared in a flash of released steam, leaving the magnetic clamps fifty meters from their original position and the bay empty.

Schlegel stood, his VR helmet covering his head, and his mechanical voice yelled, "Yeah! What a rush!" He punched his fist in the air and yanked it back even faster, doing a little dance. He yanked off the helmet; and with a big smile, as he ran his fingers through his hair, he called, "That was the best, *ever*."

Charles laughed, but for a different reason. "Liam, never seen you so excited. Our cool cucumber finally burst his skin."

"Just in this." Schlegel's smile wouldn't go away. "I always wanted to be a Sling Pilot. The program evaporated before I reached the Academy, and I drifted into education."

"How about I send a Priority Message to Command to bring all the old suborbitals back online?" Charles grinned.

The pressure wave from the *Daughter Two* hit, her drive kernel initiating her manufactured black hole and strengthening her warped quantum field. The *Higgs* vibrated, and Nielson's hands were a blur as he manipulated his virtual environment. Levitson's display of the launching bay now showed an exterior viewpoint, the *Daughter Two* alongside the *Higgs*, not yet pulling ahead, but skewing at an angle, already on an independent path. No stars were visible. At the *Higgs'* rate of acceleration, the stars weren't in place long enough for them to register in the ship's sensors. Numbers just below the *Daughter* spun, suggesting a fantastically elevated rate of travel; but then, she *had* been thrown like a lance from a crazed knight on horseback, him barreling at his opponent as fast as his animal would carry him. It was how the *Daughter* would gain so much speed. Using her forward momentum as ballast, her drive module would kick start in a moment, and she would be flung into the black reaches of nothingness, her manufactured black hole compressing space in front of her while space behind her expanded, just like a giant ocean wave, going where no ship had gone before, as far as anyone aboard would know.

Then the *Daughter* flared, her Magnetic Resonance Field winking into existence. It was huge, larger than anyone had expected. Without color, as this was the real thing and not a computer simulation, it made the edges of the *Daughter* shimmer. Out into space, spreading out from the midpoint, just where the drive magnets were in convergence with those on the ship; and held in sync, pushing and pulling at the same time, drawing in massive quantities of energy: the magnetic flux lines were the waves of the sea painted black, undulating just below the visible level, yet distorted enough that the brain was disoriented simply watching.

"Look away if it makes you dizzy," Pollock reminded everyone. "The ship will settle down as it pulls away."

Sure enough, the vibration had already lessened, and Nielson's hands had slowed. He popped off his helmet and removed his gloves, his craggy face looking more tired than it had so far on the trip.

"Ship's got control, Commander. Eighteen hours, and the oscillations between the two drives will cancel out. We'll have smooth going again then. If you don't mind, I'm chilled, and I'd like to head to my quarters." Nielson stood, rubbing his arms, and frowning.

"Everything okay, Freddie?" Pollock leaned forward, expressing her concern.

"Sure." His face brightened, whether by inclination or effort was unclear. "I'd never done that in real life, and I guess it took more than I expected. We did it, though, you, me, and Levitson over there. A cup of joe might be all I need."

"Off, then. Good job, Pilot." Pollock nodded, and she turned to her display showing Minkovski. She was still at Okotie-Eboh's side, and the Specialist seemed to be resting, her eyes closed. Pollock keyed her armrest and asked, "You two do okay during that maneuver?"

"Imani was already out, and I'm always okay." The Doctor was patting Okotie-Eboh's arm, and she turned to face the camera. "They're gone, away, no longer our responsibility. And we're still good with that?"

Pollock's eyes tensed for a moment before she could catch herself. She said softly, "We have to be, don't we, Doctor? That door's closed forever, and we can't undo the lock, even if we wanted. Me? I don't want to. Sorry, dear."

"It had to be done, for Imani's sake, if no other. You're a good Commander, and now we can all get back to our duties with no further interruptions." Minkovski smiled and looked back to her sleeping charge.

Pollock shut down the video feed, and she looked at those on the Bridge with her. Levitson was pointing out something to Charles using his hologram of the *Higgs*; and Schlegel was back under his VR helmet, this time wearing gloves, with his helmet and gloves lighted like Christmas trees, showing full immersion. They didn't seem concerned, not in the way Minkovski had been. As the good doctor said, now we can all get back to our duties with no further interruptions. Pollock decided to head down to check on Clarkson. Disassembling a bomb, even disarmed, was unlikely to promote steady nerves and good digestion. The man would probably appreciate some company. Too bad he didn't have Kirkpatrick's build. Ah, well. Jameson was with Prime, so let the First Mate have her joy for now. There was all the time in the Universe for developing a mutual attraction between the two of them, or at least the next ninety-nine days.

A Spacy Speakeasy

Crystal Hollis tumbled into the corridor, surprised when her door actually gave way under her assault. She crouched, her hands shaking, ready to kill the little flusher who'd locked her inside. Finding an empty corridor, she diagramed the ship's layout in her head and placed herself a hundred paces from the exit. Seconds at full speed, and she could be there. It was no different than the mines, learning and *remembering* layouts, doorways, and passages. Life or death, you chose by your reaction times. She chose life, always life, no matter who she had to take out on the way.

In Hollis' moment of *evaluation,* a face appeared from an adjacent doorway. She sprang, her claws extended, ready to strike. "Magill! I'll rip your throat out!" The words were little more than a scream of defiance. She landed on him, only to find his hands already holding her wrists, and he pulled her tight, his face nose-to-nose with hers.

"Thought that was you I heard. You make enough noise to wake the dead. We've got better things to do than make out in public. How 'bout we find our compatriots and see if we can locate the bridge of this boat?" He kissed her hard on the mouth, his arms around her even as she fought him for space. As soon as she relaxed, he pulled away, laughing. She slapped him, and he laughed even harder, dropping her. She fell roughly against the wall, rubbing her lips and shooting him a filthy look.

"You exhaust thruster, you," she spat, pushing her thick hair away from her face. "I'll bust that wrist for you a second time."

"No hitting below the belt, darling. Kaseem," he yelled. "Zealander!" then softer, "or whatever your name is." Abdullah stumbled into view, blinking hard, his eyes still glassy. "Know where Zealander is?"

"Don't know where *I* am." Abdullah rubbed his face, then grimaced. He looked around, trying to orient himself, then wrapped both arms around his head and doubled over, moaning.

"He's useless. Let's find Zealander. We might need his muscle." Magill motioned to Hollis to follow him. He stepped around Abdullah, leaving him sitting on the floor in a heap. Opening doors, he ducked into the third one, calling back, "What's this? We're about to die, and he's asleep?"

"The doc gave him something, for his foot, I think. Water might wake him." Hollis stepped behind Magill, taking it in. The cabin, a carbon copy of the rest, was narrow. A small mirror reflected Magill's shoulder, and past that, Zealander was sprawled on his back, his arms at his sides, fully clothed, with one ankle heavily wrapped. The cabin had a tight head, no more than a toilet and a shower built as one component, and the door was open. The toilet was a dry unit, water only present when flushed. They weren't getting water from there, and the shower head was fixed to the wall.

"Leave him. He's useless, anyway." He turned and brushed past Hollis, forcing her against the wall.

"I'm here, Mac. Did ya' even see me? It's me, Crystal." She yelled the words, but he was gone, already. In the corridor, he was disappearing into the lounge, and she chased after him, finding him in the small bridge area. He was on his knees under the console, yanking away covers to access the electronics inside.

"They've fixed us good." He sat up, tearing his hair with his hands, before rubbing his palms over his face and looking at her. "They've disabled the verbal computer interface. I have to do everything by keyboard."

"You can fix it, right? You can fix anything." She smiled hopefully.

"With time, yeah, and the right parts." He leaned inside, fiddled with something, and the terminal's display blinked and dimmed. He hit the console with the side of his fist, and it came up to full brightness. He stood and pulled up a portable keyboard. "Let me see what we've got."

The first view was of the ship's trajectory. The *Higgs* was off to the side, shown in a two-dimensional line drawing, the drive unit and the main ship two discrete images. Their smaller ship, the *Daughter Two*, was alongside, although angled slightly askew. As they watched, the *Daughter* blipped and was a fraction of a centimeter farther ahead.

"Are we off course?" Hollis had both her hands on one of Magill's shoulders, and she whispered the words.

"Probably not. They don't plan for us to tag along. If I can locate it, there's doubtless a preset course in the computer. I just need to find it and reset our destination." He tapped a series of instructions on the keyboard, and the image winked out, replaced by something similar, but showing the two ships and their drive signatures. The *Higgs* was centered in a massive Magnetic Resonance Field, deepening to darkest ruby-violet at the core. "That's not right," he muttered. "Too big. Never seen a Field that large or that color."

"What's it mean? It's pretty."

"Let me see . . ." and he began to tap on his keyboard. A series of expressions ran across his face, puzzlement, nervous understanding, then disbelief. He hit a key hard, and numbers appeared across the bottom of the display. They were big and getting bigger

90

fast. "Levitson's a good engineer. Don't know what he's done to make this happen. He's never going to bleed this much energy from the Field. Hope he doesn't—"

The ship lurched, and alarms began sounding, with flashing lights on the wall. The walls and floor vibrated precipitously, as if the ship was coming apart. The display jumped and blurred, the constant shaking making it difficult to read. One thing easy to see was the Resonance Field now surrounding the daughter ship.

"The fools! What were they thinking, and at these speeds? I've got to initiate shutdown."

"Oh, Shankie, what's happening?" Hollis, despite her rough upbringing, clutched his shoulder even tighter, and he attempted to shrug her away.

"Off!" He pushed her, freeing his shoulder, and returned to the keyboard. "They've fired us too soon, linking the drives. The black holes will merge, become infinitely larger, sucking us all in." He hit the console with his fist, turning to her, his face ashen. "The idiots have completely disengaged the shutdown procedure on this vessel. I've no way to turn it off. Their main drive's about to become unstable. It's going to be quite a party."

"You can tell that from here?"

"All master programmers with genius level IQs can, sweetie. Look, right there." He reached to the screen, used his fingers to enlarge the *Higgs*, to reveal an orange warning box around the magnets connecting the ship to her Cassel-Jackson Drive. He double tapped it, and numbers appeared, flickering, then growing rapidly.

"Explain it to me, Professor." Hollis didn't take his arm or touch him in any way, but she simpered quite well. He almost smiled at her reference to his past life.

"Two Casson Drives can normally operate quite close to one another, and the computer can damp the Envelope oscillations, keeping them stable as they push each other apart. That's at normal speeds, no more than two to three light years per day.

Faster, and the oscillations can no longer be synched. They lock, essentially becoming one drive. If I can't get this resolved fast, we'll tip into the black hole too far to ever bleed off our speed. Worse than that, if we brush too close to the edge of the warp bubble, time dilation could set in, and we'll never see home. Dear God, this could be the disaster of the decade." He grunted disgustedly and didn't go on.

"Okay. I still don't understand." She smiled, layering on the simpering quite heavily.

"There." He jabbed at the screen. "We're not at normal speed. Not even close."

"Oh!" Hollis felt her skin grow cold. The numbers were high, reading 342,589 percent of normal speed. The smallest decimal places changed to 90, 91, then 92 as she watched.

Then the *Daughter's* image caught their attention. An orange box blinked into existence around their drive connection. Words began to scroll across the bottom of the screen: "Attention required. Acceleration now reaching 345,000 percent of normal speed . . ."

Hollis gasped, grabbing Magill's arm anyway and pointing to the display and the orange box surrounding their drive unit. Her finger fell to indicate the scrolling words. It wasn't what she was pointing at, however.

"What?" he spat.

"That. I think the party's about to begin." The image of the *Daughter* blinked, returning a centimeter ahead of the *Higgs*. Then it blinked again, one centimeter farther ahead. She whispered, "We're moving faster than they are."

She shivered. Even having lived through the torture of existence in the Venus mines, she was truly frightened now.

Taking a Cold Shower

Kirkpatrick peeled back the top of his StretchSuit, exposing broad shoulders and a well-muscled upper torso. Freckles littered his flesh. His skin was red, and he gleamed with moisture. More dripped from his red hair. His eyes, a deep emerald green, sparkled with adrenalin-fueled laughter He rolled a dry towel and popped it Honda's direction. She also had her StretchSuit worked down to her waist, although a sports bra concealed portions of her upper body.

"Showers, next." Kirkpatrick shook his head, letting water fly. He sat on an observation bench, disengaging the rest of his suit and working it over his legs and feet. He wore compression shorts underneath, and when he stood, they flexed with his shifting muscles, creating tiny rolls of fabric that formed and disappeared each time he leaned or straightened. "You're a fool on the gaming mat. There for a bit, I forgot it was only a game."

"Forgot it was only a game?" Honda was massaging her feet, with her suit still covering her lower body. "I was just there to kick some butt."

"You kicked mine, that's for sure." He held his hand to a vent in the wall, moved to a temperature display just down from it, and called, "Ship?"

"Kirkpatrick acknowledged. How may I be of assistance, Officer Kirkpatrick?"

"When was the last diagnostic run on the ventilation system?" He leaned one arm against the wall, watching the temperature display intently.

"Three days ago while in dry dock. I have the results—"

"Run another. Start it now. Upload it to my terminal, marked priority, as soon as you're finished."

"As you wish. The results should be ready for your attention in five hours."

"Thanks, Ship. Out."

"Can't take losing, I see. Gives you the chills." Honda was down to her sports bra and compression shorts, and she sauntered past triumphantly, hanging her suit in the Gym's ionizer for cleaning and disinfection.

"And a good hot shower takes them away." His suit followed hers into the ionizer, and he continued talking as they stepped into the shower room. "Wasn't today a blast? I knew we had those guys, just knew it. Ain't no one tougher than the crew of the *Higgs*, don't ch'a know it, baby?" He grabbed a clean towel off a rack, draped it over a hook beside the first of the two stalls, and closed the half door. The water began to drip, then it spattered loudly against the smooth walls. After a moment, his shorts came flying out and hit the wall with a wet splat.

"Right-o, there." Honda disappeared into the next stall with a towel ready for her use. Her suit appeared on her door, neatly hung. Her water started up, and she yelped, "It's freezing!"

"I thought it was just mine. Better make it a quick one." Kirkpatrick began to sing, his voice going higher in pitch, until he cut the acapella vocals, yelling, "Enough's enough. Whew!" The sound of his shower stopped, leaving the room silent. "Wendy, you done? Wendy?" He grabbed his towel and leaned out as he massaged his hair. "Hey, Honda, where are you?"

"Dressed, already." She appeared from the direction of the Gym, and she was tucking in her tunic. Her hair was completely dry. "Just waiting on you."

"How'd you get out so quick?" The door was wide, and he wrapped his towel around his hips and stepped out, rubbing his arms. "Did you ask the ship to check on the weather in here? I didn't know she did winter."

"I didn't, because you already did. Besides, I rinsed and called it good, so I'm not flash frozen. I bet laundry's pulled all the hot water." She shrugged. "Bad timing."

"Let me dress, and I want to see how the launch went." He grinned as he pulled a folded stack of clothes off a shelf and sat on a low bench, working his hand in to reveal a pair of red plaid undershorts. He shook them out and laid them to the side before reaching for a black undershirt next.

"Off and doing well." Honda was at the door, exiting, and she leaned inside, tapping her ear. "Been following it all."

"I knew there was a reason I love you so much." He stood. "Now out, while I get decent."

"Ha! You decent? Never." She laughed and was gone through the door.

Two Heads Are Better Than One

Pollock felt the goosebumps on her legs even before she remembered her request to the ship. What was going on with the ventilation system? She paused at a readout station, tapped the pad, and chose temperature display. She frowned. It read 64. She tapped the Change icon and was surprised to find the target temperature was, indeed, 72. She rapped the readout with her knuckle, wondering if something was wrong with this station. The next one was the other side of the exit for Weapons where Clarkson was entrenched in dismembering a very deadly bomb. It might not have been enough to punch a hole through the ship's hull, but damage enough internal systems, and it wouldn't matter. The *Higgs* wouldn't get to her destination, and that was the same as destroying the entire vessel. Pollock felt her neck, rubbing it absently, acutely aware of how far south this day had nearly gone, and she pushed away the temperature issue. It could be dealt with tomorrow or the next day. Clarkson deserved all her attention. He was the ship's champion. He'd saved the day. No, more than saved it. He saved 5,000 days, times a lifetime for each one. Plus, ten more lifetimes, those of her crew. Clarkson was her superhero, and she wanted him to know.

"Welly?" She called his name softly through the door. Two lights were above the doorway, one green, telling of an empty room, and the other red, indicating a locked door, as there was danger on the other side. Neither was lighted. She knew from the Mess that Clarkson had disengaged the firing device, but still, procedure, procedure. He had a backpack of explosives in there somewhere. When he didn't answer, she knocked softly and called, just a bit louder, "Weldon?"

"Yeah? I'm busy." His voice was dismissive and completely preoccupied.

"May I come in?" Pollock smiled. Yeah, this was the real Welly, wrapped in his work and oblivious to anything else, including military hierarchy. Then, he wasn't military. He was a civilian Specialist, who happened to be responsible for 5,000 humans in deep cryofreeze, kept alive by his masterful touch at the Cybernetics Terminal, as he kept the CorpseCases fully func- tional and in top-notch condition. After all, freezer pops don't stay frozen without a well-maintained freezer.

"Sure, Commander, sure. The door's open." He sounded still preoccupied but less abrasive.

The door slipped aside to reveal a secured room with racks of instruments along the walls, but no weapons, no explosives, and certainly no detonation devices. Clarkson worked with manual, handheld tools made with rubberized handles and soft-touch metals. A giant, backlit magnifying glass hunkered between the Specialist and the bomb. He placed a small wrench on the table at his side, and without looking, picked up another. His diffusion suit gave him a bulkier-than-usual appearance, and his blast-proof helmet glowed with a white light inside. There were controls inside he could operate with the touch of his tongue or a brush of his forehead, and they needed to be visible at all times.

"There, Commander." He pointed absently with his tool, indicating a chair on the far side of the room. A clear blast shield separated Clarkson from the observation area.

"I thought it was no longer live." She looked at the chair and at Clarkson, and she did as he asked, although she remained standing. She was here to help, not observe.

"It's not." He sounded disgusted, and he tossed the instrument he held onto the counter. It bounced before coming to rest against the edge of the bomb. He removed his helmet and set it on the far end of the counter.

"I can come out?"

"Yeah. Look at this." He turned the package her direction. Taking an extendable rod, he pointed inside. It was about as might be expected, several wires, a small timer with a blank screen, and two containers of chemicals, which would combine violently when their respective vessels were breached. It was the type of primitive device that wouldn't arouse suspicion when loaded on the ship. There was no radiation signature, and if done right, the chemicals were safe, even desirable when used independently. The wires dangled freely, having been cut when Clarkson first found the package. Both containers were sliced open, and that was alarming. The contents spilled out, dangerously close to touching.

"What substances are those?" She trusted him, really, but she didn't want him to kill her ship; or in this room, her or her Mission Specialist.

"It doesn't matter. They can't explode. We had nothing to worry about. Here's why." He laughed, as much a snort as anything, and he dug in the chemicals with the pointer. "Rather, let me restate that. We *have* nothing to worry about. Six hours ago, I don't know that we were so safe."

"Okay. What does that mean?" The ventilation system, now Clarkson. Was the entire mission on the blink?

"Ice crystals. Look." He jabbed the chemicals again, and she noticed something sparkling as it slid down in a little avalanche.

"Go ahead, it's safe. You can pick it up." Even so, he handed her a pair of thin, protective gloves.

She put on one and pinched a small amount of one of the chemicals, careful not to mix the two. Holding it under the magnifying glass, an ice crystal warmed next to her skin and slowly melted away. "What is this?"

"Simple aluminum powder. It was used as a catalyst mixture as far back as the twentieth. It shouldn't have *that* in it, though." The ice crystals, but he didn't have to say that. "Be careful about holding too much of this stuff. When the ice crystals melt, we'll get off-gassing. Hydrogen gas. Not good."

"The other?" She pulled off the glove, not wishing to touch any more.

"Something basic, ammonium nitrate, used in agriculture as a high-nitrogen fertilizer. It's the same, filled with ice crystals. Here's the weird thing." He scraped a bit of each onto a glass plate and held it under the magnifying glass. "See it?"

She shifted the magnifying glass to get a better angle, and the chemicals sparkled. Her eyes blinked, the piles seeming to shift, changing shape. Not growing! She cut her eyes to Clarkson to find him grinning.

"It's growing ice crystals." He set the plate down, and he stood. He began to unfasten his suit. "Ask me how, Commander."

"How?" She wanted to hear this.

"There's moisture everywhere. Even in here. The air we breathe would dry out our nasal passages if it didn't contain some moisture. That air condenses on surfaces that drop to a colder temperature. Here's the question I can't answer. What's making that colder than the air?" As he slipped the rest of the suit off, he nodded at the bomb materials opened and spread across the counter. "The detonator's totally gone, frozen solid, a chunk of ice filled with circuits."

"It's not my area of expertise, but we remove heat to make something colder. We have refrigerant lines all over the ship doing just that." She shrugged. That was simple enough.

He pulled two metal containment vessels from a cabinet and began to separate the chemicals into them as he took her explanation one step further. "What the refrigerant really does is slow down the movement of the molecules, taking away the friction that generates the heat. The process is systemic, and if we don't continually add heat back in, eventually we get absolute zero. The whole cosmos will slow down in its old age, quit generating heat someday, freezing solid, and collapsing, before reigniting into a brand-new Universe—"

"The Big Bang, but that's billions of years in the future. I was awake in my science classes. What's that got to do with this?"

"What's sucking away our heat? Have you felt chilly, today?" He stepped over and tapped the wall. It sounded different than she expected, the difference in the sound of rapping a metal panel on a hot world, and one used on a planet that's continually frozen. "Computer, what's the temperature in here?"

"The target temperature for the Weapons section is 72 degrees."

"That's not what I asked. What's the actual temperature? Right now, in here?"

"Current temperature is 61 degrees."

"An hour ago?" He smirked, as if this would prove him right.

"The temperature one hour ago was 63 degrees."

"Thank you, Computer. See, Commander? Access one of our outside storage compartments, one next to the skin of the ship, and you'll find it's twenty degrees colder. Something's stealing our heat."

"Not the Big Bang?" She smiled as if laughing off his reference.

"Not unless we're skipping across about five billion years. I don't see how that could happen. I'm just the Mission Specialist. I report to you and let you make all the hard decisions. All I know for certain is that I'm cold." He pulled a jacket from another locker and slipped it on, then rooted around until he found some gloves and slipped them on, also.

"I'll have the ship run a diagnostic on the ventilation system. We'll see if we can get the heat back on. Stay warm, Welly."

He smiled and exited the door, letting it slide closed behind him. Pollock called to the computer.

"Ship, when was the latest ventilation system diagnostic run?"

"One is running right now, Commander."

"Who requested it?"

"Science Officer Kirkpatrick. Would you like a copy of the report when it is ready?"

"Yes, thank you. Query finished."

The ship didn't reply, which was to be expected, having been told the query was complete. The Commander was stymied. Why would Kirkpatrick have requested the ship to run a diagnostic of the ventilation system? Was it breaking down all over? What would it take to ensure the survival of the crew if that were the case? Where could they make a redoubt until the ship got to Deneb and repairs could be initiated?

She was jumping the gun. She didn't even have the diagnostic report, yet. Still, jumping the gun was how ships were saved. She smiled, thinking, I can probably wait for a few hours to jump too far. We're en route across the galaxy. What can I personally do to change the situation now?

She decided she could check on Minkovski. She was looking down when they last spoke. Maybe she would have some opinions on what was up.

Houston, Are You There?

A cup of coffee hadn't done the trick. Pilot Frederick Nielson was in his quarters, and he had an entire thermos of black gold, now half empty, and the dregs of his last cup in his hand. His mind raced, and as he set the cup on the tabletop, his hand shook, landing the cup on the surface with a clatter. It was the caffeine, he allowed, though his experience said it was more. He just needed to pay attention—and get some rest.

Shaking his head to clear his thoughts, he stood, refilled his cup, and pulled his computer screen out of the wall just over his desk. He seated himself and idly touched his input board and powered up the device. It blinked once, then displayed the message, "This station has not been powered up and left on since leaving Earth. Would you like to update and sync this station with the main computer now?"

"Sure," he said aloud. "Computer? Can you start that?" When there was no answer, he called again, "Computer?"

He sighed and clicked okay on his screen. Voice recognition was probably part of the update. The display blinked, resetting to a bar showing his download progress and his expected completion time. He used the enforced inactivity to think over the day, hoping to put his finger on what troubled him. The launch of the *Daughter Two* had gone exactly as expected, textbook, in fact. Nothing could have been smoother. The oscillations of the two drives firing in such close proximity was jarringly rough, but it was what he'd been told would happen. He'd just not expected it to be so violent. The troublemakers were gone, Clarkson had diffused the bomb, Okotie-Eboh was unharmed and resting, and they would be arriving a few days early, per Levitson's accounts. That'd be a pleasant turnaround, enjoying a few Denebian beers, a realbeef dinner under the stars of a distant constellation, and maybe a smoke or two. There wasn't much on the station that couldn't be savored with enough funds or other goods to trade.

"Levitson?" He held his finger on his console comm icon as he pushed the call through.

"That you, Freddy?" Levitson's image came up in a corner of Nielson's screen, too small to obscure the download display running in his main view. His face filled the tiny image, and it was difficult to see what was behind him. He was looking off screen. Levitson muttered, "I feel I'm schlepping around," his eyes jumping, intent on whatever he was doing.

"You still on the Bridge?" Nielson released the comm, remembering that it blinked repeatedly on the other end until he did. "Sorry about the blinky thing."

"Blinky thing?" Levitson's eyes twitched, and he looked to the side, before saying, "Oh, that. I didn't notice. It's okay. I do it sometimes, too. How can I help you?" He stopped whatever he'd been doing, and he stared directly into the screen with a smile.

"You said we were having a short trip this time." Nielson nodded at him as he took a sip of coffee. "How short? Will I have time to finish a novel if I download one from the Library?"

"You? A novel? That's a *schlock*!" Levitson's face pulled away, fighting a smile, as if he'd sat back in his chair; and he looked toward the top of the screen, punching imaginary buttons in the air. "Novels." Punch. "Risqué." Punch. "Man-on-man or man-on-woman. Hmm. I can't decide." He laughed, looking back at the screen and leaning in to fill the empty space. "What's your poison, Pilot?"

"Just remember, I control the joystick. You're only having fun if I'm having fun." The sync bar completed, stating it was about to restart. He clicked okay, and the screen blanked and returned with a welcome screen behind Levitson's picture. Softly, the computer said, "Welcome, Frederick. Please speak your full name to log in."

"I see you got the message, too." Levitson was full face in his small display, and he grinned. "It's hitting all of us, one at a time. You think they'd do this for us before we ship out across the galaxy. So, what about our travel time? What do you want to know?"

"Trying to plan my turnaround time on Deneb. Can you come up with anything specific, or at least a rough estimate? A day early, or a week?"

"Kirkpatrick would be able to give you a better estimate, but I don't know if he's had a chance to look at the drive anomaly, yet." He glanced down, looked like he was inputting information, and the bottom third of his tiny display shifted to the display of the ship's drive Nielson had been looking at earlier. "Here it is. Whoa!"

"Whoa? What does whoa mean?" Nielson watched the Engineer drop back into his chair, his face growing smaller in the tiny square. Nielson double-tapped the image to bring it up to full screen. He could see the Commander's chair in the background, empty. The large display that circled the Bridge showed a neutral image of the space they traveled through, now appearing dark blue and nearly blank. The third of the image showing the ship's drive was perfectly clear, and very different than when he'd been watching Levitson's explorations before the near-debacle with Magill and his bunch of hoodlums. He tapped it, hiding Levitson, and letting the ship's drive fill his screen.

"How much of this can you read, Nielson?"

"I can *read* it all. Understanding it might take longer. What's that skewing our Resonance Field?" The lines looping around the *Higgs'* drive extended out on one side, as if there was something there, something powerful enough to create an energy eddy around the *Higgs'* bubble of flat space. Was the energy anomaly ever a big one!

"I'm searching." Levitson's fingers were making noise, even though Nielson couldn't see them. "Oh, this can't be good."

"You like keeping secrets, Engineer, or is it just something about me?" He wanted to chuckle, but his eyes were glued on the image on his screen. He'd never seen a Cassel-Jackson Field that had absorbed this much energy. In the gap between the two magnets, the purple-violet colors deepened to near black. No drive pulled down to black, ever.

"Let me add this to your display." A smaller Cassel-Jackson Resonance Field appeared, overlaid on the *Higgs*. It meshed perfectly with the disturbance looping into space. "That's the *Daughter Two*. It appears the drives have linked. The Alcubierre Wave must be massive."

"Whoa—" Nielson felt his blood run cold, unable to think of any response other than to repeat the Engineer's word.

"Yeah, join the team. Surfing the stars, riding the biggest warp bubble I've ever seen. If we don't slip off flat space, we'll be fine. Just turn around and go home." He gave a sour chuckle. "Only thing, I can no longer tell if we're centered or not."

"This . . . at what speed can the drives lock like this?" Nielson noticed the oscillations in the ship hadn't begun to cancel themselves. They'd gotten stronger. He grasped his coffee cup, pressing the heel of his hand firmly on the table. The liquid inside vibrated, and he couldn't hold it steady. The table was moving, not his hand.

"You and I don't work with numbers that large." Levitson's

voice shook, and Nielson double-tapped the image to bring the Engineer's face back onto the screen. He looked pale. Just below the image of the ships, a bar with numbers was marked by annotated powers, and it was growing at an alarming rate.

"Computer on," Nielson called to the ceiling. "Pilot Frederick Nielson." The display changed, relating Levitson to a small corner.

"Welcome, Frederick. How may I help you?" The words were warm and melodic, unlike the pointed ones thrown back at her.

"Computer, I want a real-time link to engine function on both the *Higgs* and the *Daughter*. I want every node and sine wave variation. I want to know how these two drives are linked, and when and why. Levitson, I need to make sure the Commander is aware of this. See if we can calibrate our velocity with the nearest stars. I know it's difficult at speed—"

"But not impossible, and I'm trying, sir. Stars that should be there are in the wrong magnitude. Their luminosity's way off. Locations, too; it's like they've just jumped. Hey, they just did it again, and, nah, that can't be." He glanced up to look directly at Nielson. "Stars don't just wink out. But one just did." He looked back down. "All over the place, they're winking out like dying fireflies."

"Machinery error?"

"Don't see how. We're reading the *Daughter* just fine. There's something else I can try—"

A band of color blinked around Nielson's screen, and transparent words flashed over the images already there, screaming, Warning! Temperatures in Hull Proximity Storage Rooms Now Below Operational Minimums. Action Required.

"Never mind, Asher. We've got a whole different can of worms on our hands. Meet me on the Engineering deck." Nielson stood, calling, "Computer, tell Pollock that Levitson and I are dealing with a life support emergency in Engineering. Let me know when she has my message."

"Understood."

Pilot Frederick Nielson was already out of the room, and as the ship's voice went silent, his door zipped closed after him, catching once before whining and finally sealing his quarters off from the rest of the ship.

The Gloves Come Off

"Get in there and get Zealander off that bunk. Kick him, if you must. Whatever it takes." Shank Magill spat the words.

"And Abdullah?" Crystal Hollis had a gleam of expectation in her eyes. "Can I kick him, too?"

Magill glared at her, figuring she'd do what she wanted, no matter what he said. He shrugged. "When his head clears up, he may remember. Your call. I just want as many people as possible to help sort this out."

"Got it." Hollis grinned and disappeared out the door.

Magill dropped to the floor, his head disappearing into the underside of the console. He jerked at something, and a plug-in circuit board went skittering across the floor. Four lights went dead on the console. He jerked again, moved something, and hit it with the heel of his hand. Three of the lights came back on. He grabbed the edge of the console and pulled himself up, his eyes scanning the effects of his butchery and stopping on the dead light. He made a quick series of inputs on the console, searching for a response that satisfied him. Nothing happened, and he cursed.

"Give me a chance, and I'll wring Levitson's neck. He

shouldn't be able to override my backdoor protocols." He was determined he wasn't giving up. He was still working out how they'd made it from the LaGrange station to the *Higgs*. They'd just been *there*, and then they were *here*. It wasn't conceivable. The kid? He didn't know how he'd made the globe work. It wasn't even turned on. Still, he'd know, however long it took. He admitted he didn't have time for that now, and he pushed it aside. If he didn't get this computer interface repaired, the rest of it didn't matter. He took a deep breath. There was more than one way to trick a computer into doing what you wanted. He restarted the machine to reset its operating parameters. As it rebooted, he interrupted it with a series of key strokes he liked to call *Baby Maker*. It would start a mirror application program, one without full functionality, but also one without the restrictions Levitson had used to strangle the ship's computer. He would have access to everything. The only drawback would be the time involved in teaching the mirror application so it would perform satisfactorily.

"Computer, initiate voice-mapping protocol Alpha-C." He typed the words as he spoke them. It was the most basic of the voice-recognition programs available, but one which was endemic and most likely to be installed on the *Daughter's* mainframe. It would take him an hour to teach it enough to access what he wanted, but giving up an hour was better than nothing—if it remembered him. He prayed his backdoor was still there.

"Protocol Alpha-C initiated." The computer replied aloud, but the words were disjointed and toneless, as if the acoustic parameters weren't set properly, and the neuro-linguistic relays were dragging.

"Recognize Doctor Shankelford Magill, University of Edinburgh, Research ID Number 1178." He typed and spoke at the same time. While the computer worked, he leaned out the door and yelled, "Hollis? Are you lost?"

The computer pulled him back in, with, "Hello, Doctor Magill. It's been a long time." The words were still broken and lifeless.

"A, B, C . . ." Magill wasn't in the market for conversation with a program he'd written as a teen. The important thing was bringing it up to speed. He tapped each letter as he spoke. ". . . D, E, F . . ." Phonemes, graphemes, consonant blends, he'd have to do them all. An hour of this, however, and he'd have voice access back again, even if at a limited level.

"Hey, Professor." Hollis knocked on the door, leaning in. "Got company for you." Something meaty hit the corridor wall just outside, then it slithered to the floor. It sounded like the back of a head. A groan filtered into the bridge. She turned to the corridor and yelled, "Stuff yourself, Kaseem. No one's feeling sympathy for your empty, brainless skull."

Magill paused at his keyboard, took a deep breath, and turned to face her. He couldn't do this alone, not reset the computer and give them insurance, just in case this wasn't successful. He knew she was mechanically adept. It was part of the reason he'd included her in his team to take the *Higgs*. What he didn't know was if she *really* understood starship propulsion drives. "What do you know about Casson Drives?"

"Like on this ship?" She shrugged. "I was the best on telematics, autonomous drill rigs, and mobile infrastructure maintenance. I could merge two broken rigs into one in the dark with my eyes closed. You got something broken I need to fix?"

"Kinda the same thing, no?" Laughter erupted in the corridor. It was Zealander's voice. "How'd you know it was dark if youse eyes were closed?"

"You want another belt in the kisser?" Hollis made a fist and aimed it at the speaker. "So, Mac, what's with the ship's drive?"

"I need the three of you to head to the bow and see if you can find a way to disengage the drive. I'll keep working on shutdown from here."

"Won't that leave us stranded?" She seemed surprised he'd even suggest such a thing.

110

"You prefer dead?" He gave her a hard look, hoping she got the seriousness of this.

"Any directions? It helps to know where to start." She shrugged, with a dubious look on her face.

"Just do it," Magill barked. "You were so good at *merging* rigs back on Venus. Now get up there and *unmerge* one. Simple enough for you?"

"Sure, Mac. Thought we were getting along pretty good there for a bit. Now your true colors are coming out. Thanks for nothing." She snorted and turned away, yelling, "Get off the floor, Kaseem. No naps, and you, Zealander! This isn't a party."

"I'm saving our lives, Hollis." Magill spat the words at her. "Hear that, saving our lives!"

"Yeah, right," she spat back, before turning her anger at the two men accompanying her towards the bow.

Magill shrugged and returned to his tutorial, hoping that his genius would bleed into the computer, and sooner was better than later, if they wanted to survive this very rotten day. He took a moment to rub his arms, noticing the chill bumps that had formed. It was *cold* in this ship. He'd deal with that next. Right now, he had to get this ship disengaged from the *Higgs'* drive field, or they were all dead.

The Snow Queen's Kiss

Payload Specialist Imani Okotie-Eboh turned in her bed, pulling her blanket over her arms and sinking her head deeper into the pillow. She smiled, remembering the snow outside Bern, flying down the slopes with the wind in her hair. It was fabulous. The day had started out sunny, blindingly bright, then the smallest of flakes had begun to drizzle across the sky. Laughing, she and Henri had stopped on one slope, hidden by a copse of snow-covered trees, to embrace in a passionate kiss. Soon, however, the snow became a sheet of white, and a number of school kids had come by, bantering excitedly, and they had separated, agreeing to meet for coffee at the bottom. They'd huddled before a realwood fire, warming numb fingers and noses before making their way to a late supper—lobster and wine—casting away a month's salary in one indulgent splash.

"Turn the heat up, Henri," she called sleepily. "Either that or come snuggle with me."

When there was no answer, she opened her eyes, surprised not to see their room in the Bellevue. She pushed the covers from her face, and they crackled, causing her to come immediately awake.

It was *cold* in the room, and a layer of *frost* covered her bedding. Surveying the rest of the space, the glittering sugar also crawled up her walls. She threw the bedding back and gasped, now seeing her breath in white clouds.

"I need clothes," she muttered, beginning to shake violently. In the dream—surely a safety valve resulting from her earlier attack—she'd been warm, and in the intensity of the cold, her trauma at Zealander's hands was forgotten. Stumbling to her wardrobe, her feet dancing on the frosted floor, she pulled the heaviest clothing she could find, covering herself four layers deep before she was finished. Still, her shipboard clothing was designed for visual stimulation or gaming, not weather, and she was barely warmer than before. She held her hand in front of the vent and felt a modicum of warmth, but hardly enough to do her any good.

"Computer, where's the heat?" Her voice shook as she headed toward the door. The response surprised her.

"Heat is—" crackle "—on. Please do not adjust yo—" pop "—your local controls. Heat will be restored in approximately—" crackle, fizz "—minutes." Ship's voice tried to purr innocently, but clearly there was something going on.

"How long?" Okotie-Eboh placed her palm on the door release panel as she asked the question, flinching at the cold, and startled when it didn't immediately open. "Ship, my door won't operate."

"Crackle, fizz," the ship repeated, ending with a belated, "—minutes. Please be patient."

"Ouch!" she cried, pulling her hand away from the panel just as it blinked, and the door began to open. Halfway and it stopped. When she pushed at it, leaving blood, it retracted fully into the wall. She looked at her hand to find patches of skin ripped away. It was numb, and she could barely feel it. "Ship," she called plaintively, "you've hurt me."

"Heat is on. Please—" fizz, pop "—adjust your—" and with

a sharp electrical *bzzt*, the voice went silent.

"I need a new room," Okotie-Eboh mumbled, as she moved into the corridor. There was no frost, but it was barely warmer. Clenching her hand, she felt the pain just starting. She thought, *frostbite,* but quickly dismissed that. No one got frostbite, ever, on the Deneb run. It did need to be looked at, and Medical would surely have all the heat it needed. She smiled as she remembered Doctor Minkovski's kind words. She considered the lift, even had her bleeding hand over the access panel before remembering the ship's faltering speech and her quirky door. Medical was two floors down. She laughed at what her crewmates would say if they knew she was using the stairs. It would help warm her up. She was freezing, and she needed the extra exercise, that was all. Me? Worried about the ship? Nah, she laughed. Never. I felt perfectly safe all along.

Even so, she couldn't get her mind off her hand. It was really stinging by the time she passed Recreation, and it had begun to burn by the time she got to Medical. The heat made the snow queen's kiss central and immediate, and her frost-covered walls fell from her thoughts.

Crystal Clear Reflection

Pilot Frederick Nielson cursed as he jogged along the corridor. He'd tried the lift to Engineering The door had opened fine, but inside, the ship had refused to respond to any verbal requests. Nothing, even from the backup controls. And it was star-sucking cold inside, as if it had been turned into a temporary refrigeration unit—or a morgue. He left the door open and headed down the stairs, surprised to catch a glimpse of Okotie-Eboh exiting on Gold Floor. He thought nothing of her heading to visit Minkovski after the trauma she experienced in the *Daughter Two's* bay, but using the stairs was odd. Then, he was doing the same. Maybe the glitch with the computer was systemic. First, the ventilation system, then the computer interface, and now the lifts. What next, the main drive units? He was anxious to get with Levitson and dig to the bottom of things. Only thing about the bottom, he told himself, is that's where the muck tends to settle.

The door to Engineering was open—surprisingly—and he burst through, calling, "Ashe, you in here?"

"Yeah," the answer came, yelled from someplace Nielson couldn't see. Then, quieter, "What a schlemiel! Don't know what flash brain chose to—"

"Chose to what?" Nielson found him partially hidden behind a swing-out panel, and he knocked on the metal to get his attention.

"Hey!" Something banged, and Levitson backed out, rubbing his head. "It's you. You know, Freddie, this is a schmuck. The air handlers are freezing up. Ice crystals on the filter racks. The cooling coils are coated. Look at this." He backed away and motioned for the Pilot to see for himself.

Inside, the internal portion of the unit extended into the cavity four meters or so, and air, cold air, sucked past as Nielson leaned closer. It glittered with crystalline facets, as if filled with frozen diamonds. As he watched, it twinkled, then again, and he realized the crystals were forming as he watched. He asked, "Why's it not freezing in this entire room?"

"It was. I have the auxiliary heat on." He pointed overhead where red coils burned in the ceiling in a Dante-esque dance. "It's hardly keeping up, but it's better than it was. My concern? This is the only part of the ship with supplementary heating. If it's that cold in there, I can't imagine how we'll keep the rest of the ship tolerable."

"I think we're past that point."

The two men turned to see Commander Pollock in a massive coat, with a thick, furry lining billowing around her face and hands. Nielson laughed.

"Commander, where'd you get that?" He jabbed his elbow into Levitson's side, grinning.

"This is part of a shipment to the Deneb Archeological Museum. Belongs to an ex-polar explorer who's sponsoring a Shackleford exhibit in an upcoming exhibition. How do I look?" She paraded coquettishly for two steps before laughing. "Yeah, it's funny. It's warm, too. I spoke with Honda. We're not heating properly, obviously." She pulled apart the lapels of the coat and fanned them before wrapping back up.

"You gotta look in there, Commander. The whole thing's a freezer. If I had access to Cybernetics, I could reverse the cryogenic pumps, route it through here, and get some real heat, but . . ." He shrugged.

"Five thousand buts. Thanks, Engineer. I think we'll let them live. What are our other options?"

"Levitson, you might want to mention the stars." Nielson kept his eyes on Pollock. Under the Dante heaters, she'd tossed back her hood, and it seemed as though her head floated in a puffball of blonde hair.

"The stars are offline, now?" She crossed her arms with a smile.

"We just can't find them." Levitson looked at the ceiling and began to rub his arms. He shivered. "The heat's not keeping up."

One of the heating panels sizzled, then with a bright flash, popped loudly and went off. Sparks shot out, as hot bits of metal bounced on the floor, glowing for a moment before going cold. The dead element popped several more times as ice began to form around it. Then a second panel did the same thing, driving the three crew members into the corridor for safety. Levitson called to the computer as he ran from the room, "Computer, auxiliary heat off, now. Power down."

There was no response. The remaining panels continued to glow, the coils blinking and sizzling, and going out one at a time. "Computer on," Pollock also called, to silence.

"It won't work." Nielson jumped back as a lump of glowing metal bounced through the door. "The lifts are down, and not even the backup controls respond." At his feet, the fragment went black, before becoming white with frost. "That's odd," he muttered.

"I think I can get to the console and shut this down manually. Excuse me." Levitson ducked inside before Nielson or Pollock could stop him. A lump of glowing metal hit his leg, and he exclaimed, "*Fey!*" and zigzagged to the main console. He hit it

117

with his fist, and a thin sheet of ice broke free. He began typing in commands, becoming frustrated when there was no change. Finally, he dropped to the floor, popped a panel free, and yanked out a circuit board. The auxiliary heaters overhead went dark, as did the rest of the lights in the Engineering room. In the quiet, wind from the opened air handler whistled gently.

"Asher?" Nielson called into the darkness.

"I'm okay. I could use some help, though."

"Just come out." Pollock's voice. "We don't have a light."

"Good point. I can't."

"Why not?" Nielson.

"My clothes are frozen to the floor. Take your time, guys. It's getting really cold, really fast."

The floor had become slick, even icy, when they entered the room to dislodge Levitson from the floor. Even odder were the walls. It was, perhaps, because of the total darkness in the room that they noticed them. In the corners, around fixtures, at any seams in the wall panels, an eerie, purplish light glowed coldly, as if trying to get in and unable to quite figure out how.

"That could sap the socks off a centipede," Levitson murmured as he clambered to his feet, with Pollock and Nielson holding his arms. He tugged at his clothes without looking at himself, as he kept his eyes on the walls, tracing the purple glow.

"Your opinion, Engineer?" Pollock shook his shoulder to get his attention.

"I don't have one. Sorry, Commander. Mold, fungus, space virus? This isn't part of any course I ever sat through."

"Okay, Nielson, if we don't have an opinion on the purple light, what about the stars?" They were stepping through the doorway, and she was the last one through.

"It's Levitson's thing—" The man was still agog over the purple light and looking in the corridor, as if he might find more. "—but since he's got other things on his mind, well, they're gone."

"So, the purple stuff just fries our brains? The stars can't be gone. Levitson, snap out of it. What's with the stars?" She took his shoulder in her hand, and she forced him to look at her. "Engineer, now!"

"Yes, Commander?" He tried to brighten his face and half smiled.

"Nielson says you found out something about the stars. Well, man, what it is?"

"They're going out, just blinking out of existence, one by one." He smiled vacantly, then his eyes rolled into his head, and he collapsed onto the floor.

"To think I saw something in him at one time." Pollock shook her head. "Computer on. I need Minkovski at Engineering, stat. Computer?"

"Down, Commander," Nielson reminded her.

She turned to the manual input on the wall, only to find a thin sheet of ice covering it. She rapped it with her knuckles, and it fell away. It was dead, too.

Nielson's personal comm wasn't, and he tapped it and requested the Doctor's attention. When she replied, it wasn't what he expected.

"Nielson? Thank God someone's still active and about. Imani's shown up with frostbite on her hand. I treated it, but God knows how she got that. Now, all my equipment's failing, I can't contact anyone, and—" Minkovski's voice went silent.

"Doctor?" Nielson got no reply. His comm was dead. "Maybe we should try to carry Asher there, Commander." He looked around, wondering how long before something else went wrong. He was beginning to wish he was on the *Daughter Two*. Even if they could power up the *Daughter One*, he didn't know if the drive could come on line fast enough if the *Higgs* were truly disintegrating. Then, there were their 5,000 passengers. No way could they abandon them.

"I agree." Pollock knelt with Nielson and lifted Levitson, one under each arm, and with his feet dragging, moved toward the stairs. "I'm thinking, Freddie, if we move to the *Daughter One*, we'd have heat." She paused. "Surely."

"You'd expect so," he said, not too loudly. "If it's not infected, too."

She looked at him in a hard, quick glance, before shifting Levitson on her shoulder and heading onto the steps leading up to Medical.

Packing Heat

Mission Specialist Welly Clarkson found Communications Chief Ranson Charles in the Recreation section. Tucked under the upper-level Quarters section and above Medical, the Virtual Gaming Center was about as centered in the ship as any space could be. Clarkson still wore his gloves and jacket from Weapons, and with the center of the ship so much warmer than anywhere else, and warmly dressed, it felt relatively toasty. It had seemed odd that exiting the lift had required him to shove the door the last half a meter open, then it had remained open as he walked away; but it wasn't his area of responsibility, so he let it slide. Besides, if Charles could offer him some opinions on what had happened with that bomb, he'd be right back, and he wanted the lift available.

Through the one-way glass in the wall, Clarkson had a full view of Charles in the Gaming Center. He wore a full virtual suit, with the helmet, gloves, and sensors. On a shelf off to the side rested his obligatory ear buds. Clarkson couldn't tell what environment Charles was immersed in, but he could see it being acted out. Above the door, a light showed the room was locked and could only be entered when the program was paused or ended. The Virtual Gaming Center's main appeal over Okotie-Eboh's virtual format on the Bridge was the immersion level. The Gaming Center had full feedback, including a floor with yaw and pitch control, temperature and wind modifications, and olfactory inputs to ensure the most realistic environment possible. Impact sensations came from the sensors in the suit, sending electrical signals to individual muscles, sometimes in very painful bursts. There was no sound, as the helmet provided full audio and visual feedback. In the Gaming Center, what you saw and heard in virtual, you felt in the real world. You got broadsided with a sword, and you carried bruises for a week. Chase someone uphill, and you ended up winded. Tangle with a skunk, and you needed deodorizer before interacting with other crew members.

Chief Charles was getting pulverized. The floor shifted, and he was running uphill. He tripped over an invisible obstacle, the sensation of the object in his way fed through his sensor pads, and he was down, the floor dropping out from under his feet for a second, then jerking up to meet him and jarring him as he made contact. He stood, panting, then kicked wildly. He lifted both arms and cheered, when his back jerked, and the floor rippled. Charles dropped to his knees, with one hand on the floor.

Clarkson balled his hand into a fist and jabbed a giant red plunger on the wall that would signal Charles he had a visitor. Orange and yellow lights around the ceiling flashed in an alternating pattern. Charles continued in play for several minutes before the floor leveled, and he pulled his helmet off, exposing his shock of bright red hair. He looked to the window and grinned, as he pulled a cloth from his pocket and wiped his face. The lights above the door changed, and when Charles hit a matching red plunger on his side of the wall, the door slipped aside and disappeared, as the yellow and orange lights went dark.

"Welly!" Charles threw an arm out in an old-style Nazi-like salute, holding it until Clarkson hit his palm to Charles'. He laughed. "That was the 'Frisco quake of '06. I just fought off a group of thugs vandalizing undamaged houses. It was brutal, especially the aftershocks."

"You mean 1906?" Clarkson slipped off his gloves, worked them into a pocket, and loosened the front of his jacket. It was very warm inside with Charles.

"It's the only one that counts. How are our popsicles doing?" He grinned again, as he began working the feedback sensors from his suit.

"Fine, I suppose. I'm here for some technical advice." As Charles unfastened the front of his suit, Clarkson moved behind him to help him work it off his shoulders and to his waist. "It's about the bomb."

"Oh?" Charles turned to face the Mission Specialist with a puzzled look. As he worked the legs of the suit off, he said, "I thought you and the Commander already handled that."

"Okay, not just the bomb, but the bomb's part of it. It's what was in the bomb."

"Like, explosives?" Charles had the suit off, and he straightened his shirt and pants. His shoes were to the side, and he slipped them on. "I was in the Mess. You had it disarmed. Was there something else inside I should know about?"

"Ice." Clarkson took Charles' suit and hung it in a recess in the wall.

"Ice." Charles paused, and he ran a hand through his hair. Absently, he picked up his earbuds and worked them around his neck, letting them hang loosely down his chest. "And you stored it where, in the freezer?"

"Weapons. No freezer, not even close. Just in Weapons."

"And Pollock was there?" When Clarkson nodded, he asked, "Her opinion?"

Clarkson shrugged. "She's the Commander. She had other things to think about. I separated the chemicals into separate containers and put them in storage. Even the detonator was iced up.

Solid."

"That the reason for the coat and gloves?" Charles clapped Clarkson on the shoulder, and they made ready to exit the room.

"You *are* in the dark." It was Clarkson's turn to laugh. "Ship's ventilation is on the fritz, at least down in Weapons."

"You flashing me? Has anyone been to Engineering, yet? The air handler is probably clogged, though I don't know how. We've only been out a day—" He snapped his fingers as he moved into the corridor, his face turning hard. "Sabotage. It's gotta be it. Those four plungers on the *Daughter Two* are to blame. C'mon, I've got some ideas to get the air flowing again." He looked around as if surprised. "It's cold in here."

Clarkson didn't have time to answer. The ship creaked ominously, the way an empty building does when exposed to drastically shifting temperatures, a twisting metal sound, that of an ocean-going vessel caught in a torturous winter tempest. The lights flickered, then went dead. An alarm started up and sputtered out. After fifteen seconds, red emergency lighting along the floor gave a soft glow to the corridor. Clarkson looked in Charles' face, his eyes eerily darkened in the reddened light. He opened his mouth to speak, only to see that the window into the Virtual Games Room was edged with frost, and it was spreading as he watched. The emergency lights began to shatter, sending tiny shards of red plastic into the air. They moved slowly, as if the air was thickened, or time was running amok, and when they hit, the sound was brittle, like ice shattering on a frozen lake. Charles' face grew dimmer until the last light was gone.

That's when the blackish-purple glow appeared. Across the walls, previously imperceptible and jagged lines—cracks, if it were possible—snaked around them, glowing with cold energy, yet looking like they would burn if someone dared get too close. The light throbbed, alive, pressing in, as if it would crush them if it could.

"Your ideas? They'd be useful about now." Clarkson could

hardly catch his breath, he was so frightened.

"Ideas?" Charles' voice broke. "Man, I got no ideas that would help with this."

The ship groaned again, as if to tell Charles he was correct.

Inside the Computer's Head

Interplanetary Education Liaison Liam Schlegel had the Bridge to himself. His neatly trimmed nails tapped absently on the console, and for a change, he'd forgone his good hair and wrapped his head in a VR helmet. He preferred the ship's Virtual Learning World on the Recreation Level, but the computer hadn't cooperated. He'd asked it to raise the local ambient; and while it had *promised,* he'd been unable to get warm; so, he'd bailed to lesser connections on the Bridge, ones that were adequate for the rest of the crew but stupefied and muddied for a connoisseur like him.

It ranked shivering. He hadn't been able to concentrate in Recreation.

Inside his virtual environment, he was disconnected from the world. Unlike Specialist Okotie-Eboh's StretchSuit or Chief Charles' Virtual Gaming Center, virtual learning was less about the body and more about the mind. The point was to be disconnected; Schlegel needed his mind to be free to wander the electrical pathways of the ship's electronic brain; to peruse the rarified codices written in piezoelectric impulses; to live as a spark of life in a brilliantly expanded world, if only for the short time he could

126

steal away from real life.

Schlegel enjoyed being in his head, often more than he enjoyed other people. It was how he maintained his even keel. He was disconnected, able to view events from the outside, from a *virtual* perspective, as though he wasn't living them but observing. It was why he'd dreamed of being a Sling Pilot. Ain't no one more disconnected than a Sling Pilot. Man, they were disconnected from the *Earth,* at least for the time they were riding the rocket into the suborbital zone and back down again.

He wandered the internal matrices of the ship's mind, his presence a mere puffball of thought images and interconnected electrical motes. His existence was so delicate—even fragile— that the ship was unaware of him, unless he chose to make himself known. Today, he floated and sampled. One seed head brushed a communication from the Bridge, from Commander Pollock to Admiral Lebo Eriksson. Schlegel's touch was so gentle that it was easy to slip in and slip out, the fibrous tendrils around his inquisitive seeds caressing the information nodes, overriding careless safeguards, listening to secret whispers, and pulling microelectronic bits of information out, before returning them to their secret places when he had them mirrored at the core of his puffball. There was something about the Commander expecting more from the Admiral than he had given her; a promise incomplete; and an angry threat if it wasn't made good. The promise wasn't available to his puffball tendrils, so he floated on, letting it go. An image appeared when he came to one of Prime's connections. It surprised him, as he wasn't anywhere near the First Mate's private stash. He usually didn't bother with Honda's electronic lockbox, as her passwords and elaborate encryptions were usually unbreakable. This, however, was a fly line cast through the ether, intended to snag a glittering trout, to reel him in with a dazzling promise of favors unbounded. In the 21st century, they called it sexting. Now? It made Schlegel aware of his physical body, and he closed it out. He was *virtual,* and physical awareness hindered his ability

127

to be a ghost in the machine.

He found one thing he was pleased to uncover, an entire swath of coding with Shank Magill's signature all over it. It permeated the ship. It hit him, Shank Magill was Doctor Shankelford Magill, the eminent master programmer who'd been at the forefront of voice recognition before his inexplicable fall from academia and disappearance into the shadows of disenfranchised and black-balled Mensa members. He'd been demoted to a university in Scotland, he thought. No wonder he'd been able to infiltrate the entire ship, gain access to the *Daughter Two*, and plant the bomb in Cryo-Storage. The quantum camouflage suits were full military, and Schlegel probed for anything about that, but there was nothing. Magill was smart, he'd give him that. He'd hidden himself well, leaving nothing on the ship's servers except his voice recognition signature. Schlegel brushed Communications, looking for the *Daughter Two*. She was out there. With the Casson Fields overlapping, the connections would be brittle, ready to shatter at the lightest touch, so he was at his gentlest. He elongated the tendrils around one seed, reaching, brushing, intertwining with the signal. The *Daughter Two* whispered to him, *". . . shouldn't be able to override my backdoor protocols . . ."* Schlegel sat up straighter in his real-world seat on the Bridge, and he felt his slender virtual connection stiffen, straining to listen. It was near breaking, and he forced himself to relax. The tendril stretching from the *Higgs* to the *Daughter Two* eased, and the information began to flow again.

"Protocol Alpha-C initiated." Schlegel puzzled over that. It was unfamiliar to him. Then he heard the toneless, *"Hello, Doctor Magill. It's been a long time."* It was the sound of his first programming efforts in a grade school science project, the computer speaking with a flat voice, before he'd learned to implement voice inflection and tone modulation, although the words were different. It was the Doctor interacting with the *Daughter's* computer. His connection was picking up the back-

ground sounds of a conversation. Bits and pieces came through: *... Casson Drives ... belt in the kisser ... disengage the drive ....* That left Schlegel puzzled. Why would Magill want to disengage the drive? He had no record of the course settings, and he'd be stranded with no known coordinates to recalibrate directional headings. Even to *disengage* the drive was risky. The *Daughter Two* was propelled forward by a black hole, even if it *was* manufactured, that drove the flat space-warp bubble. Fall into it, and you were toast forever.

Schlegel withdrew his tenuous tendril, and he stiffened his dandelion puffball. With increasing purpose, he floated deeper, sampling, sometimes grabbing, and occasionally setting off alarms. They faded when he withdrew, or continued to bleat their complaints, but he looked for anything that might tempt Magill, an undisputedly brilliant man in his field, to do something so foolhardy as bring a ship to full stop light years away from any habitable planet, and he couldn't afford to be gentle. When he was done, he could massage the bruises he'd left behind, but he would leave bruises, if that's what it took.

He found what he wanted in Navigation, Telemetrics, and the ship's Log. He didn't understand it, and that frightened him. The ship's position could be triangulated with as few as three solar bodies, and there were a hundred million in the Milky Way alone. The *Higgs* was on a programmed course, so all triangulation had been done before they set out. Now, though, he searched for familiar stars and couldn't find them. The few he thought recognizable had blown into red giants or collapsed into white dwarfs, with several supernovas where he expected well-known stars to be fixed in place. Dipping into the Log, he felt his stomach loosen as he scanned the drive's power readings and speed. He wasn't the Engineer or Pilot, and this wasn't his area of expertise, but the numbers registering the speed of their vessel were enormous and increasing at an exponential rate. Brushing against the memory banks for drive telemetry, he saw with his virtual eyes something the ship's visual monitors couldn't capture. The *Higgs* and the *Daughter Two* leaped into full, three-dimensional life, surrounded by the Resonance Field held in place by the Cassel-Jackson Drive. The massive Alcubierre Warp Bubble was invisible, but the shifting light from what stars he could see was perfectly clear, revealing a ship surfing a rogue wave of unbelievable proportions across the cosmos. The ship was dwarfed by the magnetic energy contained in its Resonance Field. Schlegel shifted the light wave parameters, and the bizarre scene became a turbulent and violent maelstrom of flowing energy, with the few celestial objects still visible flinging out long arms of solar material towards the *Higgs* as if they were being drained dry, their energy lifeblood sucked away by a voracious vampire of unimaginable origins. The space around the *Higgs* pulsed with light that was purple and deepening to black, giving off an eerie glow that threatened to erupt from within. Capillaries of frozen lightning extended gnarled fingers throughout the ball of energy, nourishing the writhing mass with the lifeblood of the stars.

Schlegel desperately searched for an explanation, shifting his focus to the ship's engineering records. What had *happened?* Could it be *fixed?* Was this simply a computer-generated simulation or, and he hardly dared think it, a reflection of *reality?* It was impossible, wasn't it? The picture he'd seen could only be explained one way. Somehow, for some reason, the *Higgs* had become an energy attractant, absorbing and somehow *containing vast amounts of the Universe's energy.* Stars, constellations, nebulae, gone. Star clusters, galaxies, and more—whole galaxy clusters, simply vanished, drawn into and compressed into the sphere of the *Higgs'* Casson Field. Such an event could only transpire over billions of years, and that was impossible.

Unless.

Liaison Schlegel zeroed in on the *Higgs'* magnetics, searching the drive, observing the black hole, comparing whole data banks of historical information. He found the *Higgs'* warp bubble interlinked with the *Daughter Two*'s, forming one massive black hole. He shifted back to the view of the ship dwarfed by the Casson Field, with its massive waves of energy streaming in, and he drove his viewpoint to the core of the ship's drive. He overlaid the image with real time facts, numbers, nodes, tipping points, temperatures, and anything else the ship had available. The combined black holes had compressed the distance between the ships and their drive units, pushing them faster and faster, and pulling them over the edge, nearing the proverbial Event Horizon. It was the only answer Schlegel could come up with to explain what he saw. The stars, disappearing. The ambient temperature in the celestial void, nearing absolute zero. The massive quantity of energy contained in the *Higgs'* Field, mind-boggling.

Schlegel's dandelion began to float free. All tethers were lost. What would he tell the crew? Everything they knew was gone. Deneb Station, evaporated into the mists of time. Earth, ended. The Universe, winding down. The *Higgs*, how could it contain so much energy? It was a soap bubble filled with all the Universe had been, was, and could be. Burst the skin, and . . . and . . . there was no and. It would be the end of all creation.

Time seemed frozen to the man in the black helmet. As he lifted his arms to free his head, his limbs moved slower and slower, until they no longer moved at all. Triggered by his slowing synapses, as if living out a life he'd only ever imagined, his eyes began to jerk, the events he dreamed visible to only him.

Singing to the Stars

Crystal Hollis, veritable spitfire and child of the Venus mines, cursed Shank Magill as she fought her way into one of the two extra-ship suits available on the *Daughter*. Her olive skin glowed with perspiration, and her black eyes glowered. The suit was too *big,* and it kept *slipping off.*

"Need some help in there, little girl?" Kaseem Abdullah was around the corner pulling on the second suit. It was even larger than hers, but for him, that was about right. He still struggled with fine motor coordination, but his mouth was hooked up and operating just fine. He laughed coarsely, calling, "You got nothing I ain't seen before, girlie. I'll let you see mine, if you let me have fun with yours."

"I told you last time," and she snatched a screwdriver from a rack on the wall, holding it backwards in her hand, "that mouth of yours is about to get you in real deep." She had one arm in the suit and the other out, with her helmet still off to the side, when Abdullah stepped around the corner, leering at her. He was fully dressed, with his helmet under one arm. She stepped toward him menacingly.

"C'mon, baby." He patted his crotch through the thickly padded material. "Everybody likes a little fun." Behind him, Raytheon Zealander—the medication mostly cleared from his system—leaned against a wall, the expectation of a fight coming through in the smile on his face. His stance favored his leg, still wrapped, but his eyes were clear. He was bundled in several layers of clothing, odd sizes found in various cabins. None of them seemed to fit, but he claimed he was warmer.

"You touch me, and you won't be able to have a little fun." Hollis raised her fist, with the tool extended below, a sabretooth's jaw ready to rend him limb from limb.

"Just offering." He raised his hands, palms forward, and backed up a step. He still grinned, however, and he looked as though he was leering with the scars on his face.

Hollis lunged toward him, jabbing with the makeshift weapon, as if wanting to damage his suit. It would be a disaster for the man if she did, which seemed to be her intent.

"Baby, you do want help out there, don't you?" Abdullah finally attempted to placate her

"You want to be in one piece there?" She pointed to his crotch with the handle of the screwdriver. "If so, I expect you to shut it."

"Got it. You are some touchy woman."

Zealander chuckled, ducked his head and turned away, muttering, "Man doesn't know when to quit." He limped as he moved, favoring his bandaged leg.

Zealander was their backup in case there were problems. He had a portable comm on his belt, and the other two would use the ones in their suits. The only manual override for the Cassel-Jackson Drive was in the actual drive unit. For that, they needed to EVA the *Daughter* and enter the drive. It wasn't especially dangerous for experienced crew members. Hollis and Abdullah's resumes, however, weren't padded with lots of hours at this. Once Hollis had her suit completely on, with a spare ratchet strap cinching up the waist, Abdullah and Hollis made their way hand over hand up a metal ladder. This part of the ship was designed explicitly for maintenance of the giant, electric magnet that encircled the nose of the vessel, and when they climbed upwards, they were in the hollow center of the artificial lodestone. Much as in an electric amplifier or a loudspeaker, the magnet picked up any noise in the structure of the ship and multiplied it by a factor of ten or twenty or more, depending on the energy being fed into the magnet. That sound was trapped in the space between the body of the ship and the drive unit, but it could already be heard through the hull. In the open space between the two parts of the vessel, the ship truly "sang" its way to the stars, a melody of gargantuan proportions. Hollis notified Zealander to evacuate the air in the passageway. When Hollis hit the plunger to iris open the massive door at the top of the steps, it released with a jerk violent enough to shake her hand on the ladder. Above her, an aurora borealis of deepest purple shot through with black and overlaid with fingers of red lightning filled her vision.

"My God," she murmured, freezing in place.

"What's wrong, Hollis?" Zealander's voice fed through her helmet, quizzing her.

"Sorry." She cleared her throat. "I just didn't expect this. I'm moving out."

"Expect what?" Zealander, again.

"Forget it, Zealander." Abdullah's words had a cruel edge to them. "It's too *pretty,* and Hollis can't bring herself to get her job done. Move, Hollis. I'm coming through." He jumped, hitting against her, and grabbing the edge of the opening. His helmet was face to face with hers, and he laughed before pulling himself through. The area between the ships was gravity-free, and he floated slowly upwards toward the main drive. There were safety cables to hook to their suits, but they went unused.

"I'll frag you!" Hollis threw herself through the opening, grasping at his ankle. When she grabbed it, she began pulling herself up his body. Amid the glowing light of the purple fog, she took his shoulders in her hands, held tightly, and head-butted her helmet into his, creating a whacking noise. "Ha! Keep your hands off me, pervert!"

She shoved away, but he easily caught her as she slipped past. The throbbing hum of the ship's song reverberated around them, felt in their suits, with occasional high-pitched wails threaded through. It was a whale's song, multiplied by a thousand in volume. Their time outside was limited by necessity. The song would damage them physically if they remained too long. In the distance, barely visible through the glowing bluish-black sky, visible more by the lightning it blocked rather than by its actual shape, hung the *Higgs*. It was a hundred times as long as the *Daughter*, and fatter, too. Far ahead of them, the near edge of the Alcubierre Warp Bubble was there if you knew where to look, apparent in the stars that were shifted just out of position from where they should be.

"You're a fool," Abdullah spat at her, ignoring the gathering fingers of frost at the edges of his faceplate. "My god-niece and my *husband* died in the Camps of Sterkrivier. You think I'd want a soft thing like you? I like men, tough and with bite in their voices."

"Thank God for that!" She slammed her helmet into his again, and shot off toward the upper hatch. Abdullah was her ballast, and heavier, he floated backwards only a short distance before the magnetism between the two ships reversed his direction, and he could swim towards her once again.

"I like you better, already," Abdullah said, grinning, as he joined her. He hit the plunger, and the door jerked open. He forced himself past her once again, his trailing hand offering her a vulgar hand sign as he floated past.

Inside, there was room for two, but just. It was a maintenance shaft, built for access by unsuited workers in dry dock, not fully suited insurrectionists quarreling over insults real or imagined. There was no atmosphere, so their suit integrity would have to be maintained. As she floated in, Hollis called, "Zealander, trigger the lights."

"I have." His voice crackled, as if reception was failing.

"You get that, Kaseem?" She punched him on the shoulder. "That purple goop is providing interference."

"Yeah, why the lights aren't working. I serviced these back in my day. Let me." He pulled himself to a panel, worked it open, and yanked a lever. Numerous lights flickered on with a reddish sheen, giving the space an eerie appearance. "Now, where's the off switch?"

"You can't just kick it and make it stop." Hollis was back in her element, and it soothed her. "Once I back it down, it takes a couple of hours for the entire drive to cycle off."

"Hours?" Abdullah scoffed. "Magill said now, not hours."

"I know machines. You let me do this the right way." She already had a monitor on, and it flickered among the piping, levers, and switches. The input keys were massive, designed just in case someone in an EVA suit needed to access it someday. She had gone through three menus and started the process when Abdullah interrupted her.

"Hours, huh? It's cold in here. I'm ready to be done."

"Hours," she responded without turning. Her face plate was crackling with ice crystals, also. She'd already turned up her heat once. "Magill had this ship cycling online for a full day before we planned to use it. Taking it down in a couple hours is pushing it."

"How you doing that?" He was at her shoulder, and he seemed interested.

Zealander's voice interrupted, crackling and barely understandable. "Every . . . kay? Magill says . . . owly. Don't rush."

"Don't rush." Abdullah purred his words, now charming. "That'd the one thing I got out of that. I never rush."

"Stop it." Hollis, no longer threatened, teased with a laugh. She indicated a green bar at the top of her display, one that remained visible even as she changed menus, and she explained.

"This is the electrical feed for the magnets. Once I begin the shutdown, it'll drop until it reaches zero. Then the magnets will disengage. It's all automatic. Our speed will drop until our ship is stopped in empty space, waiting for us to start it up again."

"What's that?" He indicated a large, red plunger on one end of the console, one just like the one that had opened the hatch. A large X inside a circle covered the top.

"Full shutdown." She continued her work.

"And why can't we use that?" He was still pleasant and warm.

"We just can't, Kaseem. The magnets must remain balanced throughout the entire process. Too quick, and they can be knocked out of alignment. Instead of our black hole evaporating, we could be knocked into it. That would be bad." She made a final few taps and said, "There. Ready. All I have to do is press start."

"Like this?" He slammed his fist into the red plunger, and a siren began to wail. Then it stopped, and a large series of numbers began counting down on the screen. It started at thirty and was down to twenty-six before Hollis could comprehend what her partner had done.

"You fool! We have to get out, and *now*." She pushed off using her handgrips, her feet aiming directly for the hatch below.

"Now?" The numbers were down to twenty-one. "What's the countdown for?"

"For when the magnets shut down. Now, Kaseem!" and she disappeared through the hatch. The color of the sky had deepened, and it was colder as she fell out of the drive module, aiming directly for the ship below. When Abdullah dropped through, she hit the plunger, and the hatch slammed shut. Air filled the space, and she whipped her helmet off. "What was that about? We're likely dead."

"I want to get home now." His voice was iron. The oil and honey was gone. "Wait three hours? Not worth it. We'll be all right."

"Hollis!" Zealander was off to the side, watching, and

Magill's strident voice ripped over his comm. "All my screens are blank. All I'm getting is a countdown. What is this?"

She glared at Abdullah, and as she opened her mouth to answer, the ship jerked violently, alarms went off, the lights died, and the emergency lighting came on. For a moment, just for the barest instant, she thought she saw someone else in the compartment with them, and she wondered how he got in. The wall behind him became a vast window, and she could see the purple filling the sky beyond. He looked like a . . . a *boy.* She shook her head, dismissing the hallucination, and reached to pull herself to a communication console. The ship twisted malevolently, the walls rippling, and the emergency lighting blinked off. The purple aurora filled the ship, and red lightning crawled over the walls. Their clothing crackled with frost. Zealander's comm barked, "Hollis? Abdullah? Zealander? I've got ice forming everywhere. And, God! What's this purple fog? Oh, God!"

Zealander had started to run towards the lift. The ice shattered off his clothes with each step, crumbling in a glittering shower, falling slower and slower, a fairyland of tiny beings living out lives that could last a trillion seconds, or be gone before they had even begun.

The final pieces never hit the ground.

Love's Labors Are Lost

"This is the side of you I love." Science Officer Jameson Kirkpatrick stroked the hair around First Mate Wendy Honda's face, although he couldn't see it. Her cabin was completely dark.

"You do?" She purred her words at him, wrapping one hand partially around his thick, muscled arm. "Which side, my front side or my back side?"

"Both sides." He laughed softly, using his lips to caress her cheek before finding her ear and touching it with his tongue.

"Stop that." She giggled and pushed him away. They were very warm, under a thick blanket or two, although they'd both remarked on the chill in the room earlier when they'd tossed their clothes to the side before climbing into bed. "How'd you like my picture?"

"Oh, that was you?" He teased her. "I thought it was one of my old girlfriends, and I deleted it without looking. Too bad."

"This was better, I bet. You didn't just get to look."

"Much better." He kissed her, brushing his lips across hers. "Very much better."

"Enough." She wriggled away from him, working her way

139

deeper into the bed. "I followed the launch. Did you?"

"Never got to it." His fingers started at her wrist, traced the inside of her elbow and back again in a repeated pattern. He was on his side, with one hand holding up his head, and his elbow sunk deep into his pillow. "You did, though. How'd it go?"

"Nielson thinks it was a piece of cake, but Levitson's been in the computer. You know him. I helped him with the drive kernel earlier, a reading he couldn't get to balance out."

"And you found the solution?" He chuckled. Levitson was very good. Honda was no slouch, though. She knew her way around an engineering department.

"I thought so, but then the alarms sounded, and you know how today's gone. It seems the oscillations between the two drives should have started damping each other by now." She reached out of the blankets to place her hand on the wall to feel the level of the vibrations, only to yank it back inside and laugh when her hand touched the chilled surface. "Oh, that's cold. I don't guess the ventilation issues got resolved."

"The report was inconclusive, showing that the air handlers are up to spec, and airflow seems to be unimpeded. Temperatures across the ship are falling, but you know that. I didn't check to see if the laundry was running. Let me see if there's an update on that. Computer on," Kirkpatrick called. There was no answer. He tried again with, "Room, lights on." Again, no response.

"I take that for a no." Honda didn't sound especially worried, and she leaned onto Kirkpatrick's chest, pushing him back, and snuggling against him with her head on his shoulder. She ran her hand down his side, touching each rib along the way.

"I really should get up and check." He kissed her forehead before resting his head back on the pillow. "I really should." He didn't sound very enthusiastic.

"Okay, go." She slapped him on the chest and threw the bedding back. She gasped at the air temperature. "It's freezing, James. Ventilation's broken, no doubt. Yeah, go get it fixed, then let me

140

know so I can get up and get dressed." She pushed at him to get to his feet and laughed when he pulled himself out of bed.

"Lights, lights," he called into the darkness, as if he were searching.

"Left, door, just like in your quarters."

"I don't use the switch in my quarters." He hit something and cursed when it fell over, then laughed. "Sorry. I don't think it broke. Here, I think this is it." He hit the switch several times before the lights flickered on, dimming before brightening. They buzzed and didn't look quite right. He looked at Honda and frowned.

"Try the console. Maybe you can get the ship there. And Jamesey, maybe some pants might be nice." She giggled and pulled the covers tightly around her, leaving only the upper half of her face showing.

He looked down at himself and grinned. "Yeah." He dug through the clothes piled on the floor until he found his pants and slipped them on. Sitting in the chair, he tapped on the inputs but got no response. He held a finger on the power icon for several seconds, and the monitor blinked once and went dark.

"I guess it needed restarted." Honda yawned. "Maybe it's cold, too."

"Yeah, like me." The monitor turned on, said, *Welcome, Wendy,* then went dark. "Again," Kirkpatrick said, repeating the process. It did exactly the same as before. He turned to Honda, "No hablo Español, or finger tapping, or vocal commands. I'm getting nothing, here."

"You could come back to bed." She winked at him.

"You could get dressed and go with me to find out what's going on with the ship. Maybe we can find something that *is* working. Right now, nothing seems to be."

"Turn your back." She twirled one finger in the air, waiting until he faced the opposite direction. "Throw me my clothes."

He separated out the items, hers and his, and dressed. When

141

she announced she was ready, he stepped to her, lifted her face, and gave her a kiss on the tip of her nose. "I think I could fall in love with you, Wendy Honda. We've got three months until Deneb to find out."

"Less, you fool, according to Asher. He says we'll have an early arrival on Deneb Station. Better fall in love quick before time runs out."

"Done. I've decided. I'm in love. How's that?" He smiled, his green eyes sparkling.

"Dang, but I've got a thing for redhaired men." She laughed, drawing away. "I'm out after you."

Surprisingly, the door didn't want to open. Kirkpatrick had to use the manual release along the ceiling, then force the door back with his hands. They only thought it was cold in the room. The air pouring in from the corridor was *frigid*.

"You got anything warmer you can put on?" He glanced at her with an eyebrow raised.

"Not really, just more of these." *These* was a lightweight tunic. She lifted her earpiece from the counter and held it to her ear. "Not working. Thought I might find out what's going on. I'm kicking some butt when we get home if they sent me a faulty unit. I live for these." She sourly tossed it to the side.

The lights in the corridor buzzed and occasionally flickered. They shone with the same off-color cast as the ones in Honda's quarters. Kirkpatrick rubbed his arms as he studied one, then tapped it with an outstretched hand. It crackled, and lines spider-webbed out; and with a second tap, a thin sheet of ice fell to the floor, fracturing into glittering shards when it hit. The light in that one spot brightened.

"I've never seen that before." Honda shivered. "I think I will take a second tunic."

"Sure." Kirkpatrick grinned. "I'll check the environmental readout. It's got to be below zero in here." At the end of the corridor, a panel on the wall caught the light, gleaming in a very unnatural way. As Honda disappeared into her quarters, he tapped at various places on the walls. The ice was everywhere, including the readout. He hit it three times with his fist before the ice cracked, then twice more to get it free enough he could work the panel. The display was blank, and first, as a reflex, he tried the computer. "Ship, are you there? Computer?"

"Has it come on?" Honda walked up behind him, tugging a tunic over her head. She pushed her arms through the sleeves and straightened the waist before running her fingers through her hair.

"Nah." He pushed on the manual input panel with one finger to see if it would respond.

"Well, it didn't work in my quarters. No reason it should here. We have to find someone. How about trying the lift?" She had worked her hands up under the waist of her clothing, and she shivered.

"I want to know the temperature." His frustration was building, and he hit the display hard with his fist. The panel turned black, then a fragmented menu began to resolve. He pushed hard on the image of an air vent with arrows attached to curved lines crossing it. The response was slow, but the menu changed, and he finally got a temperature reading. As he watched, it changed, then again and again. "Oh, my God." He reached for Honda, slipped his arm around her, and pulled her to him,

"That bad?" She leaned in to see, only to find the display had gone blank again. "What was it?"

"Fifty-six below was the last reading it showed." Kirkpatrick had begun to shiver, violently at times, and his teeth chattered as he spoke. His color was off, and he didn't look well. His single layer of clothing was doing nothing to keep him warm. "I have to have more clothes. Then we need to get to Engineering to see what we can do about this. At least there, we'll have supplemental heat."

"Clarkson's right here. He keeps heavyweight items for use in the Cryo section." She pulled Kirkpatrick two doors down, and with her elbow, she cleared the area around the access panel. The door didn't fully open, but she did manage to get it to release, cracking the ice along one edge. Using her fingers, she worked at the seam until she could get a good hold and forced the door open enough they could squeeze inside. She left blood on the edge of the panel, and it had already frozen by the time they were through. The lights wouldn't respond, but the closet doors operated manually, and they located a couple of coats by feel. Honda ransacked several drawers and came up with gloves for their hands. Kirkpatrick's fit about right, but hers were massively oversized for her petite frame. She laughed and held his face for a moment with her clown hands, before pulling him down to kiss him.

"That'll warm me up." He still chattered, but he looked warmer, and he managed a half-smile. They moved to stand just inside the door, with the light from the corridor spilling over them. "You got any ideas? Any at all? I'm fresh out."

"I like your last suggestion. Engineering, supplemental heat, and then we figure this out. Kick some butt. Get the ole girl back in line." She made a couple of false punches, uppercuts, like a boxer might, and she moved her feet in a little dance step.

"Sting like a bee, right?" Kirkpatrick laughed through the chattering, leaning in to kiss Honda on the cheek, then on the lips. "I'm so glad I decided I love you. I do, you know. Maybe I always have."

"You'd be a fool not to. I suspect the lift will be out, but the computer doesn't run the backup system. If we can get the doors to the stairs open—" She laughed, not finishing. She wiped one of her oversized gloves across her cheek and looked away.

"Tears?" Kirkpatrick tried to move around to face her, and she turned away from him. "Wendy?"

"I don't want you to see." She sniffled, then let out a strangled sob.

"What?" He held her shoulders and twisted her to look in her

144

face. Wet streaks left tracks to her jaw. "Was it something I said?"

"Yeah, it was." She looked him in the eyes and wrapped her oversized gloves around his thick neck. "You finally said the words I never thought I'd hear, and it's too late."

"Nah, don't say that. Too late for what?" He pulled her to him and pressed his cheek against her hair. In the corridor, a light buzzed and shattered, changing the quality of the light leaking into the room.

"My great-grandfather was a member of the 300 Club. When the weather reached 100 below, and that's Fahrenheit, they would run around Earth's geographic South Pole naked."

"Seriously?" He chuckled. "So, we're okay, right?"

"Then they jumped in a 200-degree sauna to warm up." She looked in his face. "Once a man didn't get inside fast enough, and he died. That 56 was in Celsius. We're nearly to 100 Fahrenheit below. There's no sauna. I know what that means."

"We're not naked—"

"We were warmer when we were." Her eyes glistened as she kept them locked on his.

He kissed her cheek, tasting the saltiness of her tears. They were freezing on her face. Another light in the corridor shattered and went dark as a single tear began its fall from her chin. It released its hold on her, and as it tumbled free, it moved slower and slower, until it hung in mid-air, a sparkling jewel attesting to their love, frozen until the end of time. In that singular, unchanging moment, a new world of infinitesimal fascination danced between them as they stared into each other's eyes, a new story on a microscopic level playing itself out story by story, emotion by emotion, as real as Earth had ever been.

The last light in the corridor shattered, and the black-purple energy of impending disaster found its way inside to bathe the doomed lovers with an eerie glow. Red lightning crawled across the walls, painting tracks that threatened to rip the speeding ship board from batten.

For Wendy and Jameson, time had frozen, leaving them forever locked in each other's arms; but in the bigger universe, the
end had just begun.

The Big Chill

Time and space are terrible mistresses. They entrap the unwary, forcing them down paths they might otherwise not trod, offering seductive entreaties: promises of eternal youth, vast vistas, sweet victories, and fulfilled dreams.

Time, her words filled with honey and nectar, touches us with her magic for a moment, then bored, moves on. Space is even crueler, for her teasing charade is an unfulfilled dream, so fantastic we can never imagine the whole of it, yet the ending is written across every motion of every celestial being ever seen in the skies.

As the *Higgs* danced with the *Daughter Two*, and the two ships' Cassel-Jackson Drives held them locked on the Event Horizon of one massive space-time disturbance, five billion years had frittered itself away, and space had become shredded, tattered into remnants of what once was. The last of the Cosmos' star-stuff was being drawn inexorably into the Casson Envelope—the Magnetic Resonance Field surrounding the *Higgs* and the *Daughter Two*—compressed tighter and tighter, straining the molecular bonds of the very field that drew them in. Visible matter violently streamed toward the Envelope, twisting and churning, sensed through deadly ultraviolet radiation, X-rays, and gamma rays; seen in the blues, yellows, and reds of visible light; and surging in broad swaths of galaxy-sized microwaves and radio waves. Within a parsec of the ship's massive Resonance Field, the flowing matter was vividly intense. Farther out, the Universe had been emptied. Even dark matter had surged Higgsward, dragging all dark energy with it, crushed into an ever-tighter mass, and roiling with pent-up malevolence, wanting nothing more than to be free once again.

The Universe that once was had fallen prey to the charms offered by time and space: the promise of forever with unbounded horizons to explore. Yet, forever was a lie, even if it took a long time to play itself out; and space, once crushed by the power of the largest black hole ever conceived, was an illusion, no more than a rubber band that once stretched to its limit, violently snaps back once again, a whip with a deadly popper that would soon shatter the massively strained and compromised Casson Envelope like a soap bubble on a hot summer's day.

The lie was found out, and crack of the whip was about to find its way home. All the substance of the Universe was collapsing in on itself with a violence never before seen or imagined. Once compacted, the void would be emptied of all matter and energy for the merest fraction of a second, and the heartbeat of time would slow until it pulsed no more . . .

— Part 2 —

Gods

Book of the Gods

Roshanna 1:1-3

IN THE DAYS when the skies began to burn with fire, the gods fell to the land, though they did not become one of us. Some retained their powers, and some didn't. Four are greater gods, and these are Shosu Jabena Poll-fa, Shosu Wen Hoda-fa, Fadda Ja Kirk-fa, and Fadda Freder Neil-fa.

SIX LESSER GODS fell to the precipices with them, being Shosu Lisabet Kovski-la, Fadda Sher Vitson-la, Fadda Ran Char-la, Fadda Eidon Arkson-la, Shosu Imani Eboh-la, and Fadda Liam Egel-la.

THESE ARE THE GODS of great wisdom who desire to help those who walk our world. Some are very powerful, and some are not so powerful. Selah.

Purple Fire

High Acolyte Aaeon Hibolah had encouraged Mene to come to the storm wall at three fingers past yellow tail. This day, he'd promised, she would certainly see purple fire. It would burn in Kirk Temple today. He could feel it in his bones.

Mene had laughed at him. "In your bones? Surely not." She also reminded him with a teasing grin that purple fire had never burned in Haukberk's Kirk Temple, either in the future or in the past. Only in the Grand Temple's Chamber of Eternal Flame.

If not in his bones, he'd responded with a smirk, at least in the ions lacing the air when their precipice of rock and soil passed through the storm wall. In the last passage, the ions had pummeled the precipice. This passage, surely the purple fire would fall.

He found himself assigned to the prayer tower and watching for the lightning. It was what powered his world, and as a high acolyte, it was his duty to catch it. At the first signs of crackling energy, he sounded the alarm and prepared to dash down the stairs with his brazier in hand.

Then, green lightning had lanced out and wrapped around a Rising Stone. The warmth of unseen energy, released with the

153

green light, filled the air. Aaeon instinctively ducked behind the crenellated stone wall surrounding the prayer tower, not wishing to be burned. The colors flickering around him shifted, and as he lifted his head to peer over the wall, the color split, yellow bleeding off one side of the Rising Stone, with blue flowing down the other.

Then, he was awed to see a finger of red join the blue, and they danced in a symphony of ecstatic union. His pulse raced with elation. He couldn't see purple, not yet, but it could mean nothing else. *Purple lightning,* as he predicted. If only Mene were here to see this! Soon, as the lightning mixed in the Rising Stone, the cache of fuel would be filled with precious purple fire. He would live his dream of attending the purple flames in the Grand Temple, only these flames would be here, in the Kirk Temple, and on Haukberk Precipice.

He pulled the hood of his tunic over his head and laughed. Green flames would have been acceptable, for he could sell them to Arkson House. The followers of Fadda Eldon Arkson-la were rarely quick enough to gather their own, and they would pay handsomely for green. Even red would be acceptable, for Kirk Temple could burn red, but purple! There was nothing better than purple fire, which all houses could accept!

As the glare of the lightning faded, he thought of his friend, Regeth. Regeth Zapatha was only a neophyte—and Aaeon's truest friend—but as a lowly neophyte, Regeth couldn't retrieve purple fire. Only an acolyte, trained such as Aaeon, was trusted with such high responsibilities.

Regeth could watch, however. Even so, Regeth was not here, so Regeth was out of luck. Aaeon smiled and leaped for the stair-well.

Even so, his chance at glory—and advancement to underpriest at only sixteen crackles—was eaten by a moving haze curtain. The flowing time distortion, a wall of different *whens*, sucked the purple fire from his grasp. Through the glittering haze curtain, another person, indistinct through the shifting distortion of *whens*, also approached the purple fire. Then, unexpectedly, the haze curtain moved on, taking the purple fire and the unknown person with it, leaving Aaeon with nothing but disappointment.

It had been *his*, right *there*, just within his reach! Now, it was contained within another *when*, most likely carried into the future, for old haze curtains were generally well known and predictable—although it was not unknown for unfamiliar haze curtains to travel into the past. In his moment of frustration, he'd considered chasing down the curtain. Even the uninitiated could enter and return from an established haze curtain, as long as they could focus and hold an image of their own time in their thoughts. He'd done it enough, although he wasn't allowed. Anyway, it was of no matter. Old haze curtains only provided caches of useless stuff, ancient spears, bows, and sometimes an old-style slingshot, even if they were mostly in good condition. Hunters often made use of the older haze curtains, but they had to hunt quickly. Staying too long made it harder to return, but many considered it worth the risk, and old-time haze meat was good. Aaeon admitted that.

Losing the purple fire to the person beyond the curtain was less so, and before he made up his mind to pursue it, the curtain was gone, and he could no longer sense it.

Now, he knelt contritely on His Holiness Bishop Raymene Doitsey's thickly woven Planck gossamer carpet, thankful his knees were softly cushioned, and he pulled his tunic tightly about his neck. The scratchy neutrino filament cloth rasped against his skin, and he wished the bishop would *get on with it* and release him from this tedious confinement. He'd knelt for at least twenty thumps of the chalk while the prelate worked at his desk and pretended to ignore him.

"Harrumph."

The bishop cleared his throat, and his chair scratched on the rough, stone floor. His carpet only extended to just under the front of his desk, for Planck gossamer was very hard to gather from within the haze curtains, making it expensive. It did no good to waste it underneath a desk. Aaeon kept his head down as the shadows in front of him shifted and the hem of the prelate's robes appeared; and he tightened his fist at his collar when the bishop's woven photon slippers moved into his vision for the briefest moment before his robes covered them once again. Woven photon! He'd never seen such a thing, not so closely, anyway.

"Purple fire?"

The bishop murmured the words softly, more in disbelief than in a real question, and Aaeon didn't lift his head or reply. The resulting silence, however, grew awkward, and besides, his bladder had begun to encourage him to hurry things along. After an extended silence, he dared, "Yes, your excellency."

"You thaw purple fire, and for that, you left your poth without permithion?"

"Yes, your excellency."

Aaeon dared say nothing more, but he imagined Regeth free, probably with nothing better to do than sweep the Temple steps and actually sweeping the Temple steps. Aaeon wished he were sweeping the steps. He'd sweep the entire Temple, if he could escape the bishop's inquisition.

"And how did you thee purple fire, my dear boy?" The hem of the bishop's robe moved, allowing a glimpse of woven photon, and he disappeared. The cleric's robes rustled as he circled the acolyte, and he reappeared on the other side. "I have never theen purple fire."

"I only saw the lightning, your excellency. I mean, I knew it would be fire, for fire always gathers in the cache. Then, the haze curtain overtook me, or rather overtook the fire, and then it was gone."

Aaeon's legs quivered, and his bladder demanded his attention. Then the stones around him shifted one against the other. Minute traces of dust gathered on the floor just within his vision, revealing the movement of the building around them. Even the precipice upon which the temple rested had grown bored with the bishop and wished the interview to be done. Aaeon considered asking the prelate to be excused, but the man cleared his throat, cutting off his request.

"Ahem. Not green lightning? Are you thure? I thaw green lightning move acroth the sky justh today. And red. Red ith everywhere. It makths up our thorse of light."

Sure enough, through the window behind the bishop, a direction the acolyte dared not look, the vast sky was a backdrop of shadows, lighted only by the red lightning that was permanently frozen across the sky. Small fingers of green and yellow dotted the heavens, mere threads of color in comparison. Only when they broached the storm wall would the lightning come alive, berating the Rising Stones with their fury and releasing the energy that fueled the world.

The bishop's hem moved towards the desk, and the creak of his chair told that he was seated.

"Yes, your excellency."

Aaeon quivered with need. Anything, bishop. Whatever you want to hear.

"Tho. No purple lightning, ath I said." Bishop Doitsey seemed very pleased with himself.

"I mean, no, your excellency. Yes, red falls everywhere, but no, it wasn't red." Aaeon felt himself rambling, but this had to be wrapped up quickly. He dared raise his eyes to see the bishop writing on a pad of paper, then blotting the surface carefully, never looking his direction. He grew bolder. "Green lightning hit a Rising Stone. I dutifully sounded the alarm, your excellency. I wasn't shirking my duties. I looked up, and it was beautiful. The lightning divided, as it sometimes does, yellow down one side, and blue down the other. Then a finger of red combined with the blue, and I knew it had ignited the combustibles. I just *knew* it."

He paused, realizing how fast and loud his words had become.

"You knew it, I thee." The bishop smiled, although he didn't look up.

"It had, your excellency. The storm wall had passed, so I snatched my brazier and ran all the way. I was *there*. The fire was purple, near to black, just as in the stories in the Book. I meant to get it. I really did. I admired it for only a moment before a haze curtain swallowed it."

Aaeon sagged. The memory of the moment overwhelmed him. His time of ultimate achievement had gone from supreme victory to utter defeat, for there was nothing he could do about a moving haze curtain. A stationary curtain, sure, he'd done those plenty of times, but he hadn't received the training for a moving curtain; and he would have tried, he told himself, even as he admitted that he'd likely never have made it back to this *when* by himself.

The bishop glanced up and seemed unperturbed to find Aaeon watching him. He pointed his feather quill his direction. "Do not call the Thriptures mere thories, my son. Fadda Kirk-fa is more than an inthpiration. When he fell from the sky in the arms of Thothu Hoda-fa, we learned the true meaning of pathion, for when a man holds a woman, no thacrifice is too great to bear."

"Yeth, Bishop." Aaeon slumped and whispered, "Good advice if I ever get to hold a woman."

He closed his eyes and grimaced. His mispronunciation, why did he say such a thing? He hoped the bishop didn't call him on it. He tensed his bladder. He had to go *now*.

"We will thpeak more on thith later." The bishop stood. "You may be dithmissed, Hibolah. Kirk-fa be with you."

It was something the bishop practiced, calling the younger initiates and acolytes by their surnames, and while it sometimes irritated Aaeon, this day he hardly noticed.

"Thank you, Bishop. Kirk-fa be praised." Aaeon leaned forward and kissed the carpet, rose, and without looking the bishop's direction, he pulled his hood over his head and quickly exited with his eyes still on the floor. Once out the door, he cupped his hands over himself as he danced with need, only to bump into his friend, Regeth.

"I waited on you, Aaeon. Did you get the purple fire? I wish to see it." Neophyte Regeth Zaptha, still an unshaven boy, without even armpit hair to show he wished to be a man, smiled warmly at his friend. His hood was down, revealing that he was working, and he held a broom as if he might, indeed, have been sweeping the steps.

"Not now, Regeth." Aaeon puffed out his cheeks and danced down the wide passageway.

"Aaeon?" Regeth called to him.

"Later!" Aaeon returned the reply over his shoulder, and with a cry of relief, he disappeared into a door far down the passage-way.

Love Is in the Details

"Yes, purple fire."

High Acolyte Aaeon Hibolah was too depressed to say more. He'd traveled Upwards, nearly to the end of the precipice, and he lolled bare shouldered under the distant storm wall with its red lightning frozen across the roiling shadows. A light breeze disturbed the occasional patches of greenery erupting from the surrounding stones.

His eyes sought out the branch of lightning under which he'd been born. Sixteen crackles flickered from its bottom branch. A seventeenth was just forming, a mere bud, and he roused enough to point to it.

"See, Mene? Soon, I'll be seventeen."

"And if the crackles withdraw, what then?" Mene Zaptha, Regeth's older sister—though not too much older—rested her head on Aaeon's shoulder.

"Never!" He jerked up without thinking, and she fell back into the small patch of rough, Upward grass. He gasped. "I'm sorry, Mene. With Kirk as my witness, I'm very sorry." He reached to work a coarse blade of grass from her long, black hair, and she

160

shooed him away.

"Never mind. I see what's important to you. You're more worried about the number of crackles budding from your branch than the state of my head." She smiled as she began to sing to herself in a high-pitched, sing-song voice, and she ran her honey-colored fingers through her hair, sending a flurry of dried and fresh grass cuttings to waft skyward in the breeze.

"I like it when you sing." Aaeon dropped to the ground, yanking off blades of grass one by one and flicking them into the air. "It's only right you should join El Char-faitum. When the Temples of Fadda Ran Char-la host their Summer Festival, yours will be the only voice anyone listens to."

"So, why are you so annoyed?" She'd pulled an extra-long blade from the ground, and she traced it down the side of his face, teasing him.

"My good friend Regeth, whom you may know, received a new ceremonial robe, of sun wisp, no less, one that's far finer than anything I own." He smirked at her. "Now it seems I must wear my old one at Services, and everyone will know I'm unloved."

"Poor Regeth, who is still a neophyte, and who can own nothing because it might paint his friend Aaeon in a bad light, is cursed to have no one who respects him and wants the best for him." She looked into the sky and pointed, "There, my branch, with fifteen crackles. It's so beautiful."

"You're beautiful." Aaeon flipped over and looked into her black eyes, his shoulders wearing torn blades of grass like little green leeches. "Will Regeth's sister make me a sun wisp robe? Then Regeth can wear his with pride, because his friend Aaeon will no longer be unloved." He smiled. She still held the long blade of grass and had been poking him with it. He took it from her, put the end in his mouth, and moved his lips back and forth to get it to dance.

"I think I shall have to say a prayer to Fadda Arkson-la at bedtime tonight."

161

"Those silly dreamers?" Mene might not have the blade of grass any longer, but her voice poked and prodded Aaeon just the same. He rolled to his back and rested his head against her side. "All El Arkson-faitum are dreamers—"

"As it should be," she interrupted in a more severe tone. "I'd thought to ask Fadda Arkson-la to bless me with your presence in my dreams."

"No!" He leaned his head backwards so he could look into her face. She was smiling, and he rolled over, still watching her, and grinned. "Seriously? I thought only silly girls offered prayers to Arkson-la. Tell me if it works. I'll visit his Temple tomorrow with a gift of green fire to fortify their tiny flame. They'll be so appreciative I'll get all the dreams I want for days and days." He laughed and rolled to his back again.

"You're so mean." Mene didn't sound upset. "What dream would you ask for?"

"You." He tilted his head back just enough to catch her eye and let his head drop, laughing. "If you're nice to me and make me a sun wisp ceremonial robe."

"Ooh! Why I come here with you, I don't know." She abruptly stood. "Regeth can have you. He worships you. He does. I tell him you're a fool, and he just smiles and says he doesn't care what I say. Someday you'll get him in trouble he can't get out of, and he'll accept it as the will of Kirk, all because you're the one who led him astray."

The sound of someone approaching caught their attention.

"Mene! Have you seen Aaeon?" Coming over the rocks, Regeth's scruffy black hair bobbed as he climbed, sometimes visible and sometimes not. His hood draped roughly over his shoulders, and the slap of his sandals on the stones grew louder. He disappeared in a low space on the slope.

"There he is, your esteemed follower. Be nice to my brother. I adore him, still, even though he's chosen the priesthood, and I can no longer claim him as kin." She waggled her finger Aaeon's

162

direction. "You'll do this if you want a new robe."

"Seriously?" Aaeon was on his feet in an instant, his face in a wide grin. "Mene, you'll do that for me?" He took her arms, then wrapped his around her, pulling her tighter than was proper.

"Stop that!" She pushed him away. "Propriety. Regeth's coming."

Aaeon shrugged with a smile, although his cheeks were warm. "He has to learn sometime."

"And you'll not get a robe from me if he learns it from you. He's here." She adjusted her tunic and pulled her hood over her head, hiding her long hair except around her face. "Your tunic!"

It lay on a large stone, along with his devotional cup, his lightning match, and his flame oil in a small pouch woven with neutrino filaments and star thread stitching. His undertunic left his arms, shoulders, and neck exposed.

"Ah! He sees me without it all the time. In the baths—" He was pulling it over his head as he spoke.

"Aaeon! Don't say such things!" She paled, grabbed the throat of her tunic, and pulled it tighter at the neck as she looked away.

"It's true." He had his head exposed by then, and he grinned. He turned to his friend and waved. "Little Fish! What news?"

"Did you feel the ground move?" Regeth's face was red, and excitement danced in his eyes. "It's almost every day, now."

Aaeon shrugged. "It never does damage. Besides, it didn't move yesterday. I would have been told. That can't be the reason you came so far Upward."

"Havey wishes to see you. We must head Downwards now." Regeth panted with his climb and used his sleeve to wipe his face. He shrugged apologetically.

Havey was Underpriest Sil Havey, a learned and kindly but less-than-ambitious cleric who'd aged past the time when most candidates moved on to higher duties. He was loved, if sometimes laughed at, by the younger initiates. His heart was right, however,

163

and he was often given functionary duties no one else wanted, as he would painstakingly execute them to the smallest detail. Havey wishing to see an acolyte, even a high acolyte such as Aaeon, wasn't welcome news.

"You told him I had prayer tower duties already?" Aaeon looked pained.

"I did." Regeth smiled, and he glanced at Mene and back to Aaeon, as if sharing a joke.

"And reminded him I'm a high acolyte, and of nearly seventeen crackles?" Aaeon had his tunic belted, and he noticed his devotional pouch on the ground. Perhaps his friend was right, and the ground had shaken. He gathered his precious pouch and stored it within his tunic. He finally patted his robes to lay them flat, and he looked at Regeth expectantly, hoping for *something* that would get him off the hook.

"And that you've spoken with the bishop. It's the reason he requires your attendance, Kirk be praised." Regeth gave a quick nod of his head and briefly touched his open palm to his breastbone as he spoke the final three words.

"From your lips to the ears of Fadda Ja Kirk-fa." Mene bowed her head respectfully for a moment, copying her brother and pressing her flattened palm over her breastbone in the universal motion. The phrase came out almost as one word, not exactly rote, but said so often even a portion of it spoke all the words in the listener's mind.

"So be it," Aaeon said, again not rote, but almost as one word. "When's my audience?"

"Now." Regeth shrugged again, his way of accepting something out of his control. "It has to do with your purple fire."

"Purple fire? Aaeon, this is good, isn't it?" Mene's voice held hope.

"Aah! Who knows? I'll probably be assigned flame duty once more, and I won't be able to watch for the lightning ever again. Besides, I never got to collect the purple fire. It was eaten by a haze curtain, and a very strong one. If Underpriest Havey wishes to discuss the purple fire, he'll have to do it from inside a time pocket."

"Can I go?" Regeth's eyes were bright with Aaeon's words.

"Go where?" Aaeon led them down the rocks, jumping from the larger stones, and scrambling across those that were loose. From time to time, he paused to help Mene down an especially tricky section of the path. He called to his friend, "Where do you wish to go, Little Fish?"

"You must know!" Regeth's tunic billowed out like a skirt when he jumped, revealing thin, pale legs. "Through the haze curtain."

"No, Aaeon. You can't take him if you go there." Aaeon had his hands around Mene's waist, helping her down a steeper than usual step, and she wagged her finger at him. "Just no!"

"And if I do?" When she was down, he didn't release her but looked into her face instead, grinning. "What will you do?"

"Never speak to you again." She tried to be stern but smiled at the end.

"Then I must kiss you now." He planted a kiss on her cheek, just catching the corner of her lips, before she could squirm away.

"Aaeon," she cried, as he released her and tripped down several more steps.

Regeth grinned and careened down the steps after his friend.

Book of the Gods

Roshanna 1:4

*F*OUR GODS ALSO *fell to the land, and they have become shades: Kella Shana Gill-um, Kella Theon Aland-um, Shulla Cryst Hol-um. and Kella Aseem Dullah-um. Selah.*

Learning the Ropes

High Acolyte Aaeon Hibolah's meeting with Underpriest Sil Havey had turned into weeks of training. The repeated and long sessions brought despair to the High Acolyte. However, the outcome was something he'd looked forward to for a very long time, his hoped elevation to underpriest.

It wouldn't likely be *this* day, however.

The large room around him, buried deep within the bowels of Kirk Temple, boasted narrow, high openings along the wall that fronted the Crevasse toward Morning. A smattering of reddish light spread shadows along the ceiling, but it was weak. Supplemental lighting was by means of oil sconces, which put off excessive amounts of flame and smoke; and floating glow globes, which seemed to require no energy source and self-adjusted their positions to best illuminate the activities in the room. Thin cracks spiderwebbed up the walls, reminders of the shaking that occasionally accompanied the growing streaks of permanent lightning decorating the sky just outside.

Along with Aaeon were Underpriest Havey, his heavily embroidered tunic thrown aside across a large table; Underpriest

J.J. Abbey, a youth hardly older than Aaeon, who'd only been elevated to underpriest less than a crackle before; and Underpriest Ken Quartten, a second-year underpriest, older than some might expect but whom many thought might someday succeed the existing cardinal, Ne' Kirk-fait IX.

Abbey's red hair was sharply cut, close at his temples, high in the back, and formed a waxed bowl across the top. He wore a tunic filled out by broad shoulders. He frowned continually, both when Havey spoke, as well as when Aaeon answered.

Quartten had a quick smile, thinning hair, an ear jangle hanging from one lobe, and a staff on the floor at his feet. His chin revealed the strong beginnings of a beard. He was in his thin undertunic, with loose, flowing trousers covering his legs. The trousers were like those Havey wore, ones Aaeon would have access to once his training was complete. Quartten had been using his staff to perform a series of military-like moves, and a sheen of sweat covered his exposed skin.

"And if you should meet yourself when you step through the haze curtain?" Havey referenced a large sheaf of papers and announced the question directly to Aaeon.

"Meet myself?" Aaeon thought hard. Meet himself. Meet himself. It wasn't possible, was it? Abbey continued to frown, even as Quartten grinned.

"I should repeat the question?" Havey had his nose in the sheaf, and he raised just his eyes.

"I've never—" Aaeon stopped, realizing he'd almost said too much. He'd been through the oldest haze curtains from the time he was a boy. He'd never *met himself.*

"Never what?" Havey continued with his head down and his eyes up. It was very disconcerting.

"Never, um," Aaeon extemporized hesitantly, "I mean, you never meet anyone you know through the haze curtains. You can't, can you?"

"He'd not be worth his salt if he hadn't explored as a boy,

would he, Havey?" Quartten asked the question, and it seemed a good thing. He knelt blindingly fast, lifted his staff, and slammed the end against the floor. He called, "You, Abbey, when was your first?"

"I—" The redheaded youth broke off, looked to Aaeon, his frown growing deeper, and he glanced to Havey as if confused. "Havey, I don't have to answer . . . he's not approved. He's just a *boy.*"

"As were you a short time ago. Bishop Doitsey desires this, and the young man is learning quite quickly. I think we can safely share a few of our little secrets."

"But—"

"Underpriest Abbey!" Havey's interruption was abrupt and strong.

"As the voice of Kirk wills." He bowed slightly to Underpriest Havey and turned to Aaeon, speaking in a clipped tone, while keeping his eyes averted above his shoulder. "I was eleven."

"His first time to *intentionally* navigate a haze curtain and enter a time pocket, but not the first, eh, Abbey?" Quartten's voice was kinder than Havey's had been, and the underpriest's reaction revealed why.

"No." Abbey closed his eyes tightly, and for the first time, his frown gave way to something less angry.

"Acolyte Hibolah needs to hear what you experienced. Do you wish to tell him, or shall I?"

"I was four. My family had no warning, and a fast-moving haze curtain caught me." His eyes were still closed, and he shuddered. "The time pocket carried me to the place of the gods, and I saw them."

"Thank you, my friend." Quartten still held his staff, and his words were soft.

Abbey took several deep breaths and opened his eyes. They were red. He looked at Havey and asked, "Is that enough?"

"Yes, for now. Thank you, Abbey." Havey set his sheaf of

papers aside, and he crossed his arms at his waist, slipping his hands into his sleeves until they disappeared. "Underpriest Abbey's experience isn't the first of its sort, but it's the best documented, and it's from one in our Order. That makes him special, and it's important for you, Acolyte Hibolah."

Aaeon watched with trepidation. Abbey had been distant and even critical during Aaeon's sessions. He'd hoped his connections with the underpriest would lessen when his training was over. Now, he wondered otherwise, and his stomach turned over.

"Today's training," Havey continued, "consists of what we know about the fallen gods, the shades that wreak havoc upon our world. Do you have any questions so far?"

"I know the shades. Everyone does. There are four: Kellas Gill-um, Aland-um, Dullah-um, and Shulla Hol-um. All are taught in lexicon classes from earliest childhood." Aaeon smiled proudly.

"And taught as shadows and whispers, but never as truth and fear. If I tell you Kella Gill-um leads the shades to destroy our world totally and forever—"

"Kirk-fa be praised, may it not be so." Aaeon, without thinking, interrupted as he pressed his palm to his breastbone, and he ducked his head momentarily in respect. "Shosu Jabena Poll-fa will call Shosu Wen Hoda-fa to her side, and the gods will reign supreme. Shosu Poll-fa and Shosu Hoda-fa ruled the skies for many seasons before The Great Falling, and they will rise again when we are in our greatest need."

"So says Poll," Havey murmured, tapping his palm to his breastbone in a quick, reflexive motion.

Aaeon, realizing the level of his disrespect, fell to one knee and began to apologize. "Forgive me, sir, for my interruption. I spoke out of turn. I understand. Kella Shana Gill-um will destroy our world by the aid of his three companions—"

"Not if we can help it, by Kirk!" Quartten slammed his staff onto the hard, stone floor as he spoke.

"Sir?" Aaeon looked up, surprised and a bit frightened. If the gods chose to destroy the world, there wasn't anything to be done about it, and the shades were gods, if dark ones.

"Now, Ken," Havey admonished, the rebuke softened with the man's first name. "We are in Kirk's House. No profanity, please, and using Kirk's name in vain constitutes such."

"You are right, as always, Underpriest Havey. My apologies. Here's what we've been able to determine, Hibolah." Quartten held his staff like a scepter for a moment, giving him a kingly stance, one of the reasons he was expected by so many to assume the role of cardinal someday. As he spoke, he shifted it to the crook of his arm as a shepherd might carry it, giving him a fatherly warmth.

"Fadda Kirk's words from your lips to my ears." Aaeon felt both cowed and pulled in.

Quartten smiled and continued, "Abbey's time pocket from his childhood was moving very fast, and as we've been taught, it had to come from the future."

"As was the wall that took my purple fire!" Aaeon was no dummy. He saw the connection, even if he wasn't certain exactly what it was just yet.

"True." Quartten looked to Havey, who smiled. Abbey chewed his lips, but his forehead was smooth. "Fast-moving haze curtains connect to future events, and slow ones—"

"—are from the past." Aaeon froze, having interrupted once again, and his face went cold.

"Correct." Quartten laughed as if pleased. "I told old Ziggurat you were no fool. He'll be proven wrong yet again."

"I hope so, sir." Oh, Kirk, Aaeon thought. That was a stupid thing to say. "I mean, no, sir. I hope his esteemed self isn't proved wrong."

"Oh, we definitely hope so, or you'll be kicked out of the priesthood and sent to farm the slopes of the precipice. We can't have that, can we?" Havey chuckled and nodded Quartten's direction. "Go on."

Aaeon tried to settle his mind with thoughts of Mene, to remember the taste of her lips, but in his stress, the recollection escaped him. He breathed a silent prayer to Fadda Kirk for the memory to return, and if not, to bless him with the prowess to engage her again at an opportune time. He pulled his thoughts together and realized the underpriest was talking directly to him. His mind went white with stress. What if he'd missed a question he was expected to answer? He stared at the man's lips until the words began to sink in.

". . . and we haven't been able to determine just how far Abbey went, as he was but a child, but we know it wasn't a too-distant future. Before you ask—" Aaeon had his mouth open with a question, and Quartten brushed it aside with his hand. "—Abbey has quite a good memory, and our psychologists are very adept at retrieving images even our Abbey didn't know he'd seen."

"What images, sir?" Aaeon dared ask the baleful Abbey directly. For a moment, he expected a sharp rebuke, then the underpriest answered, and afterward, offered Aaeon a question of his own.

"Our glow globes." He motioned, and one of the orbs floated towards his hand, finally stopping within his reach. He tapped it, and it winked out. Aaeon stepped backwards, visibly shaken. "Do you ever think of these, consider where they come from, or why we use them *and* the oil sconces?"

To the side, Underpriest Quartten chuckled audibly and glanced at Underpriest Havey, who held up a hand and quieted him. He'd lifted his sheath of papers again and had his head down, looking up with only his eyes, very authoritarian. It was unlike the Havey Aaeon had known before the ever-so-tiring sessions had started but one that was becoming more familiar to him by the day.

"They are from Shosu Poll-fa, one of the miracles she blessed us with when she fell from the sky." Aaeon tried to smile. She was the Patron of Electricity and embodied in the lights in the sky. She had been secluded in her boudoir with her lover since before Aaeon's first breath, leaving the storm wall to obscure her face, but she would return. All the tales said so. Surely the glow globes were one of her gifts, given as a reminder that she was sequestered and couldn't visit her shining face upon the land.

With the dimmed globe, the red from the high openings was brighter, casting a bloody glow within the deepened shadows and drawing Aaeon's eyes upward. Outside, the red light from the lightning streaks, normally moderated by the ambient energy released from the precipice's regular intrusions into the storm wall, cast its baleful glare. He'd always considered the globes to shine for a similar reason, filled with energy absorbed from the storm wall. Of course, that was when he'd thought about it, which was only in the past few moments. The storm wall was what created day and night, although the timing of daybreak and night-fall was—of necessity and due to scientific principles—dependent upon how often the world intersected the storm wall. Today, only the red glow filtered into the interior space.

"Anything else I might have seen that would suggest the timeframe of my unexpected travel?" Abbey asked the question with a solemn face and his words devoid of emotion.

Aaeon watched him carefully for hints of what he wished to hear. Nothing. He racked his brain and came out with the only thing he could think of. "The skies would be different." He cleared his throat. "The lightning, if you traveled to the future, there would be more of it."

"More lightning?" Abbey's eyebrows lifted as if surprised at the answer.

"I tell you, the boy catches on quickly." Quartten stepped between Aaeon and Underpriest Havey. He had redonned his formal tunic, although his hood still hung loosely at his shoulders. Underpriest Abbey backed to the side. Behind him, Havey had pulled a well-worn satchel to his workspace and began laying out various cloth and metal items. Quartten nodded his head at Aaeon before speaking. "Explain your response, Acolyte. This is your final test."

"My final . . . test?" His voice cracked on the last word, and he felt his stomach turn. He'd not known today was a *test*. He tried to find a rationale for something he'd never thought of except as a general realization. Older time pockets—the ones he'd entered- —were plainer, less colorful, less *red*. The only reason for that was less lightning in the sky. He was sixteen crackles. Mene had teased about the crackles of light disappearing, but they never did. New ones grew and remained in place, only occasionally flashing from the sky when the storm wall grew too close to land. The patterns of the lightning were how they told the moments of the day, of youth versus adulthood, of before and after. He took a deep breath and bravely started, as if under the auspices of his boyhood tutor, and quoted an answer directly from his textbook.

"Haze curtains are of many colors. Very old ones are pale and washed out, and they are the safest to enter. They're easiest to find when looking from Morning to Evening." Underpriest Abbey opened his mouth as if to speak, and Aaeon tensed for a curt word. Havey shook his head, and he stepped down. Aaeon threw his shoulders back, finding new strength and refusing to be cowed. "Everyone does it. I shared haze meat with a hunter, once. It was very good."

Havey's eyebrows raised, and Quartten smiled. "Go on. We won't quibble about the taste of haze meat. I want to hear of the lightning."

"There's less of it near the oldest time pockets. There's more now than when I was a boy. It makes sense that if you could see the sky through a haze curtain, you'd know the length of time that had passed on the other side. Perhaps the sky Underpriest Abbey saw when he was four revealed the time that had expired."

"Brilliant, my boy." Quartten stepped forward and grasped both his shoulders, gripping them tightly, then clapping them twice. He seemed to glow with excitement. "When I was born, your branch hadn't budded even one crackle. Nor had Abbey's or Havey's."

"Underpriest Havey, sir? He's so . . ." Aaeon glanced at the man's graying hair and lined eyes.

"You have my permission," Havey said, forcefully and clearly, "to say it this once."

"He's so old, sir. You, you're barely older than me."

"And yet I'll be cardinal someday. Doesn't that seem odd to you?"

"It's not my place to say. If Kirk wills it . . ." He let his words die away.

"You do know Ne' Kirk-fait IX isn't the cardinal's real name." Quartten seemed to be making a point about the cardinal, and Aaeon shrugged. The floor shivered under their feet, and the stone overhead groaned. Dust filtered from the cracks that painted the walls and ceiling, but it wasn't much, and the conversation continued.

"I suppose, but I've not thought much of it."

"Have you met the cardinal before?" When Aaeon nodded, Quartten asked, "Describe him."

Aaeon frowned for a moment, looked at the three men, and began, "He's about your height, bald, I think, although he wears his hood usually, and with eyes about your color . . ." His voice failed him completely this time as the resemblance between the two men jumped out at him.

"I think you're getting it. The cardinal's name and mine are the same, or at birth they were. We were born under the same sky, sort of. It's more accurate to say we were born under the same *when*."

"Then either you—" The implications were sinking in, and they didn't do anything good for Aaeon's stomach. "—or the cardinal must have come from beyond a haze curtain. One of you is an imposter."

177

"Not imposter. The same. It's why Havey asked you about meeting yourself on the other side of a haze curtain. It's why I've never met the cardinal. This next part is important, Acolyte. Once you learn this, you can't go back. Are you ready to pledge the priesthood, to give up your home, and to only concern yourself with finding and enabling the Will of Kirk to save your world?"

"To save the world, sir? Is it ending?" Aaeon thought of Mene. Surely, he wasn't being asked to give up girls. Fadda Kirk-fa was the Patron of Passion. It was the reason he'd pledged with House Kirk as a neophyte, or one of the reasons, anyway.

"Will you pledge, Acolyte? For the good of Haukberk and all lands beyond?" Quartten took his hands, and he held them gently. His eyes glowed with warmth, and they pleaded, also. Aaeon couldn't tear his away, and he fell to his knees, more certain than he'd been of anything ever before.

"I wish to pledge all that I am unto the Will of Kirk."

"Good," Havey called. "We can get started, then. Bring the boy here." Havey had donned a long vestment cloth that wrapped his neck and fell almost to his feet on both ends. He'd thrown his hood back and wore an embroidered headpiece. A thick and well-used volume lay open on the surface before him. A pen and inkwell were to the side.

Aaeon stood, asking, "What am I to learn? What did Abbey see? And how are you the same person as the cardinal?"

"Such fire and zeal, and many questions. We should, perhaps, move this along, or curiosity will get his cat." Havey smiled as he motioned Aaeon forward. "Come, boy. Fadda Ja Kirk-fa welcomes you into the Chamber of Flames as one of his initiates. Before we can answer your questions, however, we have a few details to cover. This way. Come on."

Aaeon moved forward to stand where Underpriest Abbey indicated. Underpriest Quartten took three additional vestment cloths, although of a different design than Havey's, and draped one over his shoulders and handed another to Abbey. The third, he and Abbey ceremoniously draped over Aaeon's shoulders, kissing the ends and murmuring, "To the four greater gods, Poll-fa, Kirk-fa, Hoda-fa, and Neil-fa, we beseech your grace upon our fellow Kirk-faitum. To the six lesser gods, Kovski-la, Vitson-la, Char-la, Arkson-la, Eboh-la, and Egel-la, we humbly plead for your guidance. From the fallen gods, Gill-um, Aland-um, Hol-um, and Dullah-um, who have become shades, we place a barrier around this one that he will forever be protected from the wardings of revenge, war, seduction, thievery, and murder. Such we have asked in the name of Shosu Jabena Poll-fa, who guides all the gods and showers our world with life."

Aaeon murmured, "From your lips to the ears of Shosu Poll-fa."

"Please place your name in the book." Underpriest Havey offered Aaeon the pen. "Once you're signed, you will be a full underpriest."

"That's all?" He took the pen and dipped it into the ink, leaned forward, and put his hand to the paper. Before he could write, Havey cautioned him.

"All? This binds you to the House of Kirk for life. This isn't all; it's everything." He made a sound with his tongue, as if the boy had somehow missed the point.

"I just thought there'd be more people, a grander ceremony." Aaeon placed his name in the book as he spoke. Finished, he grinned and looked at Underpriest Quartten, who'd seemed the most convivial of the bunch. "Maybe a party to celebrate."

"There will be no party. Now, however," Havey began, carefully blotting the wet ink in the book before offering the pen to the others in the room, signing himself, blotting each signature, and closing it gently and setting it aside, "we can answer many of your questions." He hit himself on the forehead, calling to Abbey, "Before I forget, bring the young man his new devotional pouch. Quickly, my boy."

"As Fadda Kirk wishes," Abbey said, pulling a folded cloth

from a cabinet and offering it to Havey.

"Thank you, Abbey." He unfolded it to reveal a finely woven cloth pouch with a sturdy drawstring and a flap that could be tied down. A long strap allowed it to hang from the shoulder. The holy symbols of Kirk Temple ran the length of the strap: different colors of flame interwoven with images of romance and passion. He held it out to Aaeon. "This will be better than the one you've been using."

"I didn't think . . ." Aaeon's eyes teared up, and his voice broke. "I mean, I didn't expect this." He ran his hands along the strap, admiring the thread creating each symbol. Opening the flap, he found the pouch was lined with leather, and he let out a choking sob.

"What, boy? You don't like it?" It was Quartten, and he seemed to be teasing.

"Very much." Aaeon began to smile. "If my flame oil leaks again, it won't stain my tunic."

"That's the way to see it." Quartten refocused the proceedings. "About the boy's questions, Havey. Now's a good time."

"Yes, yes," and Havey chuckled. "You do understand, none of what we speak of can go beyond these walls. You are now bound by the rules and codes of House Kirk. What goes on in this room is for no one's ears but your own."

Aaeon nodded, his mind picturing every gruesome thing he could imagine, from nefarious deeds to drunken orgies to slave trading under the dark of night. He shuddered and wondered what line he'd crossed and if he could ever cross back.

Abbey brought up heavy chairs from along one wall, with high, straight, carved backs and seats upholstered with coarse but durable fabric. After some maneuvering and much scraping on the hard floor, they had them in a circle of four. Havey apologized and began to collect the vestments. He explained to Aaeon that they were not his to keep, as the Temple only had a few sets, and they were far too valuable to gift to people. It was his name in the book that counted, plus those of the witnesses that had participated in his oath. Once everything was folded and stored once more in Havey's battered valise, the four found their chairs and were seated. Quartten pulled his chair closer to Aaeon.

"So, Underpriest Hibolah. Do you feel any different?" He had a twinkle in his eye.

"Curious, maybe. Frightened a bit. Worried."

"About what?" Quartten leaned in as if really interested.

"Underpriest Abbey—"

"Surnames only, or given, if you know someone well, please, among the initiated." Quartten smiled.

"Um, sure. I'd like to know how he, um, J.J., um, I'm sorry. I don't know his first name."

"J.J. will do." Quartten still smiled. Abbey smirked, but it looked less mean than before.

"Well, how did, um, J.J. find his way back, if he was in a future time pocket? And you, um," he pointed to Quartten.

"Ken. My apologies. I think you know Underpriest Havey's name."

"Yes, sir. Sil." Aaeon gave him a quick smile and a wave. "You, Ken, how can you be the cardinal? He's quite old."

"We'll come back to that, but it's the reason I need your help. All that's *curious*. Why *frightened?*"

"If the world will end, how can we . . . I mean, we should be frightened. Right?"

"My son, it's part of Scripture. Have you forgotten? Chazah 2:8 tells us the world will be destroyed—" Havey's eyes opened wider when Aaeon interrupted him to complete the verse.

"—by lightning and fire. Still, that's not real." He looked back and forth to find no one agreeing with him. "Even if it were, we can't *know*, at least not *when*."

"Granted, for now." Quartten glanced to Havey and smiled, as if pleased, before looking back to Aaeon. "And you are worried about?"

"Well," Aaeon felt his face warm, "Fadda Ja Kirk-fa is the Patron of Passion. Neophyte Regeth—he's my good friend—has a sister named Mene, and well, do I have to give up girls, too?"

Havey and Quartten burst out laughing. Quartten slapped his leg as he threw his head back. Even Abbey smiled and turned his head aside, and his face showed red.

Quartten placed a big hand on Aaeon's slender knee, and he bunched the material under his hands and reassured the boy. "Remember, Kirk is the Patron of Passion, as you said. You've nothing to worry about there, as long as you remember your vow. All that's said in this room remains in this room."

Aaeon felt such a sense of relief that he didn't care about all the rest, at least not as strongly as he had earlier. The discussion continued, covering every topic Aaeon wanted to know about. Abbey, who, it turned out, was only distant because he'd felt Aaeon might not prove himself, warmed up quickly as he shared what he remembered. He'd been abducted into a strange metal world, where the walls were covered with red lightning. A massive window towered over his head, with the surface covered by more of the lightning. It filled the sky outside; and a deep, florid purple, nearly black wave swirled as far as he could see. At the center of it was a metal thimble, and it looked as though it was sucking the light from the sky. He'd turned away to find help to discover three people with him, two of them encased in metal and glass, and the third watching. Then he'd wished to be home really badly, and he'd closed his eyes, only he didn't get back to his exact *when*. Several eighth-crackles had passed, his family had been in despair, and that's how the priesthood had learned of his journey.

Quartten and Havey skimmed the discussion of the glow globes, explaining that occasionally amazing technologies were brought from the other side. Often they didn't work, but these did. They had been brought from behind a very red and fast-moving haze curtain. "Snatch and grab," Abbey chuckled, as if he might have had something to do with it. When asked why they didn't make more, as Aaeon saw that they could be very useful, he was told the technology to do so was *then* and not *now*.

Quartten's personal story was much more interesting. He'd been abducted by a haze curtain from his *when*. In his *when,* this Haukberk was no more than a future time pocket behind a shifting curtain. He'd been sleeping alone out on the farthest reaches of the precipice—yes, there was a reason for not allowing it—and when he'd awakened, the wall had shifted him too far away to get back. He had to return to his *when* before his *when's* Quartten was elevated to cardinal. The date was immutable, and if he wasn't there, he wouldn't be able to advance in office, and that meant he couldn't be cardinal here. He needed someone adept at navigating the haze curtains to help him find his way home.

"That's easy." Aaeon didn't know why they were telling him, although it was very interesting. "Lots of people could take you. Getting back out of a haze curtain's easy. You just, um, I mean, if you *were* to jump into one, you would *probably* just imagine you were home, and it'd *likely* take you where you wanted to go." He felt himself beginning to perspire. Was his mouth ever going to get him in so much trouble!

Quartten grinned widely. "You, my boy, are magnificent. See, Havey? He's been there, and he thinks it's easy." He laughed. "He thinks it's *easy!"*

"It's not?" Aaeon was surprised. "You've gotten through, and Abbey said he returned. And the globes . . . I assumed, um, that anyone . . . no?"

"Only a few and with any skill. And much training. It's what we've been teaching Underpriest Abbey the past year. He's learning, but even he'll admit he's clumsy."

"How do you know I'm not?" Aaeon shrugged. He'd not had any training at all.

"You saw the lightning that created the purple fire." Quartten looked hard at him, as though this was very important, and the other two men grew silent. "Do you understand what I'm saying?"

He shook his head. "Everyone can, can't they?"

"Not me," said Abbey with a shrug. When Aaeon looked at him in amazement, he continued with, "Ever, except when I was four and looking out that window."

"Only a few," Havey murmured, just loudly enough for the others to hear.

"Listen to me good, Aaeon," Abbey started, his voice earnest, "I went to the lesser throne of the gods, but those were no gods I saw. They were three of the shades. I heard the voice of the fourth. *'Hollis? Abdullah? Zealander? I've got ice forming everywhere. And, God! What's this purple fog? Oh, God!'* That's how we know who they were, even if the names weren't exactly the same. The voice I heard had to have been Kella Shana Gill-um." He looked disgusted at even voicing the name. "I can still hear every word—*in the voice of a shade*—as if I were still there. I was in the underworld looking out toward heaven. The skies burned as no one's seen them before. It was the end of time. The Scriptures are true." His voice broke, and his face twisted. "I was *there*."

"You were *then*," Havey corrected. "All whens are now, as time doesn't flow but overlaps. In actuality, there is no now and then, only when. Remember that, Aaeon. You'll need it."

"All this is good background information so you can understand what's happening, but it's not everything. Let me explain why it's so important for me to get back to my when." Quartten found Aaeon's knee again, this time with a balled fist, and he tapped it twice then pressed on it. "This Quartten, the one who's wearing the cardinal's shoes, is assembling a team of expert haze divers, time explorers, whatever you want to call them, to search for a way to reverse the effects we see in the sky. If we let it go too far, we might never correct the imbalance that's causing it. We're hoping we can at least slow it down."

"You've never met him. How can you know he's doing that?

Has he asked any of you to be on his team?" He hoped he wasn't chosen. He'd just gotten his first kiss with Mene. He wanted a lot more, not to be sent off to another *when,* never to see her again.

"Because it's here." Quartten tapped his head. "And what's here will someday be there." He pointed off to the side in the general direction of where the Kirk Temple's Bishop's Palace was located. "And if I'm not there, I can't be here."

It was indeed a predicament, one that made Aaeon's head spin just trying to figure it out. Of course, thinking about his kiss with Mene tended to jumble everything up, but Underpriest Quartten's especially difficult situation had everything so twisted that not even Mene could make it all go away.

Book of the Gods

Roshanna 1:5-9

IN THE TIME before the skies began to burn, the gods and the shades traveled together from world to world, for the vastness of Creation was theirs. Shosu Jabena Poll-fa, the Patron of the Skies, wielded great powers, and she took lovers as she would.

THOSE WHOM SHE blessed were filled with joy, and those she cast aside were overcome with despair.

SHOSU POLL-FA desired Fadda Sher Vitson-la in her deepest of hearts. She called him to her bed in the middle of the night, but he loved his machines more than he loved his mistress, and she cast him aside to be a lesser god.

FOR THAT REASON, Fadda Sher Vitson-la is our Patron of All Things Mechanical, and it's to him we pray when we gift a new machine unto the world.

FADDA SHER VITSON-LA'S followers are called the El Vitson-faitum, or followers of Fadda Sher Vitson-la. Selah.

Stranger Lands

Newly minted Underpriest Aaeon Hibolah pulled the collar of his tunic closer as wind whipped from the bowels of the Crevasse below. During his prayer time the previous evening, he'd poured a small amount of flame oil into his devotional cup, and striking his lightning match, he'd set the small blaze going. As the smoke rose, he brushed it towards his face, soaking in the sweet smell of crushed oilstone, and paused as his nostrils burned and his thoughts left his head. He'd communed with Fadda Kirk-fa, who'd reassured him he was in the Fadda's will, although as usual, he couldn't remember the actual words the Fadda deigned to share with him.

Once the oil burned away, his head cleared, pulling him back into his room, and he'd stored his devotional materials away. The warmth of the experience remained, bringing him sweet dreams. Now, he wished he could recall the Fadda's words.

The cables along each side of the open-air cable ferry between Haukberk Precipice and Gates Precipice squealed with distress each time the manually operated wheels turned. Underpriest Quartten and Aaeon's good friend Regeth operated the one on his left. Two men—not of a clerical nature and with bulging arms—stood on the right. The men with the big arms seemed to be having an easier time of it, as Aaeon's muscles could attest. They had pulled continuously since the beginning of the trip and still could carry on a conversation, with energy left over for bursts of laughter.

Aaeon looked behind him to see Haukberk Precipice, his home, jutting into the muddy maelstrom of tortured and shadowed sky. Above, casting a reddish blush, the lightning of the gods danced across the sky in ever-present constellations of fire. They were the timekeepers and life givers of all creation. The land itself glowed, absorbing the longer X and gamma rays that burned the soil during interactions with the storm wall, releasing the energy in a phosphorescent reaction that provided a mimicry of daylight and nighttime, although one that was dependable only in its irregularity. Kirk Temple was barely visible against the lightning-filled sky, with its pronounced dome, prayer towers, and large overhangs to shade the acolytes within from the flash burn that accompanied lightning strikes. Up and down the precipice walls, tiered fields of lush growth teemed with moving black beetles, though by squinting his eyes, Aaeon could see that they were ordinary men going about their business.

Closer to where Haukberk Precipice was rooted to the other precipices, the land disappeared into an especially violent maelstrom of churning, lightning-streaked clouds. There, Gates Precipice was connected to Haukberk by tightly strung rope bridges, or in places, even rigid walkways, but it was many days to travel along land to reach those conveyances. The cable ferry, while requiring strong shoulders, was very near Kirk Temple. The benefit of using this mode of transportation, Quartten had assured him and Regeth, was that they would arrive only a day's walk from Vitson Temple. El Kirk-faitum maintained a small Kirk Home nearby. It was there that Aaeon would begin his training to navigate the haze curtains from an experienced Temple Master named Ziggurat, although Quartten hadn't felt inclined to share much about him, except that he was the best. Regeth was to be Aaeon's helper, assisting in every way possible so that the under-priest's fast-tracked learning cycle could commence as rapidly as his skills allowed.

Beneath Quartten's good humor and affable nature, it was clear he wanted to find his way home with little delay.

During one discussion, he shared a time when as a boy he'd been wandering his *when's* Haukberk Precipice and collecting pockets of fire from the base of the Rising Stones. A glittering haze curtain had moved among the stones, frightening him and shifting the multi-layered puzzle pieces of the time pockets one over another. Moving on, the curtain deposited a fag of purple fire where none had been before. A dismayed youth was visible on the other side, and then the curtain moved past, leaving the fire and taking the youth with it. Quartten gathered the fire, as he responsibly should, and sold it to the clerics of Kirk Temple. Of course, that was many years before he'd pledged to the priesthood, but the purple fire that burned in the Chamber of the Eternal Flame was the same.

"Nah," Aaeon wailed, his astonished cry meant to cover his dismay. "My fire, my *purple* fire is the Eternal Flame?"

"Well, it will be eternal, so long as the acolytes at the Grand Temple continue to supply it with plentiful combustibles."

"All my life I've been desiring to attend the very flame I lost just a sixteenth-crackle ago."

"It looks that way." Quartten found it amusing. He became serious, saying, "It's another reason I'm confident you are the one to help me find my way home. You, my friend," and he jabbed him in the chest with an outstretched finger, "have a connection, however tenuous, with my *when*. You are my best chance at finding it again."

At the time, Aaeon felt honored at the future cardinal's trust in him, and somehow special, also. That sensation had come and gone, however. Now they rode the cable ferry, Aaeon's arms and shoulders ached, he was cold, and it was nearly his time to take the wheel from Regeth and let his friend rest. He scanned the upcoming shore. He'd never visited Gates Precipice. He'd assumed it was like Haukberk, with fertile fields, an imposing Temple, and massive Rising Stones covering much of the landscape. He found none of that. What he'd assumed for much of his life to be rocky spires were taking on a uniform appearance, and in several places, black smoke belched as though the very land was aflame. And buildings! They were everywhere. He'd not imagined such a thing.

"Magnificent, isn't it?" Quartten appeared at his side, his tunic across one arm, and his shoulders bare. He gleamed with perspiration even in the coolness. "All of Gates is like this, from one side to the other."

"Not at all what I expected." Aaeon blew out his cheeks, apprehensive. "It's my turn to man the wheel."

"After a time. We're taking a moment of rest. Your young friend's gone for refreshments."

Aaeon looked around to see that both wheels were vacated, and at the opposite end of the ferry, Regeth held several one-Kirk and two-Kirk coins and negotiated with a vendor. The two men with the massive arms sat on a cart among their friends and laughed at a story one of them was telling. In the distance, the tip of Haukberk Precipice grew close to the storm wall, and as he watched, whole branches of lightning peeled themselves from the sky and connected with the Rising Stones, red, mostly, but some in green and yellow.

"Any purple?" Quartten asked the question lightly, almost with a smile.

"The green would have to split first." He narrowed his eyes to see it better. "It'd turn blue after the yellow peeled away, then red would mix in. Nah, not that I can tell."

"A shame." Quartten chuckled. "There, on Gates. What

colors?" He shifted Aaeon's attention to the upcoming landmass, where lightning, far out on the tip, was close enough to interact with the storm wall. Great sheets of color rippled, an aurora borealis of sorts. The strikes landed only on the rocky spires, freezing in place as their energy was drawn off and fed into the series of identical structures.

"Fadda Kirk be praised. Those are like our Standing Stones." Aaeon laughed.

"Exactly." Quartten relaxed, pleased once more. "Not stones, though. Remember, Gates' followers worship Fadda Sher Vitson-la. He's the Patron of . . . ah, here's your friend."

He left the conversation open as Regeth arrived with three small loaves filled with meat and a large container of water, as well as a half-Kirk and several eighth-Kirks in change. Quartten murmured a short prayer, "May Fadda Kirk-fa give us strength through this meal," and the three indulged in their food for a time, only making the sounds of men and boys who have been hungry for far too long.

Licking his fingers, Regeth turned his attention to Quartten. "May Fadda Kirk pardon me for interrupting, but I heard you mention Fadda Vitson-la. He's the Patron of All Things Mechanical, right?"

"Correct, Neophyte. Can you tell us about Gates' Standing Stones?" Quartten had also finished, and he took a long drink from the container and pointed to the lightning still illuminating the heavens around Gates.

Regeth shrugged, saying they were too uniform not to be man-made.

Aaeon remarked, "Some sort of machines, right? It's what Fadda Vitson-la would gift his followers. Fadda Kirk-fa is the Patron of Fire—" Regeth snickered, and Aaeon jabbed him with his elbow to hush, "—and we collect fire from the lightning. It seems El Vitson-faitum would collect the lightning's energy to run their machines."

Quartten seemed very satisfied with the answer, even as he rose and clapped Aaeon on the shoulder. "Your turn and mine again. Our two muscled friends are waiting for us. We'll speak of this later when we reach Gates."

They abandoned Regeth to clear the remains of their meal and nurse his sore muscles. When the master of the ferry yelled, "On my mark, now!" they threw their shoulders into it, breathing easier only when the massive wheels began to move.

Conversation was related to occasional grunts and mild curses for a time, until Gates grew noticeably larger than the precipice they had left behind. The ferry rolled farther along its cables with each pull of the wheel, at times spinning on its own for some distance before dragging and needing an additional push. As the surprisingly large port grew around them, Aaeon was amazed, not having pictured anything so incredible. Carts without draft animals puffed clouds of white steam, clattering noisily as they pulled away from crowded wharfs; bridges and permanent walkways intersected jutting promontories that were crowded with buildings; streetlights burned with a startling brilliance, similar to the glow globes, yet mounted on permanent, filigreed brass stands; and the people wore exotic clothing of indefinable taste. The natural phosphorescence of the land paled against the artificial lighting along the city's streets.

"This is where the floating glow globes are from," Aaeon observed during a lull in the pulling. It had to be. There were similar examples everywhere.

His mentor didn't answer, and the ferry continued along the cable, moving slowly amid the bridges, walkways, and other traffic. A woman in a velvety burgundy gown caught his eye. She rode a palanquin, elaborately carved with a deeply cushioned seat, and was carried by four broad-shouldered men with the symbol of a compass rose displayed on their shoulders.

"I recognize that emblem. Those men are El Neil-faitum."

"The bearers?" Quartten asked.

"Yes. See, they wear the compass rose."

"You are very observant." Quartten nodded at the passing woman in burgundy.

He now worked their wheel alone, and on the other side, only one of the strong men remained. The landing approached; and propelling the ferry had become a one-handed affair. Regeth stood at the rail, pointing and laughing and occasionally calling to people. From time to time, someone acknowledged him, and he yelled to Aaeon to *look* and *pay attention*.

Quartten pointed out, "You'll find men of all faiths in Gates, more than just those who follow after Fadda Freder Neil-fa."

"Somehow, I thought . . . I suppose I expected that all followers would feel most strongly attracted to the precipice of their own beliefs. We're taught there are ten precipices, one for each of the gods, except Shosu Jabena Poll-fa, who has no home, and one for the shades where no light falls."

"I'm not so sure about no light falling." Quartten laughed. "You do know your Scripture, but the world isn't so easily described in life as in books. Have you forgotten, already? We've a Kirk Home on Gates, else we wouldn't be on our way here. Enough discussion for now. We're docking. See? The men are preparing the ropes. While I help maneuver us in, join your friend and bundle our things. I expect the boy'll find more to fill his eyes than he ever dreamed."

Aaeon nodded, murmuring politely, "From your lips to my ears," bringing a smile to Quartten's face. The newly minted underpriest moved to Regeth's side, and he clapped him on the shoulder. "Did you expect this?"

"Kirk be praised, I'm the most blessed neophyte in all Haukberk. Look there." He pointed at a mounded protuberance of wheels, gears, and levers that rose nearly a full story high as the ferry glided slowly past. It chimed twice. He held up two fingers to the sky, parallel to each other, just where a branch of red lightning dropped a yellow fingerling, and he measured the

195

distance from the horizon. "See? Two fingers past yellow tail. That machine tracks the movement of the skies."

"That means it's time to sort our things." Aaeon was less concerned about the state of the skies than he was in catching another glimpse of the velvet woman. "Ken says we're to disembark soon. Remember my pouch with my devotionals."

"May Fadda Kirk forgive me, I didn't think. The wonders of the city distracted me—"

"Not to worry, my good friend. All transpires as Kirk wills. Now, busy at your tasks."

Aaeon smiled. He could grow to enjoy being an underpriest, especially now that he had Regeth as his own to do whatever he required of him. He rested his elbows on the rail and took in the sights. The burgundy woman was long gone, but there were many others just as fanciful. Few wore the discreet tunics of Haukberk, with their hoods modestly over their hair, revealing no more than their faces. Where the women of Gates were concerned, Aaeon thanked Kirk, and he wondered if Mene could someday be convinced to wander the streets of Gates with him. Perhaps he could serve at the Kirk Home on Gates, if it was large enough and could find room for him. His attention was taken with a girl about his age bound in a tight-fitting bodice who carried a woven basket of laundry on her head, her arms high to balance the load. His eyes followed her eagerly.

"I see turning the ferry's wheel has had little effect on your interest in the local wildlife." Quartten popped him good-naturedly on the back of his head. He had donned his tunic, and attaching it at the neck, he drew his hood over his head. "Hood, Aaeon. I also see you have *delegated* your work."

He looked away, as if searching the wharf.

"With Kirk as my witness, I was told to use Regeth's services as I saw fit." From the heights of superiority to the depths of his own clumsiness, Aaeon watched himself fall. Would he never get this right? He slipped his hood over his head and turned to find

Regeth bundling the final few things in their packs. There were five in total, giving each person at least one to carry, although Quartten's two were the largest to suit his bigger frame and greater endurance.

"As you should." Quartten held up his hand, palm exposed, as if the words were distracting. He replied, almost as though quoting by rote, "Except when the duty is already yours. There!" He waved an arm high in the air and called, "Luttrell, you old fool. I've come. I have the boy."

An older man in a similar-style hooded tunic worn with loose trousers, his hood only partially covering a mostly bald pate surrounded by a fringe of bristly hair, narrowed his eyes and searched the ferry. The cloth of his tunic was plain, with only a contrasting band around the wrists and cuffs, but the cut was good. He carried a staff similar to Quartten's, but he used it for balance, as though that was its primary duty. He caught sight of Under-priest Quartten, and his stubble-covered cheeks dimpled into a smile of recognition.

"You young snapper, you. Why, it *is* little Ken. Bless my heart. Fadda Ja Kirk-fa has smiled upon me. Thought I'd never see you again."

Roughly dressed workers had grappled with the lines thrown from the ferry, and they pulled them in, calling workingmen's curses such as, "Vitson curse you," when lines were dropped, or, "Where is Fadda Vitson-la when we need him?" as they searched for tools that seemed to be mysteriously unavailable. The end of the ferry was eventually hooked to a sturdy metal wheel with a long arm that would take three men to turn, but there wasn't a handle on the wheel; instead, the men climbed on the drum that spooled the cable and walked it manually, using the weight of their bodies to slowly pull the ferry in.

The ferry hit the end of the cabling that had guided it across the Crevasse, and it jerked, causing the three travelers on board to stumble. Quartten called, "The ramp will be down shortly. Hold there, old man. We'll be across as soon as we're released."

"Where's the boy with the magic?" The grizzled smile fell away, and the man's lined eyes squinted, darting across the passengers gathering to exit the ferry.

"Here and here." Quartten threw one arm across Aaeon's shoulder and then pointed to Regeth with their packs. "I brought you two!"

"Eh? Fadda Kirk be with me, I didn't agree to two. Take them home. They're no good to me. Two will only make trouble. They're *boys*." He waved his hand dismissively and turned heavily, as if it pained him, before disappearing into a growing crowd of people.

Boys? Aaeon didn't know who the old man was, but *boys?* Perhaps Regeth, yes, he'd give him that. Regeth was indeed a boy. But him? It was an insult. He lifted a hand to get Quartten's attention, when the underpriest turned to him and smiled.

"That went better than I hoped. A good start, if I'm the one to say so. Take one of the packs, Aaeon. Regeth," he called loudly, motioning with his arm upraised, "bring your master one of the packs, and you take two. Leave mine, and I'll get them on the way." He looked at Aaeon and said brightly, "Ready, my boy? Remember, our steps are ordered by the will of Kirk, and his strength will be ours."

"From your lips to my ears, esteemed one." Aaeon wanted to fume. The old man's words cut. He heard Quartten, however, name him Regeth's *master*. Now it was all he could do not to smile. He put on his best voice and asked, "Who is that man, a servant of Gates' Kirk Home?"

"Ho, ho!" Quartten was shouldering his second pack, and he laughed, clapping Aaeon on the shoulder and speaking to Regeth. "Your friend thinks old Luttrell is a servant of the local Kirk Home. Oh, that's a good one."

Regeth smiled in a pleasing way, which meant he was thoroughly confused, and he looked between the two men before asking, "Esteemed one, just who is he?"

"Old Luttrell was my teacher, Underpriest Abbey's teacher, and the man that ordained Bishop Doitsey." He began to move with the throng across the ramp, and he called back to Aaeon. "His name is Bishop Luttrell Ziggurat; he's become the Temple Master; and he's over the whole Gates precipice. He's agreed to be your teacher."

Aaeon's stomach jumped. That was *Ziggurat, his esteemed teacher,* the man who was to *train* him to navigate the haze curtains and return? He looked to find Haukberk in the distance. The lightning had ceased, and there was little more than the glow along the precipice to show him where it was. He wished he'd never left home. Crossing the ramp, he looked below him to the cloud-shrouded sky that encircled their world, then to the lightning overhead, and wished he had the nerve to step right off. It couldn't be worse than training with *Ziggurat,* could it?

Book of the Gods

Roshanna, Chapter 1:10-13

SHOSU WEN HODA-FA has always been a favorite of Shosu Poll-fa. For many seasons, they ruled side-by-side in the sky, and they were never separated. When Shosu Poll-fa took her rightful place in the sky, to bring life to those who walk the soil, she left Shosu Hoda-fa to carry her blessings to all who welcome her into our homes.

IT'S THE REASON we open our morning windows as Poll-fa rises and our evening windows as Poll-fa sets, so the queen goddess can send her whispered blessings of warmth and goodwill by the arms of Shosu Hoda-fa, who dwells in the wind.

SHOSU HODA-FA is the Patron of Weather, and we entreat her good wishes each time we step outdoors.

SHOSU HODA-FA'S followers are called El Hoda-faitum, or the followers of Shosu Wen Hoda-fa. Selah.

Rising to the Challenge

"So," Bishop Ziggurat tossed out, his lined face frowning and his voice brittle, "this is the boy who can traverse the haze." He paced the massive room, his staff in his hand and tapping with each step across the undressed stone floor.

Upon entering the building, a neophyte even younger than Regeth had collected their outer tunics. The bishop wore no more than a simple white sheath with long sleeves to cover his arms. He reached inside his undertunic and pulled out a slim container. He worked a small amount of vicweed from it and placed it in his mouth, using his tongue to push it into place along his gums. He seemed to have no real interest in impressing his visitors, or in comfort, luxury, or finer things of any sort. He didn't wear woven photon slippers or speak with affected mannerisms. Except for Underpriest Quartten, his welcome had offered little more than the thinnest layer of cordiality, and that felt as though it was about to crumble under the strain.

Aaeon sat on a bare wooden stool. In the center, open on all sides, a carved and arched lintel topped by a towering stone overmantle wrapped a bright red, roaring flame. The flue jutted upward, disappearing into a coffered wooden ceiling. Regeth was forced to sit cross-legged on the stone floor. Outside, Gates' Kirk Home was of stone and mortar construction with unfinished walls, a prayer tower of truncated dimensions, and gray slate roofing. Inside, the furnishings—what there were—consisted of rough-hewn pieces without a cushion in sight. Surprisingly, thick cabling ran along the walls, and every six meters or so, one of the lights from the city streets was mounted on the walls, burning brightly enough to bombard the room with the brilliance of a lightning strike. Aaeon's eyes watered under the strain, and he wondered at the marvels of El Neil-faitum and the city they'd built that could so easily squander power to burn such bright and wasteful *lights*.

"And I?" Quartten stood calmly between the two youths and the old man, his arms crossed and his ear jangle catching in the fire's red light. "Was I any different from this boy? Was I smarter or taller or wiser?"

"Kirk forgive me, you were not," Ziggurat granted, his eyes on the floor. Then he turned and pointed his staff Quartten's direction. "You had *drive*. You'd lost your home and wanted nothing more than to return. This . . . *child* has no focus at all." He shifted the staff to aim it Aaeon's direction. He turned and spat green juice into a metal container.

"You can tell that in so few moments? You've hardly spoken to the boy." A hint of laughter infused the words. His ear jangle sent a shard of red light flashing across the room when he shifted his position.

The bishop sank onto a stone bench, holding his staff in both his hands, and he let out a long sigh. His eyes caught the under-priest's, and he motioned toward Aaeon with one hand. "I see it in his unshaven face, his untamed hair, and his carriage. I'm sur-prised to hear he's advanced to underpriest. This child would still be a neophyte were he under my care."

"You do mean Underpriest Hibolah and not Neophyte Zaptha, your holiness? They are easy to confuse."

"Now you cut me." The bishop stamped his staff on the floor. "Save your sanctimonious terms for Doitsey. He'll eat them from your hand. I've no time for them."

"Which is why you're on Gates and not at the Grand Temple. It's also why I respect you so much."

"And you wish to be cardinal?" Old Ziggurat's tone had softened.

"I *am* cardinal, just not yet, at least in my real when. I need you to help me get there, and this boy is key."

Aaeon watched the exchange, trying to absorb the play of words. His mentor had displayed a mastery of the discussion, softening the old man with a few chosen comments. He was beginning to understand how Quartten could become a cardinal, why Quartten *would* become cardinal. Regeth had begun to squirm with discomfort, and Aaeon hushed him with a quick motion of his hand. The bishop's next move surprised Aaeon. He rose, opened a rough cabinet, and pulled out a packet of items. He motioned to Quartten to take them.

"I've sent a missive to the cardinal requesting your elevation to priest—"

"Luttrell, Cardinal Kirk-fait mustn't know my name. There can be no contact—"

"Relax, my friend." The old man smiled as he grasped Quartten's forearm in a quick motion before releasing him. "It's my hair that's gray, not my mind. When I filled in your name, I scribbled. He'll not be able to decipher it."

"And I'm not addled, either. Now that you've told me, I'll remember, I promise you that." Quartten chuckled. "Maybe I already do."

"You haven't, yet. You've already approved it. Do I need to perform the rituals, or shall we forego the nonsense and get on with things?"

"If I accept this, you'll train the boy?"

"Aye?" He looked hard at Quartten for a moment before

turning his gaze on Aaeon. "I promised, didn't I? Kirk help us all." He looked away and shook his head.

"And told me to take them home," Quartten teased.

"I was thinking of the food they'll consume, the small one, especially. He looks to have more energy than any neophyte deserves."

The lights flickered once, returned as bright as before, then flickered a second time before dimming to a pleasanter level.

"About time," Ziggurat spat. "The lightning overloads the capacitors. Always blinds me before the excess bleeds away. Now, we have someone to meet to start our training." He rapped his staff on the floor. "You, and you, too, boy. I'm teaching both of you to navigate the haze, an heir and a spare. No sense in training one when I can get two for the same work. And you better keep up. I've no patience with slackers. Neither does Fadda Kirk-fa." He rapped his staff again, turned, and made his way out the door.

"Boys," Quartten called, snapping his fingers. "He means it. Don't make him wait. Let's go."

Aaeon got to his feet, but Regeth's leg had gone to sleep. Aaeon helped him up, and with Quartten egging them on, they headed toward the door with their tunics in hand. Aaeon walked next to newly promoted Priest Quartten.

"Your holiness, I understood Bishop Ziggurat would be my trainer. Is he handing me off to another?" The possibility had him nearly giddy with relief.

"Perhaps." Despite his vague answer, Quartten seemed to know exactly what was about to transpire.

"And I'm being trained, too?" Regeth limped a little bit from his sleepy leg, but he'd managed to draw close enough to join in.

"It would seem so, Spare." The priest hiked his hood up, and he indicated for the boys to do the same.

"Aaeon, you'll thank Fadda Kirk-fa for me in your devotions tonight, won't you?" As a neophyte, Regeth hadn't yet earned a pouch of his own.

Aaeon didn't answer. Ahead of them, a heavy door stood open, and the noise of the city bled in. Gates was raucous with the sounds of commerce, people, and machines, so very different from the world of Haukberk. Ziggurat stood just outside, his tunic belted at the waist and cinched at the neck, with his head partially covered.

The brilliance of the city washed out much of the sky, but the dark purple of the storm wall and the familiar scribbles of lightning told the story of the gods that lived among them. The fantastic designs painting the heavens seemed to breathe as he watched, swelling with energy, then relaxing once more.

Aaeon was relieved to see that they hadn't come so far from home that *everything* was different.

When the Lightning Strikes

The teacher they were to see didn't live in Gates City, nor anywhere near Gates City. They walked past stalls of goods, many with varying and unusual foods, and others with impressive and complex mechanical devices which Aaeon couldn't begin to identify. Music played from invisible musicians, the mounted glow globes washed all the natural color from the sky, and from time to time they passed fountains with *running water.*

Such a waste, and yet, it was beautiful and soothing to the mind.

Most striking to Aaeon were the females with bare heads and shoulders. He bowed his head several times and looked away, whispering, "Fadda Kirk-fa, please give me strength." Once, distracted, he bumped into Quartten, only to have the priest question him on his health, even holding an arm to his forehead to see if he burned with fever. It wasn't fever he burned with, but he wasn't telling the older man *that*, even if he'd been easy to approach and kind to him beyond belief.

As the walk was long, the wonders of the city fantastic, and Quartten drawn into a deep conversation with his old teacher,

Aaeon fell into step with his friend.

"You're walking normally now." He grinned at him, teasing.

"Ack, and I'm glad." Regeth nudged Aaeon with his elbow. Two years' difference in age wasn't much for many people, but Regeth had yet to hit a true growth spurt. His was hero worship for a successful older brother, something Aaeon was mostly indifferent to.

"You should be." Aaeon clenched his fist and gave him a punch to the shoulder.

"There! The thing we saw!" Regeth pointed excitedly. The *thing* was the timekeeping device from earlier.

Closer, it clicked and whirred, with giant geared wheels, popping levers that jumped from gear tooth to gear tooth, massive springs that creaked with metallic groaning, and a balance spring perhaps two meters wide. Impulse, guard, and banking pins tapped and dinged as other metal parts bumped them.

It was beyond belief and magnificent. As people young and old passed by, they ran bare and gloved hands along the metal framework, murmuring phrases such as, "From you I draw the strength of Vitson," or "Fadda Vitson bless us," or even the more prosaic, "Fadda Sher Vitson-la, amen."

The spoken sentiments of faith helped Aaeon pay attention to the people they walked alongside. As the travelers waited to enter a turnstile from one street into another, each person touched the turnstile mechanism with a hand and whispered respectful words to Fadda Vitson-la. He caught two that especially appealed to him: a woman who said, "May Vitson keep you working smoothly," and a small boy who took his hand from a pocket and piped up, "From Vitson's thoughts to you, machine," as he ran his palm over the turnstile. The boy smiled and turned back to his mother in a conversation that continued as though he hadn't said anything.

Even opening and walking through doors brought on whispered words to the divine. So did a device a businessman used to roll out an awning over the sidewalk; a wrist-sized timepiece worn by a wealthy woman; and a wheeled cart two workers were loading with bricks. As they stood to roll it inside, they stroked the rim, and their lips moved, even though they were too far away for Aaeon to hear.

One of the steam-breathing machines he'd seen from the ferry rested at the curb with a *For Hire* sign on it. The steam engine's radius bar, regulator valves, and flywheel clattered loudly as a finely dressed man walked up, dickered with the driver for a moment, and offered him payment, which quickly disappeared. As Aaeon and his companions passed, the passenger paused before boarding and said a short prayer, "Fadda Vitson, your wise design is my safe transportation."

Twice they passed underneath one of the unusually shaped Rising Stones that towered over the landscape. Each one made Aaeon's hair bristle, as if the electricity the massive transformers captured wasn't all contained, and just to be near it was to absorb some of its excess power. It occurred to him that if there was a drought of storm wall energy, Gates would become desperate for power. Did they have the capacity to generate their own? He'd never thought of it before.

Nearing a broad avenue, a passing troupe of perhaps fifty or more forced them to wait for a time. Each passing person carried either a mouth-blown instrument or one with strings. The melodies were interwoven and moving, if transient, and gone before Aaeon could make them out. Many were taken up by another of the troupe, changed, and then cast out for reinterpretation once again.

"Pay attention." The old bishop held up a hand. "El Charfaitum travel from precipice to precipice, sharing their love of music. We see here preparations for the Summer Festival."

"I have a mouth harp, your excellency, and at home, many people play instruments of one sort or another. How can you tell these people worship Fadda Ran Char-la?" Regeth's hood had partially fallen, and he could see up and down the avenue with a simple twist of his neck.

He was right, Aaeon thought. Music was loved throughout the ten precipices, just as all precipices had fire chambers even though Fadda Ja Kirk-fa was the only Patron of Fire. Just because a god was the *patron* of something didn't mean it belonged exclusively to his or her faitum.

"Ah, Ken." Ziggurat smiled, not at Quartten, but at Regeth. "This one may have an excess of energy, but his mind works well. He observes that things are not always as they seem."

"Can you answer your own question, boy?" Quartten tapped him on the back of the hood, repeating the gentle motion until the boy figured it out and pulled his hood closer to his face.

That caused Aaeon to really pay attention to the song-playing troupe. Their tunics, while different from his and Regeth's, were nothing special, a variation of colors ranging from light gold to sea green, all very pleasing to the eye. It was their hoods that stood out. The base of their hoods draped loosely over their shoulders, creating a waterfall effect that tumbled halfway down their arms, backs, and chests. Their sandals, while also differing in color, were of comparable cuts, but there was nothing unusual about that. He'd worn similar ones at various times.

Regeth pronounced proudly, "They all carry an instrument."

About then, just in front of them, a man came by, waltzing as much as walking. He was painfully thin, with arms too long for his tunic sleeves, and hair that formed a curly halo around his face where it escaped from his hood.

"Look closer, boy." Quartten leaned next to him and whispered seductively. "Closer." The curly-haired man held a stringed instrument he played with his fingers, and where his arms protruded from his cuffs, musical symbols flashed in the light from the stationary glow globes. They seemed to float above his skin.

"Holo tattoos," Aaeon breathed. "They're beautiful."

"Correct, young man." Ziggurat glanced at him, holding his hood aside for a short time. "Something worn by none other than the Order of Fadda Char-la."

"But we have a small Char Home on Haukberk. None of the priests there have these." It was Regeth again, and Aaeon put a finger to his lips to shush him.

"Good point. He's observant. You've not *seen* them, but that doesn't mean they don't wear them." Ziggurat didn't turn this time. The last of the musical troupe was making their way by, and the crowd waiting to pass was getting restless. "Why do we see them now?"

"Aaeon," Quartten whispered. "The time to answer is passing you by. He's *testing* you."

Aaeon's heart sank for the umpteenth time in one day. *Testing!?!* Would he never get relief? He glanced at Regeth to see if he was about to answer and was relieved to see him laughing at a small, two-legged, furred pet with a tail that walked with one of the troupe on a leash. Aaeon tried to think what was different, and when it came to him, it was obvious.

"The light. The reddish energy from the sky is in the wrong wavelength for the holotats to be seen clearly from a distance. The glow globes operate at a different wavelength, giving them a greater reflectivity and making them more visible to our eyes." Aaeon knew beyond doubt it was the correct answer.

Bishop Ziggurat had already moved on, and Priest Quartten stepped briskly after him. Aaeon was just close enough to overhear the priest as he leaned toward Ziggurat and said, "I told you he works things out. He may not be as observant as the younger boy, but he's the very one we need to overcome the difficulties of moving about within the haze curtains."

Aaeon didn't get to hear the bishop's response, because just then, Ziggurat lifted his staff high and called out in a singsong voice, "Ai-ee, the love of one calls to another. Who opens her arms for our embrace?"

Aaeon looked to where the bishop pointed his staff to find a willowy creature in a highly embroidered floor-length tunic standing on the balcony of a slender minaret that stretched nearly as high as the Rising Stone capacitors. Large, burnished earrings shifted and sparkled where they protruded from her hood, and the inside of her tunic was of purest yellow. In his mind, she was a vision of beauty.

"It is I," the beautiful woman called, "the priestess of all El Hoda-faitum." Her words flowed in a beautiful melody, filled with honey, longing, and relief in one. "The Scriptures tell us that Shosu Hoda-fa fell from the sky in the arms of Fadda Kirk-fa, forever binding her followers to those of Fadda Kirk-fa in an embrace that warms the goddess when Shosu Poll-fa must be obscured from the sky. Priestess Shel Burne welcomes the eminent Bishop Luttrell Ziggurat to warm me with his presence."

As soon as she spoke, Aaeon knew he was in love. He wasn't sure *exactly* what she was saying, but he knew what it'd mean if he said that to Mene. He felt his face burn.

Regeth tugged on Aaeon's arm, asking quite loudly, "Are you sick, Aaeon? Your face, it's all red and splotchy."

"Shush," he hissed to his friend. His stomach churned, and he pulled his hood tighter around his face.

"Is everything okay back there?" Quartten glanced at them for a quick moment, before turning back to the bishop when Aaeon waved his hand that it was.

"Who is that, esteemed one?" Aaeon tried to keep his voice from shaking but knew it was practically impossible. This woman was so *beautiful*. The priest was focused on the conversation between the bishop and his siren, and Aaeon got no answer.

"I know," Regeth said brightly and helpfully. "She's a priestess of Shosu Hoda-fa, Patron of the Weather. Her name is—"

"Great Kirk, you're so stupid, Regeth. You can't know this woman. You've never been to Gates!" Aaeon was fed up with his observant friend, and he began to wish he'd left him behind.

"He knows, because she said her name aloud. In the name of Kirk, be kind." Quartten reprimanded him. "Apologize, please."

Aaeon turned to his friend, bowed his head, placed his hand to his chest, and recited the most formal apology he knew. "With Kirk as my witness, I come before you and offer you my inner-most self. Please accept that I was wrong. I will know you've accepted my heartfelt regret when you return my inner self to me."

"Gladly, I return your inner self to you. Kirk be praised." Regeth ducked his chin with his final words, placing his hand at his chest, and when Quartten nodded at them, pleased, Regeth leaned in toward Aaeon and whispered, "I wasn't upset. I think she's pretty, too."

"Oh, Kirk! You keep your trap shut about it, you hear? And Mene had better never know."

Regeth grinned as the gate before them opened, and they started towards the base of the tower. Aaeon squeezed his eyes tightly for an instant, hoping beyond hope that this priestess was ugly up close. If not, he would be in all sorts of hot water, water he didn't know if he could ever get out of.

Book of the Gods

Roshanna, Chapter 1:14-15

SHOSU LISABET KOVSKI-LA is our Patron of Healing, for she comes to our side in our times of need, returning our health to us, if we pray to her with a sincere heart. Shosu Kovski-la is a lesser god, because in the time when the heavens burned, she rendered aid to Kella Theon Aland-um, a shade banished from the sky.

SHOSU KOVSKI-LA'S followers are called El Kovski-faitum, or the followers of Shosu Lisabet Kovski-la. Selah.

The Gods Speak

By the time they reached the top of the tower, Aaeon wished for electrically powered steps.

He'd heard stories of El Neil-faitum building lofty towers for their Patron of Directions, and he supposed this must be one. When the heavens darkened and the land no longer glowed with energy, the clerics lighted the towers to guide travelers from precipice to precipice. Wasn't it written in the Scriptures that because Fadda Freder Neil-fa had failed to guide Shosu Poll-fa through the troubles of The Great Falling, he had been cast down to become the mountains? The very hills they walked were the cheekbones of Fadda Neil-fa's face, and the valleys were his laugh lines. The light towers were his eyes, and through them, he saw all that occurred throughout the land.

Still, did Fadda Neil-fa's eyes need to be so *tall?*

The priestess opened the door into her priestly abode. Underneath her hood, her pale gray eyes spoke of wisdom. The yellow inner liner of her tunic's hood gave an ethereal glow of warmth to her skin. When she invited them in, she *sang.*

"Priestess Shel Burne's heart is open, as is her home. Come, be comfortable in your rest as you are now weary from your climb." She bowed her head slightly, with her palm at her throat, almost as if she were the supplicant and they were the gods, ending with, "May Shosu Hoda-fa be with you at all times and in all ways."

"So be it, most gracious lady." Ziggurat bowed deeper than Aaeon thought possible, although he held tightly to his staff with one hand. "As always, your beauty is a credit to Hoda-fa, and your kindness exceeds that given to Shosu Eboh-la when Kella Aland-um held her for ransom."

Ziggurat's reference to the gods was insightful. Shosu Imani Eboh-la, who was a lesser god and not a greater god, had fought unsuccessfully during the Battle of the Knives; and the shade Kella Theon Aland-um had attempted to betray a fellow god for his own benefit. Fadda Freder Neil-fa swayed Kella Aland-um's depraved mind and saved Eboh-la. For this reason, Shosu Eboh-la was the Patron of the Ill and Disenfranchised and the very embodiment of kindness and goodwill towards those who had lost all hope.

Priest Quartten had found himself in much the same position as Eboh-la. He'd exhausted all hope for returning to his respective *when* until he'd chanced on Aaeon and his news of purple flame lost in the haze curtains; and yet, his continued hope came only through the help of the priestess.

The room they entered was broad and circular, much larger than it appeared from the ground. An imposing half-round table anchored the space, with a notch in the flat side for a person to sit or stand. Multiple couches and divans filled with pillows on thick, pale rugs were everywhere. It was light and airy, with a raised ceiling in the center encircled with a tall expanse of glass. A collection of perhaps a hundred glow globes, the floating sort from Haukberk, hovered. None were lighted as far as Aaeon could tell, but as each person took his or her place in the tower, the globes shuffled their positions to center above those who had arrived.

Once Burne's visitors stood by their respective soft, cushioned chairs, she positioned herself in the notch in the table and reached to her throat. With a sweep of her hands, her hood fell back, revealing a stunningly bald head decorated with holotats of weather symbols: swirling wind, clouds and sun, and driving rain. There were also those that no one recognized anymore of hurricanes, snow, sleet, and more. They were beautiful and complemented Burne's slender features, as if she might have been born with them, the most beautiful child in the world.

They were also the reason the priestess had to wield caution in removing her hood. Her tats carried power and exposing them without care could wreak devastation on those nearby. The yellow cloth inside her hood was her warning to those who walked at her side.

Aaeon was more entranced than before. He tried to tear his eyes away and endeavored to picture Mene. When the priestess dropped her tunic to expose a silken undertunic, she filled his mind with a warm haze. Then she sang to them.

"The House of Hoda occupies the House of Neil as a gift from one god to another. I welcome the House of Kirk to share in Shosu Hoda's bounty. You may remove your tunics as you wish." She bowed her head, her eyes downcast, and placed her open hand over her breastbone, giving them the opportunity to do so in the semblance of privacy.

"From your lips to our ears," Quartten and Ziggurat intoned together.

Aaeon glanced at the priest and the bishop to catch them respectfully mimicking the priestess' hand. They pushed their hoods back and released their throat bindings and belts. Regeth watched him with a question in his eyes. Aaeon smiled, nodded, placed his hand on his breastbone, and began to slip out of his tunic. He noticed small racks by each chair, and he draped his tunic and devotional pouch over his, adjusted his undertunic, and kept his eyes respectfully on the floor. It was then he took notice of the carpets. They, also, were filled with weather symbols.

"Hoda has willed this day, enabling the skies and the winds and the storm walls to combine in perfect harmony. Much good will come of your visit to the tower." Priestess Burne's voice shifted from true song to her earlier singsong lilt. "Please be seated with me, Hoda be praised."

"Hoda be praised, and Kirk also," her four companions recited, as they followed her example and took their seats.

"Which one is the acolyte?" Burne found the two youths, smiled, and motioned with an outstretched hand, her palm raised, as if inviting the answer rather than expecting it.

"Neither." Quartten cleared his throat, trying to stifle a laugh.

"So, our savior is lost already?" Burne's eyes drifted Quartten's way. "The haze curtain has consumed yet another willing youth?"

Consumed? Aaeon was startled out of his complacent admiration for the room, its luxurious seating surfaces, and the beautiful woman speaking to them. *Consumed?* He didn't come all this distance to be *consumed.*

"Not today." Quartten chuckled and shrugged. "Perhaps we'll lose one tomorrow. Who knows? However, the acolyte has become an underpriest, by the will of Kirk, and his youthful companion is a lowly neophyte."

"Huh?" The word burst from Regeth's mouth before he could contain it. "Lowly?"

Ziggurat opened his mouth and raised a hand to correct the neophyte, but Quartten interrupted him with a loud bark of a laugh.

"Yes, my boy, a lowly neophyte. It's the lowest of our Order, a mere pledge who knows nothing yet wishes to someday be cardinal. However, not at this time, even if you are to be trained to navigate the curtains."

"The small one? He is my trainee?" Burne laughed lightly. "He's so young. His skill must be great, indeed. May Hoda be with us in our endeavors."

Regeth turned brilliantly red.

Ziggurat rapped his staff on the carpet, found it ineffective, worked it to the hard surface underneath and rapped it again. "I'm silent for a moment, and confusion reigns. Quiet, priests and neophytes. I will speak. The youths have had no training, but each comes with a strength. As a team, they will be stronger than alone. The elder of the two advanced to underpriest in preparation for his training, and the younger travels as his aide." He blinked twice as if that said everything.

"And their strengths, excellency?" Burne smiled.

He accepted the question graciously and nodded as if he expected it. "Observancy is the strength of the younger and understanding of the elder. What the younger can see, the elder can work out. Through the zeal of Fadda Kirk and the blessings of Shosu Hoda, they will find success."

"From your lips to the ears of Shosu Hoda-fa," Priestess Burne murmured, her hand momentarily finding her breastbone before returning to her lap.

"So be it." Ziggurat flicked his fingers but did nothing else to indicate respect or subservience. "You will train them as requested?"

Her shoulders shifted underneath her undertunic, and Aaeon so hoped the priestess agreed to do this, even with Regeth as part of the new plan.

"There's one other thing. Ken, if you please?" The bishop indicated the younger man.

"More?" The priestess held up an open hand, and her earrings caught in the light flooding in from the windows above, scattering color throughout the room. She spread her golden hands on the table in front of her, looked directly at Aaeon, closed her eyes, and bowed her head before speaking in her singsong voice. "Youth, the connection is with you. Our dear Ziggurat tells me you work out what others see. I see you in the Tower of Neil, and you are barely more than a boy. You travel with a companion your junior, and he admires you greatly. Priest Quartten shepherds you as a treasure, and even the bishop finds great value in you. Through the eyes of Shosu Hoda-fa, this is what I see. What is the path you wish to walk to uncover the will of the gods?"

Quartten grinned, and the bishop nodded in satisfaction at the younger priest. Aaeon's jaw quivered as he attempted to answer what must be said.

"Boy?" The priestess repeated her entreaty. She looked up, and her earrings flashed with a light that was greater than that coming from the sky above. "Where will your feet lead you?"

"I follow after Kirk in my search for the purple fire, for I saw purple lightning fall from the sky." *And after the priestess, if she'll lead me,* for he would follow her anywhere. Mene was far from his thoughts at the time, and if he'd been able to remember her name, her face would have fled in despair.

"Ahh!" The priestess whispered the word as she closed her eyes and lifted her hands, palms up. They hovered in front of her as if floating, and above them, the air grew misty. The weather runes on her scalp began to glow with a rippling effect, the subtle effect slipping from one to another. The room seemed charged with ozone, as though a powerful current saturated the air, ripping electrons from atoms and flinging them carelessly through the gathered motes of light. "Ahh-hh!" the priestess cried again, her face turned to the windowed recess above her head. The glow globes were in motion as if they no longer tracked those sitting far below but had found other prey to pursue. The air grew thicker, almost opaque, a curtain of undulating *time* and *when.* Within the priestess's hands, time belonged to the future or the past, not part of the *then.*

The mistiness grew thicker, and with a jerk, Aaeon was cold, then hot, then cold again, and all around him was metal, metal, and more metal. It was a metal world, and he was made of metal. He looked through a glass window, and there were metal people being eaten by purple sky. A voice rang in his head, *"You fool! We have to get out now."* He clawed at his ears, realizing he was also encased in metal. A metal person fell through the purple sky from one orifice and into another orifice. He was pulled along after her and into yet another metal world. The orifice closed, the woman whipped her helmet off, and his ears exploded again.

"What was that about? We're likely dead."

Aaeon wanted to answer but couldn't. His throat wouldn't work. He knew her, however, as he knew his companions sitting in the tower with him. He stared into the eyes of Shulla Cryst Holum, and he quaked in fear. Then, of its own accord, he heard his voice say, *"I want to get home now. Wait three hours? Not worth it."* His ears rang, his vision blurred, and he opened his eyes to an ordered space of white walls, floors and thrones. In front of him, seen with his own eyes, was the visage of the Patron of the Skies, she whom the Scriptures said wielded great power and took lovers among the gods as she pleased. Shosu Jabena Poll-fa lived, with Kirk as his witness, and Aaeon instinctively felt the urge to fall to his knees.

He had no such option, for he wasn't in control of his legs. A petite, fine-boned beauty stepped into the room, and she called to him, *"You got the last burger, Kirkpatrick, as always?"*

Him! She called to him! She could be no other than Shosu Hoda-fa, and she called to *him*, naming him Kirkpatrick. He had no clue what patrick was, but Kirk was obvious. He was in the throne room of the gods, and he shared the body of Fadda Kirk-fa.

He marveled, for Fadda Kirk-fa's lover called to him.

Then he was yanked away, and he saw a vast wall of lights. Numbers scrolled, one shimmered red, and he heard himself say, *"Sure. Why not? It's not like we're going to die."* And he knew who he was, Fadda Sher Vitson-la, for only he knew the mechanics of all things and, without question, could offer others the gift of life or condemn them to death.

The nightmare continued, and in another location, he said, *"We could do that, space 'em?"* He heard the god who spoke with his voice, and it was Shosu Imani Eboh-la, a lesser god who had once battled Kella Aland-um. Aaeon wanted to yell, "Space who? What does that mean?" but his vision blurred, and he was yanked away.

He began to feel ill as each wrenching thrust through the domain of the gods ripped a bit of him away, leaving him more and more exhausted. *"Your ideas? They'd be useful about now."* He felt the words of Fadda Eldon Arkson-la tear from his throat. His head spun, and almost immediately he said, *"Man, I got no ideas that would help with this,"* and Aaeon knew he'd inhabited Fadda Ran Char-la, the lesser god whose youth kept him from becoming a greater god.

Aaeon's tumble through the realm of the gods went on.

"Maybe we should try to carry Asher there, Commander." The voice belonged to Fadda Freder Neil-fa. Aaeon groaned, dreading the desperation that enveloped him with each change. The gods were in dire trouble, and he didn't know how to help them. In Fadder Neil-fa's words, *Asher* was certainly Fadda Vitson-la, for Aaeon felt it must be so. The word Commander he didn't know, but he knew that a god's life hung on the edge.

He was yanked, and the world around him changed once again.

"Event Horizon," and the thought surged through Aaeon's head. He reached for the name of the god, and images of black points in space filled his vision, overlaid with numbers he couldn't comprehend. And the stars! Disappearing!

What were stars? For a moment he knew, then it was gone, but the feeling remained. It was the end of everything, and it was cold, cold, cold. As the connection slipped away, he knew who had spoken, for Fadda Liam Egel-la, the lesser god, spoke through things unseen.

Then, he was wrenched once again to yet another scene.

Shosu Lisabet Kovski-la's voice surged through the darkness, calling in desperation, *"Thank God someone's still active and about,"* and Aaeon's eyes opened to a medical facility. The lights were failing as he looked around. He recognized the face of the god he'd been just moments before, Shosu Eboh-la. She was in pain. He wanted to cry, "Yes, I'm here! Regeth's at my side, as are three clerics who are helping me. Here, here! I'm active and about," yet, his voice was hers, and he couldn't speak. Would all the heavens tumble to the ten precipices before his nightmare was complete? Why was he here? What was he supposed to learn?

His final lurch told him more than he wished to discover. He was thrown from god to god in quick succession, wrenched violently, painfully, cruelly, without regards to his welfare or desire; and in each jump, he gained a little knowledge of those he'd touched.

"How'd you know it was dark if youse eyes were closed?" The voice was that of Kella Theon Aland-um, and the shade's words burned with hatred.

"You want another belt in the kisser?" He recognized Shulla Hol-um, for Aaeon had already tasted her vile soul.

"I need the three of you to head to the bow and see if you can find a way to disengage the drive." Aaeon barely survived his hit into Kella Shana Gill-um's mind. He was the Perpetrator of Revenge, and the shade's thoughts seared him with cruelty.

"Won't that leave us stranded?" No! Aaeon rebelled, fighting Shulla Hol-um's touch.

"You prefer dead?" Yes! The thought escaped Aaeon's mind before he could focus. He admitted with remorse that even death might be better than the touch of the minds of the shades.

"Any directions? It helps to know where to start." Shulla Hol-um seared him again, and he tried to run and hide. She was the Perpetrator of Seduction, and she attempted to pull him in.

"Just do it. Simple enough for you?" He slammed back into Kella Gill-um, broken and no longer caring. Let it end, Aaeon

pleaded.

"Get off the floor, Kaseem. No naps, and you, Zealander! This isn't a party."

Aaeon recognized Kella Aland-um and Kella Dullah-um in Shulla Hol-um's words, and he leaped, certain the Perpetrators of Battle, Thievery and Murder were preferable to Revenge and Seduction. He reached and nearly caught them, then Kella Gill-um erupted, pulling Aaeon in, and crushing his soul.

"I'm saving our lives, Hollis."

"Yeah, right," she yelled back, her anger ripping Aaeon through the mists, absorbing him, and with careless disregard, flinging him from her.

Aaeon floated free in a haze of purple fire, not knowing if he still dreamed, and he felt his consciousness dissipate into a tattered remnant of what he'd once been. As parts of him released their hold and fluttered away, he did the only thing he knew to do. He held to the thought of his friend Regeth and the good times they'd known when they were boys. He remembered Mene and the kiss he'd stolen from her sweet lips. He drew strength from Quartten, for he'd been kind to him, and from Ziggurat for believing in him. In his thoughts, he pictured the Eye of Fadda Neil-fa filled with the symbols of Shosu Hoda-fa and the beautiful priestess who called it home. He wiped everything from his mind except the images of those five people, and with a wrench, he fell, broken, back into the Tower of Neil.

All the King's Men

Aaeon opened his eyes, surprised to feel his head on a pillow and a thin blanket covering his legs. Looking up, an unfamiliar ceiling indicated a smaller room than before, and even more surprising, a cleric of Shosu Lisabet Kovski-la stood to the side. He recognized the white robe with its blue stripe at the hem as belonging to the Patron of Healing. The width of her stripe said she could be no higher than underpriestess. Her hood was thrown back, and her sleeves, normally long and loose, were rolled nearly to her shoulders and tied with small cords. Chocolate hair, straight at the crown, twisted into lively curls at the tips. Over her robe, she wore a pale, salmon-colored apron that had eaten something red.

"Your excellency," he began, as he struggled to raise himself on his elbows.

"Ah, the adventurer awakes." She turned, tutted at him, and pushed his shoulder to the low couch. "Not yet. I'll get your master. He'll want to know you've recovered."

"I was . . . in Neil-fa's eye—"

"In *Fadda* Neil-fa's eye?" She stressed *Fadda*, crossed her

227

arms, and looked at him for a moment. Her eyes twinkled. "I've never heard of anyone being in *Fadda* Neil-fa's eye. How did you manage that?"

"I misspoke." He released his head to the pillow, picturing Fadda Neil-fa as the spine of Gates Precipice, and the tower as his eye. Of course, she wouldn't understand that. Through the windows far overhead, the dark of the storm wall revealed jagged red slashes streaking across the sky. Glow globes bobbed about, with three hovering just over him and the underpriestess.

"You did, did you?" She took his arm in her hand, and as she lifted it, blood-soaked bandages revealed the reason for the red on her apron.

"Where has the day gone, and … and how did that happen?" His stomach surged as she unrolled the bandaging to reveal scoured skin underneath. A green poultice filled the bandage, and exposed, the wound began to sting. "Are there more like that?"

"Some worse." She cleaned the area and, from a small jar, added more of the poultice, easing the pain. She wrapped it with a long cloth. "You have burns on your leg and a sprained ankle, perhaps. Maybe damage here, if I'm any judge." She chuckled and tapped his forehead.

"Hey," he said, flinching. "Nothing's wrong with my head. Do you have a name?"

"Do you?" She washed her hand in a basin of water using a gritty-looking bar of soap before shaking them off and drying them on her apron. She studied him for a moment. "Come now, name?"

"You, first." He felt better and suspected there was a strong soporific in the paste. He wondered how long before he would fall asleep again.

"Very well. My name is Ana Bethl, and you mustn't call me *your excellency* again. I'm only an underpriestess. You are Underpriest Hibolah. See? I already know." She laughed lightly as she folded the bottom portion of the blanket back and began to feel his lower leg. Using a small pair of shears, she clipped at a bandage carefully while watching his face. "Let me know if this hurts. It's the burn. Sometimes the bandages don't release easily."

"It's fine." Aaeon could feel his words slipping away. "This is Neil's Eye." He motioned with his good arm to the ceiling above them. It felt as though the arm had a life of its own. His hand flopped and twisted, and when he went to lay it down, the arm fell without warning, bouncing on the bedding.

"Do be careful," and Bethl giggled. She'd finished rewrapping the leg, and she pulled the blanket back over it. "It won't do for you to be injured while under my care. Tell me how this is Neil's Eye."

"It's like a prayer tower. Only taller." He blinked and yawned, his thoughts becoming disjointed. In his jumbled grasping, he pulled at his memories of the Kirk Temple in which he'd served faithfully on Haukberk. They were good memories, made up of good friends and adventures up and down the precipice. "You can see everything from my prayer tower, even blue lightning when it combines with red. You know blue and red? They make purple babies. Purple lightning is so pretty."

"Silly." She worked on a place on his temple with a damp cloth. It kept coming away red. "No one sees purple lightning. It's a story from the Scriptures, and we're supposed to keep in mind that analogies help us apply the lessons we learn, even if the ancient events aren't real. Otherwise, we'd never develop modern medicine."

A door opened, and Priestess Burne entered. Her yellow-lined hood covered her head, and as she drew closer, in her singsong manner, she inquired about Aaeon.

"May Shosu Hoda-fa pardon me for interrupting, Ana, but how is our charge?" She brushed back her hood and, for the briefest moment, nodded her head with closed eyes before letting her gray orbs find the underpriestess.

"The vicweed poultice has taken his thoughts to another

place." The damp towel finally remained white, and Bethl rinsed it in the bowl and wrung it to dry.

"He sleeps?"

"Near enough but not yet."

"Thank you, Ana." Burne motioned at the open door behind her, calling softly for the others to enter, and Regeth was the first to join her. His hood remained in place, leaving his smooth face just visible in the shadows cast by the glow globes.

Aaeon chuckled, and he waved a hand wildly, only to have it drop off the couch and dangle, no longer his to command. "Regeth!"

The young man ran to his friend's side, his hood falling back as he grabbed Aaeon's hand and wrapped it in his own. "Aaeon, you're well. Where did you go? We thought you were lost, and then you returned injured, everywhere!"

"He was, indeed, very nearly lost." Quartten and Ziggurat followed him in, and Quartten put his hand on Regeth's shoulder. "We are lucky he returned to us."

"Not luck," Burne sang. "The one who sees the purple lightning is stronger than you believe. He returned because he could do nothing else."

"It's true?" Bethl paled. "He's truly seen the purple lightning? It's real?"

"And stepped beyond the haze curtain to commune with the gods." Ziggurat's hood still wrapped his face, and he adjusted it tighter at his neck, as if unnerved by it all. "The proof is the frost burn on his leg. The gods have made their mark on his person to let us know they wish to be left alone."

"The Kiss of the Gods," Bethl murmured, her hand at her mouth.

"I had so much fun." Aaeon laughed at their discussion of the gods, but of course, no one could understand his words. To be truthful, they couldn't be certain he laughed. He was too far gone in the vicweed for that.

Having fun wasn't exactly what he meant, but when in a vicweed fugue, things tend to get a bit disconnected. Just after that, he began to snore, and the Eye of Neil was no more.

Book of the Gods

Roshanna, Chapter 1:16-19

*F*ADDA FREDER NEIL-FA *is a greater god, for he guided Shosu Poll-fa through the troubles when she fell from the sky.*

*F*OR THIS REASON, *Fadda Freder Neil-fa became the mountains from which we take our guidance, for we travel Upwards along the precipices that form the world, or Downwards to the storm wall from which the world springs, to Morning to face the early light, or to Evening to pray to Shosu Poll-fa.*

*F*ADDA NEIL-FA *is our Patron of Directions, for he is always there to guide us. If we know Upward, we can find Downward, and if we can find Downward, Morning and Evening fall into place.*

*T*HE FOLLOWERS OF *Fadda Neil-fa are called El Neil-faitum, or the followers of Fadda Freder Neil-fa. Selah.*

Fractured Loyalties

"I believe you are completely well."

"Perhaps." Aaeon shrugged. He was on his bunk with his devotional pouch beside him and polishing his devotional cup with a thin cloth. He smiled at Underpriestess Bethl. Her hood draped casually across her shoulders, and her hair danced around her neck.

The four visitors to the Eye of Neil had found there was more to the high tower, for on the outer ramparts, a ring of small rooms encircled the large, central chamber, providing sleeping quarters, personal facilities, and even a place to prepare simple meals. Aaeon's sleeping area contained little more than a narrow bed, a built-in chest, and a chair to sit and read, with a small kneeling rail alongside a wall niche, but it was private with a full door. Priestess Burne had generously offered to provide him an icon of Kirk to help him in his evening prayers, but he had declined, requesting his devotional pouch from his pack. Regeth had retrieved it, and until Aaeon could manage, Regeth poured flame oil into the small devotional cup and set it ablaze with his lightning match each evening at three fingers past. Aaeon spoke his prayers from his bed, while Regeth knelt at the kneeling rail, whispering in union with him all the while.

Only once had Aaeon needed to remind his aide to crush additional oilstone and add it to the flame oil to ensure the fire burned brightly each evening. After all, the intensity of the flames signified the depths of one's devotion to the fadda.

Today, his tunic lay across the chair, filling the seat, and he wore full leggings and his undertunic. His shoulders and arms were bare, revealing the patch of white skin where he had recently healed.

"I'm sure of it." Ana Bethl laughed. "Shosu Kovski-la's healing touch was the miracle you needed for your broken body. Your frost burn, no more than a ripple of rough skin. The poultices have worked wonders on your ankle. Do you even limp now?"

"You know I don't."

"Let me have one last look at your temple." She brushed his hair aside. "As I thought, no blood and no scabs, only a patch or two of lighter skin. If I may say so, Shosu Kovski-la's healing touch flows well through my well-taught and practiced hand."

"It does, does it?" Aaeon had grown to like the underpriestess, and he teased her.

"Yes. I serve as the hand of Kovski, for as the Scriptures tell us, the goddess once rendered aid to Kella Aland-um, and the shade received relief from his travails, so, through me, the goddess does mighty works of healing. After all, you traversed the curtain to her world and back again."

"Don't remind me."

"Don't doubt the good you might do. Priestess Burne believes in you, as do your companions. You must believe in yourself."

"I will try to remember that." He smiled. "You've taken good care of me."

"The neophyte has taken good care of you." She laughed brightly. "He worships you, I think."

"His sister and I . . ." He shrugged, not finishing the sentence, and felt a twinge of guilt. "She's a friend. Regeth and I have known each other since boyhood."

"So that's why he sleeps outside your door, says prayers with you each night, and asks me four times a day if you're yet well. I believe I may be able to finally tell him yes. I think he'll wish to move into your room."

"Ha!" Aaeon laughed. He'd finished polishing the cup, and he rolled the items in the cloth and slipped them into his pouch. He leaned back, resting on his elbows. "Where? On my bed? Not with me in here. The floor hardly has space for me to walk, much less for another person."

"He's certainly devoted to you. Be grateful."

"He's my aide, assigned by the bishop before we left—" he shrugged and smiled, "—and my friend. Devoted? I don't think so. You, tell me about you. If I'm well, then what?"

"I have my duties at the small Kovski Home here in Gates."

"But you're not from Gates. Your accent, your calling." Aaeon sat up and leaned forward. While ill, she'd been at his side daily. He'd not thought ahead to when he was well, and already, he realized how much he would miss her.

"Of course I don't sound like I'm from here." She stepped into the room, handed him his tunic, and took the chair. She crossed her hands in her lap and leaned forward. "I was raised on Hopkins Precipice, as are all the followers of Kovski-la. I was *born* here, however, which is why I choose to serve here. Our Home is very small and but one of many, but I have relations nearby and I get to see them occasionally." She dropped her head and sighed. "*Had* relations nearby. Of course, I have none, now."

"As with me and Regeth, also, although his sister is still his sister to me. And she still considers him a brother, although she says so only to me."

Bethl looked up, and her face brightened. "You understand, then."

"Yes. Are you ever lonely?" His heart pounded at the question he wanted to ask, although he hardly dared. Still, just to think it was exciting, and Mene was very far away. He was no longer sure he'd ever see her again.

"That, I wouldn't admit." She stood, holding her hand out for his tunic. "Let me return that to the chair before I go."

"I thought, perhaps," he felt himself warm with chagrin, "you might travel with us. I might get injured again."

"The tunic?" She smiled. "If you get injured again, there are other Kovski Homes. You'll not be without healing for long."

When he didn't offer the tunic to her, she stepped beside him, lifted it from the bed, and returned it to the chair. She raised her hood to wrap her face. She kept one hand at her throat as she turned and said, "Your aide is just outside the door. I had him wait while I spoke with you."

"Oh, Kirk! He heard everything we said?" Aaeon's heart sank. What if Mene found out? Why hadn't she said anything?

She laughed. "There was nothing to hear. I've cautioned Priestess Burne that you mustn't be allowed to wander in and out of the gods' realm without better training." She seemed to tease with her words. "I sent a message to the Kovski Temple on Hopkins for advice, and my superiors have counseled guidance from two Orders, those of Fadda Arkson-la and Fadda Neil-fa."

"Dreams and Directions." Aaeon smiled. "I have dreams enough. Directions? If we know Downwards, we can find Upwards, and Morning and Evening follow in their stead. The Scriptures tell us so. I can't get lost, not really, even if I try."

"Such is reality only for the landbound. Traveling the *whens* of the haze curtains is very different. Your frost burn is healed, but it speaks the truth in my words." She smiled from the shadows of her hood. "I must be off."

"I'm searching for a reason for you to stay."

"And my duties insist I leave." As she turned, a cough came from outside the doorway.

Aaeon rolled his eyes, calling, "Are you getting an earful, my friend?"

The underpriestess smiled and dropped her eyes. "May Shosu Kovski-la be with you in your travels, and may all your prayers reach the ears of Fadda Kirk-fa even before you speak them aloud." She held her hand at her breastbone as she intoned the words, then dropped it away.

Aaeon replied, "From your lips to the ears of the gods."

"You may come in, neophyte. Your master is once again yours," and she was gone. The room seemed devoid of life without her.

"Quartten and Ziggurat are on the way." Regeth's words spilled from him. He wore his tunic, and it was open, revealing his undertunic; and his hood formed a thick collar of fabric at his neck. He dipped his head in a slight bow and said, "Fadda Kirk-fa has smiled on us. We travel to meet with priests of the Orders of Arkson-la and Neil-fa."

"So I've heard. I'm ready to see something besides the inside of this tower. Are things prepared?" He stood, picked up his devotional pouch, wrapped the decorative strap around it several times, and held it out. "Don't forget to pack this with my tunic."

"Fadda Kirk be praised, certainly." Regeth took it, smiled, and nodded. A clearing throat brought Aaeon's attention to the door.

"Still having the boy do things for you that you could do for yourself?" Quartten was in his tunic, the waist secured, but with his hood at his back. His ear jangle caught in the light. His expression was neutral, but he held his arms at his waist, one laid atop the other. His high forehead with its receding hairline gave him an unusually somber look.

"He *is* my aide." Aaeon let the words slip before he realized how didactic they sounded. Of course, the priest knew that. He dropped his eyes and glanced toward Regeth to see if he was smirking at his reprimand. He held the devotional pouch respectfully. Aaeon turned back to Quartten. "My apologies, esteemed one. I spoke out of turn."

"Learn from it, and Fadda Kirk will guide you. The neophyte is along to aid you, not serve you. There's a difference, young underpriest. Our companions await. We travel Upwards to meet with Priest Kel Tjark, who adheres to the Order of Arkson-la. We hope to be joined by Priest Darby Pitt—"

"Oh, Fadda Kirk, how exciting!" Regeth interrupted, his hand to his breast, and he tucked his chin for a moment. He looked up and grinned. "My sister's father was given guidance by Priest Pitt as a young man, and that's how his travels led to my sister's mother. Priest Pitt is held in high regard by my sister's family."

"And not by you." Quartten's familiar smile began to break though.

"Yes, your eminence, especially by me. I wouldn't be here, otherwise." He looked to Aaeon to find him frowning, and he pulled the devotional pouch to his chest, snatched up the tunic, and exited the small room.

"Priest Pitt worships Neil-fa?" Aaeon smoothed the bedclothes in hopes it would reflect well on him in Quartten's eyes. His fortunes had gone topsy-turvy since the underpriestess exited, and he hoped to put himself in a better light.

Quartten cleared his throat, motioning for the youth to join him in the main room. "You're aware, then?"

As they exited, Aaeon shrugged, commenting, "Under-priestess Bethl said her superior advised us to contact clerics from both Arkson-la and Neil-fa. You said Priest Tjark is from Arkson Home, so Priest Pitt must be from Neil Home."

"You encourage me." Quartten chuckled. "I thought we'd lost you in there, maybe your head got scrambled in your sojourn with the gods."

"Your eminence?" Aaeon swam in his confusion. "I . . . you censured me in front of my friend. Now I encourage you? I don't get it."

"The neophyte is still your friend? Another encouraging sign." They approached the bishop and the priestess. Both were

240

suited to exit the building, though both had their hoods around their shoulders. Regeth stood to the side by his and Aaeon's packs, holding Aaeon's tunic for him.

"Certainly, he is. Is there something I'm not aware of?" Aaeon looked to see Regeth grinning at him.

Quartten stopped the youth and looked him in the face, holding his attention with his eyes. "Only your carelessness."

Aaeon dropped his eyes. He got it, and he mumbled, "My apologies, your excellency."

"Tell your friend that and treat him like one. He waits for you. Don your tunic. We have quite a journey today."

The priest clapped the underpriest firmly on the shoulder, and he sent him on his way. Quartten joined the bishop and the priestess, greeting them loudly, and telling them their charge had healed nicely and could withstand the rigors of a long and strenuous day. Aaeon didn't know that he was prepared to withstand long and strenuous rigors. He blew out his cheeks and headed to Regeth.

"I'm sorry, my friend." He held out his hand, and still smiling, Regeth placed his tunic in it. Taking it in one arm, Aaeon pulled his friend to him and punched him on the shoulder, saying, "Ready for an adventure?"

"I am, sir. What should I do now?"

"Sir?" Aaeon glanced at the other three to find Quartten looking his direction. The priest nodded at him, and Aaeon broke into a smile. He wrapped his arm around his friend's neck and began to rub his knuckles hard in his hair, teasing, "Sir? I'm sir, now? What happened to Aaeon? Did you forget who I am? I'll make you remember so much you'll never forget."

The younger boy was beside himself with laughter by then, and he called out, "No, no! Stop, Aaeon. I haven't forgotten who you are."

The roughhousing seemed to lighten the mood of the entire group. Quartten patted Aaeon on the shoulder, clicking his cheek

241

at him in approval. Priestess Burne smiled, more beautiful than ever as she pulled her hood over her tattooed scalp. One could never be quite certain about Bishop Ziggurat, but as he shouldered a small pack, he watched the two young trainees tug on two packs each, sharing the load evenly.

He did study the sky carefully through the glass walls before they exited the spacious chamber. The sky loomed over them, leering, as if it waited for only one thing: five small tidbits it could snatch away as an easy meal.

Book of the Gods

Roshanna, Chapter 1:20-22

FADDA ELDON ARKSON-LA is the Patron of Dreams, for in a former life, he watched over the Lesser Five Thousand who slept as they traveled among the stars. He is an inner god, rather than an outer god, and for that reason he can never meet in the heavens with Shosu Poll-fa, for they are forever separated by nature, by nurture, and by desire.

WE KEEP STATUES of Fadda Arkson-la near our hearths to remind us of the importance of each individual; we rub Fadda Arkson-la's round stomach, for each person deserves a life filled with goodness; and we kiss Fadda Arkson-la's bald head to remind us to think before we speak, for wisdom comes from words not spoken, just as from those we let escape from our lips.

THE FOLLOWERS OF Fadda Eldon Arkson-la are called El Arkson-faitum, or the followers of Fadda Eldon Arkson-la. Selah.

A Dream by Any Other Name

Bishop Ziggurat hired one of the clanking, spitting steam conveyances Aaeon had seen when first arriving in Gates. Theirs boasted a massive engine topped with a silvery water tank, held up by trusses of filigreed metal worked with brass designs of the Order of Vitson. The seating compartment was an open framework with padded benches, and the passengers were shaded from the intensity of the storm wall's radiant heat by brightly hued fabric stretched over a lightweight frame. As the vehicle's engine began to roar, and gurgling steam set the pistons clattering, the wheels started to turn, and the canvas flexed and popped, making conversation difficult.

The overly bright, stationary streetlamps on their worked metal stands made the red-threaded sky darken into a semblance of true night, and they cast rippling shadows across the steam cart's passengers as they traveled.

The clerics and their charges kept their tunics and hoods closely fastened, as their cart rode high off the ground, and they had no wish to broadcast their urgent mission to those who walked the streets. Gates held its share of devout believers, but some claimed truth came only from the mechanisms men could create and not from the gods who claimed to have created men.

In addition, there were reports of dark-robed visitors from the one precipice that was only whispered of, Xibalba, the home of the dark gods, where the shades roamed free to do as they pleased. The wicum, or followers, of the shade Kella Aseem Dullah-um were known to strike down the unwary in the dark of the night.

Even so, the danger of traveling through the city wasn't extreme, although putting oneself on a pedestal and appearing free with coin—and the steam cart was expensive—could irritate those with already-thin skins. It was wise to appear contrite when traveling among those who might try to abuse them of their perceived wealth.

"If I may be so free as to ask, your excellency—" Aaeon leaned forward, resting his elbows on his knees, and spoke to Priestess Burne. "Something very dramatic happened when you conjured the haze curtain, although I've lost much of what occurred." He noticed her eyes closed in prayer, and he shrugged and smiled as if to laugh it off.

It bothered him, however, and he hoped the kind priestess would provide him a sincere answer, not the bland platitudes from his days lying in the bed being nursed by others. The cart bumped an uneven place in the road, and everyone on board jerked sideways. The priestess' eyes came open, and Aaeon held to one of the roof supports as his tunic jostled around him. His devotional pouch fell to the floor, and he bent to pick it up.

"Wouldn't walking be better?" In frustration, he put the question to Quartten.

"Better, perhaps. Quicker, no. Another half-kilometer and we're there. Be patient, my impatient charge." Quartten nodded to him and returned to a hand game with Regeth, one that involved a covered container and a small stone.

"He thinks of you as a child." Burne smiled at Aaeon. Her mouth was wide, and her teeth glistened. "I think you're more."

"More?" Aaeon felt himself break into a grin, unable to stop it. Of course, he was more, and it excited him that she noticed.

"To respond to your inquiry, I didn't summon a curtain. I am a mere priestess of the weather, may Hoda-fa be praised. My Order is a very important one, to be certain, but to summon haze curtains? Not even I, or perhaps it would be more accurate to say, especially not I, can summon the time vortexes to do my bidding."

"Yet, you waved your hand, and it was there." He knew what he'd seen. The cart jostled again, jerking roughly up and down. Aaeon let out a "Humph!" and the driver called out, "Fadda Vitson isn't with us tonight. My machine is cursed." The driver hit the rear of the water tank and cried, "Where is Fadda Vitson when we need him?"

"From your lips to Fadda Vitson's ears," Bishop Ziggurat murmured, his hand very briefly making contact with his breast-bone. "We are fine. Drive on."

"Certainly, your eminence." The man ducked his head in chagrin at the bishop's soft rebuke. "My apologies, your graciousness."

Aaeon nodded to the priestess and said, "Mine to you, also. I cried out rudely."

She returned his nod in acceptance of his apology, and she began to share. "I lifted my hand, and you saw what you were sup-posed to see—"

"That's right, the haze curtain. Everyone saw it."

She held up her hand. "Nay, patience. Not all, just you."

"But . . . it was there. You held your hand in the air—" and he held out his to mimic her motions at the table, "—and it just appeared." His eyes caught Bishop Ziggurat's and saw clarity in them. The bishop worked his face, adjusting the vicweed that lined his gums. He knew the truth, and it wasn't the one in Aaeon's words. Aaeon jostled Regeth's arm to get his attention and pleaded with him, "You saw the haze curtain, right?"

"Haze curtain?" He glanced to the priest who held the game

pieces in his hands.

"At the table, the first day." Aaeon felt desperation crawl over him as though he was about to tip over the edge of a dark crevasse. "Remember, the priestess? She held up her hand, and I fell into the curtain."

Regeth grinned. "You fell, yes, from your chair to the floor." He shrugged. "It had to have been. You disappeared from your seat, and a few moments later, we heard a thump, and we found you lying down. You were mumbling about the gods and were injured, so we knew you'd been with them. The priestess said so."

"But I was pulled into the haze curtain . . ." They all turned compassionate eyes his direction, and he felt his face burn. Overhead, the cloth popped, and the cart's framework creaked as it worked its way over the uneven ground. The engine was a roaring demon, and even the people walking alongside screamed for his attention.

"It's okay, Aaeon. If you saw it . . ." Regeth shrugged again, giving in to his friend.

The cart turned up a deserted street and stopped, and the engine let off a tower of white steam. The driver called for his fare, and the bishop opened a small bag and handed over several coins.

There were fewer streetlights here, and the red lightning glowed vividly in the sky, bringing the storm wall especially close. They were at a stone archway leading to a building carved from the hillside, and the reddish light caught on a crenellated roofline. Away from the single glow globe mounted a dozen meters away, the ground and buildings shimmered with the energy soaked up from the storm wall in the way a moonlit night might shower a landscape with a soft coat of effervescent snow.

Two windows in the building pulsed with light, as if brightened by glow globes, and one darkened as the light moved to another window.

"It seems Tjark has arrived. Two are within the walls."

Ziggurat stood, adjusted his cloak, and made his way down the steps to stand at the archway, waiting expectantly.

"And that Pitt has welcomed him inside." Quartten chuckled.

"I wouldn't say that. Kirk might strike me dead." Ziggurat laughed, and surprisingly, it was warm and filled with honey. He spat a wad of vicweed juice to the ground at his feet. "Let it suffice to say he allowed him in."

"Speak only kindness, sirs. Shosu Hoda-fa favors us this day, and the storm wall remains at bay." Burne bowed her head with her hand to her breast in a silent prayer. When she raised her head, she took Aaeon's hand and pulled him to his feet. "We'll discuss more about the curtain when we are with our advisors."

"Dreams and directions," Aaeon muttered, naming the two Orders to which the unknown men adhered.

He felt empty, as if the world had moved around him, and he hadn't been there to see it. He stepped after Burne to find Regeth had already disembarked and was collecting their packs on the curb. The house door had opened, and several sconces deep within were lighted by flickers of flame. Closer, the barest outline of a glow globe floated behind a man, shadowing the person, and making him into a figure of darkness deeper than the sky overhead.

Behind them, the empty cart's engine clattered and surged, heated water gurgled, and the pistons began to shake and spin into action. The machine's wheels ground against the stones on the street, and within moments it was gone, leaving a damp and unexpected silence in the air.

A fresh capillary of lightning twisted across the sky, revealing the heavens as no more than a bloodshot eye growing more tired by the hour. To the side, another and another crawled through the cloud-banked vistas, leaving a permanent stain that would never fade, for they never died. A distant crackle followed, and a second and a third, then the world stilled to silence once again.

Aaeon watched for a moment, seeing and hearing no others. The additional heat they shed was noticeable, and he wanted inside. The silence followed him to the door. This street was empty of people, save a couple in matching pantaloons and puffy-sleeved jackets on the far side. They laughed and held each other arm in arm as if ignorant of anything else in the world. Aaeon thought of Mene. He'd felt that way with her when they were alone on the Upward point of the precipice, but it seemed a very long time ago. He turned to follow the others up the steps, and when he passed through the door only a quarter meter from their host, he still had no idea what he looked like. Inside his hood, he was black as black, as though darkness had stolen his face and left him an empty vessel ready to absorb the secrets of the night.

Aaeon shivered, the itchy fabric of the neutrino filament cloth around his neck digging in and sending a cold chill down his spine.

Staring Into the Rabbit Hole

For four thumps of the chalk, silence reigned in the darkened foyer. The space was barely lighted—and close—as the ceiling wasn't high enough to fully admit the glow globe, and it hovered up a broad set of three steps.

Cloth rustled, and packs and tunics found their way to benches and pegs. Even Aaeon's devotional pouch made its way to a shelf along one wall. They were left in their undertunics and loose trousers, except for Priestess Burne, who retained her tunic with its yellow lining. Her hood still covered her head, and she moved up the steps ahead of the others, warmly greeting someone Aaeon couldn't see.

The man who had stood at the door, whom the three clerics seemed to know by sight, let his outer tunic fall away, and Aaeon couldn't tell where his undertunic stopped and his skin began. The undertunic soaked up the light, becoming a whirlpool of nothingness that disappeared from the eyes. Looking higher, Aaeon saw that the darkness hadn't stolen his face. It *was* his face. From head to toe, his skin was painted with midnight, even his eyes. The light from the glow globes and the burning sconces struggled to find him.

It was when he noticed the man's clothes were of powdered anthracite that the young underpriest understood that he could be none other than Priest Kel Tjark, adherent to Fadda Arkson-la, the Patron of Dreams. The charged matrix in which the ground-up anthracite was suspended insulated him from the electrical impulses of others' bodies, enabling his dreams to flow across his synapses without interruption. Only the Dreamers were allowed license, for the manufacture of the suspensor field generators that powered the anthracite fabric was a proprietary secret belonging to El Vitson-faitum.

The exchange between precipices was one of necessity, for to build the machines, one had to dream the machines, and dreams only came through Fadda Arkson-la. Those who rose in the clergy of the Dreamers were sensitives who needed special protection from the raging skies, even more now that the lightning in the storm wall had begun to burn so strongly. The followers of Fadda Vitson-la had risen to the task, and an alliance had been formed.

Aaeon also understood why Priestess Burne had retained her tunic and its hood. The holotats that crowned her head weren't put there simply for appearance. They imbued her words, her actions, and even her predictions with power. They *interacted* with the world around them, and in that interaction, the world was changed. It dawned on him that they were likely part of the cause for his recent trip into the haze. He just now recalled she'd been weaving her hands in the air, and her holotats had *glowed*. He was determined to find out more. The priestess had said they would speak later, and now, he was certain they would.

Upon entering the main salon, he found his companions grouped and already in conversation. The two glow globes were overwhelmed with the number of people, and they couldn't pick a location, jumping and bumping against the ceiling, and causing shifting light and odd shadows. The flickering of the sconces was worse, and their light struggled to fill in the areas just underneath them. A broad, finely woven carpet, heavily trafficked and worn on one side, swept across the floor. The stone and timber walls were plastered and heavily textured; and a massive rock fireplace had a small blaze slinking in one corner with barely enough flame to warm a rock hornet. Smoke escaped the edges of the flue, seeping into the room and covering the ceiling, which was low and filled with rows of darkened beams.

What furniture there was seemed to grow out of the walls. A stair led to an upper floor, but the landing was dark and Aaeon could see nothing beyond a curtained window that looked as though it was never opened. To one side, Tjark, the Dreamer, smoothed oil over his exposed skin, revealing twisting designs etched into his flesh. They seemed to jump in the reflections of the flames.

The second surprise of the visit was Priest Darby Pitt. As a cleric of Fadda Neil-fa, the Patron of Directions, Aaeon had expected someone youthful, a traveler, an explorer of intrepid stamina. Not so. He was *ancient* and morbidly obese.

Aaeon chided himself. Regeth had shared that the priest had counseled his father before he met his mother. Of course, he would be old beyond years. Yet, he was disappointed. The man was a near-cripple and confined to a Curtain Chair, with thick rolls of flesh billowing from under layers of fabric and a bald head, except for a wisp of white just above his fleshy neck. Surely he couldn't be lifted except by three or four strong men. If the power in his Chair were to fade, it would be impossible to assist him.

"Ah, this must be the boy!" Priest Pitt called to Aaeon, lifting one fleshy hand and swinging it in an arc through the air. His voice belied his appearance, leaving Aaeon surprised. It was soft and welcoming. "By the footsteps of Neil, you didn't tell me he'd be so *virile*. He's a strapping lad. How old are you, boy?"

Aaeon hesitated, searching the other faces for direction. He tried to find his voice and couldn't. Warm and welcoming or not, he was used to priests who, if not youthful, at least maneuvered through life with a certain amount of *flair* and a great deal of mobility.

"Traveler?" Priestess Burne's singsong voice called to him from within her yellow-lined hood. "Now's your time to greet the master. With Priest Pitt's assistance, we may well return our friend Ken to his *when* before many more days pass. Come."

"Yes, come. I would greet you in the name of Fadda Neil." Pitt's massive hand toggled a control on his chair, and with a whir, it lifted a few centimeters from the floor and floated Aaeon's direction. The others deferred to the moribund priest, murmured soliloquies of obsequious platitudes, and moved out of the way before returning to their conversations.

"Your eminence." Aaeon placed his hand at his throat and bowed deeply, even falling to one knee. He was reminded of his audience with Bishop Doitsey. He thought to look for this man's slippers of woven photons, yet to lift his eyes was to add insolence to insult.

"Nay, child. Rise." The priestess cupped Aaeon's elbow in her hand and lifted him to his feet, although his gaze remained down.

"Shel is right, boy." Pitt's gentle voice warmed his soft rebuke. "You are what, seventeen, eighteen crackles? Surely not more. With my news of you, I expected a greybeard, an old warrior of many travels and perhaps a widening girth."

"A widening girth?" Aaeon repeated the phrase, his eyes leaping to the priest's face. Was he *teasing* him? Perhaps he'd expected someone of Priest Tjark's experience, for he was scrounged with scars. Aaeon cringed to admit his youth disappointed the man.

"Yes, widening girth!" Pitt patted the mounded flesh that filled the chair in front of him. "Am I a warrior? If I judge by my girth, of the most prodigious sort." He laughed heartily.

"Sixteen, sir, almost seventeen." Aaeon whispered his answer, hoping it would be overlooked and not asked again. He was embarrassed he hadn't lived up to the priest's expectations. He couldn't fix it, either, just because this man expected it.

"Say it again?" Pitt put his hand to his ear and called loudly. "Sixteen crackles, you say?"

"My seventeenth bud has already started."

Priestess Burne fought a smile. The priest constructed of the fabric of night was to one side in discussion with Priest Quartten and Bishop Ziggurat, and the three stood under one of the flaming sconces. Priest Tjark caught Aaeon's eyes. His blackness was fearsome, and his skin shimmered under the flickering fire. The raised-flesh tattoos under their coating of oil seemed to crawl over his skin, giving them a life of their own. Whelps of bruised and torn flesh, healed in great lumps of skin, lashed his face with reminders of battles long over. He was enough to make an honest bishop quake, and Aaeon wanted to be this man. He wanted his strength and his somber disdain for what was around him. He wanted to not care what Priest Pitt thought of him. He wanted to return to Haukberk and spend a light-hearted day Upwards on the precipice with his Mene.

"The *almost* is important, is it? I thought so. Come, boy, and you, Shel. I wish some peace." Pitt touched the arm of his chair, and he floated off to the side and up several steps through two heavily carved columns.

They traversed a short passageway lined with display niches and a low ceiling before coming to a room swelling with books, chairs, and a large desk. A small oil sconce simpered sullenly, giving off a thin stream of smoke. The priest's massive chair traversed to the far side of the desk, slotting itself into a recess just its size, and with a practiced hand, he tossed a lightning stick to Burne, who struck it, flaring its small flame into existence. She touched it to two open-topped braziers on the desk. Flame leaped, and the lighting improved considerably in the room.

Aaeon dropped to one knee, bowing his head in shame. "May Kirk grant me forgiveness. I apologize for disappointing you,

255

eminent one. If I had known an older adherent was desired, I would never—" He was jarred from his self-abasing speech when Pitt's massive fist thumped his table, causing the young underpriest to jump.

"I see your education is lacking." The man's words held laughter, not contempt. "It's surely Shel's fault. Eh? Is that so, Priestess Burne?"

"From your lips to Hoda-fa's ears and back again." Burne nodded her head slightly, but not enough to be called a bow, and her hand barely touched her breastbone.

"Come now, Shel," the priest called. "Old Tjark isn't here. Throw back your hood and let me see those wonderful toos."

As she lowered her hood with a smile on her face, Aaeon took in the interaction between them. They seemed to be close in some manner, yet the priestess was still youthful and beautiful. Master and protégée? They were of different Orders, so he didn't consider that possible. Lovers? By the gods, he hoped not.

"You really haven't told him, have you?" Pitt's easy temperament hardened, and he looked sternly at the woman.

"Truth is in the timing." She smiled, not put off by Pitt's question. "There have been interruptions, none of which I could avoid."

The walls trembled around them, and the priest and priestess looked upward at the ceiling. Minor amounts of dust floated from the beams overhead.

"This place is secure, or as much as any other." Pitt rapped his desktop, the meaty knuckles softening the sound. He looked at Aaeon. "You, my boy, are our hope, and Tjark and I are the ones who will guide you, with Shel's assistance. Nothing happens without Shel. I gather you've already learned that."

"I've learned nothing, eminence." Aaeon dropped his eyes.

"Nah, don't be bashful. You're as arrogant as I was at sixteen. I tried to hide it, also, but everyone could tell. Anyone who can ride the haze curtains *and at will,*" he coughed, "well, that's a man we can use."

"Use for what?" Aaeon was as confused as he'd ever been. Ride the haze curtains?

"Tell him, Shel." Pitt rapped his desk again. "He needs to know before this goes any further."

"Aaeon," and Burne faced him, bowing her head gently, then looking him in the eyes, "you have misunderstood the nature of the haze curtains. All your life you've traversed the time anomalies, never realizing the true nature of who you are. You've never found a haze curtain—"

"I have!" He refused to be mocked, even here, especially in the presence of two clerics of high standing. He wouldn't allow it.

"Nay," and she held up one hand. "Listen for a moment. I only realized the truth of this when you fell into the realm of the gods. You saw the haze curtain appear when none of us did. The truth is, you don't find your haze curtains. The curtains find you."

"They . . . find *me*?" Aaeon was so stunned he couldn't speak.

Priest Pitt laughed and called to Burne, "Enjoy the silence now, Shel. It's probably the last moment of peace we'll have from him until all this is done."

257

Book of the Gods

Roshanna, Chapter 1:26-29

FADDA JA KIRK-FA is a greater god. The Patron of Fire and Passion, he embodies the male passion, and we pray to him before we take a woman. We do this because Fadda Ja Kirk-fa fell to the ten precipices embraced in the arms of Shosu Wen Hoda-fa.

SHOSU HODA-FA tried to protect Fadda Kirk-fa, but she is only the wind, and Fadda Kirk-fa was too heavy for her to hold. Fadda Kirk-fa burned as he fell, so he was made a greater god.

FADDA KIRK-FA and Shosu Hoda-fa still love one another, and it is the reason a flame burns hotter when the wind sweeps down from the mountain, and it is the reason a bonfire will create a whirlwind that tries to lift the flame into the sky. Wind and fire are trying to reunite once more, but Fadda Kirk-fa fell to the ground long ago, and they can never be reunited again.

THE FOLLOWERS of Fadda Kirk-fa are known as El Kirk-faitum, or the followers of Fadda Ja Kirk-fa. Selah.

The Flick of a Switch

Underpriest Aaeon Hibolah was sequestered, together with Priests Pitt and Tjark, as well as Priestess Burne.

Pitt's home was strategically positioned on Gates Precipice, allowing him direct access to a vast network of underground caverns. The window on the stair landing, which hadn't seemed to be a window, was indeed not a window. It was a wooden door as wide as two normal doors and two times the height.

Iron hooks the size of a man's foot held a beam across its girth. Once it was removed and standing alongside, a tarnished brass latch was undone and hefted out of the way. When the door swung wide—after much effort from Aaeon and Tjark's strong shoulders—it proved itself to be two hand-widths thick, nearing a third of a meter.

Aaeon wondered as he daily passed through the opening what it was designed to keep out, or perversely, keep in.

He sat up on his sleeping mat. The world was black, with no lightning-littered sky overhead or phosphorescent ground under his feet. He wasn't happy. Angry? Maybe. Irritated, for certain, and perhaps a bit frightened.

Well, he'd admit, a lot frightened. And frightened made him touchy. He couldn't get the priestess' words out of his head. *The haze curtains found him.* He'd begun to look around every corner before stepping past and into every doorway before moving through. He dreaded waking in the dark, and he wondered if he'd wind up like Priest Quartten, a man out of his time and unable to return home.

He also thought about Mene—a lot—and how she'd feel if he never returned home, or at least never returned *when.* What would Regeth tell her? That he'd been *eaten?* That he'd *vanished* into thin air? That Aaeon had been there one moment and gone the next? Would he even know?

No one had been able to see the haze curtain above the priestess' head in Neil's Eye. Only him. Would they think he'd abandoned the quest to infiltrate the time vortexes and return the future cardinal to his own *when?* How would they know, if the haze curtains simply sought him out and *took* him?

The four living together in the caverns had shared meals, times of new and awkwardly worded joint prayers, and many hours of silent contemplation. Priest Tjark had laid out weapons, shown Aaeon how to use them, and then refused to let him touch a one. The priestess seemed to delve into his psyche, drawing out his past and revealing nothing of herself. Priest Pitt often watched from his floating chair, sometimes with a smile on his face, giving little more than pithy remarks at opportune times. More than once, a simple task Aaeon was given turned out to be rigged and impossible to complete, bringing a smile to the old cleric's broad face. Aaeon had practiced controlling his thoughts and emotions, though not always successfully. He was certain Pitt was playing jokes on him to teach him something, but he wasn't sure what he was being trained for.

It was the first time in his life to spend more than a few hours without some reminder of the magnificent complexity of the world in which he lived, even if he was only recently aware that his existence on Haukberk had been pastoral and backward compared to that on Gates . . . and they were only one Crevasse apart. He stood and called to the glow globe that hovered somewhere overhead.

"Hey, I'm up." When the room remained dark, he groaned and intoned, "All thanks to Fadda Kirk-fa, from whom all passions flow."

The light winked on, slowly at first, then gradually growing brighter. This one had been linked to him and instructed to follow him through the caverns, lighting his way and keeping him from getting lost. It wouldn't go into places that were off limits to him or dangerous, and in the blackness, he would be forced to turn around. He'd decided Pitt had programmed it to require the religious phrase to turn itself on and off just to amuse himself. He'd turned out to be a prankster, leaving Aaeon in constant fear of which practical joke would next bring the day crashing in on him.

He heard the whirring of Pitt's chair, and he turned to see the priest float through an opening roughly cut in the chamber wall. Aaeon adjusted his lightweight sleeping gown. His full set of clothes was folded neatly on a large round cushion used as seating.

"How did you sleep, my boy?" Pitt asked the question as if he sincerely wanted to know. His chair whirred louder, and he slipped across the open space faster. A second globe followed him, helping brighten the room but only making partial progress. The blackness overhead was Priest Tjark's fist, and it soaked up radiance like a leach loves blood.

"Fadda Kirk-fa guarded my dreams throughout the night. Praise be to Kirk-fa." He nodded his head in a minimal bow and touched his palm to his chest. He was too sleepy to do more. He hadn't rested well, and his dreams, nay, his *nightmares* had been of haze curtains eating the walls of the cavern and spitting them out into other *whens*, both future and past, that he could hardly comprehend.

"You may speak freely with me. I'm your guide, not your

263

guard. I see the circles under your eyes, and they've grown worse for three nights. Tell me what bothers you." Pitt rested his thick arms on his broad, blanket-covered girth. Realizing the man didn't intend quick action, the chair slowly dropped to rest against the floor.

"You truly wish to know?" The old man might prank him, but he spoke kindly, also. He also kept the secrets Aaeon shared, at least those he'd drawn from him. At the priest's nod, he let his words fall from him in a torrent. "I miss my friend. Why can't Regeth join me? Then at least I'd have someone to talk with. And Priest Tjark says nothing good about me. Half the time, I can't see him in the darkness, and he's so silent he could be a shade—"

"Respect, boy." Pitt held up one finger in warning. He fought a smile. "Be careful with your words but continue."

"Okay, not a shade, but his tattoos. They're never in the same place twice." Aaeon shivered. "Would it hurt him to say one nice thing about me?"

"Has he criticized you?" Pitt's face was neutral, as was his voice.

"No, I guess not. He says nothing, mostly."

"If he disapproves of your progress, you'll know." The priest did smile at that. "Consider yourself praised in his lack of criticism. Anyone else?" His smile broadened. There were only two other people in the caverns, and Pitt was one of them.

"I . . . um, I guess not." He wanted to say that the priestess, as soft-spoken and beautiful as she was, seemed too oddly intimate with Pitt; and that he understood why she must remain robed in her outer tunic with her hood raised when around Priest Tjark, but it made him feel like she was hiding from him.

"About me? Surely you must have something about me you find irritating."

Aaeon jerked his eyes to Pitt's face, expecting to find an accusing stare. The man was smiling, and in that moment, Aaeon was certain he could see the man as he used to be, not exactly youthful—he doubted he'd ever see *youth* in the old priest's face—but finely boned under all the layers of excess and age. He knew that smile, and his stomach jerked. He thought of Quartten, a younger version of His Primate Cardinal Ne' Kirk-fait IX, who'd been stolen from a distant *when* and dropped into this *when*. Then he realized he'd been stupid. Quartten couldn't have been the first. There must be others, there must be.

"You see what you've not been told. My confidence grows in you daily." Pitt nodded his head in an approving manner. "Now, tell me. What do you see?"

"Priestess Burne's smile in your face." The implications chilled Aaeon, washing nightmares over him. It had happened to this man. He was proof of Aaeon's worst fears.

"And?" Pitt prompted him to continue.

Priest Tjark appeared behind the crippled cleric, silently listening as if he'd been there all along. Aaeon blinked twice, trying to think what he'd overheard. He concentrated on Pitt's question and said the only thing that made any sense. "You couldn't return, either, could you?" *Like Quartten,* but he didn't say that. He didn't need to.

"Ha!" Pitt laughed out loud, and he touched the arm of his chair and turned it just enough to be able to see Tjark. "Now? You see? He's ready." In his excitement, his words caught a melodic lilt and held it for a moment.

"He sees it all?" The man's words rumbled his doubt as the etchings on his skin rippled in the globes' half-eaten light.

"Eh? Underpriest Hibolak?" Pitt goaded Aaeon with bright and anticipatory laughter, and the sound rang against the distant walls.

"Great Kirk, I'm tired of this. You torture me with your half-spoken suggestions, both of you." Aaeon felt his eyes burn. Thoughts poured into his head, epiphanies of upwelling magnitude, and he spat them in a torrent. "She's your sister, isn't she, except not really. The priestess you knew is already old, caught in a *when* you can't return to. Or," and it dawned on him, "you don't want to return, do you? You've achieved a sort of immortality. You *manipulated* the curtains to trade places, so the *young* you could have a fresh start. That's what you want for Priest Quartten, isn't it? Send the cardinal off so his younger self can take his place? Did the cardinal not want to uphold his end of the bargain? If you can do this, why do you need me?" He fell to his mat and dropped his head, pulling his arms over his face, too distraught to comprehend his new revelation. "I want to go home."

"Aaeon?" It was the priestess' soft, singsong voice. She was at his side, kneeling in front of him, and she took his hands, pulling them from his face. "Will you look at me?"

"Why?" Yet, he raised his eyes. Within her yellow-lined hood, her face, so beautiful, now reminded him of Pitt's. He saw what he'd missed all along. "You're part of it. I can't believe you're part of it." He was appalled to feel the warmth of tears streaming down his cheeks.

"Yes, I am a part of it. Do you want to know what the 'it' is?" She smiled.

"What?" He pulled his hands free and wiped at his face. "I mean, yes. I'm trapped in here and can't get away, so I might as well know."

"Not trapped—" Priest Pitt's denial was interrupted by Burne's upraised hand.

"As my *twin* says, not trapped. All this," and she indicated the caverns with a look of her eyes, "is for your protection. There've been, shall we say, disagreements in the streets. Some nonbelievers feel the clergy saps energy that would be better fuel for science. We disagree. You've lived your life on Haukberk, where the Temple still reigns supreme. The rest of us fight a losing battle."

"Not losing," Tjark's deep voice intoned.

"See, Shel? I told you Kel would come around. He's finally on the wagon. Give him food and a place to rest his etched skin,

266

and there's no end to what we can achieve together."

"Do not bait me, old man." Priest Tjark's voice dropped an octave. His expression didn't change, but his meaning was very clear. "Explain your purpose to the boy."

"I'm not a boy," Aaeon mumbled, unsure and uncaring if anyone heard.

"You've seen the skies." Burne settled at his side, taking one of his hands and holding it gently in hers. "They grow red with the energy leaking from the cracks in the clouds. Even now, we hardly go out uncovered when the storm wall approaches. My brother can tell you that in his when, it's worse. You see him as crippled. The truth is much more. The angry skies cursed him with boils that ate his legs. The twin I knew—" and she put her balled fist to her chest, with two fingers extended, "—took this one's place forewarned. Priest Pitt has little time left to live, and his work in the other when couldn't be left undone."

"Your brother went forward first, then his older self returned?" Aaeon pictured Quartten. Could it be a similar situation, and that the cardinal had reneged? It surprised him this twisted ruse had already been consummated once before, and by people he knew. He felt a gullible fool to have fallen for the man's game. "You don't want to return Priest Quartten to his when after all, do you?"

"Yes, to your first question, after learning all his older self knew. To the second question, we do want to return Quartten, just not the one you know. Let me explain. The cardinal is pivotal to my brother's success in saving our world. Yet, the current cardinal—an older version of our friend Quartten—is very near death. He must not be allowed to die in office, or my brother's sacrifice will be pointless. Does this make any sense to you?"

"No." Aaeon's head swam with the implications. "Let the cardinal die and Quartten can take his place."

"And there's our predicament." Priest Tjark strode forward, a shadow moving among the shadows, with only the glimmer of his oiled-and-etched skin revealing his presence. "One Quartten has to be in that *when* for this one to survive. You've been told this, only holding back that the elder of the two needs to give up his hold on this *when*."

"Or our world ends." Aaeon *knew*, for it was written in his mind, but he couldn't *believe* his world was about to come crashing to a stop. What were a few more crackles in the sky? It was what *happened*. It was how life was measured. His seventeenth crackle had just budded. He wanted to be seventeen, and eighteen, and with Mene. He didn't want it to simply be *over*.

"Not today, and perhaps not in your lifetime, but certainly in your son or your daughter's lifetime. That's who we're saving, if we can. We must try." Burne's voice pleaded, the lilting tones crying tears of desperation.

"I gave up my life, boy." Pitt said the words forcefully and convincingly. He murmured his next words. "Or my other me did, anyway."

"But why me? If it's not happening now, why can't I go home?" *And be with Mene?* He was emotionally exhausted, and he didn't want to decide to save the world. He couldn't save it, not if these people couldn't.

"And the boy seeps out again," Tjark murmured, stepping away and turning his back. He disappeared into the shadows, and only his carven tattoos revealed his presence.

"Patience," Burne cautioned the man. To Aaeon, she said more softly, "When Underpriestess Bethl sent her request for aid, we arranged for my brother and Priest Tjark to be recommended. We three, together, are adept. We can do what we ask of you. We *could* do what we ask of you. My true twin could." Her voice broke for a moment, and her face twisted before she cleared her expression and went on. "Priest Pitt's legs weren't just disfigured by his boils. They were eaten away altogether. Without them, he cannot achieve what we need of him."

The priest leaned forward to pull his blankets up to reveal two fleshy stumps that ended just below the knees. He dropped the cloth and chuckled, calling in a good humor, "So, my boy, you must join us. So that all isn't lost, eh?"

"But what can I do?" Aaeon was consumed by his question.

"You, alone, can do what it takes three of us to do." Burne caught his chin with one finger, and she looked him in the face.

"You can get on board." Tjark still faced into the darkness.

"You can save the world." Pitt encouraged, with a pleading tone.

"Can I ask Regeth," and Aaeon pulled up the front of his sleeper to drag the cloth across his eyes, "if he wants to come with me?"

"That's the spirit!" Pitt tossed an arm into the air, calling out, "Quartten, Ziggurat, get in here, and bring that youth with you. We've got some timelines to untangle, and the boy gets the crash course."

Aaeon smiled. He hoped one thing, that Regeth didn't take as much convincing as he had. He didn't know if he had the energy, and he didn't want to have to send him home. His good friend needed to be at his side if he was going to survive.

If he was going to survive. He didn't want to think about that, and he didn't think it would be smart to tell Regeth. His friend might abandon him for sure, if he learned that.

Book of the Gods

*F*ADDA RAN CHAR-LA *is a lesser god, for his youth keeps him from being a greater god. Even so, Shosu Poll-fa, the queen of the gods, was entertained by Fadda Ran Char-la, and that's why we honor Fadda Char-la as our Patron of Music and Dance. It is he who sings to us through the instruments we play and the words we voice in song.*

*T*HE FOLLOWERS OF *Fadda Ran Char-la are known as El Char-faitum. Selah.*

The Flip Side Flips

"This way!"

The pack on Regeth's back jostled wildly as he leaped from one moss-covered stone to another. Form-fitting clothes of durable fabric, unlike the hooded tunics he'd worn as a neophyte, suited haze travel. A waterfall tumbled overhead, sending spray washing the sky. The day was bright—surprisingly so—and the view was clear for kilometers. Looking to see if Aaeon followed, he slipped on the moss, and one foot landed in a pocket of water.

Aaeon caught up with him, leaping past and slapping an open palm against his friend's head. He was dressed in similar clothing with sturdy shoes. He carried his pack in one hand, dragging it through the underbrush with him. They had irritated a rock hornet, stirring its anger.

He called, "It's going to catch you!"

Aaeon darted around a tree and tumbled down a grassy slope. At the bottom, he turned to search the foliage for his friend. It was their tenth time through the haze curtains as a team, and the first so far back. In this *when,* the sky was a pale wash of gray, and the bloodshot spiderwebs that crisscrossed the sky formed little more than faint impressions of a future that hadn't yet arrived.

Regeth burst through, scattering greenery through the air, with both arms in front of him. Having zigged where Aaeon had zagged, he skidded to a stop at a steep drop-off. Behind him, the bushes thrashed with the advancing rock hornet. The youth ripped the pack over his head and tossed it down the escarpment. Grabbing a low branch on a thin tree, he bent the slender trunk low, grabbed high in the crown, and leaped over the edge. The trunk of the tree popped several times, then snapped with a loud cracking sound, slamming its passenger against the side of the low cliff.

He held to the tree for a moment, waiting motionless for the broken trunk to give way. He slipped a third of a meter, then a third more. With his feet scrambling, the trunk gave way completely and, using the friction of the broken tree over the lip of the cliff to kill his speed as much as possible, he tumbled, slipping and sliding the rest of the way to the bottom. At the top, the rock hornet stood on the edge of the drop-off and screeched in fury, its long tail whipping the air, and its forearm-size teeth flashing in the light.

"Run," Aaeon yelled, motioning with his arm to his friend. He hiked his pack to his shoulder.

"Wait on me!" Regeth searched frantically for his pack before finding it in a stand of low, flowering shrubs. He yanked it out and scrambled to Aaeon. He panted as he asked, "Did we get it all?"

"Enough." Aaeon patted his pack. At the top of the escarpment, the rock hornet leaned over the edge as far as it felt safe, prodding the soil with a large paw. When the loose dirt crumbled, it jerked back and roared in frustration, sending the youths scrambling behind an outcropping of rocks. They leaned with their backs against the stone, panting. Aaeon grinned. "Are you ready?"

"Never more." Regeth wrapped one arm across Aaeon's shoulder and they leaned in, touching forehead to forehead. The rock hornet screamed. In the distance, foliage thrashed, and

Regeth hissed, "Now, Aaeon."

"Give me a moment." Aaeon concentrated, keeping an image of his friend in his mind, and picturing them back in the caverns underneath Priest Pitt's house. He also pictured their packs. He had to have it all, or something might be left behind.

This was the reason for their journeys, ensuring that Aaeon could return from the time vortexes across the haze curtains with his friend in tow. It did no good if they both made the trip across and Regeth was lost, forever stranded. They'd confined their journeys to the past—thanks to help from Priestess Burne and Priest Tjark—straying only a few months from their *when* at first, then venturing slightly further each time. Aaeon had learned that attracting the haze curtains might be an innate ability, and returning home might be simple for a natural, but controlling it to travel to specific times and places was something else, as much taste and sensation and *feel* as anything else, very much like taking a wrong turn down a lane that looks familiar, and you walk for a time thinking this must be the right path, except it doesn't *feel* right. You may not be able to identify what's off about it, but you know the right path when you return to it.

Aaeon was learning to feel his way around the time vortexes. In his pack were rock samples, hand-drawn maps of the landscape, and watercolors of the sky for the clerics on the other side of the curtain to identify just where and how far they'd gone. If he was correct, they were on Kravitz Precipice, the future home of El Char-faitum, what many considered the happiest of the Five Thousand who'd fallen with the gods. Mene had described her Patron's precipice often enough that he recognized it. Regeth and he had attempted to reach as far back as possible on this trip, but to find no people and just wild rock hornets? Surely, they were near the time of creation. Wouldn't Priest Quartten be surprised? And he'd never seen such a clear sky Surely next time they'd find the gods, themselves, perhaps before the battles in the heavens had decimated their heavenly home, and he could ask how to save their world.

Surely the gods would have the answers Priests Pitt and Tjark required.

The air around them grew thicker, the sky waxed hazy, and the sound of the rock hornet faded to a distant wail. The ground at their feet began to blur. The two youths felt the chill of the haze curtain grow around them. Somewhere overhead, invisible in the solidifying mist, lightning crackled, and the smell of ozone assaulted their nostrils. It *smelled* like they were crossing the time barrier into another *when*. Aaeon concentrated on his image of the caverns and standing inside with their packs. Then a cold wind hit them, and they stumbled, having crossed the barrier, albeit not quite at floor level. The few centimeters of air between their feet and the floor caught them off guard, and Aaeon's knee buckled, sending him crashing into Regeth and nearly bringing them both down.

They had returned to darkness. Sensing Aaeon's presence, the glow globe winked on, giving off a dim glow in the vast space. In the silence, water dripped in the distance, and the sound echoed in an eerily repetitive parody of a near-forgotten dream. The under-priest called, "Brighter!" and when the mechanical lighting system refused to brighten, he sighed and repeated, "All thanks to Fadda Kirk-fa, from whom all passions flow."

The room brightened, revealing a darkened shape off to one side.

"You have what you were sent for?" The low-pitched words seemed to come from all sides in the hard-walled space, not from the darkened shape, which remained immobile.

"We think so." Aaeon dropped his pack, still in adrenalin overload from the chase with the rock hornet, and now he fumbled to separate the two packs.

He'd hoped the old chair-bound priest would be present. He was excited to share what he'd learned, including the adventure of the rock hornet and the clarity of the skies. He was disappointed to find Priest Tjark. If he would only be *nice* once or twice, it would make things smoother, but he was the one that could call the curtains through Fadda Arkson-la. Priest Pitt was the one who determined where the curtains took them, although Aaeon was learning. Pitt would be excited with him, but Tjark would only want the results; and Aaeon's enthusiasm would simply get in his way.

"Bring them with you. We await in the dining hall." The black-skinned priest with his tortured and oiled flesh disappeared into a passageway, the soft whisper of powdered stone shifting within the field of his body-hugging clothing trailing after him into the night. He hadn't even brought a glow globe with him into the caverns.

"Thank Kirk he's gone," Regeth said, laughing softly. "He gives me the willies."

"Shush." Aaeon held out an opened palm, cautioning him. "He'll hear you. He has big ears."

"Yeah," Regeth snickered. "Big black ones."

"Careful now," Aaeon cautioned.

As he dropped to one knee, the single glow globe sensed his action and mimicked him, lighting the space just around him. He untied the packs to go through them and sort their things. This trip, they had three types of stones, those from atop the soil, dug from within, and broken from a sheared upthrust of fractured rock. Each was likely to tell a different story, indicating the *when* they had visited. Aaeon sorted the maps and drawings. Small markings on the maps matched those on the stones. The clerics would want the stones matched to the maps to understand their true nature. Pitt would praise him for organization, and if Pitt was pleased, Priestess Burne would grace him with a warm smile. He enjoyed the company and kind words of the priestess, at least until he could get back to Mene.

"What are you smiling about?" Regeth looked up from sorting the stones they'd recovered.

"I'm not smiling." Aaeon tried to look stern. He thought of Mene and her love of song, and he realized why the priestess captivated him. Her singsong speech reminded him of Mene's habit of softly singing to herself when she thought no one was around. He wanted to be able to tell her about Kravitz—if the clerics agreed it was their location—and the early *when* of her proposed Patron's precipice.

"You were," Regeth teased.

"Just forget it, okay?" Aaeon sat back on his heels and asked, "Why Kravitz, Regeth? Surely Pitt knew where he was sending us. There was no one there. All we got was this." He motioned to the stones and the drawings.

"And chased by a rock hornet." Regeth grinned. "Nearly eaten by a rock hornet."

"Never!" Aaeon jumped up, rolled the papers with their rocks and stuffed them into his bag, and he jabbed Regeth with his elbow. "It'd get a taste of you, spit you out, and leave me alone. Remember when I used to call you Little Fish? You'd taste so bad it wouldn't be able to eat for a sixteenth-crackle."

The youths continued to tease as they traversed the corridor and foot-worn stone steps up to the house proper. Today, they would lay out what they'd brought back, the clerics would be as excited as they were, and they would soon be on their way through yet another haze curtain. There was no better life to lead than the one they were experiencing right then. They had already done impossible things, traveled to amazing places, and ventured further and further from their *when*. With the priestess, the bishop, and three priests to guide them, how could they possibly fail?

Their first sign something was out of place was the noise coming through the massive wooden door separating the caverns from the dark pile of a residence Priest Pitt called home. The age-darkened monstrosity was often left open wide, as it took two strong backs to move it. And as Priest Tjark had just come for them, he would have only recently passed through.

Now, it was almost closed.

"They've very nearly shut us in." Regeth dropped his pack and pushed on the door. It didn't move, but he laughed and called, "Together we can do it, except you're too slow and lazy. I'll be tall as you before I have it open at this rate."

The truth was that Aaeon hesitated as he drew closer. On Haukberk, with Underpriest Havey as his mentor, one of his acolyte classes had been in swordplay. For days they'd brandished weighted, wooden weapons, standing across from each other in pairs, throwing them about in an anarchic cacophony of youthful motion. Their dances were an attempt to knock an opponent from his feet. Aaeon had been more successful than some, but not as outstanding as others, and he'd struggled with the oddly balanced weight of the weapons.

It was the better-balanced steel swords that felt at home in his hand. The brittle *ching* and the high-pitched ringing as blade met blade was life in the marrow of his bones. He'd graduated to heavier and longer weapons before their training was complete, surprised to discover that the last and best one he was given was incised with runes and other symbols. A long, unbroken line of unreadable text tumbled down the blade. He'd traced it with his fingers before standing against his opponent, and as his fingers moved over the surface, the designs caught the light. He'd sworn it seemed to glow with an internal gleam before laughing off the idea. He knocked down his opponent handily, though, and he hadn't tired, even wielding the weight of the weapon with both arms.

Havey was apologetic when Aaeon asked him if he could read the scrawling script. The weapon wasn't intended for use by the acolytes. He couldn't explain how it was mixed in with the practice weapons and placed in the acolyte's hand. When Aaeon pressed the underpriest, he told the youth to walk at his side as he returned the sword to its chamber of safety. On the way, he pointed to the lettering, showing Aaeon where certain peaks and

279

valleys were recognizable when compared to normal script. He refused to read the words aloud, but Aaeon knew his letters well, and he soon figured out the script emblazoned on the metal.

By Theon Aland-um's strong fist.

Everyone knew the battle cry. It was from the Scriptures, found in the *Book of The Daughter*, which told the story of the Battle of the Knives from the time before The Great Falling. The dark lord had stood upon his chariot of metal and light, held his sword high, and proclaimed his battle cry. The heavens had shuddered at his words, and the gods had come crashing down, tumbling towards the storm cloud. At the last moment, Shosu Poll-fa had brought the precipices into being, and the gods and the Five Thousand had dwelled in and on the precipices ever since.

It was a dark book not accepted by everyone as valid Scripture, one telling of the shades and their deeds at the end of the gods' heavenly reign, and not read openly in the Temples. Kids were kids, however, and copies did surface from time to time. With Havey's guiding counsel, Aaeon came to understand that weapons of steel were accursed things from the hands of the dark gods, and they should be used only as a last resort in the most desperate circumstances.

It was Theon Aland-um's strong fist that Aaeon heard coming through the partially open door. The metal sang with dark voices crying for blood to quench their thirst.

"Back, Regeth," Aaeon called, breaking into a run. He let his pack fall to the floor.

Overhead, his glow globe, caught off guard, dimmed for a moment as it changed position to follow him. In the flickering shadows, the door was clearly being forced open. The blackened hinges creaked as the opening into the abode let chaotic light seep through, the opening growing wider, then metal sang, someone wailed in pain, and the song moved farther afield.

Aaeon yelled through the opening, "Priest Quartten, are you there?" Rapid breathing answered him, and looking down, the bloodied chest of a man heaved heavily in a prolonged gasp, then stilled.

"He's dead?" Regeth crowded close, and he peered through. In the distance, down the half stair, a fire still crackled merrily in the fireplace, sending light to flutter around furniture tumbled across the broad carpet they'd walked on only hours before. His voice shook. "What killed him?"

"Theon Aland-um." Aaeon spat the word as he wrapped his arm in the thick brass ring used to pull the door to from inside. He remembered the time he held one of the shade's swords and the strange power that seemed to come over him. It was addictive, and only by the grace of Kirk had he managed to break free. He wished to be prepared in case someone from the outside decided to force the door open without their permission. He wanted to seal off what was just on the other side, but he hesitated, for once fully closed, it could be barred from outside, and they couldn't escape.

"Theon—" The younger boy's voice broke in shocked under-standing, and he didn't finish the shade's name. His eyes were riveted on the narrow opening, although the weapons had carried their song to another part of the house. "The dark gods are here?"

"Their weapons, at least. You never advanced to swordplay at Temple, did you?" Aaeon yelled through the opening, "Priestess Burne? Bishop Ziggurat?" He paused to listen, then called, "Priest Pitt? Can anyone hear me? Do you need our assistance?"

"No, I never did. I would have after pledging to become an acolyte." Regeth whispered the words, then asked in the same, soft voice, "Why aren't they answering?"

"I don't know." Aaeon had seen the weapon in the dead man's hand, however. The sword, long and blackened, and now painted with red, glowed with runes and a series of letters twisting down the blade. He didn't have to read them to know what they said. Metal against metal still sang distantly in the familiar rooms on the other side of the door. He refused to imagine whose blood still dripped from the tip of the blade.

281

Their answer didn't come in the form they hoped. The light through the door darkened as a midnight-black figure slammed into the wall centimeters from their watchful eyes, startling them both into sharp exclamations. They had little time to react otherwise as Priest Tjark hissed through the narrow space, "Are both of you uninjured?" The whisper seemed especially ominous from the mouth of a man who had only ever spoken in solemn tones of rumbling thunder.

"We're well, eminence," Aaeon replied, also in a whisper. He hoped his voice didn't shake. Now wasn't the time for fear.

"Your tunics, you have them?" Tjark carried a sword, and it glimmered blackly. It carried runes, also, even if they couldn't be clearly seen.

"On the chair behind the desk," Regeth yelped. "What do we do, eminence?"

Tjark's eyes found Regeth through the opening, and for the first time since they'd met, the black face relaxed into a hint of a smile. "Prepare to open this door." Then he disappeared from their view down the steps, just as the stones under their feet began to shake.

Book of the Gods

Roshanna, Chapter 1:32-35

*S*HOSU IMANI EBOH-LA *is also a lesser god, for when she fought the shade Kella Theon Aland-um in the Battle of Knives, she was near defeated, and her rescue came at the hand of Fadda Freder Neil-fa.*

*S*HOSU EBOH-LA *was near death when Fadda Freder Neil-fa came to her rescue, and with words of mighty wisdom, he tricked Kella Aland-um into accepting his greatest desire rather than killing Shosu Eboh-la.*

*F*OR THAT REASON, *Shosu Eboh-la can never become a greater god. Shosu Eboh-la is the Patron of the Ill and Disenfranchised.*

*S*HOSU EBOH-LA'S *followers are called El Eboh-faitum, or the followers of Shosu Imani Eboh-la. Selah.*

My Cup Runneth Over

The frame around the massive wooden door was of fitted stone, and one ground against another as Gates Precipice writhed under their feet.

Regeth fell to his knees, and Aaeon wondered desperately where the priest had gone. Were the others okay, taken captive, perhaps? Were they to join them? He looked up at the falling dust. Would the entire precipice collapse on their heads? He breathed somewhat easier when the shaking stopped and the dust began to settle. Seeing the sword still in the dead man's hand, he recalled their trip across the city on the steam cart and the warnings about the wicum who followed the dark gods. His back trickled with sweat, and moisture beaded his upper lip.

"Take these." Tjark's dark fist thrust one tunic into the opening, then a second. "Wait," he said and knelt to the sword in the dead man's hand. He pried the gloved fingers apart and yanked the weapon free, offering the hilt to Aaeon through the opening.

"No, eminence," Aaeon gasped. "It's . . ." He'd seen the runes. He knew what they meant.

"Take it, boy." Tjark pressed it farther in, insistent.

"I've held one before. I know what it does. It steals your soul."
For weeks, he and Havey had sent extra prayers heavenward, and
at one point, Aaeon had thought he was lost. Only by not having
access to the sword had he been able to fend off its dark magic.

"Take it," the priest insisted. "If you know of its evil, you can
resist it. Keep your skin from the blade, and it can't harm you.
Then, help me get this door open, both of you."

"Yes, eminence." Aaeon took the hilt. There was blood on it!
He drew it carefully through the opening and stood it on the tip
against the wall.

"Push!" Tjark commanded.

The sound of a commotion had begun on the priest's side of
the door, and it grew louder as he struggled to widen the opening.
Yelling, a voice accosted them, "In here!"

Tjark cried, "The door, now, fools!"

Aaeon and Regeth threw their shoulders against the wooden
behemoth. It moved only slightly.

"I think the shaking has it seized," Regeth gasped, as his feet
slipped on the stone floor.

Aaeon kept his arm in the ring to be able to pull it to once the
priest was inside. His feet also slipped, and he scrambled to
remain upright. Tjark yelled at someone they couldn't see, and he
disappeared from the opening.

A fresh singing of steel filled the youths' ears, and Tjark
yelled at an invisible foe, "For Fadda Arkson-la!" An unseen
voice grunted wetly. The black man slammed into their view once
more, his back hitting the wall, and his sword flashed. It now
dripped red. He yelled, "The door, or I'm dead!" Blood ran from
a wound on his face, and his shoulder revealed raw muscle.

"The way is clear," Aaeon called, still pushing. He hoped so,
anyway. It would be, if they had to pull the priest through, leaving
his undertunic of powdered anthracite to grease the frame of the
doorway as they departed deep into the caverns.

The priest hit the opening, shifting his sword from right hand to left, still swinging as one side pressed into the opening, leaving his other vulnerable. Aaeon's optimistic assessment was close, but the big man didn't fit as yet. Aaeon yelled to Regeth to grab the man's arm and *pull,* while he slammed into the door over and over. Steel danced and clanged in sharp, metallic reports. After several hard blows with Aaeon's shoulder and both of Regeth's hands on Tjark's arm, the big man fell inside, sending his sword clattering into the rough-walled space.

The priest called as he fell, "The door! Pull it to!"

A dark-robed minion tried to ensure otherwise. He also fell against the door, one arm reaching through, while brandishing a blackened, gleaming sword to cut and maim anyone he could reach. Aaeon fell away, grasped the hilt of his new sword, and hacked at the arm, cutting, he was certain, to the bone. The man dropped his sword and yanked his arm back, leaving a portion of his bloodied sleeve on the floor, giving the youths the opportunity to lay hand to the brass ring and tug on the door. Aaeon dropped his frightful, freshly bloodied sword and let it clatter to the stones. The door began to move when Tjark placed his massive arms next to theirs and joined in the effort. The hinges squealed in protest, but the door drew to just as a band of reinforcements filled the stair landing to relieve their injured attacker.

Aaeon dropped the inner bar into place, and he drew in a ragged breath. His eyes found Tjark, and he pleaded with the last remnants of hope he could muster. "What of the others? What survivors can we claim?"

Tjark closed his eyes for a moment, becoming a shadow in the shadows, and he whispered, "Shosu Jabena Poll-fa has joined arms with Fadda Arkson-la, and they dream in their care." Dimly, through the door, axes could be heard biting at the wood. "We will dream also if we don't find a way out of here."

"And there we have a problem." Aaeon dropped into a squat with his back against the door. It was a problem of unimaginable proportions. The caverns were secure. There was no way out except through the door.

"We have three swords," Regeth reminded them. "We can hide and gut them as they come through." His words were strong, but his face was pale.

"You are filled with the courage of your god. Fadda Kirk would be proud to hear your words." Priest Tjark motioned to the sword their attacker had dropped. "Pick it up, boy. Handle only the hilt, and it'll do you no harm. Go ahead but use both hands."

Regeth stood over the weapon and grasped the hilt in a two-fisted fashion, and he lifted it, attempting to keep the point high. When he got his hands to waist level, the blade began to drop until the tip rang against the floor. He gasped, "It's heavy!"

"And is the reason we won't remain to fight." The priest smiled when the youth let the sword clatter to the floor.

"We can't escape." Aaeon had his hand in his hair, and he twisted his fingers tight. Quartten, dead. The priestess, also. Old Pitt, whom he had learned to love for his kind spirit. And Bishop Ziggurat. He hadn't liked the man, but he had respected him. They were just *here*, his companions and mentors. He couldn't imagine them *gone*. He fought to keep his eyes dry, but his head pounded, and he felt he wanted to smash his fist against the wall.

"There's a way." Tjark stood and collected the two tunics he'd forced through the door. The attack on the wood rang louder, repeated and often. He nodded its direction. "They'll be through soon. They don't mean to let us live."

"We've done nothing. Why?" Aaeon looked up, wiping his cheeks. He'd not been quite successful with the tears.

"We worship the true gods. That's all the reason they need. You led a sheltered life on Haukberk. Have you not wondered at my face? I wasn't born this way." He offered his hand to the youth, pulled the young underpriest to his feet, and offered him the larger of the two tunics. He handed Regeth the other.

"I didn't suppose you were, although I didn't think about it much." Not at all, actually. He'd accepted the man as he was and tried not to be too frightened of what he might have done to look the way he looked. With the blood running from his wounds, he was beginning to understand. The others might be gone, but this was the man who would keep them alive if anyone could. He felt of the tunic and exclaimed in dismay, "My devotional pouch. It's fallen out." He held out a wide leather strap he hadn't expected to find in the tunic and looked at it, puzzled.

"And is, therefore, lost. Can you worship without it?"

"I can't go back for it, can I?" he muttered, new tears filling his eyes. It was his one treasure. He'd polished his cup daily, and his lightning match had been a gift from his parents, the one thing he could bring with him when he pledged as a neophyte. He held out the strap, asking, "What's this?"

"I have one, also." Regeth had his tunic on, and he clinked two iron rings, one against the other. They were attached at one end of the strap.

"Mine." Tjark took the strap from Regeth. "Watch, under-priest. See how I do this, and then put on yours." The priest didn't have his tunic and wore only his powdered anthracite. His generator was enveloped within the pitch-dark fabric, and the whole melded against his skin as one. He wrapped the strap around his torso and across one shoulder, fitted one end through the iron rings in a double loop, and tugged it tight. He adjusted the portion on his shoulder to avoid his injury. One section of the strap across his back was a double thickness, and he retrieved the cloth from the man's arm, wiped his blade, reached over his head, slipped the point of his sword into the doubled layers of the strap, and let it slide through to rest with the cross guard against the leather. Now he could bend and twist, even sit, without having to remove the weapon. With a jerk of his hand, it would be ready for battle, able to fend off any comers that might think to go against him.

"I see how it goes. Let me help you, Aaeon." Regeth took the strap from his friend's hand and dropped it to the floor. He also

289

pulled the tunic from Aaeon's motionless hands and shook it out. Bunching it to slip over the older youth's head, he held it out, motioning to Aaeon to duck. Once he did, Regeth quickly fitted it and helped him place his arms in the sleeves. Tjark watched with an appraising eye as the young man accurately draped the strap across Aaeon's shoulder and belted it properly by looping the end through the double rings.

"You impress me." The priest nodded at Regeth and patted him gently on the head. He knelt to retrieve Aaeon's bloodied sword. He wiped the blood with the cast-off sleeve, put his hand on the youth's shoulder, then gently slipped the weapon into its resting spot. He turned Aaeon to face him, grasped his shoulders, and looked into his shocked face. "You'll work this out. This is what Priest Quartten and Bishop Ziggurat saw in you, and I've found the same. Your aide is your strongest ally, and you must trust him. I am your strong arm, and I will be at your back. You must learn to lead us and learn quickly."

"All my mentors are gone. Who is there to guide me?" Aaeon was numbed by the turn of events. He wanted back his success on Kravitz Precipice. His time there had reminded him of Mene, and then it was yanked away. Now, he wore a massive sword on his back and had bloodied a man's arm; and the minions of the shades wanted him dead.

"Will you try?" The priest squeezed the youth's shoulders. His words held no stringent demand or accusing tone. He simply placed the question before the boy.

"For me, Aaeon?" Regeth's eyes kept going to the door. The whacks of the blades on the other side were growing brighter and louder, as if the wood was becoming thinner.

"I . . . I'm empty inside. I can't focus my thoughts."

"Hopefully, we can do that for you." Even Tjark's eyes found the door. It had started to splinter. "Find your strength, boy. Find a thing you want to live for, a thing that will be forever changed if you should expire in the next few moments."

"Maybe sooner," Regeth whispered, his eyes red with concern.

"Mene. I'd never see her again." Aaeon's heart twisted inside. The sun wisp robe she would never make for him. Her kiss, as sweet as the day.

"Then she is your strength. Make her the core of all that you think." He turned to Regeth, telling him, "Gather our things. Leave the sword you cannot carry, but all else goes."

"Our packs, too, and the rocks and maps?" He was already gathering them.

"You have those? Excellent. Nothing is to be left." He brought his scarred and bleeding face nose-to-nose to Aaeon and said, "I am a priest of Fadda Arkson-la, for my strength is in my ability to dream that which I desire to come to pass. You are now a priest of Fadda Kirk-fa—" Aaeon's eyes jerked to the priest's face at this revelation, "—for you know the fire of passion in your breast. You, my son, have a strength inside that you have yet to tap. Without the priestess and the cripple, I am unable to navigate in the haze curtains or return us home. My ability to dream, however, remains unfettered. If you are willing to test your limits and move three across the curtains, I am willing place my dreams in your care."

"Three?" Aaeon's eyes went wide. It was too much to ask. "I've never . . . three? I've not learned the control to move three."

The first axe head pierced the door, and an unseen man cursed as he worked it free. Shards of broken wood littered the floor. A voice called, "They are just inside. By the power of Kella Shana Gill-um, they'll join their fallen brethren before another bud forms on the branch of my birth!"

"You can do three. I know you can." Regeth danced just behind Tjark, keeping as far from the door as possible. He held a pack over each shoulder, and his hood hovered halfway down his neck. His face shimmered with fear.

Aaeon straightened his back, truly feeling as if he gathered strength from the priest's strong fingers. He found his image of Mene in his mind. He pictured her standing on the Upwards stones of Haukberk with the lightning-studded cloud wall at her back. The ground glowed, and she laughed when he made a joke about the baths.

"You're there?" Tjark looked him intently in the eyes. "I see strength if I'm not mistaken. Let Fadda Kirk gird you, my boy. Offer me your best, and I'll not let you down, with Fadda Arkson as my witness."

"What do you need from me? With Fadda Kirk-fa as my witness and Shosu Poll-fa as my guide, I'll do as you request."

Aaeon had taken all the time he could. The door was splintering at their backs, and their enemies would soon be through. Regeth—his trusted friend, Regeth—depended on him. Mene. If he wanted to see her again, taste her lips again, he had to become a stronger person than he'd been in the past. And this man standing before him, scarred in battle and now bleeding, banked his survival on Aaeon's cooperation. This was no time to feel sorry for himself, to wish for other lives to lead, or to blame those who were gone for the danger he faced. Now was the time to act, for success or failure, and it was time to commit with his full measure of strength.

Priest Tjark nodded in acceptance. He held one arm to pull in Regeth, and they stood as three points of a single triumvirate. "Hoods up, youths, for your protection as we traverse the haze. Arms just so." He wrapped his across their shoulders and waited until they copied his stance. "Heads in to touch, forehead to forehead."

The glow globe overhead mimicked their posture. Sensing Aaeon's attention focused downward, it dropped to just over their heads, casting a halo of light and sprouting long shadows at their feet like the legs of a massive creature crouched and ready to spring. Behind them, more axes breached the failing door, this time in several places. The voices of their attackers grew louder.

Tjark drew the trio together with his deep, resonant voice. "Priest Hibolah, I am not a follower of Kirk and cannot access your Temple's book, yet you must trust in your heart that your bishop and priest wished this for you and gave up their lives to allow you to live. As Shosu Eboh-la fought the shade Kella Alandum and nearly perished before Fadda Neil-fa came to her rescue, so Shosu Eboh-la is now the Patron of the Disenfranchised. We carry weapons born from the fires of Xibalba, the dark precipice, and ready ourselves to step past the curtains of time. May Eboh-la guard our journey, may Kirk-fa impassion our hearts, and may Fadda Arkson-la gift us a strong dream where all will be well."

"From your lips to the gods," Regeth automatically murmured.

"And now?" Aaeon's heart thumped in his chest. The door that had kept them safe fully split, giving way to the axes as it cracked with an explosion of thunder. Hands grabbed the broken remains, clearing a passage for the intruders.

"Take us through the curtains, all of us, and now!" Tjark gripped their shoulders, pulling them painfully tight.

Aaeon had no destination in mind. Before, the priestess and Pitt had provided both direction and location. All he'd had required of him was to return home, making sure Regeth was at his side. He had nothing in his head except his image of the haze curtains as he imagined them, a vast puzzle of interlocking steppingstones that fit together seamlessly, shrouded in multiple layers that could rise up at any location, one piece at a time, shifting those inside to any possible *when* as easily as stepping from one room into another. As he focused, the air around them thickened. The floor grew indistinct, and the sounds of the splintering door grew faint. A cold wind swept across them, bright light consumed everything they could see, and they fell through the haze curtain. They tumbled onto a softly padded floor, with gentle muzak filling their ears.

"By the gods!" Priest Tjark was the first to his feet.

293

Underneath a high ceiling, a vast window of unimaginably clear glass filled the far wall. The sky on the other side whispered in tones of pale blue, and thin white clouds partially covered a brilliantly yellow sun. A band of green bordered an uncovered body of water that expanded until it disappeared in the distance.

Closer, inside the vast structure, hundreds of priests in white tunics—shrouded but not hooded—gathered in long rows before individual windows of their own, each staring into their minute worlds. None looked their direction. Surprisingly, the glow globe had followed them through the haze curtain, and it floated over Aaeon's head.

"Where is this?" Aaeon whispered.

"A place no mortal has ever visited." Tjark's eyes took in the scene, and he glanced at Aaeon and to Regeth. "Keep your heads covered. In this place, I must find a tunic soon. The gods won't tolerate disrespect."

An amplified male voice echoed, and Tjark dropped into a crouch, adjusting for his sword, as though he had worn one continually in the past.

"Mission Control to Commander Pollock, thirty seconds to ignition. Are you good to go?"

Aaeon's heart pounded in fear. He was certain it would give their location away. He sucked in a sharp breath as a new voice began to speak.

"Are my freezer pops in orbit and ready to fly?" A female voice as loud as the first. Priests throughout the room laughed at the words.

"All five thousand CorpseCases sealed and loaded." The male voice chuckled. "Keep your nine crewmates in line for us, Commander. Five thousand passengers are riding on their skill."

"So am I. Just get me to the *Higgs*, and we'll deliver our payload and bring our ship home. Pollock out."

A new voice picked up, counting down evenly, "Nine, eight, seven, six . . . ignition."

Through the window, just where the water ate the world, a flame erupted, a conflagration white hot, even against the brilliance of the sky. The building around them shook, increasing in violence as the fire grew bigger and brighter.

None of the priests looked their way. All remained focused on the massive window or on the smaller windows they worshipped, many of which carried smaller views of the catastrophe happening just outside.

"This is the end time spoken of in the Scriptures?" Aaeon whispered to Tjark. His weapon at his back fought him, catching on the soft flooring.

"I'm unsure." Tjark noticed his difficulty and instructed him, "Bend the spine. It gives the weapon its freedom." He nodded, satisfied, when the youth adjusted his position successfully.

"It's just," Aaeon frowned, "that I've read the Scriptures. The gods and fire." He shrugged, hoping he didn't appear frightened. He was, however. It was foretold that the world would be destroyed by the gods, that it would end in lightning and fire. Here were the gods—their priests, anyway—and fire was consuming the world. There was no lightning yet, but who knew what the gods were capable of?

"The sky, see the color?" Tjark lifted his hand and swept his open palm over the scene. "The oldest stories tell of a *when* that held skies of such beauty. I think, perhaps, we've traveled to a when *before* the time of the gods. The name, Pollock. Perhaps we are brought here to witness Shosu Poll-fa's elevation to the rank of true god. Even now we could be looking over the shoulders of Fadda Kirk or Fadda Arkson." He seemed in awe.

"Or the shades before they were fallen," Aaeon remarked dryly.

"I wish to see Shosu Eboh-la. The stories say she was the most beautiful of the gods." At the prospect of such a sight, Regeth had calmed his quaking and joined them. The fire outside caught his attention, and he sank back to the floor, pulling his hood over his face, still wrapped in his two packs.

He missed the inferno as it blossomed into a massive red flower. The world rumbled, the building truly began to shake, and the flame leaped heavenward. The white-robed priests stood and cheered as the echoing voice intoned, "Launch achieved. *Daughter One* is away."

"Hey!" A sharp voice broke the castaways' isolation, telling them that their attendance at the unfamiliar ceremony was no longer a private affair.

They turned toward the voice and found three black-suited men holding what must be weapons, although they were of a sort they'd never seen before. Before they could reply, one of the men hit a large, red pad on the wall, and lights strobed. The bright lights shot pain into their eyes. Alarms wailed. A loud voice intoned, "Intruder alert. Hostiles have breached the perimeter. Intruder alert."

"The gods have found us," Regeth moaned, his face green.

The men aimed their weapons at them, and one called, "On the floor, now! Hands away from your weapons where we can see them!"

"You, in the black," another man called, equally loud and even harsher, "away from the other two. You with the packs, toss them away from you, and *power down that white device.*"

The panicked voices of the white-robed priests wove a static background to the events as they evacuated in a frantic and haphazard fashion. The building still shivered, but the rumbling was less; and through the window, the fire had leapt skyward and was trailed by a thick column of smoke. The voice that had counted down the launch overrode the alarms and said, "Booster separation in three, two, one." A muffled explosion and short but intense vibration shook the glass in the windows, and the voice said, "Separation complete."

"Shut that noise off," one of the black suits yelled over his shoulder. "The alarm, too. We've got this."

Tjark, Aaeon, and Regeth remained bunched, and the midnight-skinned priest hissed to the newly-minted Aaeon, "Be ready to send us. Touch foreheads now." He grasped the youths' shoulders and pulled them in as the wailing alarm went silent. The rumbling of the launch was faintly audible in the background.

"Hey," the black suit yelled. "I said separate. Down, now."

The travelers ignored his words, and they threw their arms around each other. Regeth was overbalanced by the two packs, and he stumbled while trying to lean his forehead in. Tjark grabbed the strap of one pack and jerked the youth to him. "Now, boy, or we die."

"On my count!" The black suits lifted their weapons and braced their feet. "Last chance if you want to live. On the floor, hands out. Three, two—"

Aaeon grabbed at his mental image of the puzzle pieces rising from the soil, and as the scene grew in his mind—the multiple layers of time separating one atop another—he searched for something familiar. All he could find was a vortex of unfamiliar events. He vaguely felt Tjark jerk their small group sideways, and as weapons fired, he fell jarringly and hard towards an unknown piece of the puzzle. The yelling voices grew faint, and a cold wind blew a chill up his tunic. Then he was blinded by a flash of light, and his thoughts went blank.

Book of the Gods

Roshanna, Chapter 1:36-37

FADDA LIAM EGEL-LA is a lesser god, for he is rarely seen in the true world. Fadda Egel-la speaks to his followers through meditation, for he finds his strength in things unseen.

FADDA EGEL-LA IS the Patron of Inner Peace and Emotional Well-Being. His followers are called El Egel-faitum, or the followers of Fadda Liam Egel-la. Selah.

Star Light, Star Bright

Aaeon first felt warmth.

He breathed deeply, and the weight of layers of bedding pressed against him, holding him, as his chest drew in air. It was quiet, with the only sounds being a low hum that seemed to vibrate the surface he rested on and the occasional ding of a bell in the distance. The bell came at irregular intervals, but it was always the same, one quick, high-pitched tone, and it was comforting.

He opened his eyes to a blank ceiling in a gray color, flat and uninteresting. Across the space were two doors, one closed and the other open. His glow globe was off to the side, resting on a low table, apparently powered down. He smiled at that. The black suits finally got what they wanted.

Black suits! He sat up, too quickly, apparently, because his head began to spin. He let out a deep breath, muttering, "Fadda Kirk, give me strength," and sank back to the bed. His head continued to spin, and he put his hand to his forehead, finding not skin, but bandaging. He remembered the countdown and the words, *Last chance, if you want to live.* They'd done it, attacked! They'd *done it!* He was furious.

He was also grateful to be alive, and then it hit him. *Regeth!* Sorrow welled inside, and he regretted the times he'd taken his friend for granted, brushed him off, even forced him to act as his slave, giving him duties that weren't his friend's to perform. He lifted a special prayer to the Patron of Inner Peace and Emotional Well-Being, whispering, "Fadda Egel-la, I offer my friend into your hands." It was the most he could do. His friend was gone, and he could never tell him how much his friendship meant to him.

Had the rugged priest also been taken, killed as he protected his wards? Aaeon hadn't liked the man at the beginning, had actively *disliked* him, but he didn't wish him dead. He'd been the one person who'd risked everything to return to the caverns and save them. In one day of frantic survival, he'd realized the man was a warrior priest, with unknown but quite formidable skills; and without him, Aaeon was lost. He murmured, "Fadda Arkson-la's dreams are forever yours, for you were a great warrior."

He pushed the bedding back—slowly and gently this time—and swung his feet to the floor. He didn't recognize his clothing, a snug, white top, and white bottoms that fitted him closely, with built-in legs that stopped halfway to his knees. He checked his limbs and his chest and found no additional wounds.

On the floor beside the glow globe, the two packs Regeth had carried leaned against a slick and seamless wall. One was whole, and the second was tattered along one side. The strap on the tattered bag hung lifeless, trailing along the floor. *The floor!* It glowed and writhed with colors where his feet touched. He lifted them, and the colors faded to a neutral sheen that appeared to be flat and to have no solidity at all. It made him nervous, as if he might sink into that surface if he placed his feet there again. Still, it had been firm when he'd not known its appearance. There was no reason it shouldn't hold him. He touched his feet to the floor again, and the colors swirled where his skin touched, spreading out in ever-fainter patterns until it hit the farthest walls. He breathed deeply, refusing to let it overwhelm him. It was the same as Haukberk, he accepted, in the way the land glowed from the energy of the storm wall. The floor lighted the room as it should. It just didn't *feel* like home.

He felt his chest. The strap. *The sword!* The men in black had taken it from him. How would he fight? Could he fight? Could he call a curtain, perhaps escape that way? Or would he be in a different *when,* yet still in this room? A confinement room was a confinement room, no matter how many whens he skipped over in his travels. That had been the priest's duty, to dream new locations, while Aaeon's was to take them there.

There was no escape. He realized that, and despair washed over him. There was no escape at all.

Rising slowly and carefully, the pulsing floor too dizzying to watch, he made his way through a doorway he hoped led to personal facilities. A light flickered on as he entered, and his immediate view was of himself reflected in a large pane of mirrored glass. It was a long time since he'd seen himself outside of his acolyte's tunic, and never since his surprising promotion to priest.

He studied his head, with its pale shock of hair askew on its crown and the cloth he'd felt earlier wrapping an injury. A spider-web of darkening stain revealed the reason for the bandage. His eyes spouted dark smudges that bled to his cheeks. His face, still smooth, wrapped a strong chin and dropped to a long neck and narrow shoulders. His unfamiliar clothing revealed a tight torso with narrow hips and slim legs. He felt himself redden at the snug-fitting shorts and wished for his tunic. Turning from the mirror, he found equipment that, while not exactly familiar, was easy to work, and he availed himself of it. The water in the small sink came on as he placed his hands inside, and he cleansed them, wiping them on his shorts before returning to the disturbing floor.

He knelt at the bags, opening the undamaged one to find the maps and drawings. The stones he'd wrapped inside still revealed where they'd been found. The second bag carried the remnants of some of the larger stones they had collected. An unfamiliar strap kept them from falling out, and when he untied it, he reached inside to find little more than crumbled shards. Only at the bottom were the stones he remembered whole. He worked out one laced with red veining. It had reminded him of the storm wall, and he'd hoped Quartten or Pitt could tell him if it was a fragment of the sky that had fallen when the precipice was created. It seemed reasonable. The precipices had to come from somewhere, and the storm wall was the logical place.

Now, his two mentors were gone, and he'd never know the answer to his question. He placed it back in the pack, and his finger brushed something cold. He lifted it to find a segment of cylindrical metal, pointed on one end, although twisted. They hadn't collected anything like it on Kravitz Precipice or put it in the pack. It must be what had shattered the stones, he thought. He dropped it back inside and stood.

Folded neatly behind the glow globe, he discovered his tunic. He carried it to the bed and shook it out. His clean, form-fitting clothing from his trips into the haze fell from inside, tumbling to a lump on the bedding. A sound made him turn, and a medium-size man stepped into the room. His dark hair clung to his head, neatly clipped, sporting a well-groomed sheen. He wore tailored clothing, dark, banded in lighter fabric, with a stiff collar and cuffs at the wrists. Insignia and a name were on one breast. His shoes gleamed as if they were a point of pride with him. He held out a hand in a quick motion and smiled.

"You're finally awake. Liam, and you're Aaeon, right? Sit and let me check that head."

Aaeon looked at the hand, and realizing what the man intended, he grasped the proffered limb and held it. He studied the man's name, Schlegel, wondering what it meant, until the man cleared his throat and looked away.

"I'm sorry," Aaeon mumbled, releasing the hand. He'd

flubbed again. He felt his earlier embarrassment return, and it reminded him of what he was wearing. He looked to his tunic hopefully but was distracted by his visitor.

"Nothing to worry about. You've been out nearly a day. I really need to check that head, if you don't mind." He grasped Aaeon's shoulders and pressed him to sit on the bed. He retrieved a small scissors from an invisible pocket and held one hand against the bandage while he snipped it free. As he worked, he talked. "Normally I'd have Elisabet do this—she's the flight doctor—but as you're not *official*, I'm filling in. The station medic?" He laughed. "I trust my own skills better. I can't let you anywhere near the *Higgs*, you understand, but here on the station, you're fine. Lots of people visit the station, and not much vetting goes on. I mean, it's not like it's a *military* operation." He chuckled as he unwound the bandage, dropping it into a waste basket at the end of the bed. "Ah, not too bad. I keep telling my dad I could have gone into medicine. It's what I *do,* education, and that's all medicine is, that and a bit of practice. You're my first patient, my friend, and I think I'm doing very well. If anything happens to Elisabet while on our flight, I'm ready to step in."

"Flight?" Aaeon remembered the longest trip he'd ever taken, the cable ferry from Haukberk to Gates. Was that what the man meant? They had been suspended over the Crevasse for quite some time.

"That's what your friends asked—"

"Regeth and Tjark are alive? Where?" Aaeon jerked to his feet, ignoring the man's attempt to hold him back. He leaped toward the door, not knowing how to open it but needing to find his companions. At the quick motion, his head spun, and by the time he got to the door, he collapsed against the wall, barely able to stand.

"That wasn't wise. You've a head injury. Take slow moves for a while." Liam stepped to him and supported him as he made his way to the bed, talking the entire time. "Your older friend wished to replace his ceremonial robe, and the boy went with him."

"Ceremonial robe?" Aaeon watched his feet, each vibrant step making his head spin.

"Your hooded . . . thing? He said it was urgent for his head to be covered." He shrugged. "I liked his skin etchings. I explained there's a religious festival this week in Vatican City. That's the section just past the Mediterranean Sea Water Park. That's the best place, ever! Anyway, I said he'd find what he wanted there if it was anywhere."

"My friend went with him?" Aaeon felt vaguely disappointed, as if Regeth had abandoned him.

"I insisted. His first time on the station, and he needed to see the sights. I promised I'd check in on you, to practice my medical skills, you know. Don't expect him back soon. It's on the other side of the ring, and the station computer didn't recognize him. He'll have to walk the entire way. He left you your things and asked you to wait here until he returned."

"Can you turn this floor off?" He no longer cared about his companions. Well, he did, but his head was spinning so fast, and his stomach felt like it was about to empty itself. He just wanted to sit.

"Yeah, I didn't think. It's probably not helping that head of yours. Let's get you seated—" He cut his words off as he took Aaeon's weight, releasing him as he sat fully on the bed. "Computer?"

"Liaison Schlegel acknowledged. How may I help you, Liam?"

He laughed. "That's a pretty girl. Set the floor to default in this room, warm glow only. Thanks, sweetie."

"You're welcome." The colorful swirls faded, and the light in the room softened.

"Thank you," Aaeon said. His head swam, and not from his

run across the room. He couldn't get over the relief that his friends were alive. Even Tjark. After thinking him dead, he wished to claim him as a friend, along with Regeth.

"I get it. You're a nature-type guy, like your friends. Sure. I should have left you a view." Liam touched a panel at the end of the bed, and the wall behind them opened to a panorama of a space station comprised of a massive torus, with thick spokes interlocking at a center hub. Lights glimmered across its surface. Docked below the hub, partially obstructed by the station, an outsized ship hovered, attached by an extended gantry. In letters large enough to be easily read, *UEF Higgs* scrawled down her side in a sculpted and flowing script. Underneath, block letters a quarter the size, though still clearly visible, proclaimed that the vessel belonged to the United Earth Federation. Past that, the giant, glowing form of the water planet Earth swam against a background of stars, forming a pincushion of light in the darkness. The moon, half in shadow, hung to the side. "Sorry it's not an unobstructed view. You take what you can get, sometimes."

Liaison Schlegel laughed at his joke.

Aaeon's stomach twisted, and he felt ill. It was all so . . . *vast.* Before he could ask again where his friends were, or if he could cover with his tunic, or if his new friend was named after Fadda Liam Egel-la, his head began to spin, he grew dizzy, and the world around him faded away.

A Goddess Speaks

"I'm sorry, Doc. I thought I was doing the right thing."

The words swam in and out of Aaeon's head. He tried to grasp them, but they kept slipping away. He seemed to remember *walking* somewhere . . . leaning on someone's shoulder?

"The commander won't be happy when her shuttle arrives, but I think he's better here than out on the station. Was he vetted for ship access?"

A woman's voice. Vetting, vetted . . . Aaeon caught the familiar word. The man—Liam—had used it, and now the . . . *doc* had used one very similar. He tried to concentrate. What was a doc? A mooring station, such as for the cable ferry that ran from Haukberk Precipice to Gates? No, no . . . He fought uphill toward the bright light suspended just overhead. *Doc.* The man had been speaking to the *woman,* so a doc must be a person.

The doc's voice said, "You cleaned the wound as well as you could without surgical instruments. It was nicely done, Liam. Don't be displeased with yourself, and you brought him to me when you saw things were beyond your skills. You're a credit to this crew." A hand touched his face—*her hand?*—and she said,

"He's barely more than a boy. I'm surprised he's aboard the station, if he's here to work. His chip didn't register in the databanks when you brought him across on the gantry elevator? He shouldn't have been able to get past security."

"I don't think he *is* chipped."

"Not possible. Hand me the portable scanner from the cabinet just behind you."

Aaeon forced his eyes open. A bright light overhead glared. So, *that* was the light that had drawn him upward, not the light of survival or a beckoning of the gods toward their heavenly realm. It was just a light, and he tried to turn his head and lift his arm to shield his eyes.

"No, you don't." The woman grasped his arm and gently forced it back to his side. "Ship, surgical light at twenty percent."

"Acknowledged, Doctor Minkovski." The glare faded as the ship's computer spoke.

"Where . . ." Aaeon struggled with his words.

"Easy," she said. "You've been under, and you'll take a bit to come around. Say your words slowly, and you'll do just fine."

"You . . . you're Doc, but . . . Liam? He was with me earlier."

"Right here, Aaeon. How are you feeling?" The neatly trimmed man appeared in Aaeon's vison. He was blurred, but it was definitely him, and he leaned in and said, "We're on the ship. Bet you never expected that. So, maybe medicine isn't quite like education. You're all fixed up, now, thanks to the doc."

"On the ship?" Aaeon blinked several times, the room trying to come into focus, and he found the doc. She was beautiful. Old, but beautiful. Well, not *old* old, but at least as old as his mother before he joined the Temple. Her dark, thick hair tumbled around her shoulders, and her bright, full features contrasted with her clear, pale skin. She smiled at him, and he felt his pulse race.

"On the *UEF Higgs*, one of the lucky few. Well," and Liam chuckled, "not *too* few. We've got five thousand popsicles in the hold, ready for delivery to Deneb 4 Station, but they hardly count.

309

It's the ten up top that matter, eleven, with you. Except, you can't stick around much longer. If you're on when we launch, you're on for the duration, a year of your life gone like that." He snapped his fingers and laughed.

"Don't tease, Liam. He'll be back on the station long before we make our departure." She stepped to the bed and spoke to Aaeon. "Liam tells me your name's Aaeon. Is there a last name?"

"Hibolah. I'm feeling better, now. Can I sit up?" He was cold, but his vision had cleared, and he could tell he was speaking more clearly.

"Certainly." She touched something on the side of the bed, and it whirred as it lifted him. She pulled her hand away when he was at a comfortable angle. "So, Aaeon Hibolah, what do you do on the station? You have a job, I suppose?"

"Is the station the big circular thing Liam showed me through the wall?"

"Liam?" She didn't look away but kept her eyes on Aaeon.

"I just opened the wall, and that's when he conked out—" He sounded apologetic, and she waved her hand at him to let him know it wasn't his fault.

"Yes, Aaeon, the big circular thing is the station. What's your job here?" She continued to smile.

"I'm not from here. I'm an acolyte on Haukberk, but when we were attacked—that was on Gates—we used the haze curtains to escape." He grimaced. "Sorry, I'm a priest, now, but it was sudden, and I keep forgetting."

"A priest." She smiled.

"A priest?" Liam stepped into Aaeon's view again, grinning. "Like, inner peace to the masses. I'm so glad I saved your skin. Wait till I tell the rest of the crew."

Doctor Minkovski laughed. "Liam, get on out of here. You said two men were with him? See if you can run down this boy's friends and let them know he's all right."

"I know exactly where they are." He hovered at Aaeon's side

310

and whispered, "A priest? So cool!"

"Go, Liam. I want to scan this boy, and you don't have to be here for that."

"You want I should bring 'em back here?" It seemed exactly what *he* wanted to do.

"Might not be possible. You *can* check out a job assignment for our young friend. He'll fit in better if he's got an official placement. Now, out. I'm busy." She'd picked up her scanner, and she'd already tuned out the liaison officer. She spoke to Aaeon. "Everyone on the station has to be chipped, and Liam said he couldn't locate yours. I'd like to run a scanner over you. It won't hurt. May I?"

"If you want. Despite what he thinks, I'm just recently a priest, and barely that." He sent a mental apology to Kirk for not being clear. "Can I see my head, first?"

"I forgot." She chuckled. "You must be, what, I'm guessing, about fifteen—"

"Sixteen!" He didn't look fifteen. No one ever told him that. He proved it by adding, "Going on seventeen."

"Most sixteen-year-olds are. Appearances are everything to a boy your age. Here." She opened a drawer and pulled out a square made of mirrored glass. "My work is neater than Liam's. You can thank a real doctor for that."

"A doc is a doctor?" He admired the patch on his head. His hair fell over it, covering a portion of it. "You cut my hair under this?"

She shrugged. "You can call me either one, and I couldn't dig out the stone shards otherwise, but I expect it'll grow back. Where did you say you're from? I've never seen stone like that. The mass spectrometer couldn't give me a chemical makeup that matched any known rock sample."

"From Haukberk Precipice. How did the stone—" He remembered the damaged pack and the pulverized rock inside. They'd been in the house of the many gods—or at least their priests—and

311

they were fired upon. Priest Tjark had jerked him sideways—saving his life, he now knew—because the weapons had impacted the pack and not him. *The metal cylinder!* It had come from the weapons. Shards of the stones must be what ricocheted off and hit him in the head. "The stone wasn't from Haukberk. We traveled the haze curtains to Kravitz Precipice and collected the stones there." He handed her the mirror, satisfied.

"Okay. I'll go with that. Where's Kravitz Precipice?" She asked the question in an easy tone, still holding the scanner in one hand.

"Not where, Doc." He looked into her eyes and smiled. This was easy to explain. "*When.* You can scan me, if you want. I don't mind."

"When?" She pulled the blanket back to reveal his snug clothing still covering his slim form. "How can something be when?"

"Because it's not now. The curtains always take you to other *whens.*"

"Oh?" She seemed amused as she moved the scanner over his body, keeping about a quarter-meter distance. "You can't travel to a different where?"

"Oh, sure." He continued to smile. "With a dreamer's help. That's why Priest Tjark's helping me. He dreams different locations, and we can travel there. My friend Regeth—he's just a neophyte—is my assistant. He runs my errands when I need him to."

"Is that so?" She seemed to find his story amusing. She'd finished with the scanner, and she was puzzled. She looked at the readout and shook it as if it might give her a different reading. "How'd you say you got aboard with no chip?"

"The men in the black suits were shooting at us, and Priest Tjark said *now, Aaeon,* and we wound up here. You can ask the priest how he picked this place, but I bet it was an accident. We were about to be killed, and anywhere would do."

312

"Anywhere would do." She repeated his phrase, thinking. "Where were you almost shot?"

He shrugged and tried to explain it as best he could. He didn't think she'd want to hear of the priests, so he tried to describe the place he was in. "A big building with a clear wall. Fire outside shot into the sky, and everything shock. A loud voice was counting down and said launch had been achieved."

"There were lots of men wearing white coats?" She indicated the one she wore. She was no longer interested in the scanner.

"Yes!" He smiled that she knew the place. Then his face fell. Maybe they hadn't been priests after all. That disappointed him in some way.

"You," and she stepped closer to him, "were at Mission Control?"

"Mission Control?" He felt panic set in. Her question didn't sound like a good one.

"Oh, my God," she said. "Ship, put the news summary from earlier on screen." Across the room, a large display lit up, and images flickered across in a jerky, quick motion. She called, "Stop. Replay in real time."

There, on the display, were three soldiers with weapons aimed at a trio of people huddled on the floor. Two were hooded, and the third was ebony dark with designs etched over his skin. Two long swords were just visible. A glowing globe hovered over their heads. A banner of words across the bottom of the display said, *Live Earlier Today.* Covering a portion of those words, it added, *Prerecorded Yesterday.* In the background was the vacated command center in Mission Control, backed by a vast and stunning panorama of greenery, sea, and sky. The remains of a fiery torch leaped through the air, supported by a strong fist of billowing smoke. As the three soldiers fired their weapons, the air around the hooded trio grew thick, filled with haze, and fell out of focus. Then, with a bright flash, the place they'd occupied was empty, with nothing to show they'd been there. Two of the projectiles impacted the floor, ripping carpet and gouging the concrete underneath. The third? There was no sign of it, anywhere.

Book of the Gods

Roshama, Chapter 1:1-5

THE FIRST OF THE four fallen gods is Kella Shana Gill-um. When he resided with the gods in the heavens, he was the wisest of all who walked before him or after, and he created great wonders for the gods to enjoy.

HIS DOWNFALL WAS to hold grudges against those who failed to live to his standards.

HE ATTEMPTED TO cast fire and destruction across a portion of the Five Thousand as retribution for failures long forgotten by other gods, and for this reason, he was banished from Paradise and is a fallen god known as a shade.

KELLA SHANA GILL-UM is the Perpetrator of Revenge.

KELLA SHANA GILL-UM'S followers are known as El Gill-wicum, or the Minions of Shana Gill-um. Selah.

The God Gene

"It's not possible." Doctor Minkovski had an incredulous expression on her face as she looked from the wall display and back to Aaeon's face. "That was you?"

She asked her question as if she wanted to be convinced otherwise.

"Maybe." Aaeon began to think he'd said too much. Oh, his mouth liked to run on! He wished Priest Tjark were around to give him guidance. "Is it a good thing or a bad thing if that was me?"

"That depends." She leaned against a cabinet about three meters away, with her arms crossed over each other. "If that was you, how'd you get from there to here so quickly? That was the Commander's launch, and with a stopover at the Metagalactic Transfer Depot, she's still in transit. There's no way that I know of to get here quicker. So, I suppose it's wishful thinking on my part." She uncrossed her arms and turned to a stack of folded clothing resting on a chair. "Something to wear, for you." She lifted it and held it out to him.

He stepped her direction and took the stack, saying, "Thank you, but I have my tunic. It's . . . it *was* wherever I was before. In

Liam's quarters, maybe? Was he," and Aaeon laughed awkwardly, embarrassed he was actually asking the question, "named after Fadda Egel-la?"

"Who?" She frowned and laughed at the same time, bringing out a bewildered look.

"The Patron of Inner Peace, and well, Emotional Well-Being, also, although most worshippers don't care much about that. If you're blessed with inner peace, your emotional well-being is nothing to worry about." He said it proudly, having memorized something very similar in his catechisms years before.

"I don't know this . . . um, patron. Where did you hear of him?" She seemed interested again. She pulled the top item off the stack he held and shook it out. It was a jacket similar in design to Liam's but in different colors and sturdier, as if for a service worker or a member of the guard. It had a standup collar and black banding around the cuffs, with the body of the jacket in light charcoal. She held it up to him and smiled. "Liam's good. This looks to be an exact fit."

"You must know the patron." Aaeon was shocked she'd never heard of Fadda Egel-la. The names of the gods were taught in children's earliest lessons in all the cities. It was an adult's *responsibility*. How else would a youth know whether they wished to pledge to a particular Order, if they were unaware of those not on their own precipice? Of course, it was rare to pledge off-precipice, but it was done. Mene, for example, had long harbored dreams of doing so. At the thought of her, his heart swelled, and for a moment, the room around him blurred. He missed her so very much.

"Nope." She shook out a pair of long pants in a slightly darker color. A belt was already woven through loops around the waist. She laid them over the chair and draped the jacket over them. "So, who is he?"

"Liam Egel-la is one of the fourteen gods, though only ten are real gods." He glanced at her, realizing she wouldn't understand

318

that if she didn't know the Patron, and he tried to explain as simply as possible. "Four are shades, and they mean no one any good at all. No one sees Fadda Egel-la, except El Egel-faitum, his followers. Even they rarely see him, it's said."

"Then I think Liam takes after your god very nicely. We hardly see him, either, even during training exercises. He'd just as soon be in the ship's Virtual Learning World as out on the town with the other crew members." She had a pale gray shirt out, inspecting the fasteners to see if they worked correctly, and she tucked it under her arms and smiled at Aaeon. "You've sure brought him out of isolation. Thank you for that."

"You're welcome." He wasn't sure exactly what she meant. He tried to bridge the gap by saying, "Your name's similar to one of the gods, also. A goddess, actually." He was unfamiliar with the clothing styles, and he asked, "Do you wish me to wear those?" She'd been measuring them against him, and he couldn't retrieve his tunic wearing the things he had on. He was far too *exposed.*

"So, what does my goddess do, hide in the air ducts?" With a chuckle, she pushed her hair on one side behind her shoulder, and she held out the shirt. "Try on this first."

He placed it on the bed and began to pull his snug top off. He had it worked to his chest, about to pull one arm out, when she put her hand on his arm, telling him to put the new shirt on over it. Mortified he'd missed yet another cue in this strange place, and certain he'd soon be laughed at, he mumbled his apologies and pulled the white shirt back down. He smiled contritely before slipping into the gray shirt.

"Very nice." She smoothed the fabric as he fastened the front. "You'll want to thank your god. Liam, I mean." She covered her mouth with her hand, but her smile came through.

"That's funny," he said, at ease again, working the pants from under the jacket and slipping his legs inside. "Shosu Kovski-la's the Patron of Healing, like you."

319

"Shosu, um, Kovski what?"

"Kovski-la. Like your last name. She's a lesser god, because she rendered aid to one of the shades when the heavens burned and the gods fell from the sky. Kella Aland-um, I think." He shrugged, hoping she didn't blame him for perhaps misstating such a minor detail. He explained, "It's been a long time since my catechism, and we never spent much time on the shades."

"Kovski-la. I'm a lesser god. Oh, that's rich." The door opened, and Schlegel leaned in. She motioned to him, calling, "I have a goddess that's in my line of work, and we've got similar names. Mine's a lesser god. You're named after the god of inner happiness. I'm not sure if you're upper or lesser."

"It's *greater* or lesser gods, and Fadda Liam Egel-la is a lesser god, also, the Patron of Inner Peace," Aaeon corrected, as he tucked his shirt in and did his belt up. He looked up and smiled apologetically. "I'm sorry. I didn't mean to correct your termi-nology. I talk too much, my teachers always said."

"That's rich! You're a priest, Aaeon, and I'm a lesser god." Schlegel grinned, but he remained at the door. "You couldn't make me a greater god?"

"He didn't say you *were* a god, just named after one." The doctor shook her head and chuckled, picking up a handheld computer and scrolling with one finger.

"Yeah, I'll take what I can get. You through with him, Doc? Does he pass your approval for job assignment?" He looked behind him and held up a hand with one finger raised, and he mouthed a silent, "One moment."

"Certainly, if you brought him shoes. I didn't find any in the clothes you provided." She already seemed preoccupied, and she waved at him absently.

"On the floor. Sorry. Hey, can I bring someone in?" He was still at the door, and for the first time, Aaeon noticed a person just outside, dressed in colors similar to those he now wore.

"I do have a research project to monitor and a launch to

prepare for. Make it good, Liam." She looked up, pointed out the shoes to Aaeon, set the computer aside, and she crossed her arms again, this time with a harsh look Liam's direction.

Schlegel motioned the new party in. He touted thick and wavy hair, very dark; and although light-skinned, his features hinted at an African ancestry. He moved with a fluid, long-legged walk. In a glance, he took in the room, and he nodded to the doctor. His jacket read Shank in a cursive script across one breast.

"Ma'am, pleased to meet you." He had a cloth cap in his hands, the type assigned to laborers aboard the station, and he turned it in his fingers, following its circular shape. It was a very casual, off-hand action, something familiar someone would do without thinking; but the way he moved two centimeters and stopped before repeating the pattern gave it a calculated feel.

"I thought I'd been introduced to all the workers assigned to be on and off the *Higgs* while we're prepping for transit. I haven't met you." She wasn't curt, but she didn't smile, either. She waited on him to explain why he wasn't someone she knew.

"My fault." Schlegel laughed with a shrug. "I assumed you knew, and I shouldn't assume. Nielson tells me that all the time. You hear about that decompression blowout on Station Level C a couple weeks ago?"

"What about it?" Again, waiting patiently but ready to move on.

"So, you don't know. Sorry, Doc, for leaving you out of the loop. Acee Deesy, the drive technician assigned to the ship, and Pearl Jham, his helper, were both in the decompression zone. Mac's one of our backup crew, pressed into service for us by the station."

"Shank, or Mac?" She seemed to thaw, but she looked at the writing on his jacket questioningly.

"You noticed that." He dropped his head for a moment and chuckled, then he looked up. "I asked 'em not to, but you know the station. They do what they want. That's my name, but I go by

Mac. I know you'll be off in a few days, but I'd appreciate the Mac."

"You're replacing Technician Deesy?" She said it like a question, but her eyes made it a statement, one he didn't have to answer. "What about Jham? I don't follow up on the drive systematics closely, but I don't see how you could work alone, not with our eminent-departure timeframe."

"That's what makes this perfect." Schlegel shot two thumbs up. "Our man here—" he chuckled, "—needs a job, and Mac needs a helper—"

"You're vetted through the station," again, a statement, "I suppose."

"I wouldn't be here, otherwise, ma'am. Sorry about Deesy and Jham. I'm just picking up the slack. I want you folks to be off the line in time to get your job done, that's all. I'll be glad to take this young'un off your hands if it helps you out." His tone was submissive, but his eyes were sharp, taking in everything in the surgery, as if he were soaking it in.

"We're fine." Minkovski reached for her glass, already returning to other priorities. She watched his hands: shift, shift, pause. Then repeat. "The boy needs his injury checked by the station medic. The bandages will need changed. He needs to be vetted if you bring him back aboard the *Higgs*. Full documentation, Mac."

"Yes, ma'am." He nodded his head in a subservient manner. He stopped turning his cap just before he lifted it to his head, and smoothing his hair carefully, he worked his cap on his scalp, leaving the bill jutting high in the air in a cocky, jaunty pose.

"Aaeon, I'm sorry about your injury, but I'm glad I was able to help. Take care and follow Mac's instructions. I'm sure he'll set you up adequately for life on the station."

"Thank you, Doc."

She'd already turned away, and Aaeon looked to Schlegel and Mac. Schlegel motioned him along, and as they walked from the room, Mac asked, "You got a room, boy? Me, I'm from Glasgow Section, and it's a long way to work. I could use something closer, if you've a mind to share."

Aaeon shrugged and looked at Schlegel. "I was in Liam's room, I think. It's not mine—"

"You can have it. I'll set your permissions into the system." Schlegel gave another thumbs-up. "We're close enough to departure I can move onto the ship."

"—so I don't know. Oh." The liaison's words soaked in, and Aaeon smiled. "I guess I could, though I suppose I should find my two friends before I make any commitments."

"No worries," Schlegel reassured him. "I haven't found them yet, but they're on station. I'll tell them you'll be back at, what, Mac? Eighteen hundred at the gantry elevator?"

"Will be there," he said.

"Oh, before I forget." He palmed a panel beside the door, keyed in a series of instructions, then told Aaeon to press his palm to it. It turned from orange to green, and Schlegel told him it'd now work back at his quarters. His friends would know the directions from the gantry elevator to his room. He nodded to Mac, "The kid's not chipped, the Doc said, so tell them to contact her if that's a problem."

Mac's eyes lit up, and he smiled. "Taken care of."

"Take care, kid, and you might name a god after this guy, too." He laughed. "I'm off."

As soon as Schlegel walked away, Mac's speech patterns and subservient mannerisms changed. He grabbed Aaeon at the base of the neck with a big hand, and he asked—not unfriendly, but very much in control—how large the room was and if another friend could stay there, also, as they, like him, were from Glasgow Section. Things were moving so quickly that Aaeon felt he was being swallowed in a Crevasse, and he sidestepped the question with one of his own.

"How do I get vetted?"

"You're probably a good kid, right?" Mac ruffled his hair.

"I'm sixteen, nearly seventeen. I'm not a kid." Aaeon pulled away, not liking his hair messed with by the stranger.

"And not chipped." Mac grabbed his neck again, and he grinned.

"I guess not." He didn't know what chipped was, just as he didn't really know what vetted was, except it had to be done if you wanted to work here.

Mac stopped him in the corridor, and he faced him, with one big hand on each of Aaeon's shoulders. Workmen, most dressed like Mac, worked their way around them, some talking and some not, in a live static that Aaeon recognized from the many people who'd crowded the streets in Gates. The flashback brought on another memory: the attack and the reason they'd escaped through the haze curtain, only to find themselves in a very bad situation. His gut churned.

"If you're not chipped, my young friend, that means you don't have to be vetted, which makes you a very important person in my world." He smiled, and it didn't seem as pleasant as the one he'd given the doctor. He balled up a fist and gently tapped Aaeon on the nose. "How'd that injury happen, if I might ask?" His eyes searched the bandage.

"Some men shot at us—"

"On Earth Station LaGrange?" He laughed, returning his fist to the boy's shoulder and letting it rest there. "Not possible. All the weapons on this bucket are locked up tighter than a spare oxygen bottle on a leaking transport."

"The doc said it happened at a place called Mission Control." Aaeon was ready for the man's hands to be off his shoulders. "I've got the projectile to prove it in my pack, I think. With Kirk as my witness, I wouldn't lie."

"You? *You?*" Mac laughed loudly; and he released the boy's shoulders, pulled him close with one arm, and started down the corridor. "That was you on the news?"

"I think so." He wasn't sure he'd wanted to admit it with the doctor, but Mac seemed to approve. "They were showing it on the wall in the surgery."

"Well, well. If you aren't a prize beyond my wildest dreams, I don't know what is." Mac laughed again.

Oddly, that left Aaeon pleased, and he relaxed in the tall man's embrace. He liked being a prize, although he wasn't sure what was special about being shot at by the warriors of the gods. He marked in his mind that he'd ask Priest Tjark about it at eighteen hundred, whatever that was.

He risked a question. "Can we find some food?"

"You're hungry, are you? While we're headed that way, answer me this. Liam there said you should name a god after me. What god would I be if I became one? Can you tell me that?"

Aaeon laughed and shrugged. He found he liked this man, even if he had no god he knew that was named for him.

Over Easy

Mac's chosen eatery required a ride along the gantry that connected the *Higgs* with Earth Station LaGrange, the massive satellite that was home to nearly ten thousand souls and provided the vital link between Earth and her far-flung colonies. Earlier, Aaeon had struggled to surmount the overwhelming *size* of the vistas exposed to him; and fighting repeated dizzy spells wasn't conducive to taking in the scenery. Now, he looked and enjoyed. The gantry elevator was a glass box with room for a hundred, as big a space as any the youth had ever seen on Haukberk. He and Mac had a corner to themselves, seated in stiff, no-nonsense plastic seats. Confirming that the youth was only just arrived, and that this was his initial visit to Earth Station, Mac shared that this was a world unto itself, with gravity provided by the spinning of the outer torus, and Earth-normal weather—including rain, day, and night—to simulate as nearly as possible a standard Earth environment. Sculpted trees, small grassy plots, and profuse flowerbeds gave the station a warmth and illusion of perfection only akin to the proverbial Garden of Eden.

What he didn't say was that too many inhabitants of this

garden were the snakes that Earth hacn't quite managed to vet out of its worker documentation system. More managed to escape the planet's gravity well than were good for a small, enclosed community; and when rubbed the wrong way, friction sometimes produced fireworks. Despite that, Mac had found a solution to a problem he'd struggled with since arriving on the station, and he was on his best behavior. He *needed* this boy to like him.

"I've got something for you, kic," Mac said, as they neared the transfer point connecting the gantry elevator to Earth Station LaGrange. They readied to disembark, along with the dozen or so other people heading into the station.

"What's that?"

Their conversation was interrupted as the elevator slowed to a stop, and they stood to exit. The gantry framework surrounding the elevator created a series of shadows that crisscrossed the floor and moved steadily around them. As the station shifted in its position around the Earth, one of the arms of the station blocked the sun, and the entire elevator was swallowed in shadow. Lights came on, making the glass a mirror. Aaeon looked up and found himself standing next to Mac, his dark clothing contrasting with his light-colored hair. His eyes, even in the partial reflection of the glass, were dark with the rings he'd seen earlier. He was surprised at how ordinary he appeared. With the close-fitting clothes, he imagined himself as a child who'd yet to receive his first tunic. He'd tried to fend off the feelings of humiliation, recognizing that Liam and Mac didn't seem bothered by their clothing. Now, he realized he looked perfectly ordinary, like a man, even. The bandage was a shock. He'd forgotten it was there. His new friend, his *boss,* he supposed, towered over him, his cap on his head matching his clothing. His arm was draped casually over Aaeon's shoulder, much as a father's might guard a favorite son. As he watched, Mac grasped the bill of his cap and tugged it lower over his face, nearly hiding his eyes. Aaeon tried to remember the color of his father's eyes. He hadn't seen him since joining the Temple some years before.

"Follow me, kid," Mac muttered, nudging him in the side.

Aaeon and Mac moved forward as one wall of the elevator slithered aside, stepping through a gate that beeped with each person that walked past. When they stepped through, he noticed it only beeped once. It seemed unimportant, so he filed it away as something to remember to tell Regeth later, if he was interested. They passed two guards dressed very like the ones that had shot at him earlier, but they had no weapons. They seemed focused on the people lined up to board the elevator, not those exiting.

"This, a present." Mac seemed to relax, and he pulled the cap off, ran his fingers through his hair to fluff it into place, and slipped the cap onto Aaeon's head. He looked around as if taking charge of his surroundings, and he turned the youth's face to him and adjusted the cap, telling him, "You can hardly see it, now. No one will know you ever went to see the good doc."

He cuffed Aaeon on the shoulder and laughed before grabbing his neck once more and moving to a wide opening just along the side of the corridor. Words in bright blue flashed overhead proclaiming Zander's Zuider Zee to be the best fish and chips on three levels. People were moving in and out, more than just the somberly suited workers they'd passed on the *Higgs*. A girl, one no more than Aaeon's age, walked out of the opening, crossing just in front of them, her slim fingers picking something out of a small bag and popping it into her mouth. Her leggings trussed her thighs like a smoothly recited love poem, and her lips were done in a bright red. Her hair matched her lips and stuck out more haphazardly than Aaeon's. He could barely keep his eyes from following her as she moved past.

He nearly bumped into a nattily dressed man in what could only be a business suit. The man had a microphone on a thin wire perched in front of his mouth, and he spoke into it, dodging Aaeon and nodding as he moved hurriedly past to whatever destination called him.

Mac guided him inside the opening to a restaurant with a long counter on one side and brightly colored booths filling the other. About half were occupied, and several brightly dressed people stood at the counter. One spoke to a woman on the other side, and another picked up a tray of food and walked deeper into the space.

"You really are a country bumpkin, aren't you?" Mac smiled and guided him to an empty seat.

"I don't know." Aaeon shrugged. What was country, and what was bumpkin? He watched a tray of golden food waft by, and his stomach growled in response.

"Will one of those do?" Mac nodded at the tray of food. Steam obscured the air just above it.

"Sure." Aaeon looked at him to see a white card in his hand. "What's that?"

"This, kid," Mac held it up, "is how we eat. You, not being chipped, can't get one, but don't worry. You stick with me, and I'll make sure you get all the meals you need to stay happy and healthy. I want to hear about your two friends when I bring your food."

He walked away, heading toward the counter, and Aaeon watched the people around him. He hadn't seen any truly small children, but then, the people he spent most of his time with at the Temple on Haukberk were adults, with none so young as to be considered a child, so that didn't make a big impact on him. Overhead, the ceiling was high, with exposed pipes and ducting. He knew of those things but had never seen anything so elaborate and precisely done. Each one appeared to be a different color or design, which made sense to him when he thought about it. How else would a person keep straight what went where if there wasn't some principle behind how it was laid out? Through the opening, reasonably a door, although one larger than he'd ever used, the corridor teemed with people at times, then thinned. On the opposite side, a shop was filled with clothing, although for what purpose was impossible to imagine. Whether male or female, he had no idea, and he shrugged off what he had no answers for.

Closer, the table resembled the floor he'd walked on in Liam's quarters. When he touched it, the surface swirled in a kaleidoscope of colors. He used a finger to draw the letters of Mene's name. It held the shape, with the colors pulsing behind it. Then the table spoke to him, saying, "Invalid menu option. Please try again," and the letters faded away. He wrote, "Please turn off," and he smiled with the table said, "Thank you," and the colors went blank. He placed his elbows on it and sighed in relief that it remained just a table, with no movement and no colors.

Mac still had two people in front of him, and the person behind the counter had disappeared through a disguised door. Aaeon drummed his fingers on the table, waiting not so patiently. Being alone, however, gave him time to reflect on Priest Tjark and Regeth. Apparently, by Liam's report, they were occupied at locating a new tunic for the priest, though Aaeon couldn't imagine why he hadn't used his. He supposed it wasn't sized large enough. No one seemed concerned that he hadn't seen them since waking this morning, and he'd been so busy that he hadn't had time to be worried. He shrugged it off. His stomach had to be treated fairly, and besides, he'd found that the pretty girl with the love poem for leggings and the bright red hair wasn't the only alluring sight on the station. It seemed everywhere there were women wearing less clothing than he supposed Mene wore even when she visited the public baths. He'd spent a lot of time supposing that, too, so he should know.

"Daydreaming?" Mac tossed several paper-wrapped items on the table, a tray with a few disposable towels, and a basket of steaming chips, fried to a golden brown. He set a clear cup down and placed one beside it filled with a foaming beverage. He nodded to a display of drink choices and open nozzles on the far wall. "Drinks that direction, kid. Help yourself."

"Sure." Aaeon peered into the empty cup and was relieved to see a heavyset man with a close-cropped beard waddle to the display, tap a drink icon, and set his partially filled cup under one of the nozzles. Yellow fluid spurted out, and when he removed the cup, it stopped.

Before standing, Aaeon took one of the chips, realized it was hot, and popped it in his mouth, licking his fingers and trying to catch his breath. "Oh, Kirk, that's hot," he gasped.

"Don't burn your throat." Mac laughed. He'd unwrapped one of the packages to reveal a steaming bun filled with juicy meat and placed it in front of Aaeon. "Thought you might like to try this. It's for you. It'll be here when you get back." He pulled the second one to him and began opening it. "Go ahead, kid. Fill your glass. Your lunch isn't going anywhere."

Moving toward the nozzles, Aaeon was aware of three people at another table, their eyes following him. One of the men had black eyes and an intense look; the woman was beautiful, with olive skin, and eyes and hair as dark as the man's; and the third had scars running down his face, reminding Aaeon of Tjark, except for his short, tight hair. Their tabletop was as smooth and empty as if they either hadn't started or had already finished their meal. He tried to slough it off, but their interest in him made prickles shiver up and down his back. No one else sat at an empty table with nothing to do but watch people walk about. The drink machine filled faster than he expected, and it overflowed the top, distracting him from his spectators. He jumped back, exclaiming, "Oh, Kirk!" just in time to keep the liquid from cascading all over him. He found a tray with the small, disposable towels he'd seen on Mac's tray, and he pulled several free, wiping his hand and the outside of the cup. It was mostly full, so he dropped the towels in a bin and turned to head toward his table. He took a drink and was surprised at the sweetness. He looked up to find Mac handing his white meal card to the scarred man, who palmed it and slipped it inside a pocket.

When he got back to the table, Mac was already started on his sandwich. He took another bite, smiled as he chewed, and tapped the table beside Aaeon's food. "Eat up, kid, before it gets cold. The afternoon's gonna be slow on an empty stomach." He spoke around what was in his mouth, and as he finished talking, he took another bite.

"Afternoon?" He slipped into his seat, looking for the three people. Their table was empty, and he found them at the counter, ordering. "Are they friends of yours?"

"What'cha talking about, kid?" He downed a slug from his glass, leaving it half empty. He pushed it aside and crunched on a chip from the bowl, watching Aaeon with a focused, interested look. "You seeing things I'm not?"

"At the counter, they were watching me." He didn't mention the card. It was none of his business.

"The ugly guy with the other two?" Mac grinned, making light of it.

Aaeon hesitated, thinking of Tjark. He no longer saw him as ugly, and the man with the scars had reminded him of the priest. Agreeing felt disloyal, but he reluctantly nodded his head.

Mac chuckled. "They're always in here at this time. I suppose they thought it odd to see me with you. I usually come alone. Hey, we're going to be regulars from now on. They'll get used to it. You gonna eat that? If not, I will, but it's a long while till your next meal. It's about time to get back to the ship and wrap up our afternoon chores."

"Like what?" Aaeon prepared his sandwich and thought of his lost devotional cup. He took a deep breath and apologized to Fadda Kirk-fa for not being able to properly dedicate his food in a moment of prayer. There was nothing to be done for it, so he bit in and began to chew. Sensations of flavor that surpassed anything he'd ever consumed on Haukberk flooded his mouth. He exclaimed, even as he chewed, "It's good!"

"Thought you might like it." Mac grinned. His was gone, and he wadded the paper and placed it on the tray.

"What chores are we assigned?" Aaeon swallowed his food,

almost before chewing, and he pressed his mouth around a larger bite.

"Slow down." Mac grabbed his wrist, pulling the sandwich back a few centimeters. "We've got time for you to eat. A few minutes one way or another won't matter. *You* have a very special chore, one only you can do. I need to tweak the drive parameters, but that's me sitting at a terminal for the first part of the afternoon, and you can join me later. The first thing when we get back on board, you've got a delivery to make."

"By myself?" He took a drink from his glass, his eyes on Mac. He was used to chores, especially carrying messages and making deliveries. It's what acolytes at the Temple were expected to do, that and sweeping floors, fetching water, and anything else the priests felt was beneath them.

"Sure. Can you follow a map?"

"Follow a map?" He repeated the words as he lit up inside. "I can draw them. I have two handfuls in my pack that I drew on Kravitz Precipice, both of the precipice and the storm wall. I'm good at maps."

"I don't know about Kravitz or any storms, but this is simple. It's a location on the *Higgs*. I trust you can read?" He made it sound like a joke, and he pulled over one of the napkins and fished a pencil out of a pocket.

Aaeon held up the glass, pointed to the side, and read, "Zander's Zuider Zee Fish and Chips."

"Okay, okay. Put the cup down and pay attention. I've got a case that needs to be on board the ship before she launches." He had drawn several lines on the towel, and each place they intersected, he marked in symbols and numbers. At the end of one, he drew a box and wrote Cryo-Storage. He marked off three sections in the box and drew a circle with an X in it. "Now here," he began to explain, pointing to the very first line he'd drawn, "is where I'll leave you once we get off the elevator. Follow this corridor . . ."

Book of the Gods

*T*HE SECOND OF *the shades is Kella Theon Aland-um, who is revered by his followers as the Perpetrator of Battle.*

*K*ELLA THEON ALAND-UM *is not his true name, for his true name has never been spoken.*

*K*ELLA ALAND-UM *defeated a goddess, and when she died, her power became his. He took a portion of her name to retain her power, and he killed three others so his power would never be equaled.*

*I*N THE BATTLE *of The Great Falling, Kella Theon Aland-um's foot bore great injuries, and Fadda Freder Neil-fa prevented him from killing Shosu Eboh-la with words of great wisdom.*

*K*ELLA ALAND-UM'S *defeat was so great, he was cast from Paradise and became a shade.*

*K*ELLA THEON ALAND-UM'S *followers are known as*

El Aland-wicum, or the Minions of Kella Theon Aland-um. Selah.

Death Masks

The cloth cap was Aaeon's disguise.

That's how he felt. Of course, on Haukberk, his tunic with its expansive hood had been much more concealing, but he'd worn it to express his identity, that of an aspiring cleric. It was never to *hide* who he was, but rather to keep from brandishing his individuality, as doing so would subjugate his holy calling to the services of Fadda Kirk-fa. To be a cleric was to be about their *Order,* not about *standing out* in their Order.

Mac had insisted his head injury must be hidden, and that the cap covered it, if he kept it pulled low. It *disguised* what had happened to him, as if it had never occurred, as if Priest Tjark hadn't rescued him with his instructions to traverse the haze curtain, and as if his friend Regeth hadn't carried the pack that had stopped the projectile from injuring one or more of them—thank Fadda Kirk, as well as Fadda Arkson-la, for their miraculous aid in a time of great need.

Now Aaeon carried a different canvas-covered pack with him. It was larger than the ones he and Regeth had, and fatter, rectangular, with something rigid inside. It didn't fit on his back, but had sturdy straps sewn onto the sides that formed loops he could grasp in one hand. He carried it at his side, awkwardly, doing his best not to bump anyone or cause anyone to notice him.

One thing Mac had insisted was that he wasn't to *look like* he was unsure where he was headed. He couldn't ask directions or study the map in his pocket. *"Only take it out if necessary, and then step into an unused corridor or empty room. Don't ever look at the map if anyone can see you."* Then, he clapped him warmly on the shoulder and told him how proud he was of him for making this very important delivery. No one else could do it, he stressed, and he was counting on him.

Aaeon felt his face warm at how he'd smiled back, so quick to agree, and so willing to let Mac convince him to do this thing. He'd ignored every signal that should have gone off in his head. Of course, the signals weren't ringing then, were they, he consoled himself. They were sitting at the table; the map seemed perfectly innocent; and Mac had given him his cap. He smiled and told Aaeon kind things. He bought him *food.* What was there not to like?

It was what occurred after leaving the restaurant that made his gut churn.

He'd let the man's arm rest on his shoulders, the crook of his elbow cradling the back of Aaeon's neck, and they'd fallen into an easy rhythm together as they traversed the broad corridor away from the familiar checkpoints and transfer spot back onto the gantry elevator leading to the ship. His eyes had been so full of wonder that he let himself be led by the nose to where he never should have gone. He cringed to think what Priest Tjark would say about his weak spine and willingness to trade a few moments of warm affection for something that had left him with the feeling of a shady affair.

He could still see the glittering facades that lined the walkways, hidden behind banks of clipped foliage, the doors bordered by elaborate displays of brightly colored blooms. In even the most

338

crowded locations, the hurriedly moving masses sidestepped the small, tightly cropped patches of green grass. Bright squares of sun flickered across shiny surfaces, crawling with unending motion past ornate lampposts planted near casually arranged benches, all of which were empty. Vast swatches of the ceiling were clear, something dizzying to Aaeon. He missed the storm wall, that well-defined boundary that determined what his universe was and wasn't. This, this was just *too much*.

They'd taken a turn, with Mac laughing and pointing the way, past a red-flowering tree and a mechanical man that waved a metal arm pointing toward a store, repeating over and over, "Sale. Buy now. Your chip is your personal discount." Aaeon had turned to look, amazed, but Mac pulled him along, never releasing his hold, and taking him through a door that opened to a narrow, low-ceilinged corridor filled with more doors. They climbed a staircase and stopped at a pale, painted metal door with the identification 2-B Sector A at eye level.

"You live here?" Maybe, Aaeon thought, Mac needed another cap. Aaeon still wore his. He liked it, as though it made him a part of whatever this place was, this amazing place that both frightened and excited him, and he hoped he wasn't expected to return it.

"Um, maybe, kid. You let me talk." He rifled the hair on the back of Aaeon's head, shifting the cap, then reseating it and pulling the bill down. He reached forward and tapped on the door three times, paused and did it twice more. "I've got some convincing to do."

"Um, sure." Aaeon readjusted the hat and grinned.

"Good boy." Mac patted the side of his face with his big hand, then released him and stepped away to leave some space between them.

The door opened to the dark eyes and the intense look Aaeon had seen watching him in the restaurant. Behind him was a blank wall, and the floor was hard and plain and scored with rough use. It needed a good cleaning. Aaeon took in the broad shoulders he hadn't noticed before, and how the man's shirt revealed a strength that was an animal poised and waiting to pounce. He wanted to run, but Mac was at his side, and he didn't want to disappoint him. He knew no one else, except Liam, and the clean-cut man who'd befriended him was lost with the changing events of the day. Even Tjark and Regeth, who knew? He was on his own, and Mac was his connection with anything familiar.

"Nah, Magill, not happening." Dark Eyes took in Aaeon's presence and didn't invite them in. "You know the plans. No outside people, no romantic entanglements, no contact until we get the package on board."

"Not out here, Zealander. Besides, they're *my* plans. Let us in." Mac's voice was as hard as the man's through the door.

"Didn't know you went for boys this young. You want a room? There's plenty elsewhere."

"You're an idiot. Step aside." Mac moved forward and found himself blocked by one of Zealander's arms. His hand rested right in the middle of Mac's chest.

"We discussed this after seeing you with the kid today. Hollis wants to remove his head so he doesn't give us away. Abdullah thinks he's cute." His eyes were on Aaeon. "Fertilizer or play toy. Your choice, Magill."

"Get your hand off me, Zealander. You jump Abdullah and leave this boy alone. We need him." He pushed past, grabbing Aaeon's arm and pulling him through after him. They moved into a narrow hall towards an open door at the end.

"Abdullah needs him," Zealander called with a laugh, "after lights out." The door closed, and his footsteps followed them down the hall.

Mac pointed Aaeon to a low couch, and he seated himself on the edge, leaning forward with his elbows on his knees. He didn't feel comfortable enough to lean back. His eyes trailed Mac as he entered a small kitchen and pulled two boxes from a closed cabinet. He tossed one to Aaeon, calling, "Something to drink, kid." It was surprisingly cold, and unsure how to get inside, he watched Mac pop up the end and drink from the spout he'd made. Aaeon did the same and found it turned. He coughed, barely avoiding spitting out the liquid. When he looked up, Dark Eyes was across the room watching him.

"Why do we need this boy, Magill?" Only his mouth moved, and his eyes remained locked on Aaeon.

"Because I'm brilliant." Mac walked past Aaeon, set his box on a side table, and dropped into an adjoining chair, propping his feet on a center table, one foot, then the other, very precisely. "Oh, and I need another cap. You got an extra?"

"You know exactly what I've got," the big man growled. His eyes were still glued on Aaeon, and he'd started to feel more than a little nervous, taking another small sip from the box and choking. He swallowed it by sheer will.

"Let me have it. I'm scheduled back on the ship and can't stay." Mac took a long swig from the box, shook it, took a final drink, then tossed it, hitting an open refuse bin in the corner.

"Explain first." Eyes still on Aaeon.

"You *are* a big, dumb brute. Special Ops, and you still carry your brains in your biceps. No wonder that woman died during your martial arts phase." He laughed then leaned forward, mimicking Aaeon's stance, whether he realized it or not. "He's not *chipped,* Zealander. And get this, the doc aboard the *Higgs* requested, *requested* him to be my personal aide. You taking out Jham as well as Deesy has turned out to be prescient. I thought I'd have someone looking *over* my back, and now I've got someone looking out *for* my back."

"Yeah, so he's not chipped." Black Eyes seemed to relax, and he wandered in for one of the little boxes. "How's that help us?" He took the couch next to Aaeon, and he smelled of exercise and muscle—and threat.

"You don't get it, yet. He has free reign on the station *and on the ship.* Nothing tracks him. He's our ticket, man." Mac had his

341

hand out, and he twisted and clenched it in a quick and hard fist. "I need the package."

And *that's* why Aaeon carried the package in his hand, trying not to forget the directions he'd memorized on the piece of paper, and wishing he had Priest Tjark here to guide him.

He looked at the symbol on the corridor wall. With his cap so low on his face, it was hard to see without leaning his head back, and he wasn't supposed to be obvious. He did have to find his way, however. His instructions were clear. Find the Cryo-Storage, use the white card Mac had retrieved from Black Eyes—the same card as the one from lunch—to gain access to the room, and find Section 8. All he had to do was leave the pack, the *package,* in an inconspicuous location, and return to meet with Mac. Once the package was placed, he could ask all the directions he wanted. He wasn't to tell anyone about the package, as Mac was his friend, and friends did things for friends when they asked them nicely, now, didn't they, kid?

Aaeon shuddered, even in memory. The threat had come through plainly. He wasn't stupid. Regeth might have seen through the man at the beginning, but it'd taken him longer. He saw it now, though. He finally figured it out. He just didn't like what he'd figured out, and he didn't know what to do. Mac had said to Black Eyes, "While we're gone, the kid has two friends. They're on station somewhere. Schlegel, the Education Liaison, sent them to Vatican. Find them."

"Done," Black Eyes had said, in a voice that was ominous and filled with threat. He shifted position, his muscles flexed, and Aaeon felt panic wash over him.

He breathed a sigh of relief to see the words Cryo-Storage on the wall. A workman carrying a ladder and dressed very much like him crossed behind him. Aaeon said, "Kirk-fa be with you," and nodded. The man gave him a strange look and replied, "And with you." He didn't seem to think too much of it and soon disappeared around a bend. Aaeon worked the white card from his pocket and held it to a glowing panel beside the door. With a quick movement and a suction of air, the door moved aside, and he stepped through. The air smelled clean, antiseptic, unused. It was cold. He'd been warned to expect a space so vast he'd be lost if he misplaced his directions, but this, this was so much more. His head began to spin. It was as vast as the view had been through Liam's wall that morning, and he felt about as sick.

That morning. Aaeon let himself be distracted for a moment. It was just one day, right? Not more? He'd awakened in an unfamiliar room, then again in the doctor's surgery. He'd traveled the massive gantry elevator *twice* and visited a man that had nearly frightened him into soiling his trousers. Now, he was in a room filled with rows and rows of . . .

He glanced into the one closest to him. A glass panel comprised a portion of the top, and he found a woman inside. Her skin was pale, almost translucent. A tight cap covered her head, bulging as though a full head of hair was gathered inside. Her lips looked falsely red against her skin. He stepped to another and found a youth about his age. A tight shirt covered his narrow chest and stretched over broad shoulders. His hair bristled on his head as though tightly sheared. His eyebrows. He had none. They'd been shorn off. Aaeon's heart twisted inside.

People . . . rows and rows of people. A network of pipes and tubes, a single color instead of coordinated like in the restaurant, filled the ceiling, one breaking off and connecting to each cylinder. Were the people ill, sleeping, or dead? He didn't know. He didn't know the purpose of this room, or this . . . *vessel* they were on. He didn't know anything except that he had to find where to place his *package* so Black Eyes wouldn't let *Hollis* separate his body from his head. He didn't want to be fertilizer, no matter how pretty he made the flowers grow.

He pulled the disposable towel from his pocket and glanced at it. Section 8. He searched the space and saw labels on the ceiling. Not too distant, one read Section 2. There were more, some too far away to make out, and he looked overhead to see Section 1 above him. On the first cylinder, below the window, was a name. Cynda Aafjes. 0001, Section 1. He stepped to the youth. James Aaldenberg. 0002, Section 1. He moved past them to find 0003, 0004, 0005, until he reached 0010, and an aisle opened up. Looking down it, the cylinders stretched fifty deep. He took a deep breath. He had a job, and he had to get it done, so he moved on briskly, past the dead-looking people, and on towards his goal, occasionally glancing to catch the names and the numbers that went with them. *Albero, 0099, Albers, 0100, Amatore, 0123, Azarola, 0197, Baaiman, 0201,* and so on. He began to slow when he reached the letter H. Hibolah. Would it be there? There were so many, and only a few had repeated, so far. *Haak, 1403, Hawking, 1433, Hendrix, 1444,* then another *Hendrix, 1445.* He stopped for a moment, peering inside the two cylinders with matching names. They could be twins. He wondered if they were, or siblings, perhaps, with the same shoulders, and a similar facial structure. He wondered if their eyes would be the same color if they opened them as he watched. Did they die together, or would they come back awake together? He'd seen no injuries, so he didn't think the cylinders stored the dead. He felt a level of excitement as he searched for his name, for validation that someone who carried his name might actually be aboard. He turned down an aisle and followed the names. *Heymans, Hibbert,* then Aaeon laughed. There it was, *Hibolah, 1473.* His heart leaped into this throat as he read the rest. Aaeon Hibolah, 1473, Section 3.

His blood ran cold. He wasn't stupid. Why hadn't he thought this possible? He'd been stepping through the haze curtains all his life. He knew what was on the other side, different *whens.* Time pockets of the same *where,* only different *whens.* If he was in one place at a certain *when,* what made him think he wouldn't stumble across himself in other *whens?* Priest Quartten, Fadda Kirk rest him, had been caught in the same *when* as his older self, and he'd had to hide to keep from meeting him. Then there was Priest Pitt.

He'd traded his old life for a young one, stepping from one *when* to another in the same *where*. Did Aaeon dare look inside to see if this was him? If it was, would it break the rules of haze travel and bring this *when* cascading around him? He took a deep breath. He was sixteen crackles. He was a curious youth. He was inquisitive, bright, and able to work out things in his mind. He had to *know,* to figure this out, if he ever intended to get back home and see Mene ever again. Dear Kirk, he thought. *Mene!* Would he find her name in here, also? His heart pounded in anticipation at the very possibility.

He set the canvas pack on the floor, stepped to the window, and looked inside. His first glance, after identifying the face he'd seen in the mirror only that morning, was to look for the bandage on his temple. He breathed a sigh of relief. At least he hadn't died from his injury. His next thought was of dismay. His hair! It was shorn tight, just like the boy in the second canister. Who would have done this to him? He looked at his closed eyelids. He'd never seen his closed eyelids before. They were veined with red lines, just like the lightning-streaked cloud walls at home. He never realized his lips were so full or his shoulders so broad. A taut shirt of the same design as the youth at the front stretched across his chest, only in a different color. He stepped back, and, yes, everyone here wore the same. They'd been a different color in the other sections. He grabbed the pack and ran to the main corridor, jogging toward the final section. Zaptha. Mene Zaptha, would he find her? And Regeth? He smiled. Was it too much to hope for?

And there she was, Mene Zaptha, 4,912, his beauty, in her tightly fitting cap, wrapped in her smooth honey skin, with wisps of black escaping from her cap on one side. He pressed one hand to the glass, soaking her in.

"Mene," he whispered. "I've loved you. I've always loved you. I kissed you and fell in love with you forever. I'm coming home. I promise." He leaned his forehead against the glass and prayed, "May Kirk-fa be with you until you awake, and may you

345

dance and sing with Fadda Char-la's heart while you sleep."

He tore his eyes away and found Regeth Zaptha, 4,913, Section 10. He laughed. His friend was so short his face barely showed in the window. The top of his cropped head caught the light on the ceiling far overhead, and it shimmered as Aaeon walked up to look in at him. His could see his thin chest and his weak shoulders. Oh, it looked just like Regeth! Aaeon took a deep breath. He missed his friend. "Fadda Kirk smile on you, my friend, even if I will see you before the day is done."

Tjark! He jerked away from his friend's canister. He would be here, too, wouldn't he? He must. Then he thought of Quartten, killed by the shade's minions. Would he find him? And Priestess Burne? He had to know. He carried the pack, running the aisles, looking for familiar names, finding each one. He was surprised to find Priest Pitt to be young and fit, with a firm face and a full mouth. And Tjark, black as night, but with no whelps gracing his skin. He said a short prayer of benediction for each person he found, to their particular god, when he remembered what they were.

Dreading what he might find, or if he would, he searched for Mac, then Magill with no success, then Zealander. They weren't there. The others? Hollis, he thought he remembered, and Abdullah. First names or last? He didn't know. Either way, his search was pointless. He desperately wanted to visit Mene again, but the cylinder had been cool to the touch, and there hadn't been any life there. His job was to deliver the pack, which he'd stashed behind a row of cylinders after he located Priest Pitt's name. He was at the beginning of Section 8, and Aaeon thought it a fitting memorial for the crippled man he'd befriended for such a short time. His prayer to Fadda Neil-fa had invoked the deity's power of directions to lead him home before too much more time had passed. Aaeon thought the old priest would be happy for Aaeon to claim part of the prayer, for he'd always seemed generous, and he surely wouldn't mind sharing. He never had before.

The cold in the room had soaked through Aaeon's jacket, and he'd begun to shiver. His teeth chattering, he looked around and soaked up his final view of the unusual room. Wait until he told Priest Tjark and Regeth he'd found them, alive or dead, he didn't know, but they were all here.

Except Mac and the three at the restaurant. When he thought of them, he began to shiver uncontrollably, and he fled the room, urgently needing to find someplace warmer to think about his day.

Auld Lang Syne

Aaeon wound up on the scenic tour as he searched for Mac. The terminal for tweaking the drive's parameters wasn't in Engineering, and that's where everyone kept trying to send him. Using Mac's white card added to the confusion. The ship's computer wasn't set to respond to his voice, and each time he swiped the card against a wall comm—after he'd been told repeatedly to get back to work and quit bothering busy people—the ship politely responded, "Technician Magill recognized. How may I help you, Technician Magill?" He'd ask for Mac's location, and the display would light up, showing a map of the ship with Mac's location identified by a combination of symbols and numbers. When he began to search, he'd learn he was already at that location.

He was fully frustrated when he finally discovered a worker in Engineering with red hair and a beard who was wearing a jumpsuit discolored down one side with grease and oil, and who proved to be just bored enough to take the time to search out where Mac might be. He pulled out a stained cloth, wiped his hands fast and hard, and logged into a terminal; and taking Aaeon's white card, he passed it over the data reader and made some adjustments.

"Telling it to look for your chipped friend," the man said, with a grin. "Sometimes she finds us, and sometimes she don't. Gotta stroke the girl's thighs to get her to open up to you sometimes, if you know what I mean." He winked with his words, expecting Aaeon to read his lascivious meaning. It turned out Mac wasn't on the ship at all, not the life-viable, environmentally sealed section, anyway. He was in the drive module, and that required an extra-ship suit.

"I'm supposed to join him. I'm his helper. I had to run an errand, and today's my first day."

"Ah, laddie. You're the one to fill in for Pearl. She was a sweetheart. Too bad, the accident. It was convenient for Mac to be on station to step in when that stateroom decompressed. Never seen the likes of it. Come, now, and follow me." He shook his head and held out a hand as they walked. "Ailbeart O'Cain. Been up from the Highlands for over a year. Quite a place, this. You, where you from? Never heard the likes of your accent before."

"Haukberk. That's near Gates." Aaeon grinned, pleased at the warm conversation and personal interest the man showed toward him.

"Never heard of Gates, nor Haukberk. Never heard of a lot of places. You got a girl back in your 'Berk?"

"Yeah." He pictured Mene, and not the frozen one from the ship. He remembered her on the Upward rocks of the precipice, her hood thrown back, and offering him her hand for his help. He smiled.

"She must be a special lass." O'Cain stopped at a door, and touching a pad, it opened to an elevator. He spoke, "Drive module."

"In transit," the ship replied in a clean voice with no inflection. Lights began to change, indicating motion, although the floor remained stationary and there was no apparent shift in acceleration or direction. It felt as though they were standing still.

"She is special," Aaeon replied. He started to say more, when

349

the doors opened, and his guide stepped out, and he was forced to follow into a locker-lined room with suits in niches beside each one. O'Cain eyed Aaeon and took him to a suit that seemed about the right size. He pulled it down, held it to the youth, and nodded, satisfied.

"Off with your things, now. You gotta wear this to go where your boss's gone."

"Strip?" Aaeon looked around at the people in the room. Two men and a woman had a panel off the wall, and they were testing relays with a handheld device they'd touch to each one, holding it until it responded with a flashing light. They were currently removing a faulty relay, and the woman was lifting its replacement from a foam-lined chest.

"Aye, no other way about it. Shoes, jacket, and pants, now. You can keep your underpants, if you like." O'Cain grinned and winked.

"Thanks," Aaeon grumbled, as he stripped his things off. He saw one of the niches empty and decided Mac was in that suit. Above the empty niche was a plaque that said Nielson in block letters. He read the name twice and thought of Fadda Neil-fa and how the gods were reverenced across this world in people's names. His suit had Levitson on the chest, and looking up, he found the same name emblazoned across the space above the niche. Fadda Vitson-la, of course! He chuckled, trying to imagine a god wearing a suit to protect himself from anything. Even so, Fadda Vitson was the Patron of all things mechanical, so it stood to reason . . . He laughed as he dropped his trousers.

"So, you find this amusing, do you?" O'Cain had a grin on his face, and he teased the youth.

"The names above each of these. They're very like the gods we worship at home. This one," and he tapped the suit in O'Cain's hand, "is our Patron of Machines, Fadda Sher Vitson-la."

"Aye, we see them as gods, also, laddie. Those that travel between the stars have a god's perspective, and no one can say any different. Now slip into this, and I'll be on my way. I've still got a day's job to finish. I'll be wishing you the best of luck with your girl back home, as I'll chance as nay be meeting you again. Now," and he pointed inside the first hatch, "when you get the signal, go straight across. Don't be looking around too much. It'll be pretty, so remember, you've got a job to do, and being a tourist, it's not." He laughed at that and clapped the boy on the back.

O'Cain had him in his suit and up and into the passageway, offering him a thumbs up, before sealing it off and leaving Aaeon alone to meet the man who had demanded of him a deed that on one hand had seemed innocent enough, and on the other had been fraught with unwelcome overtones of shady dealings and ominous threats.

When the hatch opened, and he pulled himself out, he understood the redheaded man's instructions. To one side, the darkness reached its maw for him as it ate the heavens, blacker than the darkest storm wall just before the most ferocious of lightning jumped from the sky to writhe over the Rising Stones and fill the chambers inside. Distant points of light, small and great, were eyes, accusing him of weakness, of seeking out the man who had shown him a kind word in exchange for a deed that Aaeon felt in his heart was wrong. Turning his head, his heart doubly jumped in his throat, for above him, the gantry leaped skyward; and Earth Station LaGrange stretched its arms sunward, hovering over a crescent Earth like a goddess extending her blessing toward a favorite daughter and giving her absolution for her sins. The sun caught on myriad glass panels, shifting and sparkling as the station turned about its axis to create a semblance of gravity for her inhabitants. On the distant globe, wispy clouds covered breaking seas, creating a jeweled crown of vivid colors and unimaginable beauty.

"Great Kirk," Aaeon whispered, his sense of self stolen from him. After longer than he thought possible, he inhaled a great draught of air and began coughing. He'd forgotten to breathe, and

351

his chest burned. He was jarred out of his reverie when three sharp knocks reverberated against his helmet, and he glanced upward.

"Hey, kid! Coming up? Or you just doing the tourist thing till I'm through for the day? Hey? Hook up and come on." The knocking had come from the shell of his helmet, but the voice rang from speakers inside. Mac had floated down from the drive unit a hundred meters overhead, and he was tethered with a strap that attached inside the hatch he'd dropped through. He pulled himself toward the *Higgs*, reached beside Aaeon's waist, and pulled out a retractable tether with a clip on the end. He snapped it onto a hook on Aaeon's suit and pushed off for the drive unit. His tether billowed out for a moment, then it began to retract into the open hatch.

Aaeon looked around him and saw no one else. Mac seemed to think he knew what to do, and he didn't want to embarrass himself. After the meeting with Zealander, he didn't want to create any disruption that would call attention to himself. He grabbed the edge of the open hatch, braced his leg, and shoved hard, leaping for the overhead hatch. He shot forward surprisingly fast. The effect was what he'd expected, although he pictured quick acceleration then slowing as he covered the distance. Instead, he maintained his speed and would have crashed into the drive unit had Mac not leaped to intercept him and break his forward momentum.

"Newbie, newbie." Mac chuckled. "You *are* fresh at this. I thought you were playing innocent, and now I see it's no act. I've got some cleanup for you to do. Oh, tongue your mic on. It's there by your chin." His tether began to retract, and when he could grasp the edge of the hatch opening, he pulled them forward and shoved Aaeon inside. As he did, he unsnapped Aaeon's tether, released it to snake through the air towards the open hatch in the *Higgs*, and snapped a new one on from inside the drive module's hatch. He slapped him on the calf as he disappeared inside, then pulled himself through afterwards.

"What's there to do in here?" Aaeon looked around at the space, trying to decipher it in comparison to what he'd experienced during his challenging and eventful day. It was a framework, like the gantry, sturdy-looking but more space than spaceship. Titanic mountains of machinery filled different areas, but there was plenty left over. A generous data terminal was mounted in the morass, but there was no floor or place to stand. Mac was pulling himself that way.

"Mac?" Aaeon called before realizing he'd not tongued the mic, whatever that was. He leaned his head back, looked down, and found several switches. He pressed his tongue against one, and his field of vision went dark. "Oh, Kirk," he muttered, extending his tongue and feeling for that one again. His vision returned. The next one didn't seem to do anything until he called, "Mac?" and the man's voice answered.

"You found it finally. Get on up here." Mac had settled at the terminal, floating, and he hooked two clips on short tethers to his waist. He was already tapping on the terminal input sensors.

"What am I to do?" He was beside the older man. He found the hooks and attached himself to the terminal console.

"You figured the mic out?" He ignored Aaeon, still on the terminal and entering information and checking the display overhead.

"Sure—"

"Practice," the word came short and hard. "Off, wait to the count of ten, then back on. I want to know you can use it."

"Okay, but why?"

Mac turned to Aaeon, glaring, his face no longer friendly. "Do I have to explain everything to you? Just do it, kid."

"Here goes." He tabbed the switch, waited, then tabbed it back on.

"Now the one next to it. It cuts out your receiver. Try it, count to ten, and reset it."

"Sure—" At the man's look, Aaeon quit talking, felt, found it, and clicked it off. He looked at Mac to see him talking to him and grinning, and he heard nothing. It *looked* like what he was saying was very crude. He clicked the receiver to catch Mac finishing a word. He cringed at the vulgarity and tried not to show it.

"Now do them both. You need the practice, kid."

As soon as Aaeon had them both off, Mac grabbed his arm and forced their helmets together. He yelled through the touching faceplates, the sound coming through as a tinny, high-pitched imitation of a man's voice.

"Don't turn them back on. Did you get the package delivered?"

"Yes, Mac," he yelled back, guessing Mac heard him in the same, tinny voice.

"Section 8? This is important, kid. Section 8?" His eyes were a tenth of a meter away, and they spit fire Aaeon's direction.

Aaeon wanted free of the man's hand. He remembered the suits and the niches they were in. Above each one had been a variation of one of the names of a god. Now, this man's eyes. His mind made an intuitive leap between the Scriptures and the stories they told of the gods and lightning and fire. Just that morning, he, Tjark, and Regeth had viewed the fire of the gods leaping through an impossible sky that could only be from the land of the gods. Could the gods also shoot fire from their eyes? He'd located no one called after the name of a god in the Cryo-Storage room deep within the ship. He'd also not found anyone by the name of this man. Perhaps, perhaps, although it was surely impossible. A god wouldn't need a boy to do his work for him, would he? And just because a man was named for a god didn't make him a god. Gods were all powerful. *People* required help from the *gods,* not the other way around.

"Yes, Mac," he said, more afraid to speak than he'd ever been before.

"What?" Mac yanked his arm, twisting, as he pulled the boy closer. Both hands were now on the youth, one on each arm, and they floated, suit to suit, in a chilling embrace.

"Yes," Aaeon yelled, anger flooding in to replace the fear. "I left in in the P's, right in Section 8. That's what you said, and that's what I did. I'm not stupid. Let go of me!" He jerked away, freeing himself, and he jabbed his tongue at the switches. Not having his receiver and mic on was something else that seemed dirty. Wrong, as if he was keeping a secret from someone who might not like what was happening.

"Good." The voice flooded Aaeon's helmet. "Now stay there while I let the others know it's done."

Mac began entering instructions into the terminal, password after password, until the words Encrypted Channel appeared. Mac smiled, and he began to speak, glancing at Aaeon from time to time.

"The package is delivered. Have you located our two guests?" His eyes were on Aaeon when he said *guests*, and he smirked before clearing his expression. He nodded as though he got the answer he'd wanted. "You located those quantum camouflage suits, yet?" After a pause, his face turned red, and he yelled, "Then find 'em! We're not getting off this station without 'em, and I don't intend to be here when the *Higgs* implodes on her run to Deneb. Got that?" He hit the terminal with three quick jabs, and the display cleared. He unhooked Aaeon's clips to the terminal, then his own, and he linked his arm in the boy's and held him as tightly as the suits allowed. He spoke in a voice that was pitched low and spoken softly, but it seemed to yell in the youth's ears. "You're not leaving my side, boy, not as long as I'm on this station. You do one thing I don't like, one thing, and I'm done with you." Mac drew a finger across his throat and smiled wickedly.

Aaeon felt his gut churn. Now was the time to find a haze curtain. Now, now, now! He had to run. He couldn't, though. He couldn't leave Regeth behind, or Tjark, and he couldn't take them if he couldn't see them or touch them. He'd never find them again

355

if he left them now. His throat filled with bile. He followed Mac out of the drive unit, and somehow, he no longer seemed interested in the way the sun had shifted on the planet, the way the arms of the station now seemed to whisper good night to her sleeping child, or that the brilliance of the nearby star hit his faceplate, and it darkened to near black. He only saw the sky eating the world, and for once in his life, he wished for lightning, for familiar red lightning to fill the skies, and to take him home. He remembered his face through the chilled glass, just one lifeless person among many in the banks of frozen people. His eyes had been closed, and red veins had painted his skin. It was as though his frozen self looked at the world through eyelids of lightning, the life he lived wasn't real, and everything he knew was a dream to the person locked inside his head.

Dear Kirk, how could his day have come to this? He didn't know what do to. He couldn't help his friends, because he couldn't even help himself.

He dropped back into the *Higgs*, released his tether, and watched it float gently across the void to the far hatch. When it disappeared inside, the drive module's hatch swung closed, and then his own did the same.

He stripped the hated suit off, returned it to its niche, and it never occurred to him to say a prayer of thanks to Fadda Vitsonla that the suit had kept him safe in the harsh environment between the ship and her drive section. It took everything he had to not look at Mac as he pulled his clothing on and followed his captor out the door.

Book of the Gods

Roshama, Chapter 1:12-14

THE THIRD OF the shades is Shulla Cryst Hol-um. She is the Perpetrator of Seduction, for her beauty is beyond compare. Beware those who follow after Shulla Hol-um, for her black eyes flash fire, and her love turns to anger at a word.

BORN FROM THE Underworld of stone dust and dead men's souls, she knew no parents and draws life from the dying breaths of those she kills. Shulla Hol-um is the Perpetrator of the Dead.

SHULLA CRYST HOL-UM'S followers are known as El Hol-wicum, or the Minions of Shulla Cryst Hol-um. Selah.

Beauty and the Beholder

The arm draped across Aaeon's shoulders chafed him to the core. It rubbed his sense of rightness wrong, and it burned away his thread of attraction to Mac.

The memory of how easily he'd let the smooth-talking man suck him in made him dislike him the more. He wanted to hit himself in the head for being stupid, but more, he wanted to punch Mac in the gut for what he'd forced him to do.

He had to remind himself he was a faithful adherent to the precepts of Fadda Kirk-fa, and while Fadda Kirk might be the Patron of Passion, he was also the Patron of Fire, and fire must be controlled, or it consumed everything. Aaeon wanted to consume Mac with his anger, and he couldn't. He *couldn't*. He had the priest and his good friend to consider.

Besides, how does a sixteen-crackle-old kid fight back against a grown man a full head taller, a man who has friends who seem to be connected to something dark and shameful, even evil, when as a kid, he didn't know *anyone,* not even the people who'd tried to help him earlier?

He knew one thing. Once he found Tjark and Regeth, they

were out of here. He didn't care where they wound up; he'd leap as many curtains as it took to get away from Mac and his bad friends.

Aaeon felt his eyes burn, and he realized they were watering. He squeezed them tightly, forcing the tears back. He wouldn't wipe them, either. He couldn't. Mac might see, and he'd know he was weak. He couldn't be weak. He had to be strong for his friends.

He sniffled, and he cringed, fighting off what he knew was coming.

"Gotta a cold there, kid?" Mac chuckled and pulled him tighter. His arm remained crooked around Aaeon's neck, and he slapped him on the chest, digging his fingers in hard before releasing him to let his hand dangle loosely against Aaeon's shirt.

"Where are we going?" It was a fair question, and he deserved to know.

"Some friends of mine are waiting. You've met Zealander. He sure charmed up to you." Mac chuckled again, and it sounded ominous. They were passing Zander's Zuider Zee, but he made no move to turn in. He'd been generous with Aaeon before he'd taken care of his "delivery," but he didn't seem inclined to offer him special incentives now.

"I didn't like him." Thinking about Black Eyes made him grind his teeth.

"No skin off his back. He didn't like you much, either." Mac gave him a squeeze, and he leaned in and laughed. "But I guess you got that."

They didn't take the turn to Black Eyes' apartment. On farther down, past a fountain that sent glittering water spitting upwards through a fretwork of levels, the water at the top rising slower as it reached the stream's apex in the decreasing centrifugal force, then falling back more and more swiftly as it reached the concourse floor, a single, black door hunkered in a recess in the wall. A small panel on the wall lit up when they were close, revealing

360

the name of the establishment: *Woven Lips*. The thrum of a heavy bass beat ate at the floor. Mac pressed his hand to the panel, the area just under his palm glowed, and it turned green. The door slipped back, revealing a shadowy, elaborately decorated interior illuminated in the flashes of white and red strobe lights. Sound poured from the opening.

Aaeon pulled back, and Mac clapped his big hand to the back of the youth's skull, pressing him forward, and causing him to stumble. Once through, the door whipped shut behind them, and the big hand shoved Aaeon sideways and his shoulder slammed into the wall.

"I told you, kid, you don't leave my side. Come on. We've got a gaming room reserved." He wrapped his hand around Aaeon's forearm and pulled him into a wide foyer with blood-red carpeting, heavy ormolu furniture, and couches lining the walls. At a small desk tucked in between two flowering trees, a thin woman with black hair tied in a severe bun flicked a long cigarette at them.

"Mr. Magill." She spoke with an accent Aaeon could barely understand. "You have a friend with you today. Your usual room?"

"I have two more friends arriving shortly. Send them on in." He held out his white card, and she waved it over a scanner and returned it with a smile.

One of the couches, along with the wall behind it, slipped aside, revealing a disguised passageway. Mac yanked Aaeon's arm, pulling him roughly into the waiting maw. The youth turned to see the wall closing again. Small openings overhead gave out regular pinpoints of lights to guide them. Doors cowering in shallow recesses decorated the walls every dozen meters or so, and they came to one with a green light above it. Mac stopped, pulled Aaeon into the recess, and the door opened for them. Once inside, the throbbing music stopped, sealed outside, and Mac released the youth's arm.

"Over there," Mac growled, indicating a comfortable-looking armchair next to a floor lamp.

Aaeon fell into it. The space consisted of a round table in the center with various designs on its surface. The center was covered in dark green cloth. Armless chairs surrounded the table, with three more armchairs like Aaeon's in the other three corners. Each was paired with a lamp, although all were in a different style. Several doors melded neatly into walls, nearly disappearing into the dark-colored surfaces. The ceiling was ornately carved and covered with a yellow, gleaming metal.

"Personal facilities?" Aaeon realized he hadn't relieved himself since lunch, and now that they were no longer moving, it had become urgent.

Mac looked at him sharply. He sat on the edge of the table with one leg up and the other down. He picked up a set of cards, and he thumbed through them, once looking up to glare at Aaeon. He pursed his lips before pressing them tightly together and growling, "Third door." He jerked his head to one side of the room.

Aaeon lurched to his feet, giving Mac plenty of space, and found an actual knob on the door. It was a small reminder of home, where all doors were equipped with knobs. He twisted it, slipped through, and watched the light automatically turn on. That wasn't like home, except for the glow globes. He saw that the knob locked, and he flipped it to give himself a chance to decompress. The space was small but luxurious with a stone sink, highly polished, with a spigot just over it. The whisper of moving air came from a grille in the wall. Soft muzak filled the room, setting a mood of elegance and distraction from the gaming area on the other side of the door. An upholstered armchair hovered in the corner by a small table with a shaded lamp at its side. The toilet facilities were through an additional door. The lights hadn't turned on there, but he assumed they would. A mirrored panel stared back at him, his reflection not what he'd expected. His jacket and trousers went well with his cap, and the stand-up collar looked crisp, still. He turned his head to see how well the bandage was covered, and Mac had been right. With the hat pulled low, it was barely visible.

He debated the possibility of escaping from Mac and finding his friends. Back doors. Secret exits. Disguising himself. Even considering that filled him with a sense of overwhelming frustration. He hadn't been able to find the Cryo-Storage without a map and substantial confusion. To find Mac afterward? It had taken a willing hand from a local who knew a lot more than him. He closed his eyes, in desperation picturing his home on Haukberk Precipice. He leaned forward, his hands on the stone sink, forming an image in his thoughts of Priest Tjark and Regeth. He could see himself there, standing on the Upward stones, looking out over the Crevasse. It felt so real, and he sensed the disconnect of the haze curtain surrounding him. The music faded, and he could no longer hear the air moving past the grille. He opened his eyes to see the soupy fog obscuring the things in the room. He hesitated . . . Haukberk Precipice was just there . . . he could see it, smell it, *feel* it. One step, and he'd be home.

He tried to bring Regeth and Tjark into focus at his side. He named them, imagined them there, placed them as he last saw them, yet they were only place holders, faded ghosts, wisps of memories that wouldn't follow him through. No matter how hard he tried, he'd step through to Haukberk, and as soon as he reached for his two companions, they'd evaporate like fog against the heat of the storm wall.

Fighting tears of frustration, he let the image of Haukberk fade from his thoughts. The music returned, the air still whispered, and the haze curtain he'd pulled up evaporated into wherever they resided when they weren't moving across the face of the precipices. It was him in the room, just him, and there was no way out, not unless he wanted to abandon those who counted most on him.

Mac rapped on the door three times, calling, "You about done in there, kid?"

"Yeah, about." Aaeon stared at his reflection, finding his eyes and studying them. His responsibility was to locate Regeth. Doing so included Tjark. It was about getting all three of them home. It was about Mene and her kiss, and not letting her think he'd simply disappeared out of her life forever. He released the stone and moved to the open door. The lights did flicker on, and he took care of his needs, returning to the sink to place his hands under the spigot and rub them vigorously when warm water flooded out. As he drew his hands back, a curtain of heated hair flooded them, and by the time he retrieved them, they were dry.

"Interesting," he murmured, studying his fingers. He'd never seen that before. He jumped when someone started banging loudly on the door. "Yeah?" he called.

"You want I should come in there and help you evacuate your internal waste system?" A woman's voice!

"I'm finished." Despite his dry hands, he wiped them nervously on his trousers and grasped the locked knob. He turned it, heard the lock release, and swung it back. The light in the small room clicked off, leaving him in blackness and facing the muted light in the larger room. After the brightness of the restroom, the area seemed dim, and he blinked hard, pausing to reorient himself.

"This is your spare part?" The woman's voice, louder and cutting. "What's this, Magill, we need to convert schoolboys to our cause? Zealander and Abdullah can't perform any more? Thought those two had vacuum on the brain when you hired 'em in, but this one has nothing going on at all." She laughed, and it was harsh.

"Kid, meet another of the team. Crystal, say hello to—" He paused, then laughed. "Tell her your name, kid. I forget."

"Aaeon." Without thinking, he offered her a hand in greeting. He recognized her from Zander's, the pretty woman who'd sat next to Black Eyes. When she didn't take it, he let it drop, rubbing his fingers against his palm.

"Polite, too." She laughed harshly. "Doesn't change anything, Magill. He's space junk, and he'll give us away. We're better off to take care of things right here." A folding knife, the blade enclosed in a handle that was little more than a protective framework, appeared in her hand, and with a touch, the blade was exposed. It gleamed in the gold light reflecting off the ceiling.

"How many people you know on this station unchipped and invisible?" Mac moved closer to her, two smooth steps, his voice dropping in timbre. He looked at Aaeon and nodded, before taking another step and partially obscuring Hollis from Aaeon's view. He cajoled her, his voice smooth and warm. "We're not off the station, yet. The kid might still be useful. Stay with me on this."

"The plan?" She leaned sideways a bit to look at the youth before fully facing Magill. As she shifted her position, her hand stirred, and the knife was gone, disappearing into some part of her clothing as if she'd never held it. "And how's he unchipped? You, me? Even Kaseem, it's cost us lifeblood to get our identities altered."

Hollis was correct. It'd cost them, but not in cash or credits. Magill was the master programmer, and it was his expertise that had stroked the electronic airwaves just so, flipped piezoelectric pathways to lead to new batches of imagined identities, and created file packets with histories as long as the station was old. To become new people who could move in and out of the system, Hollis, Zealander, and Abdullah gave up social connections, family bonds, and any claims to material possessions, either earned or stolen, that might lead back to their original lives. All but Zealander also gave up their names, but Zealander had forfeited his right to his original identity so far in the past that for all practical purposes, he was the only one who recalled it, anyway.

There was no way to completely scour them from the system. Magill had known that. There would always be isolated packets of data stored in unaccessed niches that would come to light only when the correct information gates were powered up and the search engines were sent inside at just the right time. All he could do was deflect, redirect, and propose easier identities for people to find so that they didn't feel the need to dig deeper.

Yeah, it'd cost them lifeblood. They'd had to become really and truly dead to their old lives, so they could live out their new ones.

"I don't know, Hollis. Here's what I do know." He called out, "Computer, news report, Mission Control, Florida. Time frame, yesterday noon. Play until I say stop."

One wall turned from a blank surface to a giant screen. A reporter was large in the image, with the call letters of a news channel across the bottom. The scene shifted, with white bands of static briefly filling the display before clearing to reveal the inside of Mission Control. The reporter's voiceover boomed, "This is footage captured earlier this morning, as three armed terrorists unexpectedly breached U.E.F. security and made it all the way to the control center . . ." The guards raised their weapons, the terrorist without a hood jerked one of his accomplices sideways, and Mac called, "Stop."

The accomplice's hood shifted just slightly as the person was yanked aside, and a glimpse of a youth's smooth face appeared, topped by a shock of light-colored hair. Mac said, "Enlarge image. Center on the hooded figures."

Aaeon felt chilled. It was clear it was him. Earlier, he hadn't seen this. Mac must have spent time studying it while Aaeon was delivering the canvas pack. He felt found out, somehow guilty . . . exposed.

"So?" Hollis' patience was worn thin, and it came through in her voice. "Those Schwinger-woods wouldn't know their frontal lobes from an ultrasonic probe. So they got hacked. I hope those guys blew the place up."

"Nah, better—"

The door whisked open, interrupting him, as Black Eyes appeared. His shoulders filled the doorway, and his eyes leaped from Hollis to Magill to Aaeon, and to the image on the screen, taking in an evaluation of the entire situation in that singular sweep of his eyes.

"Ah, Zealander." Mac had his back to the scene from Mission Control, but his posture said he still controlled what was displayed there, along with Hollis' fiery form, Aaeon's frightened figure, and now, the massive brutality that had entered the space.

"Are the boy's friends accounted for?"

"Yes, with Abdullah." His reply was terse.

"Have you spoken with him?"

"What do you wish to know?" His eyes lingered on Aaeon, narrowing in disgust, but they shifted, leaping from Magill to Hollis. Hollis seemed to interest him more.

"The camouflage suits. Do we have them, yet?" Said like someone would ask whether an expected delivery of electronic replacement parts had arrived.

"He's running the overrides you gave him now. He had trouble finding one Hollis' size." He grinned at that.

"Don't you make this about me, you space junket!" She whipped around, the knife reappearing, the blade already exposed. "C'mon, flash brain. Give me a reason. Just one reason, and I'll do it this time." She swayed, with one hand out, motioning him her direction.

"Crystal, not on the station." Magill gently placed his hand on her forearm and lowered it. He smiled, but it wasn't from friendliness, more as though this was something he'd been keeping under control for an extended time. She relented, and the knife disappeared. The anger on her face didn't.

"That's him?" Zealander nodded toward the image on the screen. He looked more closely at Aaeon, and then walked to the wall. He thumped it with a knuckle, then asked Aaeon, "You in a cult, or what?"

"Forget it, Zealander. You want to watch this. Computer, eighth speed forward." Mac positioned himself next to Zealander,

367

keeping them both between Hollis and Aaeon. In silence, as the scene moved forward, the air seemed to solidify, and a quick-moving projectile—moving rapidly even in slow motion—hit one of the packs worn by the trio, sending shards of rock into Aaeon's face, then a bright flash washed out the scene. When it faded, they were gone. Two additional projectiles slammed into the floor just where they'd been, tearing into the carpet and leaving dust-filled gouges in the concrete below. The dust from the pulverized concrete hung in the air, the particles' slow-motion dance resembling the thick fog from earlier, but not the same by any measure.

Mac strode to Aaeon, whipped his hat off, and took his jaw in his hand. He roughly twisted his face sideways to expose the bandage. "Tell me this isn't the same kid from that clip. He got on the station quicker than the shuttle launching at the same time just outside the control center. Like, instantly. That's how he's not chipped."

"My God," Hollis said, her entire demeanor changed. She smiled, and she walked up to Aaeon. He cringed as she reached a hand to his head, laying her palm on his hair and stroking the bandage with her thumb. "I see what you mean, Mac. The kid gets prettier all the time. I might just like a taste sometime." She tiptoed, leaned in, and licked his face from his jaw to his cheekbone.

Zealander began to laugh. "That's a good one, Hollis. You better give Kaseem first dibs. He might fight you for this one."

Aaeon's stomach began to churn. He suspected he knew exactly what they meant.

"Were you paying attention?" Magill stepped between them. "Did you watch what was on that clip? This one and his two companions, whom Kaseem's located, by the way, were able to transport from Earth to the station *without a ship.*"

"If that's possible, I wouldn't have spent half my life below-ground in the mines. I'd have left Venus to those who wanted her." Hollis spat, although no phlegm escaped her lips, and then she grinned as she raised her nose confidently in the air. Her knife had reappeared in her hand. "I can get him to share how they did it."

"She'll do it, kid. If she doesn't, I might offer my services." Zealander had his arms crossed, and he didn't smile as he made the suggestion. "Empty your pockets. Let's see what you got."

Aaeon was too frightened to speak. He looked at Mac. He didn't trust him anymore, but he trusted the other two less. Mac nodded, and Aaeon felt to see if he *had* anything in his pockets. The jacket had two pockets on the outside, and inside one was a small slip of paper. He laid it on the green-topped table. He lifted the hem of the jacket and reached into his trouser pockets. He pulled them out to show they were empty.

Mac stepped to him and reached inside his jacket. He pulled out the directions to the Cryo-Storage from earlier. "Forget this, kid? I wonder if you've forgotten something else? Check 'im, Zealander."

The big bruiser positioned Aaeon with his hands on the table and his legs spread. He frisked his upper body, then moved to his waist and down his legs. He lifted each trouser leg and felt around his calves. He stood back and pronounced, "Nothing. You can stand, kid."

"How'd you do it?" Mac had taken one of the chairs, and he had one leg crossed casually over the other. "Maybe something in one of those packs? Where are those stored?"

"Th . . . that's not it," Aaeon finally stuttered, his heart pounding. He felt violated, and he knew what he said determined whether he lived or died. The knife . . . he pictured it at his throat, or in his side, and he was glad he'd visited the facilities. "I left the packs in Liam's quarters, I think. At least that's the last time I saw them. It's nothing to do with the packs. I . . . I mean, it's something I just do."

"C'mon, Mac. He's a lying little exhaust thruster." Hollis sneered. "Kaseem has the suits, and he's installing the overrides.

Me? I can handle what he can't. We've got a shuttle to steal, and we're not taking extra baggage with us. This kid? He's dead weight."

"He's dead weight *if* he can't repeat that trick. Or, maybe it's your friends? Is that it? You're protecting your friends? Yeah, Zealander, Hollis, I thought to hole up here until Kaseem was ready for us, but now I'm thinking we need to visit our collection of extra *spare parts*." He looked at Hollis and smirked. "Let me locate Schlegel's quarters, because I want those packs. That's where we'll find the mechanics, if they weren't damaged back on Earth. Then we'll find our kid's friends and see if we can get some real answers."

Book of the Gods

Roshama, Chapter 1:15-17

THE LAST OF the shades is Kella Aseem Dullah-um.
His face is the color of the midnight sky and bears the
tracks of the fallen stars. Before the Battle of The Great
Falling, Kella Dullah-um was a lover of men and had
great love for his daughter.

WHEN HIS LOVER and daughter died at the hands of
his enemies, Kella Dullah-um swore eternal revenge. He
is the Perpetrator of Thievery and Murder.

KELLA ASEEM DULLAH-UM'S followers are known
as El Dullah-wicum, or the Minions of Kella Aseem
Dullah-um. Selah.

Spare Parts

The oversized display on the wall proved to be more than a video display. The room, ostensibly for nefarious gaming, was better equipped than it first appeared. The tabletop retracted to form a full-on interface terminal, and Magill began keying in requests, trying passwords, and working his way through the system—all reflected on the wall for all to see.

"Lost your touch, Magill?" Hollis slouched in one of the upholstered chairs in a back corner.

He spat, "It's that star-sucking Levitson. He's good, got all this locked up tight." Then he hit his head. "Get over here, kid. Schlegel gave you palm access to his quarters, didn't he? Why didn't I think of this?

He gave the terminal a series of instructions, causing a large rectangle to appear on the display. He had Aaeon press his hand against a similar shape on the terminal, and the image of the youth's hand appeared on the display. The whorls and arcs of his skin glowed, and in a rapid-fire flicker, each finger lit up and faded, then his palm repeated the process. A smaller rectangle superimposed itself over Aaeon's hand, giving both a level and a corridor and room assignment.

"That's it?" Zealander still stood at the door.

"For now, from the kid. Let me check in with Kaseem." He spent several minutes working through the same encryption processes he'd initiated in the drive module, until the screen displayed Encrypted Channel. The image of the hand disappeared, and a grainy picture of a man with short, tight hair appeared. He was looking down, as though working at a terminal. He glanced up, revealing scars running down his face. His eyes jumped back and forth across the screen, reading, then a sour smile crawled across his lips. It didn't extend to the rest of his face.

"Yeah, Magill? I told Zealander I got this."

"We're meeting you early. We'll be bringing something special. There's a chance we can get off the station without stealing a shuttle. You know where our two guests are, right?"

"With me." He reached toward the screen, his arm grew huge, then the view changed. Behind him, he revealed a brightly lighted cargo bay. Equipment was nestled neatly into scaffolding lining one wall. More pertinent, four quantum camouflage suits hung on rolling stands, all just behind Abdullah. Each had a thick cable running to it, coming from Abdullah's location. The third one over flickered, first turning transparent—although looking closely revealed that the image, as seen behind the suit, was warped slightly, and the edge of the suit didn't quite match the background—then solid again. A row of lights blinked on the collar, indicating a diagnostics program in process. The helmet—with an opaque face shield—was to the side, and it flickered when the suit did. Behind those, several large fuel tanks nestled, with a larger one only partially visible. At the base of one of the tanks, a bald black man and a hooded youth were gagged and tied to the framework holding the tank in place.

"Regeth!" Aaeon leaped forward, to be caught by Zealander. "What have you done?"

"Shut him up, Zealander. Kaseem, I want those suits up and

374

accessible."

"Like I said, Magill." He readjusted the camera, shook his head, and looked away, once more focused on his terminal.

"Kaseem, get him to show you what we're bringing." Hollis called it loudly, and she laughed.

"What's that?" Abdullah looked back into the screen. He kept looking around the Encrypted Channel bar, and clearly, he had one on his screen, too.

"Nothing. Ignore her—"

"It's a plaything, about fifteen!"

Zealander had walked the youth over, and he stood him behind Magill, with one hand on each shoulder.

"What's that?" Abdullah sat back in his chair, his eyes narrowing.

"A present, for you," Hollis cackled. She threw a wadded piece of paper behind Magill, and Abdullah's eyes tracked it.

"Magill, you said us four. Now you have a fifteen-year-old kid involved?" He snorted in disgust.

"Sixteen," Aaeon muttered. He didn't know what years were, but he'd left fifteen behind long ago.

"Shut up, kid," Mac growled. "You just be ready, Kaseem. This *kid* might be our ticket out of here. We'll talk more when we get there. Remember, don't come here. We're vacating, *now.*"

He hit the disconnect icon, and the screen returned to a blank wall. The top of the table transformed back into a gaming platform. Magill stood—smooth and liquid, as though his joints were buttered with warm oil—and he opened a panel in the wall. He palmed a hand-sized screen, and when an inner door swung open, he removed a case. He closed the panel and motioned for the others to follow.

They didn't take the front exit from the room, the one with the couches and the receptionist. When they exited, they turned the opposite direction and headed deeper into the bowels of the station. Zealander walked just behind Aaeon, with the boy's arm sharply twisted behind his back. Each time Aaeon struggled or cried out, the big man twisted the arm painfully until he got what he wanted.

Aaeon did have the presence of mind to note one thing. As they left the room, with a look of disdain, Mac pulled the white card from inside his shirt, and he tossed it carelessly on the table. It tumbled twice before coming to rest. It landed almost upright, leaning against the stack of cards Mac was flipping through before the other two arrived.

Aaeon didn't put anything to it, other than coincidence. One card was still standing, while the others were holding it up. It was a survivor, tumbling wildly and yet landing on its feet by nothing more than chance.

Luck, in other words.

Even as he cried out, the youth knew he needed more than luck. He had it, too. He had Kirk on his side; he now knew where his friends were; and with Kirk as his witness, if it was possible, any way at all, they would escape this deadly situation. He didn't know where they'd land when they traversed the haze curtain, but anyplace was better than this.

His feet caught on an unlevel doorway, and he stumbled. Zealander yanked his arm, causing Aaeon to gasp in pain.

Anyplace was better. Anyplace at all.

Nobody's Home

"There, Mac." Hollis had taken lead of their search for Liam Schlegel's quarters. She strode on ahead, her shorter legs working faster than the tall man's lanky ones. The easy-to-navigate public corridors required a different set of skills than those in the service corridors, and she had been living in and out of these for some months. "That door should exit two corridors from our destination."

"Good. We're not lost." Magill moved up to take charge again.

"We would'a been one corridor away if you'd let me guide us from the start."

Zealander laughed. "She's right. Give her her due."

Aaeon tried to keep up without stumbling again. He was certain his arm would never be the same. The low-ceilinged and barren corridor ended in a metal door with a dull bar across the center. Mac shifted his case to his left hand and bumped the door with his right hip. It released to the hubbub of a busy station corridor. The first thing Aaeon saw was a wall of greenery. It blocked the door completely, and when they stepped around, he couldn't see the door at all.

This was a residential corridor, with a high, arched ceiling, and clear insets between the arches opening to outside. The lights inside were bright, and the insets were jet black, with not even stars visible. Doors with stoops and potted plants lined the narrow street; and from windows, some open, curtains fluttered. A man rode by on a two-wheel conveyance, peddling easily, and within seconds, a woman followed him. Zealander ignored them as he identified the correct door and spoke first.

"There, I see it." He leaned next to Aaeon's ear. "Like a good boy this time. No broken arms needed."

"Yes, Fadda." Aaeon said the word bitingly.

"Smart-mouth kid." He yanked the arm higher, twisting it at the elbow, as they stopped to let a couple pass. The two women didn't even glance their way.

"Okay." Aaeon gasped, with tears running from his eyes. He was half doubled over in an attempt to ease the pain. Zealander relaxed his hold, and the youth straightened and was able to breathe normally. A man in an elaborately stitched jacket and coordinating pants looked at them questioningly, and when the big man glared at him, he paled and walked on by.

"Get my point?" The man's hot breath warmed the youth's neck, and it was moist and distasteful.

"Be nice," Magill hissed, walking past them. "We're in public."

"And he's got an attitude problem," Zealander groused.

"We'll be inside in a minute. Bring the kid along. I need his palm." When Zealander got him on the stoop, Magill jerked his free arm up and pressed it hard to the wall. The area changed color, and the door unlocked. Magill dropped the arm carelessly.

"I would've done it," Aaeon offered. "Ask, why don't you?"

Once they were inside, Mac offered his first taste of real violence. He swung around, and the back of his hand impacted the youth's face, cracking his jaw sideways and sending spittle flying.

"Kirk!" Aaeon exclaimed. "You didn't have to—"

"Again? Is that what you want?" Magill's long arm drew back, ready for a second impact.

Aaeon shook his head no. Three against one. This wasn't the time to fight. The door only opened to a corridor, and Schlegel's quarters were at the back, nestled against the skin of the station. This time, Mac motioned to the access pad, and Zealander released him enough to step forward and place his hand against it. The door slipped sideways. When they were in, the big man tossed the youth against the bed, telling him to stay, much as an owner might instruct a pet. They found the packs and dumped them, unimpressed with the rocks and handmade drawings. The glow globe was much more interesting.

"This was on the video clip." Hollis zeroed in on it while the other two searched through the packs. She lifted it, calling out, "Star-sucking proton flush, this is heavy. It's got to be something good. What do you think, Mac?"

He stood from the scattered things in the packs, looking at the papers surrounding him. "It's sure this is nothing," and he looked at Aaeon, tilting his head toward the glow globe. "Can you work that?"

"If you let me turn it on." He was angry, and his face hurt, but he said the words evenly. "May I?" He shifted as if to stand, and Zealander moved in the way.

"Nah, boy. You stay right there Magill, he's not touching that. Are we good with that?"

"Not now, anyway. You're right, Zealander, and that's good thinking. Hollis, see if it'll fit in the good pack. The one is too badly damaged to hold it." He kicked the torn one aside.

She worked it into the undamaged pack. It fit, but barely. Hollis and Magill searched the room for anything else they hoped to find, while Zealander stood guard, ensuring that Aaeon didn't move from the bed. They came across the swords in a storage closet, still in their leather harnesses.

"Weren't they wearing these?" Hollis held up one by the straps. The sword gleamed brighter than it ever had in Aaeon's hands.

"Careful, babe. Might be sharp," Zealander cautioned her. "Throw me the other one."

She lifted it and tossed, the letters and runes glimmering brighter than the ambient lighting allowed. Zealander caught it in midair, and with no excess motion, drew the sword and dropped the leather harness at his side.

"This is a fine piece of weaponry," he bragged, extending a finger toward the wording to trace the letters. Just before he touched them, Hollis called to him, "Then take this one, too, if you like them so much." It flew through the air, and catching it, Zealander held one in each hand.

"You can leave those here," Magill remarked. "They're a dime a dozen, if you like that sort of thing."

"Then maybe I can take them with me." Zealander set the sheathed one on the floor, leaning against Aaeon's bed, and he flashed the unsheathed one in the air, just to watch it shimmer. "It's a fine piece of steel."

Aaeon watched the sword against the bed, the handle just within his reach. If it wasn't sheathed, he'd grab it and begin fighting. He remembered the feeling it had given him in the caves under Priest Pitt's home. His heart dropping, he realized it'd likely give Zealander the same advantage. The whole time, Aaeon kept hoping Liam would return, maybe had forgotten something, or would stop by to be sure his head was all right. Maybe the doc remembered that Liam had offered him the room, and she realized she needed to change the bandage. He'd even let her cut off more hair, if she'd just come back to see how he was doing. With the room overturned, and having no success, Magill indicated that Zealander should prepare his captive to head on out.

As they exited, carrying the swords on Zealander's back and the glow globe in Hollis' pack, they walked over the maps and layers of lightning patterns, grinding them into the floor and smearing his images. That made his eyes burn almost as much as his arm, once again twisted behind his back. His time on the bed hadn't given it the chance to quit hurting, and this time, it was worse than before.

Three Blind Mice

The service corridors had been core to three of the four conspirators remaining at large on Earth Station LaGrange, and Hollis and Zealander navigated them with skill. Magill had hidden the team behind false digital facades, allowing them to transport their various skills out of Earth's gravity well and into space where they were needed, but he was the only one without a past waiting to erupt through the thin veneer of station life and spew destruction over their little project.

Magill was a professor in good standing—and with tenure— at the University of Edinburgh. His voice recognition program— Protocol Alpha-C, crafted when he was still a teenager—had earned him a spot at any university he desired. He'd wanted the best, and he'd gotten it. He just hadn't been able to hold onto it, hence his position at Edinburgh. If he'd chosen to reveal himself, his Research ID Number 1178, though tarnished, would have afforded him all sorts of perks on the station, including the most luxurious suite available, two floors of glassed-in glory with a view of the heavens from every room. It *wouldn't* have allowed him access to the drive systems of the *Higgs*, with the ability to make adjustments as he chose, and glory of all glories, to actually have an *unchipped teen who couldn't be tracked by the station* and who was gullible enough to *plant his bomb for him.*

Sometimes life smiled on those either brilliant enough or daring enough to risk everything for what they believed in. Magill believed in justice. He could pass for white, allowing him inside the white man's mind, and giving him insight to the prejudice that still infiltrated the ruling class. Things hadn't changed so much since the Klu Klux Klan had dragged his fellow brothers in the streets of Birmingham and burned crosses in Atlanta. Justice didn't skip generations. It followed blood, and the children of the children had to pay for their forebears' sins. Magill was filled with more satisfaction than he'd felt since he'd used his influence to ban segregationists tied to repression in whatever form from sitting on the Board of Regents for universities in places as far-reaching as Jakarta, Rio, and Oakland.

This time they wouldn't be able to crawl out of their holes and stain the new order of justice and revenge.

Along with the pack filled with the glow globe, Hollis carried a stolen access card that allowed them to traverse the various sealed doors. The access card imbued them with permissions to go where no conspirators had dared for the past hundred years. The readers picked up their chip codes, compared them against those in the station's computers, and seeing nothing in the system tagging their specific markers, let them pass. They never saw Aaeon other than as a ghost in the system, a phantasmal heat source that warmed an occasional corridor and then was gone, a wisp in the night, as though he never was.

Aaeon caught all this in bits and pieces. When they passed someone in the narrow passageways, they nodded and even wished them a good day. Once, they were greeted by a person who recognized them, and they answered questions about status reports in other parts of the station, how the hydroponics were doing this week, and whether they knew of any available quarters, as a friend was hoping to come up from Earth as soon as a spot opened up. Aaeon was held in check, his arm tight, with Hollis' knife in Zealander's hand pushed sharply into his armpit. He didn't intend to try to escape, although they didn't know that. He hoped they kept him alive until he found his friends. He was finally feeling optimism for a possible getaway opportunity, and his mood was lifting by the footstep.

It was when the corridors and passageways were clear that he learned the most about his captors. He was surprised at how freely they talked among themselves. After several slick-walled passages and a shortcut through an air-handling plant, where the massive fan precluded any talking, he realized there were no monitoring devices about. No audio pickups, no video cameras; in fact, the only time he sensed anything was the three separate beeps made by Magill, Hollis, and Zealander when they crossed thresholds from one area to another.

They were deep within the station's entrails when they stepped onto a metal-framed catwalk that wound through the vast digestive tract of the station's concealed underbelly. Magill paused, holding the others back. Hollis spoke first.

"C'mon, Mac. I'm ready to get out of this hamster cage." She made to push past him, shoving the heavy pack ahead of her, and he strong-armed her to a stop.

"Ten seconds, Hollis. Can you give me that? If Kaseem's compromised, this is our last chance to avoid the same fate."

"He's right." Zealander still held Aaeon's arm, his massive hand gripped ruthlessly on the youth's slender wrist. "If he's compromised, I get to throw the boy off the side, right Magill?"

Hollis chuckled.

"Follow me and no noise." He didn't turn to look at Aaeon but simply moved ahead.

Aaeon saw the problem when they'd moved down several levels. He began to catch glimpses of massive ships, flying ferries by all appearances, surrounded by men and women doing something even he recognized as care and maintenance. He was familiar with the steam vehicles on Gates; and as workers, wearing clothing very like his, opened panels and plugged and unplugged umbilicals, shots of steam burst forth. These were streamlined transport machines much like he already knew. He couldn't locate the area where his friends were trussed and imprisoned, however, and as they reached the floor, his vision was cut off by large pieces of machinery moving about. His captors walked in a purposeful line, and he calculated the door they would intersect. They rounded a large, rectangular container on wheels and almost ran over a tall man with a generous waist and stained coveralls coming their way. He carried a cargo manifest, and he flipped through it as he walked. He looked up just as they were about to collide. His shirt said *Rager*.

"Mac!" He held out his hand.

Magill transformed from a confident and erect man of power to his *Higgs* personality without a ripple. He shifted the case to his opposite hand, and dropping his shoulders, he laughed disarmingly while glancing at the man's shirt. "Rager! Didn't fancy meeting you down here."

"I'm also surprised to meet you, being starship class." He laughed as though it didn't mean much. "What're you doing in the belly of the beast?"

"You know how it is. Errands, and with the ship launching tomorrow, gotta tie up loose ends." Magill's posture spoke of urgency, and he kept in motion, as if ready to step out as soon as Rager released him to go.

"We don't normally see your people here. What did you say you were doing?" Rager had his hand on a comm device, and his eyes narrowed at the people with him.

Aaeon stood very still to keep his arm from hurting worse than it had to, but he noticed that the knife had moved from Zealander's to Hollis' hand. She gripped it at her side, and her arm tensed. Her eyes searched, looking to see if they were being observed. He wanted to say to the man, "Leave. Leave now, if you want to live."

"You see," Mac's voice sauntered, "I wasn't regular. Nah, I just stepped in to fill in for Drive Technician Deesy when he decompressioned. I guess that's what you call it when the wall blows out. Terrible, that's what it was. They're through with me. I won't see the inside of that ship again, less she comes back and there's another accident." He laughed as if unconcerned. "That's not likely, now, is it?"

"Nah, guess not." Rager released his comm, and he nodded at Magill. "Take care, Mac, and you, Miss, and you, too." He tilted his head at Zealander and Aaeon as one, and he returned his attention to his manifest and disappeared around the container.

Magill straightened, closed his eyes, and took a deep breath. Then he began to move on. Zealander hiked up Aaeon's arm, causing him to go to his tiptoes to keep from squeaking in pain.

"Kirk! I'm doing what you want," he hissed, but not too loudly, afraid Mac would hear. The man yanked his arm again, bringing another round of tears to his eyes.

"What I *want* is back on Earth where I can access my performance bonus. Magill owes me big time. He owes all of us. That's not happening dragging you around this space station. Inside!"

Aaeon saw through his pain and watering eyes that Hollis had carded the door, and she and Magill were inside. Zealander shoved him through, releasing his arm, and causing him to stumble. As his arm came back around, fire shot through it, and he crashed against a metal cabinet before catching himself. The door behind swished shut with a hermetic whoosh. Zealander discarded the swords, sending them clattering to the side. Standing, Aaeon recognized the room as seen through the camera on the wall in the gaming room. He searched, found the four unusual suits hanging on their racks, and in the distance, discovered Regeth and Tjark, still trussed and gagged. Before he could move, Zealander grabbed him from behind, threw an arm around his chest, and with the other, began wrapping one wrist with a cord before binding the other to it.

"Oh, not that!" Aaeon regretted his words immediately, as the big man pushed his knee roughly into his back, knocking him to the floor, and began tying his hands to his feet with quick jerks of the cord, tighter than Aaeon thought possible.

"That's better, huh? Like it, little man?"

"You do it good." Hollis' voice.

Aaeon turned his head to see her standing and watching. She knelt at his side and brushed a hand down his face, then across his arm. "So pretty. Such a waste. Maybe Kaseem can convince Magill to keep you alive." She put her fingers to her lips, kissed them, then tapped them against his cheek before standing and walking away, as though he was forgotten.

"The lady and I think alike, except I hope ole Abdullah over there doesn't want you alive. I'm also hoping your little magic trick doesn't work. I want to be the one to gut you. Come on, let's let you join your friends." He stood, and taking hold of Aaeon's arms just where they were attached to his feet, he yanked him from the floor like a sack of refuse, hauled him across the floor, and dropped him unceremoniously near the other two.

As Aaeon caught Priest Tjark's eyes and started to speak, Zealander jerked his head back, stuffed cloth inside his mouth, and tied another cord around his head. He left him face down on the cold floor, his hands and feet bound together, and forced to breathe through his nose. The worst part of it? The cloth in his mouth tasted like a cleaning rag that hadn't been laundered in a very long time.

Book of the Gods

Chazah 2:7-8

SHE WHO SAT upon the Throne vowed that one day She would triumph over the beasts who stole Paradise from the Five Thousand. Time would be restored, and the fist binding all Creation would be released. All things would be restored to their rightful place in a great conflagration such as had never been seen before.

IN THE DOING, the world as we know it will be consumed by lightning and fire. Selah.

Reality Is All in the Mind

Aaeon couldn't speak, and he sure couldn't move. He could see the priest's face, however, and just beyond, Regeth. His aide was pale with despair, although determination filled the priest's countenance. The two contrasted like opposite sides of a two-Kirk coin.

He noticed Tjark hadn't located a new tunic, either that or had it stolen from him again. His injuries from the fight with the swords had been neatly stitched. He was certain Liam's fingers had done that. Regeth, as always, was dressed respectfully, as a neophyte should. Even in the seriousness of the situation, Aaeon's biggest disappointment in the gag was being unable to tell about the fantastic people he'd found in Cryo-Storage. Regeth, and a young Priest Pitt, and Mene. Mene! Wouldn't his friend be surprised? He was sure the priest could explain it all, given the proper chance.

Across the room, an argument ensued. Aaeon could only see a portion of it with the way he was turned, but he could hear it quite well. Magill had the glow globe out, and he was attempting to persuade Abdullah that it was seriously possible it was an instantaneous transport device. He explained about the news clip, finally slamming his fist on the console and turning away to hit himself on the forehead with the heel of his hand in exasperation.

Zealander and Hollis were watching, but they were having their own conversation, and Hollis held the knife out, blade exposed, cleaning her fingernails. Finally, Abdullah jerked to his feet, knocking his chair over backwards, and he took the glow globe from Magill. He walked quickly and with hard steps toward the three captives, and when his feet were huge in Aaeon's vision, he stopped.

"So, who's the magician?" He called to the other three.

"The one trussed like a bird," Hollis called out, laughing. "He said he knows how to work it."

Abdullah squatted, and Aaeon could see his face clearly. He wasn't like Tjark at all except for the color of his skin. His disfigurements were battle scars, or from being tortured or worse. Aaeon shivered. He'd get no mercy from this man. He looked to Tjark and saw his eyes following the events. Regeth, he couldn't tell.

"So, boy, you can work this, can you?" He lowered the glow globe into Aaeon's vision. It seemed as light as Planck gossamer in his hands. Aaeon nodded as best he could. "Hollis? Come cut these cords. He can't *work* it, if he's *tied up.*" He looked her direction, waiting on her.

Aaeon couldn't see her, but he heard her speak as she lifted his hands and began to pick apart the knot, slicing through one layer at a time. It began to loosen until one leg fell free.

"You got all the suits up, right, Kaseem?" Snick, snick, snap! Aaeon's other leg was free.

"All of them calibrated and in harmonic resonance with one another so we can communicate when in stealth mode, all thanks to no one else." He said the words with an edge. "And now Magill showing up two hours early. Why?"

"You're looking at him. Zealander and I don't trust this kid.

What if this thing works, and he uses it against us? They could all escape, and we couldn't do anything about it." She'd stopped cutting the cords, and Aaeon shook his hands to get her attention to finish the job. She ignored him, and he groaned inside.

"So, this is a secret military device no one's ever heard of, is that it? Those ridiculous swords over there are more likely to shoot laser beams." He snorted in derision. "His hands, Hollis. We'll never know if we don't get his hands to where he can use them."

"Sure." She lifted one of Aaeon's arms, and she worked the knife in, not being especially careful. She caught his skin more than he liked. She whispered to Abdullah, "Should we have those suits on, you know, *before* we give the kid access to that ball?"

Abdullah rocked back and looked at her. He began to smile. "Now, girl, you're finally starting to think like a real operative." He called louder, "Mac, you and Zealander start to suit up. If this works, and we're transported to an airless environment, I want full environment up and running. Then, if this fails, which I fully expect, we're in position to take us a ship and get off this starsucking hunk of metal."

"After we pulp them, right, Kaseem?" At that moment, her knife snipped the final cord, and Aaeon was rolled roughly to his back to see her grin wickedly and stand, backing away.

"We can't leave them here." Abdullah stood, still holding the globe.

"And we're not taking them with us." Zealander had joined them. "I'm with Hollis. No witnesses left behind. Magill brought the distraction. We can place it right in their midst, and no one'll find them. Ever. Hand me your knife, Hollis."

He placed his foot on Aaeon's chest, and kneeling, he put his hand over his face, worked the knife under the cord across his cheek, and pulled sideways *hard*. The cord split, and his hand yanked the gag free from the youth's mouth in one motion. Before Aaeon could react, Zealander was standing, the knife still in his hand.

Aaeon rolled to his side and sucked in air. He looked at the big man with the black eyes and said, "May Kirk forgive you. You are as one of the shades, and your actions will return to haunt you."

"Hey!" Zealander called to the rest of his compadres. "The kid's praying to Kirkpatrick to forgive us. How about that? Who knew old Kirk would become a god and be able to forgive us our evil ways?" He knelt once again, and he laid the knife at his side and grasped the youth's jaw in his hand. His dark eyes grew blacker, and with his other hand, he backhanded the youth's face, knocking his head sideways and leaving Aaeon's eyes unable to focus.

"My turn?" Hollis looked excited, and she simpered the words, putting both of her hands on Zealander's upper arm as he picked up the knife and stood. He shook her off.

"After we try this." Abdullah blocked her view and knelt once more, holding the globe. "Boy, you said you can work this. What makes it come on?"

"I can show you." His hands were free, but he'd bitten his tongue and he tasted blood. He spat, leaving an elongated wad of watery-red phlegm beside him. He tried to sit, but it was painful. Abdullah offered no assistance. On one elbow, he held out a hand towards the globe, but the man pulled it out of his reach.

"Not so fast. Tell me, not show me." He called over his shoulder to Zealander, "I want this boy's leg affixed to something. If he tries anything, I want part of him to remain here."

"A cable wrapped around my arm? Then I can yank him back into line if he tries to go AWOL." Zealander's voice, but not Zealander. There was no one there.

"Better, and good thinking. You might be useful on this team after all. Take care of it." Abdullah stood again, and he looked at Aaeon hard. "We'll see if that clip was real or fake, see if you can do what Magill thinks you can do. He's not going to be happy if you don't pan out." He turned, patted empty space, and walked towards the other two, now climbing in their camouflage suits.

Aaeon narrowed his eyes, and he could see the edge of Zealander's suit. The lines were off just enough that if he looked closely, he could tell. The rest of the figure wavered slightly. He understood now. The suits provided total disguise. They could move around through any part of the station, and no one would know they were there. It was like what he could do, only better.

"You located me, kid. Not bad. Most people can't see it. It's the red-shift that usually reveals us. You must be sensitive to red light." The shape flickered, and the suit became fully visible. Zealander placed his hand to his faceplate and slipped it upward, and his black eyes gleamed with anticipation.

"The image wavers when you move, and the edges aren't smooth. Can you release my friends?" Please, he pleaded. All we want is away. You can do whatever you want when we're gone. He couldn't say that aloud. They'd never believe him. They didn't even trust each other.

"No can do, but I think I have something that'll keep me connected to you." He smirked as he reached above them, slipped a thick power cable from above the fuel tank, and yanked until it was tight at the wall. He wrapped it firmly in his exoskeleton-empowered fist and punched the opposite direction. A light overhead sputtered and went out. With several twists, it was tied firmly to Aaeon's leg, and he wrapped it several times around his arm. A thick coil separated the knots, leaving him more than adequate maneuverability.

"The suits multiply your strength?" Aaeon eyed the extra cord and determined that he could get to his friends with little trouble if he could distract the man.

"You're not as dumb as you look, kid. Maybe you're smart enough to help us if you value your life. Do you operate that globe thing alone, or does it take all three of you? You look smooth-faced to be the operator if it works." Zealander seemed to be softening in his attitude to the youth, whether in response to

Aaeon's intelligent questions or to ply him for more answers, Aaeon couldn't tell. If he was beginning to believe, he had to capitalize on that.

"The three of us together." Aaeon was certain he could pull Tjark and Regeth with him through a curtain—any curtain—if he could get close enough. He could unbind his friends afterward. "I'm not strong enough to do it on my own."

"You need that globe thing?" Zealander turned his head, looking for Abdullah. In that fraction, Aaeon caught Tjark's eyes, and the old priest nodded at him. He glanced at Regeth to see only fear.

"Yes, if you can bring it to me. I don't have to touch it—" He'd seen the black man's wariness. He didn't want that to erupt again. "—just have it near. I can tell you how to turn it on."

"Magill, you all ready?" Zealander turned his back to Aaeon and his companions, watching his compatriots, as the last of them pulled their suits on. Hollis was the final one, slipping on her helmet. Their faceplates were open and the suits fully visible. He called out, "I need the globe, Abdullah, and you, Hollis, bring me those swords. I'm taking them with me."

"Get 'em yourself, flash brain. I'm not your slave." She shot him an offensive gesture, one fist in the crook of her elbow, and the other thrusting upward.

"Catch," Abdullah called, and he lobbed the globe Zealander's direction. He caught it easily, as if it were no more than a wisp of light dappling through a partially obscured port. "Leave the swords. We can't risk the exposed metal. Anything we can't carry inside the suits won't be camouflaged."

"I don't think so," Zealander muttered. He turned, gave Aaeon a hard look, and set the globe down. "This sits here," he said, "or there'll be trouble. I'm getting my swords."

As soon as Zealander turned and the coil began unraveling, Aaeon began crawling towards Tjark and Regeth as rapidly as he could. He knew he was making noise, but he had no choice. He had only moments. If they could make contact, even briefly, Tjark could guide them through the haze curtains and possibly back home. Please, Kirk, back home!

He was within a meter when he was jarred to a stop by an impact to his side, and he gasped and collapsed to the floor. It was fire when he breathed, and he knew something was broken. Kirk, it hurt!

"Hollis and I told you, Magill," Zealander yelled across the empty space. He lifted a foot and kicked the youth again in the same location, this time lifting him from the floor and tossing him against the fuel tanks with the force of the impact. Aaeon landed half a meter from the other two. "Can I gut all three of them now?"

Aaeon lay as still as possible, willing the pain to ease. He forced his eyes open to see Black Eyes with the swords in hand, both removed from their sheaths. The runes and words glowed with impossible ferocity. He whispered the remembered words, *"By Theon Aland-um's strong fist."* He recalled the extra strength the sword of the shades had impressed into his arms as he had held it many crackles ago in his practice sessions, then again at the death of Priest Pitt and his other companions. The man's mechanical suit of disguise held even more strength. If this man chose to kill him now, there was nothing he could do.

Priest Tjark shifted position the barest amount, all that his tightly trussed bonds would allow, making no more than the lightest scratching on the floor, and Aaeon turned his bleary eyes his direction. The priest closed his eyes and nodded. Aaeon understood. He was ready if Aaeon could raise the curtain walls and give them escape to another *when.* His head throbbed, however, and his side filled with unendurable flashes of pain each time he breathed. He tried, truly tried, but it was impossible. He couldn't see anything except for the *pain.*

"Me first?" Hollis had joined Zealander. She knelt beside Aaeon, pressed the blade of her knife to his cheek, and she dragged it down his face. "Now, kid, is a good time if you want to use your power. Oh, that's right, your little toy is still off. You're stuck with us. Too bad. You're not going anywhere. I never believed in you, anyway. Kaseem's not going to have a chance to claim his prize. Zealander and I'll see to that."

When she lifted the knife, the edge of the blade gleamed red, and the line on Aaeon's face began to seep. She wiped the blade, snapped it into its casing, and wrapped her hand around one of his wrists. She yanked, flipping his torso face down. Before she could drag him away from his friends, she was stopped by Magill.

"What's this?" Magill's voice left no room for discussion. He stood at Hollis' side and drew a deep breath. "This is our consensus, then?"

"Yeah. It was our consensus all along. I don't guess you got that memo."

"It seems Kaseem agrees. We're better to break out with a shuttle and forget this. Too bad. I'd hoped it would work. Dispose of that ridiculous power cord, Abdullah. I've set the timer. This'll remove the evidence." Magill had the case in his hand, and he set it beside Tjark. "Make sure the kid's close so it gets all three of them."

"You kidding? That fuel tank's going to get this whole bay." Zealander looked flummoxed, now thoroughly confused, and standing with the cord still dangling from his arm.

"We're taking no chances. Do it. And leave those weapons. We'll be found out before we get halfway across the docking bay floor." Magill nudged Aaeon's shoulder with his foot, and he murmured, "Sorry, kid. It was a good dream," and he turned and walked away.

"Shees—" Zealander cut the sound off. He glanced at Magill and back to Hollis, still holding the youth's wrist, and hissed, "One day. One day, I'm gonna punch that man's face."

"And me, after he gives us the access codes to our pay accounts," she agreed. "Want a go, first?" She pulled Aaeon to his feet, cursing when he couldn't stand on his own, and he cried out when she wrapped her arms around his chest, facing him towards Zealander. "Make it good."

He hit the young priest in the gut, causing him to convulse. The youth jerked his legs off the floor and flailed his arms in pain. Hollis stumbled backwards. She ended up backed against one of the fuel tanks, and she shifted the youth in her arms for a better grip, calling out with a laugh, "Once more."

Aaeon heard her, and he was just cognizant enough to try to jerk away. He twisted his torso, and the big man's hand skidded off Hollis' arm, hit Aaeon's chest, and caught him on the jaw. With the upward power of the thrust, aided by the suit's exo-skeleton capabilities, the youth's neck snapped back, and white-hot pain filled his world. Somewhere in the brilliant brittleness of his slicing agony, he heard yelling, and he felt his body go fully limp as he was thrown down. He tried to focus. He tried, but his eyes wouldn't open, his voice was impossible to find, and he could barely feel his hands. He flexed them. One pressed against skin, tortured into elaborate designs of ornate complexity. He felt a cord and padding. He pulled weakly, working his fingers underneath, and trying with all his strength to expose what it tried to silence. After repeated tries, he heard a familiar, although hoarse, voice begin to speak.

"Excellent, my young priest. In the name of Fadda Arkson-la, you must take us through the curtains, now!"

Aaeon tried, he really did. The light that blasted his head was too bright. It swallowed everything. He couldn't find his way.

"Find your strength in Regeth," the voice encouraged. "Do this for your friend."

Aaeon felt his lashes separate, and through the glimmer of light that entered, he found the face of Mene's brother. His friend's terror-filled eyes were just above him, his mouth wrapped in silence. He'd fallen with his head in his friend's lap. His arm rested on the man at his side, his hand against his face. Aaeon tried to remember home. The last warm memory he had was of people he hardly knew: Liam, who'd been kind to him, and the doctor, who'd cleaned his wounds. He felt himself fall into the memory, and he sensed it was growing cold. The fog of an impending curtain filled the air, blurring Regeth and Tjark's faces. It was more, though. He twisted his head and looked into the room. The four suits were missing, either powered up or out of the room, but the power cord still wrapped his ankle; and the air thickened along its length, faster and faster, until Zealander in his suit was caught in the viscous air, his quantum suit wrapped in the ghostly outline of a man. Then it leaped. The suits were tuned together, and the power triggered by the youth's pain-filled mind whipped through the room like it was alive, grabbing suit after suit, making them into living ghosts. The suits began giving off sparks, and then the entire room exploded with light, filling the space, as though a sun had become encapsulated in the station and now demanded its freedom without discussion and without delay.

Then they were gone, with only a dead light overhead, an empty canvas pack, one dark glow globe, and two swords with glowing runes to attest to their passage. The designs on the swords began to fade, and with no one in the room, the lights eventually clicked off, and all was darkness.

The Yellow Brick Road

Stepping across the haze curtains was as simple as stepping from one doorway to another. Yet, it wasn't simple at all. The dichotomy erupted when placing that first footstep as one moved from one *when* into another. The traveler had to be able to *find* the doorway first, then—and equally important—had to be able to visualize the *when* on the other side. If he—or she—couldn't find a *when* to step into, the landing was likely to be *anywhen*. The young priest, so skilled at exactly this, had reached into the haze curtains with a fractured sense of awareness, searching for a destination he recognized. With the exoskeleton-powered strike to his jaw, his brain had roughly impacted the inside of his skull, and he couldn't, he *wouldn't* be able to focus clearly for some time. He was traveling blind, by touch, to put it one way. He was feeling his way with tortured nerves, the blistering pain of several broken ribs, and a total lack of understanding of where he needed to guide them.

Tjark and Regeth didn't have *some time* for Aaeon to recover. They lurched, and as the cold of the passage through the haze curtain dissipated, lights flickered on at their presence. Racks of weaponry nestled along the walls, some small, and a number intended for greater damage. Metal lockers interspersed the weapons, and there were aisles leading into unknown territory. The fuel tanks were no longer at their backs, and they arrived slightly above the floor. Regeth and the priest tumbled backwards, with Aaeon limp across them and jarring heavily against their legs. With the framework around which they'd been tied gone, Tjark rolled from underneath Aaeon, slipped his arms under his feet, and began to tear at his bonds with his teeth. Regeth still had his hands behind his back, and he struggled to extricate himself from underneath the heavier boy.

The cord still wrapped Aaeon's leg, and their four captors had been pulled through the curtain with them. The shock of the haze curtain had created feedback in their powered-up suits, and the cord sparked and jerked across its length. Each time it did, the young priest's body danced in a spasm that painted a semblance of impending rigor mortis on his face. The feedback transferred to Regeth, as evidenced by his muffled yelps of pain.

His hands finally undone, Tjark kicked the explosive case from them, and it slid near Magill. He watched the sparks, counting, then looking to see that Regeth wasn't injured more than was acceptable, yanked at the power cord's knotted grip on the youth's ankle, occasionally hissing when he misjudged the pattern. When the cord was loosened, he cast it aside. The sparking stopped, and he cautiously observed the four suited figures. Although enclosed completely in the suits, the saboteurs were fully visible, and none moved.

Counting to ten before turning his attention to his two charges, the priest felt of Aaeon's face, and satisfied he still breathed, pulled the gag from around Regeth.

"Are you well, my son?" Tjark immediately began work on the boy's hands and quickly had them free.

"I hurt all over. Is . . . does, I mean, is he alive?" His eyes were on his friend. Aaeon was injured and bloodied with the beating and the sparks. Regeth was near to tears.

"Untie your feet and be quick about it." Tjark said nothing about the youthful and unresponsive priest. He worked at his own legs. As soon as he finished, he leaned over the youth and patted his face gently. "Aaeon, we must step through yet another curtain, and now. We cannot remain here. Aaeon, wake. In the name of Vitson, you must open your eyes."

The captor by the name of Abdullah started to stir first. He'd been the farthest from Aaeon's intensely strong blast of power, and the impact on his brain's electrical signals had been mitigated by the other three. He pushed himself up on his elbows, exclaiming, "What the holy exhaust thrusters!"

"Aaeon!" Regeth watched the man stirring, and the sight created desperation in him. He shook his friend's shoulder, and he pleaded, "Take us away, Aaeon, please!"

Aaeon shifted his head. He was still cold. He heard Regeth's voice, and he wanted to smile, to do as he asked. For a moment, he was wrapped in the comforting sense of having stepped from time pocket to time pocket, as though the storm wall had recently passed, leaving the smell of ozone and burnt rock to cleanse the smells from the air. He drew in a deep breath and fell into a fit of coughing when his side was sliced with knives of pain.

"That's it. I see your strength as even you do not." It sounded like Priest Tjark, and Aaeon fought to find meaning in the words. The insistent voice continued, "With Fadda Arkson as my witness, I will protect you, boy. But now, there must be a change in *when.* You must wake enough to take us through. Our enemies are *awakening!"*

Enemies! Who were their enemies? Who was *his* enemy? At one time, he'd thought Bishop Ziggurat was against him. Then Underpriest Abbey, who hadn't trusted him until he was inducted into the priesthood as an underpriest. And Priest Tjark, who'd frightened him most of all, until he'd learned what it meant to have a true protector watching over him. He had no enemies. He had only friends who wished him well.

"Now, Aaeon!" Regeth shook him again, his tone desperate and bordering on loss of hope.

"What's this?" The four in their camouflage suits had all recovered, although not all were fully alert. The question was Magill's, and he answered his own question with, "The Weapons Bay of the *Higgs*. This isn't where we want to be."

"The *Higgs*?" Hollis seemed to be having a worse time than the others in gathering her wits. Her suit was the first to return to full camouflage. It flickered with a static-filled pattern of broken lines and white bars before she faded from sight, leaving only a ghostly impression of *otherness* when she moved a limb or adjusted her position.

As the other two groaned into wakefulness, Magill fell onto a console, working the inputs until an image appeared on the viewscreen. The station was visible in the distance, and it grew quickly smaller. He turned to glare at Aaeon. "Not Earth. It worked, but we're headed into space."

"The *Higgs*? We can't be on the *Higgs*." The shifting image that was Hollis seemed to grasp the concept this time, and she moved, just visible if one knew where to look. Then her faceplate rolled back, and her face could be seen. As she turned to Magill's display, she became invisible again, her face hidden by the back of her helmet.

"We can power up one of the daughter ships. Four Thrusters, too, in case we're discovered. The ship'll take a day to come on-line, but it'll get us home, as long as we're off by the time the package in Cryo-Storage explodes."

"Star-sucking headache. What happened?" Abdullah had his face exposed, and he rubbed his eyes and forehead with one hand. "Did the bomb ignite the fuel tanks early?"

"Thanks, Kaseem." Magill turned from his console, and his eyes darted around the bay. "I'll bet our *diversion* came through with us." Seeing the case, he yanked it off the floor, set it on the terminal, and opened it. A light blinked in a regular pattern. He punched in a code, and it went dark, at which time his shoulders relaxed. "We've got two days on the other one. We'll be okay. Ain't nobody stopping us. I'll get the *Daughter Two* online and prepped to go."

"I expect a bonus on this, Mac." Hollis spat the words.

"Yeah, second," Abdullah barked.

"Wha—?" Zealander was coming fully awake last. "What's second?"

"You want it. Trust me," Hollis said sourly.

"Somebody, take care of our three friends. They've become a hindrance we need to clear off our bocks." Magill didn't even look as Hollis whipped out her knife and extended the blade.

"Aaeon!" Tjark slapped his cheek roughly and hard, jerking his head sideways. "Now!"

The young priest was hardly aware enough to understand Tjark's request. What he felt was the pain of a hand striking his face. *That* he shied away from, and since he couldn't physically move from his present location, he did the only thing he could. He escaped to the only safety he knew, a different *when,* and the two people who were touching him were pulled along after him, riding along on a trip to everywhere and nowhere, lodged somewhere inside the head of a very ill young man.

Reality Fractures

The cold wind of stardust, hydrogen gas, and ultra-high-energy cosmic rays whipped around Aaeon, Tjark, and Regeth. Deadly ultraviolet radiation, X-rays, and gamma rays tore at their skin, burning them in unseen and deadly ways. The skies screamed with tortured light that was twisted and ripped into every color of the spectrum as the different wavelengths were yanked down the biggest black hole in all creation. So far away as to be a pinprick, the *Higgs* hung in space, with a daughter ship at her side. There was no air to breathe, and it was cold, cold, cold. Aaeon's body jerked, forming an arch as he convulsed. This was not better, not better, not better! His mind leaped, and he grabbed. The vacuum around them thickened, seizing what it could reach, forming a gel of dust that coalesced around them; and flashing brightly, the three out-of-place humans disappeared almost as quickly as they had appeared.

Searching for the Sandman

Still cold.

Yet, air; there was air, and they could breathe. They were in a room Priest Tjark recognized, although he'd never been in this one. It was a small surgery, with an elevated bed centered in the room, blankets, and other medical supplies he recognized. There were many other items he found distinctly unfamiliar. His head spun from *wherever* Aaeon had taken them, and he had to break down events into manageable segments of reality, searching his thoughts. He was incredulous the youth had transported them on his own. He had never dreamed such a place, one that contained such impossible structures and colors. He held the injured priest in his arms, and he called to Regeth.

"Boy, get blankets. There, behind you." He watched as the youth looked behind him, visibly pulled his tunic tighter to fend off the chill, and reached to a stack of blankets on a shelf. He brought three. "Good. Lay out one to keep the chill from seeping in from underneath. We'll use the other two over him."

"Y-yes, eminent one." The boy's voice shook with the cold. He dropped the blankets on the floor, then lifted one and spread it over the bed.

"Then get one for you. Wrap yourself in it." He laid out the youth, centering his slender legs on the padded surface. He placed his arms at his side and took the other two blankets from Regeth. The boy scampered away to retrieve another for himself as Tjark shook out first one blanket and then the other, spreading them over the injured youth. He heard distant yelling but could do nothing about it.

"Where is this?" Even wrapped in the extra blanket, Regeth's teeth chattered.

"Have you forgotten your lessons?" Tjark smiled, even as he felt Aaeon's face for the warmth of life. "We're taught that *where* is unimportant. *When* is our destination."

"Then, *when* is this?"

"I can't say. Please hand me a cloth." He pointed, and the young man gathered up several from a stack on a counter. "Wet this one." He offered him a single cloth and pointed to a spigot. "I'm sure you'll figure it out. Don't ask me how. I'm as fresh here as you."

"Is this very long ago or in our future?" Regeth found the spigot worked with a foot pedal. Water dripped from the cloth, and Tjark squeezed the excess onto the floor.

"They are different sides of the same curtain. When your friend awakes, we'll ask him, and he may be able to point us in the right direction." He noticed writing on the cloth, and he straightened the corner to read *Daughter Two*.

"To find home," Regeth whispered hopefully.

"Yes, so one might wish." Tjark gave the boy a smile, but it offered consolation, not encouragement.

Tjark began to sponge blood from Aaeon's head. The bandage still held, but it had started to seep, and there were several red stains. Worse were the bloody nose and the busted lip. Red from the knife cut painted his cheek. Tjark worked up one sleeve to discover a swollen wrist and a darkening joint around his elbow.

He felt of his shoulder, and the youth's eyes squeezed tighter for a moment, relaxing when he released it. He studied the boy's face as he cleaned it. The skin was pale and smooth, nearly translucent as he lay injured on the table. His nose, fine and straight, quivered just a bit around the edges of each nostril as he breathed in and out. That was a good sign, for breathing through the mouth only could be an indicator he neared death. His eyelids drew Tjark's attention. The skin, so clear, revealed a minute network of blood vessels, scattered like fingerlings of light exploding across a pale sky. Or a storm wall. One of Aaeon's eyes twitched, and Tjark smiled at the small movement. There was thought behind those lightning-etched lids. Where thought lived, life existed. Aaeon dreamed, and if the young priest still dreamed, then along with him, they lived, also.

His attention was drawn away as the lights in the room began to flicker. As they dimmed, they sputtered. It was the cold, Tjark was certain. He felt his muscles react to the extreme temperature, and his shoulder twitched repeatedly and uncontrollably. In one sputtering gasp, the room fell dark for a full moment, and red lightning crawled across the walls, as though this place was no more than an extension of the storm wall. Then, unexpectedly, the lights returned, and the room was as before.

"Are we safe, eminence?" Regeth whispered the question.

"I suppose not. Perhaps, if you could lift a prayer to Fadda Kirk, he might see to giving strength to our injured one."

"And to Shoshu Kovski-fa, for added health?"

"Certainly. Your wisdom is beyond bounds." Tjark looked up as the lights flickered once more, then held.

"He's my friend, your eminence, my most treasured friend." Even as his teeth chattered and his skin began to turn blue, Regeth's eyes were red, and his heart was exposed.

"The prayers of a friend are the ones the gods most often hear." Tjark bowed his head for a moment with his eyes closed in a moment of offered respect.

Then the lights went fully dark, and red lightning arched across the walls, lighting the room in an eerily red cast. When it crawled across the floor and up the base to the elevated bed and wrapped around the young priest, Tjark was already in motion, slipping his arms underneath the youth to lift him to safety. Regeth leapt for him, also, his blanket flying free, and just as he grasped his friend's arm, the blanket froze in its downward fall. Regeth's feet remained poised in flight above the floor, and Tjark, determined to protect the two young men as he'd failed to do earlier, held his mouth open, but no words came out. In that singular moment, Aaeon's eyes shifted the smallest amount under his lids; and in a flash of light, they were gone, leaving Regeth's blanket waving in the air, never to touch the floor again.

Lightning and Fire

Aaeon opened his eyes to a hellish nightmare not even he had dreamed possible. He stood on his home, Haukberk. The storm wall painted the sky with churning ash, and the sky-bound bands of lightning had opened their souls; fire poured forth. The ground rumbled under his feet, and he looked Upward to the tip of the precipice to see a portion of the ground crack, sending dust and debris into the air. With a rending noise as of a hundred rock hornets in severe pain, it turned loose with screaming anguish and disappeared into the Crevasse. In the far distance towards Morning, he could just see Gates. He located it because the city glowed with disaster, as flames taller than the tallest structures licked the sky. Then a section of the flames collapsed, and beneath the precipice, a portion of the city fell, still in flames, through the stone and rock of the precipice and into the void. He thought he heard screams but pushed the thought away; it was so far, it must be his imagination.

He searched and found his Temple. The prayer tower he'd stood at so long ago was still there, but the Temple dome had fallen in, and dust rose from where it once stood. The sound of rock churning under his feet filled him with fear. His feet rested on his favorite stones, and he looked for any comfort he could find. Far down the tumbled hillside, he caught a hooded figure, and he recognized the slight, narrow-shouldered Regeth. He raised an arm, and the figure returned the gesture. Behind him was the burnished sheen of a bald pate. He yelled, "Priest Tjark!" The man's arm lifted, and Aaeon knew it was him.

A voice called, one he knew, and he turned. Mene stood on the stone above, her hood thrown back, and her hair silhouetted against the red sky. He leaped to her, nearly stumbling as the stones picked that exact time to shake especially hard. He caught himself and laughed.

"You're so beautiful to me, Mene." And she was.

"You've kept my brother safe." She held out her hand, waiting for him to take it. When he did, she smiled.

"What's all this?" He motioned to the disaster overtaking the world.

"You've been gone for a long time. I'm sorry, Aaeon." Tears filled her eyes.

"For what? Tell me, my sweet. I must know."

"The ground began to shake daily, and then the news came. His Primate, Cardinal Ne' Kirk-fait IX—" she placed her hand respectfully at the base of her throat, "—died, and everything we knew began to come apart." She sniffled, and her eyes glistened. "I wanted you here, and you were gone. No one knew where, even when the Temple sent a message to Gates."

"May I hold you?" He wanted to so badly. He thought of Priest Quartten, lost and unable to return to his home. His ear jangle, tall staff, and kind words had made him a man to be treasured. He'd thought it impossible for the man's dilemma to truly wreak havoc on all creation, but it was proven true. The ground shook worse, and the sound of cracking stone tortured the air, making it hard to hear.

"Please." She smiled, and her red eyes made her even more

beautiful.

He wrapped her in his arms, and he drew in the aroma of her hair. In that moment, he pulled strength from the warmth of her skin. She was all he'd ever needed. Priest Tjark was right. He drew his essence from her, and she'd drawn him home where he belonged. He never should have left her to travel the precipices or jump the haze curtains.

An arm of lightning so massive as to seem impossible reached a fist to the precipice and slammed into the rock, uprooting plants and overturning stones all around them. Regeth now huddled under Tjark's sturdy arms, but there was nowhere that was safe. The heat from the sky and from the lightning began to scorch skin and clothing and rocks and sky.

Mene held Aaeon tightly, and as the maelstrom swirled around them, she bled her final words into his ear. "Chazah 2:8. In the doing, the world as we know it will be consumed by lightning and fire. Selah. I've loved you, Aaeon, always, since we were children."

Aaeon's heart swelled within him, but he didn't get a chance to reply, for at that moment, the ground tumbled from underneath them, and in a vast cataclysm, their world and all they knew, their places of worship, their homes, and all the people they'd ever loved, were, indeed, consumed by a conflagration of unending lightning and fire.

— Part 3 —

Rebirth

Whiplash

The *Higgs* creaked as the metamaterials of her hull, arranged in their periodic patterns; the nanodiamond coatings, able to deflect microscopic dust; and her amorphous metal framework with its disorganized atomic structure approached the critical levels of absolute zero. The massive lightshow that had whipped across the known Universe, creating an unprecedented aurora borealis of cosmic proportions, was feeding its final remnants of life into the black hole dragging the *Higgs* and her daughter ship forward. Her speed now approached the absolute limit of what was possible, and in her massive rush across the cosmos, she teetered on the edge of oblivion, about to tumble into the vast and chaotic cesspool of time and energy she had created.

Inside the ship, anything that could be frozen was. The ship's electronic brain had long since succumbed to electrical cessation, sending its final dying sparks along wires that could no longer arouse the electrons to send them along their way. Even the minute fraction of helium in the ship's air slowly cooled into a superfluid and seeped through cracks in the hull brought on by the shifting of the carbon nanotube sheathing that flexed and crackled in the extreme cold. The engines, driven by their own internal heat, and having outlived the trace gas' abandonment into the vacuum surrounding the ship, felt the frigid fingers of the slowing of the Universe in the final moments of time as they embraced the vessel and chilled her beating heart.

Her forward moment was unchecked, however. There was nothing left to slow the *Higgs*: no space dust, no solar wind, no X-rays, nothing. Even the fabric of space-time had succumbed to the massive gravity well that had virulently consumed all matter as it screamed in anguish, shredded and consumed by the beast's hungry maw.

Commander Jebena Pollock, just thirty and not yet a mother—although that had been her dream—carried the insensate Asher Levitson, his arm over her shoulder, towards a lift. Pilot Frederick Nielson, his craggy face twisted into a grimace, had an arm around Levitson's waist, taking much of the weight off Pollock's smaller frame. Nielson, in death as in life, was as he lived, whip-sharp, emotionally stable, and exhibiting a dependability made of stone. Ice crusted the trio's skin as they poised in mid-step, the Commander and Pilot doing their best to help a fallen comrade, even as their lives were stolen from them.

First Mate Wendy Honda, with her petite, fine-boned features, had tossed away her ever-present earpiece that had connected her to her world. Instead, she clung to Science Officer Jameson Kirkpatrick. His reddish-blond hair burned like cold flame underneath its coating of ice, as though his passion for her and for life still reverberated through his soul's eternal spark. One hand, encased in soft, woven gloves, wrapped Honda's neck, his fingers just in the trailing ends of her hair. His thumb brushed the underside of her chin, and he held his lips against her cheek, forever offering her a reminder of his love. Honda's eyes looked into his, still open under their coating of ice, and a joyous smile graced her lips, one that would never fade until the end of time.

Communications Chief Ranson Charles and Mission

Specialist Weldon Clarkson had thought they could expedite repairs if they could make it from the Virtual Games Room to Engineering. Charles *understood* the ship, how it worked. He was on a first-name basis with *computers* and *electronics*. His life was inside the mad demon, and like his red hair, he was on fire with the need to make them *work*. Clarkson was the solid anchor, the even keel that brought others' enthusiasm back into line. His gray hair and perpetual rosacea were misleading. He was responsible for all 5,000 colonists, and he refused to let even one die. The two men never made it to Engineering. They approached the door, their legs in motion, one foot lifted and the other pressed against the ice-encrusted floor. Clarkson's hand was already outstretched to trigger the door, and Charles' mouth was open as if he had something to say. The air around them, frozen and coating their rigid forms, sparkled with reddish light as lightning crawled along the walls. Deep purple energy seeped in like a fog, painting the world into a Goya-esque interpretation of *Dante's Inferno*.

Flight Doctor Elisabet Minkovski was in her surgery, doing as she always did, offering her services to others. Her goal in life was to locate the God-gene, the specific fragment of human DNA that when massaged just right would allow humans to live forever, essentially making them gods who could survive until the Universe wound itself down around them. She held one hand to the comm on the wall with a puzzled expression on her face, as though unsure why Pilot Nielson had ceased speaking with her. Behind her, Payload Specialist Imani Okotie-Eboh sat on the surgery table with her hand wrapped in gauze. She peered at the bandage as though it couldn't be on her hand, not *her* hand. The air in the room was gone, littered upon the floor, and the last remnants of liquefied helium curled in a smoky dance as it seeped through the fissures where the red lightning leaked through cracks and crawled across the walls.

Interplanetary Education Liaison Liam Schlegel was on the Bridge, his head wrapped in a black VR helmet. His perfectly coiffed head of hair might be hidden, but his immaculately kept nails reflected the care with which he had lived his life. He was cool and collected even when the world seemed ready to collapse. This time, however, he'd seen too much. He'd searched the *Higgs'* magnetics, observed the black hole, and compared what he'd learned with reams of historical information. The ships' warp bubbles had become interlinked and were now dwarfed by the Casson Field. The *Higgs'* drive information, containing real time facts, numbers, nodes, tipping points, temperatures, and anything else the ship had available told a truth that was beyond comprehension. The Event Horizon was upon them. Schlegel's hands reflected his last thoughts. His fingers were stretched in a rictus of terror, for Liam had seen the future, and the future was now.

The incredible stresses of the tidal forces of the black hole had become more than the *Higgs* could take. As she twisted and flexed, the ice coating her walls, ceilings, and floor began to ripple and crack. The superfluid helium, what little was left, fell from broken corridors into the void to be pulled over the edge, over the Event Horizon, and into the black hole, sucked in and added to the tremendous energy accumulated inside. The last of the ship to give up on its structural integrity was the section that had given up the least amount of heat. Deep in the Cryo-Storage vaults, the 5,000 sleeping colonists had started the journey at near zero, and the cold didn't bother them. Even when the motors and pumps driving super-cooled fluids through the CorpseCases seized and no longer functioned, the colonists' chilled micro-environments were little changed. They would be the last living creatures in the current epoch to live, breathe, and think, before all known matter collapsed and life restarted in a cosmic explosion that would mark the beginnings of new life in a brand-new Universe.

Even so, the vast room filled with 5,000 people who didn't know they were about to die suffered as did the rest of the ship. Lightning crawled across the ceilings and the floor. The air had turned to ice and coated everything, glittering with red shards of ominous proportions. The windows set into each capsule were all that kept the people inside alive. One case, marked Aaeon Hibolah, 1473, Section 3, retained a small, clear space in the frosted window that opened from the outside world into the one in which he still lived. Deep within, under his hair shorn tight against his head, his skin was clear and translucent. His eyes were closed, and red veins crisscrossed the thin skin. Just underneath, his eyes twitched one time, as though he was dreaming, when the frigid temperatures became too much for the *Higgs*, and the ship cracked, exposing the CorpseCases to the vacuum of nothingness. In that moment, the glass panel in Aaeon's capsule shattered outward.

The final moment of existence had arrived. The black hole could sustain itself no longer. The Casson Envelope surrounding the *Higgs* could stretch no farther, and it shattered like a water-filled balloon in a slow-motion video as the outer skin peels away, leaving only the liquid inside that can no longer sustain itself. The gathered matter and energy, containing everything in existence— along with the *Higgs*, the *Daughter*, and 5,014 lives—fell headlong into the unstable black hole, and for a fraction of a second, nothing existed, neither time, matter, nor energy. The past and the future, today and tomorrow, were all laid out to be perused as though flipping through a book. None of it *was*, and yet the story of all the years of the Universe were there to view, to experience, and to participate in at will. Then, that second was gone, and the collected matter and energy in the black hole shattered its weakened bonds. In a kaleidoscopic and iridescent explosion of gargantuan magnitude, a new Universe exploded in vast tendrils of expanding energy, blooming like a magnificent flower and flinging the stuff of existence into the farthest reaches of the void. Time burst into being once more, the clock moving forward, locking the past into the past, the present into the present, and the future into a world as yet unknown.

It was the moment of Creation, a time for new life to begin.

Did you en oy this book?

Find more by Levi Castle at:

 THREE SKILLET

www.ThreeSki letPublishing.com

www.ingramcontent.com/pod-product-compliance
Lightning Source LLC
Chambersburg PA
CBHW061509020726
47502CB00006B/1997